ENIGMA

Enigma

Brad Cooper

Brad L. Cooper

For the Justice League. No one in the world has the support system that I have and for that I am eternally grateful. Life-savers all.

For Wonder Woman, my lifeline. You know who you are.

For Jensen.

1

The chemical compound was simple, unassuming, but powerful: KCl.

The scientific name of the substance, potassium chloride, was innocuous but the effects of the liquid in the syringe were dependent solely upon the desired result – medicinal or otherwise.

The plan was simple, nearly flawless, the product of his training, his gifts, his experiences. This day was nothing new, with one notable exception: This was the final plan. There would not be another one crafted, another day faced, or another tear shed. The moments of disappointment and failure had faded but the years of being used and disposed of never would. The people, the self-centered perpetrators of mental and emotional trauma who consume far more from one person than they will ever collectively produce for those who they encounter and force to bear the weight of their presence, seemed to pass effortlessly through the lives of those they effect in the same manner of the daily stream of transient commuters at Union Station in the Windy City.

A deep breath.

One draw. One push.

Nick twirled the syringe across his fingers like a miniature baton, reflecting upon the other times in his life when this exact scenario had played out. Each time he had reached a mental and emotional block and, with a moment of silent prayer, relented, having been granted sufficient peace just long enough to see another sunrise. The pattern never changed, unwavering as if it had been hard-wired through a lifetime of warfare that was unseen, unheard, and unknown to everyone other than the person who looked back at him in the mirror. This time felt different, he thought, but he was certain that he had said the same thing in the past.

The use of a firearm was too grotesque, pills too obvious, the other options barbaric, if not antiquated, and entirely inefficient and unreliable. Besides, the insurance company would not pay the beneficiary in an instance such as this. So much as a note would be a dead giveaway, he thought, and smirked at the irony. No, there was another way. His education and skill set would see to that.

His plan was simple, effective, and even brilliant, if he did say so himself. Every detail was in place. Natural causes. That's what the official report would more than likely state. Stroke, heart attack, there were multiple outcomes that would be on the table for the medical examiner whose services would inevitably be retained, and even the most anal-retentive coroner would commit little attention to the single microscopic hole in the arm of a man in his early thirties with no history of intravenous drug use and a yearly checkup, complete with routine blood work, only a day earlier. Under the circumstances, the ineptitude of the phlebotomist served a purpose for Nick. Multiple attempts at drawing blood meant more than one injection site, all with plausible explanations that would prevent otherwise troublesome questions from being asked.

The potassium chloride in the syringe was potent, designed to perform its intended task with brutal efficiency. It was, in fact, one of the three substances that comprised the cocktail of drugs that was employed in most lethal injection cases throughout the United States. For death row inmates, sodium thiopental, a powerful anesthetic, is administered to render them unconscious before the second drug is added, pancuronium bromide, paralyzing their voluntary muscles including those used to breathe. Only then would the third and final drug be injected. But this was not capital punishment and the other two drugs were not in play.

Approximately sixty to ninety seconds after injection, the high dose of potassium chloride would induce certain sudden cardiac arrest. In that period of time, every action was to be carried out to the last detail. When the substance entered his bloodstream, the pain would be excruciating as the potassium ignited the sensory nerve fibers, virtually destroying the veins as it circulated toward the heart. Through the agony, he would be forced to summon the strength and concentration to throw the empty syringe out of the open window next to his bed. He would then roll onto his left side, facing away from the window and, through gritted teeth, close his eyes for the last time and wait.

Nick considered the possibilities surrounding what would be the final moment, the very last second.

Would anyone grasp the irony of it all, that he had died of a broken heart?

One would, he knew.

Would there be a moment of darkness before making the ultimate transition?

Would he even be aware that the end was *the end*?

No investigator within fifty miles would scour the grass outside of his home for an empty syringe. If they did, the pieces of the puzzle would never come together and the secret reality would remain safe. The half-a-million dollar life insurance policy would be paid out to its sole unsuspecting beneficiary. The ending would appear selfish to outside observers but feel merciful to the one in the midst of unrelenting emotional and mental battle. That was the explanation in the moment.

Still present in the bend of his right arm was the makeshift bandage, fashioned out of gauze and tape, from the drawing of blood that had taken place a day earlier. Right-handed, he would inject himself in his left arm, toss the needle through the window and into the open field outside of the house, and then lie on his left side as his final moments on Earth became his first moments in eternity. He was certain that it was an ascent, not a descent, that awaited him but it was the present that had degraded into something unbearable and unsustainable.

It was her face that haunted his dreams, their memories ever-present in his waking hours. An item she had left behind somewhere in the house, a television show or feature film that they had shared together, a scent, a taste, there was always a reminder of a future planned, a love shared, and a life destroyed. Life truly is fair, he had always said, because it is unfair to everyone, but this particular measure of circumstance seemed insurmountable.

The early afternoon sun shone through the open window, illuminating the otherwise dark bedroom on the top floor of the hundred-year-old farmhouse in the mountains of southwest Virginia. Sitting on the side of the bed, the breeze gently pushing the curtains inward and slowly drying the sweat on his forehead, Nick reflected upon the decisions that had led him to this moment in his life. An analyst in every sense, he looked back with the strange dichotomy of both regret and resignation at the series of events that had created his present state of physical and mental existence.

Thanks for everything, Mia, he thought, and held the syringe up to the light before setting it down on the nightstand next to the bed.

The long-held tradition that one's life flashes before their eyes shortly before their death was fresh in Nick's mind as he reviewed the details of the plan one last time. He paused to consider if the same was true when the end was voluntary. Before the moment arrived, he began to see his story play out before him. The images appeared and changed as if he was viewing a slideshow, moving forward in chronological order from the beginning until the end.

The images were still, in color, appearing not as photographs but instead as moments frozen in time. His childhood appeared first; the color of the images faded into gray, the details of the background blurry while key faces and moments were redacted either by choice or necessity.

Next was young adulthood, an abbreviated period of time in high school that led to an early entry into college which defied the traditional experience in American higher education.

There were five undergraduate and graduate degrees across three alma maters to his credit, his first steps on campus at sixteen years of age, and a reputation for operating in cruise control when feeling unchallenged, but the highlight of his time as a collegian was not an accomplishment but a single relationship that would forever alter his existence.

He whispered her name as he saw her face, imagining her reaction when she either heard the news or came upon the scene.

He saw her tears, heard her cry, and felt her shake.

She would mourn him, blame Mia and then herself, and suffer wounds that would never heal.

He breathed deeply, closed his eyes, exhaled slowly, and whispered a single word. "No."

The clouds that obscured the sun slowly moved to the east and the light burst through the window and onto his face as if perfectly timed by the Creator Himself.

Message received. I hear You.

In one motion, Nick pushed himself upward from the side of the bed and threw the syringe against the opposite wall, shattering the glass and sending the liquid inside onto the hardwood floor.

He walked to the antique dresser beside the doorway and looked into the mirror, scowling with anger and disgust at the image that he saw looking back at him. He thought himself to be better than this. The select few to whom he permitted membership into his circle knew him to be better than this.

The impetus was on him to live up to their confidence whether he agreed with them, or believed them, or not.

The steps of the farmhouse creaked each time his foot made contact on his way to the ground floor, turning around the corner of the staircase and moving down the hall to his office at the opposite end of the home.

He opened the middle drawer of the desk and removed a single-subject college-lined notebook, his makeshift short-form journal.

At the top of the first available blank page, he wrote the date followed by his unspoken thought of the moment:

> *Few things can match the shock, the pain, the sadness of handing someone the ability to completely destroy you, and then watching them do it without hesitation or remorse.*

Another thought entered his mind, a fleeting emotion that could be further unpacked at another time and subsequently expressed on a neighboring page. The words for the day were written. It was time to climb out of the emotional well once more.

I hope you're happy, Mia, he thought but didn't say, and shook his head as his eyes turned to the ground.

After walking back down the hall and into the living room, he powered on the stereo and pressed play on the compact disc that was always left in the tray. The motor spun to life, the laser made contact with the surface of the disc, and the song began to play just as Nick fell with dead weight onto the couch. It was the song that he heard in his dreams, the song that was nothing more than brilliantly written and pleasant to hear until he met Mia. Only then did the song take on another meaning. Nine weeks earlier, when she disappeared into the night with another man, the song shifted from a romantic memory to haunting reminder.

The recording fades in and the singer's repetition of a single phrase grows louder each time.

"Only you can save me..." the singer said.

The voiceover continues as the beat of the drums plays behind him, followed by the guitar playing a rhythmic melody that seems inescapable to the listener, taking what seems to be its rightful place as the soundtrack to an indescribable emotion and existence.

"Only you can save me..."

Burke closed his eyes and silently mouthed the words of the repetition before the singer began the first verse. The vacuum of her absence consumed him in the same manner that nearby stars are forever swept into a black hole in space. Her face, her voice, the look in her eyes, Mia was everywhere. Their shared experiences remained alive in his mind, as vivid now as on the day they were mentally recorded, but there was no video tape to erase, no files on a computer hard drive to delete. Life has no reset button, he knew, and while the windshield is larger than the rear view mirror for a reason, moving forward is not as simple as the contentions of concerned outside observers with the best of intentions. Machiavelli was a brilliant man, and Nick was a highly educated one who appreciated the Italian politician's assertion that there is nothing more difficult, perilous, or uncertain than to take the lead in the introduction of a new order of things. This, too, was simply an example of when letting go was more about acceptance than resignation, the attempt at seeing less of what might have been and embracing the hope of what might be.

In effect, a new start is often as frightening as it is exciting. The difference lies in the source of change, voluntary or involuntary. This was not a voluntary change for Nicholas Burke.

The pictures, mementos, and gifts had been tucked away in storage. Returning the engagement ring a week earlier had been the most difficult step to take. The process of removing the tangible reminders of her from his home was slow and tedious as he held out hope for an unlikely return. The one voice to whom he listened most insisted that his new Mia-free life was for the best, in her words. She was not to be trusted, not now or ever again, she said, and better things, better days, were sure to lie just beyond the horizon in spite of the long hard road that may be required to arrive there.

Before the song reached the bridge, the distinct electronic ring of the cordless handset connected to his landline telephone sounded from the office. Nick stood to begin his search for the perpetually misplaced piece of electronic hardware before the ringing stopped and the answering machine was activated. Looking at the caller ID was a pointless endeavor. He knew who was calling without looking at the display.

Gabi.

She knew.

She always knows.

Nick pressed the button to answer the call and she spoke before he could formally answer.

"You didn't answer your cell," she said.

"It's charging."

"Join us in the modern era, Nick. This connection always sounds like Alexander Graham Bell is on the line."

"Hello to you, too," Nick said, his baritone voice flat and gravelly, the product of not audibly conversing with anyone in four days.

"What's wrong? Talk to me." The sound of the wind roaring through the open window as she drove was nearly as loud as her voice.

"What are you…" he started to say but allowed the sentence to trail off without finishing. The objection was futile. She always knows.

How does she always know?

"How did you know?"

"Gut feeling. And I've been around for the last two months." Before Nick could respond, Gabi shouted an angry, "Hey!" and the sound of the horn in her dark graphite metallic BMW X5 SUV followed for what felt like five seconds before she added, "Moron pulled right out in front of me!"

"Where are you headed?"

"Don't change the subject. You were sprawled out on the couch, flat on your back, eyes closed, listening to that song again, weren't you?" Her faint, understated but endearing Southern twang was hit or miss depending on the word being spoken. Without waiting, she asked, "Well?"

"Gabi…"

She half-laughed and said, "I'm not mad. Tell me the truth."

"If you already know the answer, then why ask the question?"

"I swear to God, if you don't snap that CD in two and throw the pieces off the bridge and into the creek, I'm going to come and do it myself."

The six-cylinder engine whined as Gabi accelerated uphill, ascending the side of the mountain on the, at that stage, ironically named Moccasin Valley Road en route to Nick's farmhouse in Tumbez. There was no town to speak of, nary a traditional brick-and-mortar place of business for miles, no city hall, police or fire departments, not even a red light to slow the non-existent traffic. Even the postal service was classified as general delivery. The collection of farmhouses and small single-family homes both antiquated and modern, some even abandoned, was nothing more than quaint scenery for the occasional passerby. So seldom was artificial noise in the area that vehicles could be heard from a distance further than expected and the slow moving waters of Big Moccasin Creek could be heard from the edge of the front yard of his home that was once the modest centerpiece of a family of sharecroppers until progressive and unavoidable degradation set in following their collective passing.

The cellular signal faded to a single bar on the display as she sped down the two-lane road, sun peering through the canopy of trees covering both lanes at the points that seemed the most narrow, causing the sound on the call to scramble into unintelligible noise.

The next sound that Nick heard was Gabi letting out an exasperated snarl.

"Are you growling?" he asked.

"How is it possible to go somewhere even remotely civilized and there's hardly a signal? What year is this?"

"Where are you that there's hardly a signal?"

Gabi responded but the signal faded a second time, leaving Nick unable to understand her garbled response. The call reconnected as she let out a frustrated, "*Hello?*"

She's had a long day, the perils of working an early shift.

"What did you ever decide about work?" Nick asked but failed to wait for the answer. The noise from outside the house stole his attention. "Gabi, hang on. Someone's here."

"What are you talking about? No one's ever there."

"Stay on the line." Nick opened the drawer next to the television and extracted one of the most basic items in his cache of weapons, a Glock G27 subcompact .40 caliber pistol, and stepped toward the side door on the right side of the front porch that led directly to his living room. From the doorway, his line of sight to the gravel driveway was unobstructed.

On the phone, Gabi whispered, "If it's Mia, start shooting." When Nick didn't respond, she asked, "Who is it?"

When he heard the door slam shut in the driveway, and then echo a split-second later in the earpiece of the phone, he knew where Gabi was headed after all and sat the pistol on top of the vintage Steinway upright piano next to the door.

As his best friend began her walk through the yard, he shook his head and said into the phone, "I think we can hang up now."

Through nine weeks of heartbreak and silence there were very few opportunities or reasons for Nick to smile but there was a genuine upward tick at one corner of his mouth as Gabrielle McLane approached. He should have expected the visit. It was a matter of time considering the circumstances.

He wondered if he was getting rusty, losing his heightened sense for detail after so much time on the shelf, because the sound of the phone call dropping and the complaints over the lack of cellular signal were a dead giveaway to her location and destination.

Before, during, and after Mia, Gabrielle's presence was a mainstay. She was his refuge, his retreat to sanity and stability in an insane world. She, in every sense, made sense. Unspoken due to lack of necessity, she echoed his emotion in spite of the polar opposite background history;

Nick having grown up of modest means, she a child of privilege. Her childhood and present lifestyle of gated communities and luxuries at her fingertips, the world in which Nick chose to live was foreign in a way that drew her curiosity and interest. His way of life, his choice of location, it all belied convention. There had to be a reason for it all but she had long since given up on solving the puzzle.

The most extraordinary puzzle piece was his Russell County farmhouse, a relic ripped from the pages of turn-of-the-twentieth-century history and only retrofitted for the essential modern amenities upon his still unexplained cash purchase of the home seven years earlier. Lebanon, the county seat, was the closest incorporated area of note but the resources of the small town of little more than 3,000 in population were limited at best. The police chief and two part-time volunteer deputies of the nearby community of Hansonville volunteered their services to patrol the area of Tumbez but such activity was seldom necessary. After all, security and solitude were supposedly the chief selling points when Nick informed her that he was relocating to a familiar piece of land.

The exterior of the home was battered from years of extreme seasonal weather and general disrepair in the absence of occupants. The glass in all nine exterior windows of the home were replaced before Nick began the process of moving in but the same peeling white paint that was progressively falling to the ground on day one was still doing so on this day, and the visual was always something of which Gabrielle took notice. Each time she pulled into the worn-down grass and gravel path that Nick called a driveway at what she lovingly called *Casa de Burke*, she hoped to see some capital improvements. At least the decrepit old barn with the walls halfway broken inward, the board still intact adorned with rubber belts from trucks that were scrapped decades ago, had finally been razed. For Gabi, seeing that space now empty as she parked was an encouraging sign. Nick knew better than this, she thought, and she demanded better of him. Someone had to push the man in the matters that he viewed as trivial or somehow functional in his own twisted mind.

The porch itself was a remnant from a bygone era, a simple wooden floor set atop tons of stones stacked flat upon one another, and two levels of long, rectangular gray stones, eroded smooth and slick from years of rain and foot traffic, slanted downward from left to right, serving as steps. Nick stood next to one of the four weight-bearing poles that held up the rusted tin roof, one hand in the pocket of his dark khaki cargo shorts, the other scratching his beard that had grown to a record length without appearing out of control, and looked across the road and into the open field opposite his own. The sky was clear but there were storm clouds in his mind. Under present circumstances, a surprise visit meant a lecture at worst and an emotional discussion at best but both would originate from the same place of concern and genuine affection. He nevertheless hoped for the latter.

Her hair was mostly straight with only the slightest natural wave, the color dark brown but one that seemed to lighten in the sun without showing signs of red. On this day, it was gently parted in the front and fell to the sides, the length touching her shoulders and just beyond. Her eyes were a match, the color understated but the look that they offered to Nick was vibrant and captivating, truly the eyes to the soul that he had been privileged to know so openly, honestly, freely, deeply. They seemed magnified by the glasses that were worn when they were needed, per her discretion, and her gaze, no matter the emotion, was one that Nick Burke had not been able to escape since the first day that they met on campus at Radford University.

It was her smile that captured his attention most. In photographs it was truly picture perfect but it was the expression during personal interaction that always caught and kept his eye. She smiled as if she knew something special, a secret that existed only in her mind or a sarcastic retort just waiting to escape. When she knowingly pushed the limits with a joke, bringing the slightest blush to herself or someone else, she would look away until the tension passed and then return to normal as if nothing had happened, satisfied that an unnecessarily serious moment had been broken with something ridiculous. Rare was the occasion when hers was the only smile present in a conversation.

Jeans and the old tie-dye t-shirt? She's already been to the gym, didn't go home after work. Table for two tonight.

Their relationship was long since past traditional greetings. Gabi had the first word. "Are you *ever* going to do anything about the outside of this place?" she asked after offering a quick glance over the front of the house.

"Probably not. If the outside looks this bad, no one bothers to try to get inside. It's a different kind of security."

"Is that why you've obviously not used a trimmer in two weeks?"

When she removed her sunglasses and stepped onto the porch, he finally made eye contact and one corner of his mouth turned upward. "Three," he said, "but who's counting?" and opened the screen door for her to enter first. The breeze blew it closed with a smack the moment he passed through.

Each visit to the farmhouse echoed the sentiments of her first. It was the contrast that always stunned her. The cloak of poverty and destruction on the outside contrasted with the immaculate and contemporary interior. The doorway into the home felt like a portal to another dimension with the sudden change of scenery and Gabi always shook her head in disbelief as she looked around for whatever additions had been made since her last visit. The only notable change, she saw, was a full-color panoramic photograph of the Las Vegas skyline during the blue hour just after sunset, the casinos illuminated, the stream of headlights on the infamous strip forming a consistent white line, and the Spring Mountain Range visible in the background with a waxing crescent moon appearing against the darkening sky.

"Vegas?" she asked. "Do I want to know?"

"Of course you do."

"I know. 'I'll tell you about it someday.' Why is it that today is never someday?"

"One day it will be," he said with the first, albeit small, genuine smile of the day. Before she could offer a biting response, Nick added, "You love the challenge. Admit it." The scoff he received in return was his evidence of victory.

Deflect and she moves on every time.

Gabi sat at one end of the black leather couch, resting her head on the armrest and setting her feet in Nick's lap on the other end. She demanded eye contact for conversation, especially when talking to someone whose answers always seemed to lead down the proverbial rabbit hole. A look could mean more than a sentence, a nervous shift in a chair more powerful than a paragraph. The visit was necessary.

It was the question she did not want to ask, or perhaps it was the worry for the answer she did not want to hear for his sake. "Have you heard from her?"

"Heard from whom?"

"Don't start with me, Nick Burke," she said, and playfully kicked at his arm. "You left the CD player on. When did you hear from her?"

He let his head fall back onto the cushion and, staring at the ceiling, said, "Couple of weeks ago. It was nothing important. I didn't answer. I had nothing to say and there isn't anything I particularly want to hear."

"I can think of a couple of things you'd like to hear from her but I'm guessing they weren't included."

His head still pointed upward but he glanced toward her with his eyes. "You're right, and they weren't."

"Did you at least get the ring back?"

Nick closed his eyes, took a deep breath, and exhaled. "Let her keep it. She needs a reminder of what she threw away. I have plenty of my own."

"It happened again, didn't it?" she asked with her eyes closed. Nick broke eye contact again and returned his gaze into the ceiling fan. "Why didn't you call me?"

Not now, Gabrielle.

"Apparently, I didn't need to."

Gabi swung her legs off of the couch and stood up quickly, paced the room once, and stared at Nick until his eyes locked with her own.

"I know how bad this is but you've got to stop sulking and start rebuilding. She's not the only..."

"Spare me the benign platitudes. Okay?" Nick said, his voice breaking with a combination of sadness and defeat that surprised himself as much as Gabi. He waited through the five seconds of awkward silence that felt like ten minutes and said, "I'm sorry. It's the frustration and insomnia talking. Ignore me."

Gabi knelt in front of him and placed her hands on his knees. "Get over her."

"Gabi..."

"Be done with her."

"Gabrielle..."

"Stop trying to interrupt me. Do *not* allow *anyone* to have this kind of power over you. How dare you allow her to destroy you? You are stronger than this. You are *better* than this."

"Not at the moment. I can't just erase three years of history in a matter of weeks. It doesn't work that way when it's real, Gabi. It's not that simple."

She had been waiting for the opening. The line had come to her during her drive up Clinch Mountain and she had laughed to herself when it popped into her head before she dialed his number. "She's not your ex, Nick. She's your why."

He dropped his chin to his chest, closed his eyes, and laughed through his nose.

Only you.

"How long have you been saving that one?"

"At least half an hour," she said, and used his legs as leverage to push herself to her feet. "Stand up."

Nick did exactly as she asked. Saying no to Gabrielle was never an option. He was 6-2, 215 pounds, with brown hair and matching eyes, athletic, lean with muscle but maintaining a deceptively average build, he was agile, quicker than fast, stronger in the lower body. Next to Gabi, he was seven inches taller and seventy pounds heavier and towered over the one person who always had complete control over him at any given moment but would sooner fall on a grenade than use it against him. She embraced him, laying her head on his chest, and squeezed him at just the right moment. "It's time to rebuild. Luckily, I know what makes Nick tick."

"Only you can get away with that."

Gabi pulled away, looked upward, and asked, "So what's for dinner?" and walked to the kitchen before he could answer.

At 10 p.m., following a dinner of lobster risotto with mixed vegetables, an hour of classic game shows on a channel to which Nick had forgotten about his access, and a glass of red wine a piece as they worked through the details of Mia's recent reach-out, Gabi set out on her thirty minute drive home to Abingdon. Her rounds at the hospital would come early and sleep was difficult enough to come by, especially with the anticipation of living far too many days and nights of her life on-call. Insomnia was a trait that she shared with her best friend.

Halfway into her drive, with a full complement of 4G LTE signal bars on her cell phone, she dialed his number. When Nick answered, she asked, "You trust me don't you?"

"Like no one else, Miss McLane."

"So trust me when I tell you that it's going to be okay. Don't let the darkness win. I've always got your back, and a flashlight."

"You're not going anywhere, are you?" Nick asked, rhetorical in part but still seeking the reinforcement that there was no reason to doubt.

"Never," she said with the confidence that he needed.

Nick waited a beat and answered, "Your confidence is why I think that everything can turn out okay. Your presence is why I know that it will. Rest easy tonight."

"Now I can," she said, and added, "Love you, bye," spoken so quickly that it came out as a single word, and the call ended without warning.

I love you, too.

2

It was as good as it was going to get.

That's what she told herself with a final look in the mirror before heading out the door. Styling her hair took more than half an hour, followed by another twenty minutes on her makeup, and finally the selection of her wardrobe for the meeting. The jeans were a little tighter than expected around the waist but she hoped they wouldn't notice. The loose-fitting dress should provide sufficient cover. So much effort, such little guaranteed in return. Two different outfits. The final verdict could wait until she arrived. For now, it was the dress.

She quietly reminded herself that the absence of expectations eliminated the possibility of disappointment. It was their expectations that had to be met, whatever they might be, whoever they might be, but she was working from the position of power for a single reason: She had absolutely nothing to lose.

"Breathe," she said audibly, her eyes closed, with no one else in the room before running her hand through her long, thin blonde hair, giving it just a little shake to add some body.

Even with nothing to lose, she was nervous.

No, anxious was the right word, she thought to herself and then nodded as if there were someone else present to acknowledge.

The four days since Shelby Fletcher responded to the advertisement on the internet bulletin board had provided ample time for her to over-analyze every possible scenario. The language of the classified ad was as simple as it was intriguing to the young woman whose summer vacation following her freshman year of community college had ended and the first month of classes was proving to be a challenge. With the balance of her savings account dwindling, two credit cards maxed out in an effort to maintain her preferred image and social life, and the funding to weather the storm of mounting debt nowhere in sight, the opportunity to earn some extra cash arrived with fortuitous timing.

A childhood filled with her parents preaching the evils of debt and the madness of student loans in the modern world of higher education left her relegated to paying out-of-pocket for her Associate of Applied Science degree in accounting. The gist of her monthly bank statement was simple enough: More debits than credits, and triple-digits quickly approaching double. Pride prevented her from asking for help. The accompanying admission of both fault and guilt, complete with the unrelenting judgment and series of lectures that would follow, meant that finding a solution by any other means necessary was paramount. Tuition would be due, in full, in a matter of weeks. Her friends were not in the financial position to be of assistance and the thought of admitting her predicament to them was revolting.

The twenty minute commute from her parents' home in Meadowview to downtown Abingdon was consumed by these thoughts, moving through her mind like a carousel and gaining speed with each circuit. She lamented her carelessness, the wasteful spending, the ostensibly ever-present leeches that vanished only when it was time to pick up a check or pay off a bar tab, all of who had promised at one time or another to "get it next time". With each touch of the brake pedal, the steering wheel began to shake. Another expense, she thought, and another reason to stifle the nerves and see what this opportunity was all about.

The Wyndale Hotel and Conference Center, named after the two-lane road on which it was built, was the newest commercial building in Abingdon and strategically located near the historic downtown. Business owners on Main Street and the adjacent streets closely monitored the parking lot, looking and hoping for an influx of tourists that would lead to a momentary boost in patronage beyond the locals. The post-Millennial design of the hotel stood in stark contrast to the rest of the town, the historic Barter Theatre remaining the proud centerpiece since 1933, but only those with trained eyes and an interest in the subject devoted much of their attention to the styles of the structures.

Shelby parked in the closest available space to the main entrance of the building and kept a keen eye on the doorway. She was twenty minutes early for the vaguely described 1 p.m. meeting in one of the conference rooms at the hotel, and she craved the chance to scope out any of the other women who responded to the same post that loosely referred to itself as a casting call. There were no stipulations listed, no age minimum or maximum, no preferred body types, and no promised wage. The possible demographics of her competition were endless, if it was indeed a competition. Surely she was not the only young woman in the region to take the bait, she thought, even though the only people seen entering the building in the minutes leading to the top of the hour seemed to be middle-aged men carrying luggage with a family in tow.

12:58 p.m.

Shelby closed her eyes, drew a deep breath in through her mouth and, in an effort to slow her racing pulse, held it briefly before slowly exhaling through her nose. For a fleeting moment, she considered closing the door, starting the engine, and driving back home as if none of this had ever happened. There were no contracts, no real commitment to speak of, and, thus, no danger in leaving without speaking to a single soul. Her friends and family were none the wiser and were sure to either ridicule or shame her into backing out should they ever be made aware. But the financial pressures were an irresistible force, the weight growing heavier with each day as the end of summer faded into early autumn, and concern developing into desperation as the questions far outnumbered her answers. Whatever this is, she thought, it was a start.

The sunlight seemed to reflect off of every inch of the three-story L-shaped building as Shelby moved closer. Blue-tinted glass enveloped

nearly every visible inch of the side of the structure that faced the parking lot, the entrance in the center of the right side of the first floor that
led to the lobby, and Shelby silently noted that it looked more like a
small hospital than a hotel. She remembered watching its construction,
familiar with the process as her father had worked on the project from
the ground up, but this was her first time through the doors.

When the automatic doors opened, the desk clerk looked away from
the computer long enough to see the young blonde approaching his
desk, and then returned his attention back to the screen as he said,
"Here for the meeting?"

"Yes."

She turned and looked around the lobby, avoiding any potential eye
contact with the young man who was far more interested in the news
headlines on his computer monitor than the annoyance of the person
disrupting him with questions.

Looking up and smiling, he pointed down the hallway to her right
with a ballpoint pen. "Conference room two. It's the second door on
your left past the elevator. There are a few others in there already. You
must be the last one."

"Thanks," she said and hurried off toward the hallway. She cringed
at the thought of being the last to arrive, seeing every head turn toward
the door when she entered, every eye fixed on her, sizing her up, passing judgment, prematurely competing. The additional dose of self-con-
sciousness was the last thing she needed today. Her supply already far
outweighed the demand.

With her hand on the lever, she closed her eyes, sighed, and once
again questioned her sanity. It was still not too late to reverse course
and return to the parking lot. There were clothes to sell at the consign-
ment shop, an old iPhone to list on eBay, even the possibility of a part-
time job. The last option drew a rumble of anxiety in her stomach. She
had managed to avoid the worlds of retail and restaurants throughout
high school and had no desire to regress to that point now.

This was it.

With one last deep breath, she turned the lever and pushed open the door to the conference room.

The young man at the front desk was indeed correct. She was, in fact, the last one to arrive to the conference room but the turnout was far less than she expected. A single long, rectangular wooden table sat in the center of the hotel's smallest conference room. Three black leather desk chairs were situated on each side of the table, with an additional seat at each end. Five of the side chairs were occupied by the other girls, with a stack of folders piled in front of the chair at the end of the table furthest from the door. Doing her best to avoid the inevitable eye contact, Shelby looked at her phone the moment she sensed the others looking up from their paperwork and in her direction.

Behind her, the door opened again.

"Shelby, I presume?" a man's voice said. She heard an accent but failed to recognize it; European or something, French, maybe.

"That's me," she said, still looking forward.

The man walked around her and to the head of the table, flipped through the folders, and handed her a single manila package with her name written on the tab. He was five-foot-eight and slender, with thin blonde hair that was perfectly parted without so much as single stray strand. He wore a slim-fitting dark grey suit with a lighter grey dress shirt and a black tie. An Armani, she thought as she looked him up and down, and hoped that her evaluation would go unnoticed.

"Here you are. Please complete these before we begin," he said before extending his hand and smiling. "My name is Lucien. It's a pleasure to meet you. I remember the photo you submitted. Thank you for coming."

His teeth were perfect, all natural rather than veneers, and his smile was suitable for a male model on the pages of GQ. The high cheekbones were the proverbial icing on the cake and Shelby caught herself staring at the man who had been tasked to evaluate her along with the other five women present. She tucked her hair behind her ear, giving her shaking hands something to do, and asked, "What all are we doing to-day?"

Lucien maintained his smile, touched her shoulder, said, "That will be addressed shortly," and exited the room.

When she turned toward the table and pulled out the lone empty chair at the side of the table, the looks from the others finally relented and they returned to their forms. The other five women differed from her in every demographic and she took note of each of them: Two were white, one appeared to be Hispanic, another was Asian, and a fifth woman with caramel skin and blue eyes that she assumed to be of mixed race but decided that the accuracy of her racial identity was of no importance. She estimated that she was at least the second youngest, as the Hispanic girl was sixteen at the most; the others were in their late twenties or early thirties. Two of them had tattoos, she saw; the slender, pale brunette displayed a sleeve that covered the entirety of her left arm, and the darker woman featured a single piece of body art, a Chinese symbol at the base of her neck.

There's something here for everyone, she thought, and opened the folder to find a printed 8x10 color copy of the photo she had submitted days before and a stack of paperwork filled with questions ranging from her physical attributes to her likes and dislikes.

With each question, she read the words aloud and looked at the others to see how they matched up in comparison. Height, weight, and measurements were first. She shifted in her chair when she wrote the number of pounds in the blank: 168. No one else had a number that high but she felt confident that, at five-foot-nine, taller than Lucien while wearing flats, she was also taller than the others and carried the weight well on her frame. The belted dress she'd chosen for the day left most of her body to the imagination. Next, her measurements: 38C-32-36. Without lifting her head, she looked up and around the table to see if the others were sneaking a look at her papers but saw no one offering so much as a hint of attention in her direction and felt her shoulders relax.

It took fifteen minutes to check every box and fill in every line of her biographical information and she sat silently for another twenty as the others talked among themselves. Finally, nearly an hour after her arrival, the door opened and Lucien reappeared, moving quickly and pushing a key card into his pocket. "How is everyone today?" he asked through his distinct but not obstructive French accent. Half of the women nervously muttered an affirmative answer before he added, "All of you look beautiful today. We met with the gentlemen yesterday but there is simply no comparison."

He gathered the folders from each of the six women, stacked them neatly in front of his chair at the head of the table, extracted the third from the top and said, "Shelby, would you please come with me?"

Expecting to be interviewed in the order of arrival, not priority, Shelby lifted her head, her eyes wide, and said, "Me?"

"Yes," Lucien said, smiling and moving toward her chair. "This way, please." He extended his hand and helped her stand before moving his touch to the small of her back and guiding her toward the door.

He was reading her file as they stepped onto the elevator. "Third floor, please," he said without looking up. Shelby pushed the button and waited for the door to close. "You recently turned twenty?" he asked.

"I did. The next birthday should be a lot more fun than this one."

"I'm sure it will be. They become far less interesting with the passage time, I'm afraid."

"How old are you?"

"Twenty-six," he lied. The birth certificate that she would never see listed him as four years older but he found the sound of identifying himself as in his thirties to be revolting.

The doors opened and Lucien led her down the hallway to a room in the center of the building. His key card unlocked the door and he allowed her to enter first. Expecting to be alone with the attractive Frenchman, she gasped upon seeing three men waiting for them in front of the glass doors that led to the balcony. One was adjusting the lights that shined onto the king-size bed, another was loading a memory card into a camera, and the third was pulling the curtain closed across the window. The sound of the door slamming shut behind her seemed to echo in her mind.

"Let's take some test shots," he said.

Thirty minutes passed before Shelby slid into a white cotton terry bathrobe and walked into the bathroom, carrying her clothing in her arms. She looked into the mirror and saw the tears welling up in her eyes. Modeling was one thing but this? This was different. This was unthinkable. This was not at all what she had in mind when she walked into the building.

She closed her eyes and, in the temporary darkness, could still hear the mechanical clicks of the shutter on the DSLR camera, snapping photo after photo as Lucien instructed her to change positions or alter her facial expression. His commands sounded more like suggestions. He spoke gently, remained friendly, and was consistently encouraging. It was, after all, part of the program, one of which she remained unaware.

The men were still in the room, she knew, ready to gawk at her the moment she opened the bathroom door. She would pretend to take her time getting dressed but felt the intense desire to get back into her dress as quickly as possible. She had to get covered. The young woman, who had never taken a nude photo, not even for a boyfriend, had spent her day in front of a stranger with a camera, lying on a bed in a hotel room only miles from home and trading her public innocence for an unknown amount of currency. Desperation was indeed every bit as costly as the irresponsibility that created it.

To her surprise, only Lucien noticed when the door opened. The other three were occupied with their professional production tasks involving the lights and camera.

"You were wonderful," he said with his persistent perfect smile. "Stunning."

Shelby looked toward the covered window and then back to Lucien without speaking. She was certain that he noticed the redness in her eyes that were still puffy from the tears.

"Here you are," he said, handing her a plain white envelope with her name written on the front. "I hope we see each other again. There are so many opportunities for a beautiful woman like yourself."

The envelope was thicker than she expected. "More opportunities?" she asked.

"We have photos, much more professional, more official, and we also offer the possibility to transition into film."

"Film? You mean..."

"Yes, *Ma chérie*. I believe you would be wonderful on film. The camera adores you. You would have your choice of co-star." Lucien smiled and added, "Myself included," and made certain that his eyes met hers.

Shelby blushed at his insinuation and turned her eyes to the ground as she smiled without speaking.

"We will be in contact soon. Let me walk with you," he said and walked Shelby Fletcher, complete with her newfound confidence and sudden source of income, to the door.

Shelby rushed to her car in the parking lot. She was more anxious to open the envelope in private than she was to return home to offer a fabricated story about where she had been. Inside the envelope was a stack of crisp one-hundred-dollar bills, taken from a larger fresh stack at the bank. When she reached ten, there were more to count. The count ended at fifteen and she shrieked with both joy and relief. Three times more than what she expected, nearly a fourth of her total debt. The embarrassment and tears from moments before had vanished but the concern remained.

This is a dangerous road, she thought. This is not me, she added. Then with another look at the cash in her hand, the corner of her mouth turned upward.

She whispered into the empty car, "This is exciting."

"Three are definite, one is unsure, and one decided to leave without taking a single photograph," Lucien said into the phone. He listened for a moment and said, "Yes, we are minus one, *patron*."

His boss required five women in order to move on to the next stage of the project. He demanded that all five be secured before Lucien would be paid for his services. Disappointment was unacceptable.

"Five," Lucien said, and repeated, "Yes, five," and ended the call.

Alone in the hotel room, the photographer and other workers having exited the moment after the phone rang, Lucien sat on the edge of the bed and slowly eased himself onto his back.

"One more," he said, and blew out his breath.

3

She hated the sound of the alarm clock.

The traditional mechanical variety, a more modern electronic version, or a sound effect produced by her iPhone, which was with her at all times, it made no difference.

The blaring buzzer was among the most irritating sounds on Earth and it was a mainstay in her professional world on the days when she was on a regular schedule and not simply on-call. It was the most stressful part of working in the world of specialized medicine and feeling the strain of the constant demand of your talents. Sleep always came at a premium and rarely in sufficient quantities. The utmost insult came in the form of waking up five minutes before the alarm, sacrificing the last few moments of dark, silent, ignorant bliss for absolutely no reason.

Cardiology has been a traditionally male-dominated field throughout the country, with women making up less than twenty percent of all practitioners, and the statistics were skewed even further amongst interventional cardiologists. But defying odds and destroying stereotypes was nothing new to Dr. Gabrielle McLane. In fact, it seemed to be a natural function that was programmed into her DNA at conception. Still, on some mornings and evenings more than others she secretly wished that she had taken a slightly less exhausting course in her professional life.

A founder of Commonwealth Cardiology Associates at 29, the last three years had been eventful, exhausting, successful, lucrative, and rewarding for all of the reasons that brought her into medicine in the first place. Their approach to practice was innovative, with regular clinic hours that merged with on-call status on a rotating basis that was a creation of Gabi and her partners. In their collective estimation, their plan allowed for their patients to receive the highest standard of care while their physicians were still permitted to live some semblance of a life.

At times Gabi wondered exactly how well that had worked out for any of them but it was better than the traditional alternative endured by the majority of her colleagues.

Her regimen was her foundation. There was a calendar of important dates, a day planner with more detailed information, and a redundant calendar on her phone that included alarms scheduled for all times of day and every possible activity. Structure was the priority because it structured all other priorities. Medical school at Southern Illinois University was an effective teacher of how to properly allocate time to tasks in order of importance. Clinic days were the easiest of the work days. The alarm sounded at 6:20 a.m., then again ten minutes later if a snooze felt necessary. A reasonably long shower, half an hour to get ready, and a quick but healthy breakfast would push the time to 8 a.m., leaving a full hour to make a fifteen minute commute from her new home to the office. She was the first one there in the morning. For the office staff to arrive before her was a rarity. When the doors opened and the 9 a.m. appointment was in the waiting room, she wanted to be ready to work. Her patients deserved that courtesy whenever possible.

There were, however, circumstances that caused her to abandon her structure, and chief among them was an unexpected phone call from the hospital. Those calls had only one meaning. The Monday morning emergency calls were the worst and her work week was just starting. By 7:50 on this Monday morning, the coast was clear. Breakfast was down to its final bites, the sun was shining through the windows, and a breeze hit the memorial wind chimes set outside of her front door. Perfect.

Then it happened.

Gabi let out an extended, "No…" She felt the vibration first, and then the dreaded ringtone faded into full volume.

The voice on the other end failed to offer even the simplest of greetings when the call connected. Straight to business, as always, she thought.

"Dr. McLane? This is Regina from Johnston Memorial. We need you here as soon as possible. I understand you are not on call from Commonwealth today but you were requested."

Gabi had already abandoned her meal and was closing the front door before she responded. "I understand. I'll call the office and let them know to cover me. Tell me what we have."

"I've already called your associates and they wanted me to let you know that your appointments would be taken care of, Doctor. You're needed here for a heart cath immediately."

"One of mine?"

"I don't believe so, ma'am, but the family knows of you and asked that we call."

Gabi started the engine in her BMW X5 and the stereo momentarily blasted the most recent song on her playlist as she lunged to kill the volume. "Hold on. Let me get you connected to my hands-free," she said, and backed out of the driveway. When it connected, she said, "I'm about ten minutes out. Give me the details."

She heard Regina shuffling papers on the other end of the line and scoffed silently at the lack of preparation.

"Female, 61, suffered what turned out to be a Non-ST-elevation MI several months ago. She is still having chest pains. Diabetic, Type II; smoker but trying to stop; two EKGs were taken but with no elevation on the tracing. But all early indications are that another MI has taken place or is taking place."

"How far apart?" Gabi asked.

"Two hours and the last one taken at 7:30 this morning."

"Segment depression?"

"Some, it appears, but you can see for yourself when you arrive. How long..."

Exactly how fast do they expect me to get there, Gabi thought.

"Six or seven minutes, at most," she said. "Go ahead and get her prepped and we will start as soon as possible," she added and ended the call before Regina could answer.

"Are we ready?" Gabi asked, walking into the operating room, her nurse already waiting next to the patient on the table, her voice partially muffled by the mask covering her mouth. She was covered in light blue nearly head-to-toe, the only variations being the white latex gloves and the hint of her insufficiently tanned, in her opinion, face that was not otherwise hidden.

"We're ready," the nurse said.

The patient nodded nervously but did not speak.

"Mrs. Ellison, I'm going to talk you through every step. Okay?" Gabi said to the woman on the table. Hundreds of procedures, thousands of hours in practice, and she was nervous every time; nervous about her own performance, nervous about what she might fight, nervous about the conversation that could take place in the waiting room.

"Okay," the shaky voice replied. "Thank you, Doctor."

Unseen behind the mask, the cardiologist smiled and said, "We can't be so formal in here. Call me, Gabi. I'd shake your hand but we're sterile."

As promised, Mrs. Ellison was led through every step of her procedure. "We're going to be taking a look at your coronary anatomy. We're trying to get as much information as we can. Okay? I'm going to be going through your right femoral artery to do this. Just try to relax as much as you can. I'm sure you're nervous." Gabi was handed the proper instrument and said, "I'm about to numb the area over the vessel we need so you're going to feel a pinch and a burn followed by some pressure in your leg as we insert the tube."

She first measured the pressures both inside and outside of the heart. Gabi carefully watched the top of two monitors as the live images changed from area to area, one area clear, another with damage from the heart-attack six months earlier. Then she paused, leaned closer and, out of habit, pushed her glasses up by the bridge and changed her gloves.

"There it is," she said to the nurse. "Occluded right coronary artery, damage to the inferior wall; She's in the process of having another MI. Let's go ahead and prepare to clear it."

A guiding catheter was inserted into the artery in order to allow a wire to be placed across the blockage before a second catheter removed the clot and plaque from the vessel. In an instant, the artery opened and the image changed instantly. "That's what I wanted to see," Gabi whispered.

Having used a balloon to open the most critical blockage, blood flow was restored to the artery but more of the clot was still present. Using an export catheter and the inflation of the balloon, the vision of the area opened. As the catheter was withdrawn in reverse, the clot was almost entirely eradicated. After multiple passes, the artery was unrecognizable in comparison, the dark blue springing to life on the monitor.

One step remained.

"Okay," Gabi said. "Let's finish this off with a stent and wrap this thing up." On the outside, she was calm, leading and directing, confident. On the inside, the nerves never went away. She was apprehensive every time she looked into the monitor, looking two and three and four times, steadfast to avoid the notion that she had reached the pinnacle of her knowledge or effort, never accepting that good enough was indeed good enough and striving for improvement by the day. As she thought, she stopped moving, keeping her eyes on the monitor without looking at anything in particular.

She often wondered if she would ever be content, either in accomplishment or effort, but the OR was not the appropriate setting for reflecting upon life as a whole.

"Doctor?" the nurse said.

"Just double-checking something," Gabi replied. "Let's continue."

Another wire was inserted with a balloon over the wire. The stent was placed onto the balloon, which was then expanded and then retracted thirty seconds later, leaving the stent in the artery. Intervention complete, myocardial infarction aborted, crisis averted.

"Get her finished up," Gabi said. "I'm going to have a talk with her family. Great job. Thank you."

She enjoyed delivering good news to family members who were sitting in the waiting room, hoping and often praying for the best but expecting the worst. The sighs of relief were common, the hugs occasional, and the gratitude constant. There was, however, the flip side of the coin, the bad news, the tragic news that was met with shock, tears, denial, despair, and anger. She had experienced the full spectrum since the first month of her residency and the interactions never became any easier.

The walk into the room always felt ripped from the television or movie screen, she admitted. The stereotypes were true. The slow walk, the polite smile as eye contact was established to give the initial comfort, it was all textbook. These were the tactics that were not taught by a single medical school in the world. Life experience was the professor of medical communication with the family of patients.

For ten minutes, Gabi stood before the Ellison family, all three of whom remained seated, and explained the diagnosis, the procedure, and the prognosis. Her husband was silent, stoic but listening, his head resting in his hands by the time the final good news was delivered. Her son, who was not yet forty, not yet ready to lose his mother so early in life, was the most interactive, asking questions, nodding, looking skyward upon hearing that a heart attack had been in progress but was stopped. His hand was held by his wife, wiping away tears and squeezing her husband's hand with each revelation from the doctor.

"Thank you," the three said, nearly in unison.

"You're welcome," Dr. Gabrielle McLane replied. "You can see her shortly."

It would have been possible to make it to the office before noon but, considering the madness of the morning, there was no rush. She was a founding partner – *the* founding partner – at Commonwealth Cardiology Associates and was not about to be fired without being bought out at a premium. Gabi knew her role, her rights, and her personal expectations better than anyone.

Four and a half hours of appointments and notes and consultations followed her arrival at 1 p.m. and by the time she walked out the door, the last one to leave, her Monday had left her feeling as she would on a Friday, something that seemed to be happening more and more in recent history. The frustration had been mounting for months, from feeling underappreciated amongst her partners to the wear and tear of her brutal schedule and the utter lack of advancement in her personal life. She needed a respite, a vacation, any kind of break, for a night, a week, a month, anything.

Before she called, she knew he would answer on the first ring. If he was busy, maybe two.

Nick answered the call just after the first ring on his end of the line.

"Even when I'm not on-call, I'm still on-call," Gabi snarled. "Remind me again why I fooled myself into thinking that interventional cardiology was such a great idea."

"Because no one was born to heal broken hearts in crisis more so than you." Nick said. "Talk to me."

"I'm just now getting in the car and I'm going home. But you're meeting me for dinner."

"Gabi, I just…"

"You just nothing. I'll go home and change. That will give you enough time to pick where we're going and I'll meet you there. See? The work has already been done for you."

"I don't have the time, the energy, or the required insanity to even attempt to argue with you, Gabrielle. Peccato di Gola. I'll see you in an hour."

"That was easy, wasn't it? Love you, bye," she said before ending the call.

She never lets me answer.

The aging brick building that housed Peccato di Gola was tucked away in a cluttered area of downtown a block removed from Main Street. The railroad tracks ran fifty feet from the front of the building, a design flaw for the restaurant in the present but a characteristic originally intended by the original business and its owners for the foot traffic that left the passenger trains at stops that had been removed decades earlier. The intersection two blocks west required the engineer to sound the whistle in multiple blasts before, during, and after every pass, effectively drowning out conversations for the patrons of the restaurant several times a day.

Nick never knew what the building was used for before his favorite Italian restaurant moved in because that transition was well before his time, sometime in the 1960s according to his parents. The façade of the building was perpetually covered in the brown and black dust that was cast off by the passing locomotives. Pressure washing was futile for the brick and mortar. The owners would splurge for the clean-up once a year and begrudgingly at that. Windows were rinsed off on a daily basis out of necessity. Parking was the biggest headache. Patrons were forced to squeeze their vehicle into one of four cramped spaces in the gravel lot along the side of the building or settle for a more comfortable space along Main Street and burn some calories with a walk to the restaurant and back. Employees, with the exception of ownership, opted for Main.

His aging black two-door Honda Civic coupe was parked along the eastbound side of Main Street, at the corner of the cross street. It was hard to miss. The paint was fading on the roof and the hood, an unrepaired dent still resided in the left rear corner thanks to a hit-and-run at an interstate rest stop, and the odometer was nearing 300,000 miles. Somehow, the interior was spotless. Gabi spotted the unmistakable but reliable automobile and took the spot immediately behind it. He always arrived first, no matter where they were meeting.

Nick was waiting in the corner booth at the end of the building furthest from the entrance, his back against the wall, a clear view of both the front door and the entryway to the kitchen and a view of the parking lot from the window next to the table. It was his traditional table whenever he dined in. Two glasses of water were delivered without a word from the host, who was dressed in classic black from head to toe.

The bell over the door rang when Gabi pushed it open and walked through and she saw an elderly man walking at a pace that would set him to arrive at the table just as she did.

"Buonasera!" the man said to Nick, smiling and slowly reaching out to shake his hand.

Gabi slid into the booth and checked her phone for any texts or voicemails that could be a distraction from the conversation of which she was not a part.

"È bello vederti di nuovo, Marco," Nick replied in Italian, prompting a shocked, expressionless Gabi to look up from her phone. *"Come sta* Gianna?" he added, asking about the man's wife.

"Lei sta bene," Marco said. After a glance at Gabi, he said, *"Bella signorina."* Beautiful young lady.

Nick looked at Gabi and said to Marco, *"Così tanto."* So much.

Marco left the table as their server for the evening arrived. She was short, barely five feet tall, thin but toned, and all of her features seemed dark, Nick saw. Her hair was black, her eyes a bright green and the shape narrow and surrounded by dark-rimmed glasses, and her lips were painted a dark red that seemed to complement the rest of the profile. Her ears were pierced multiple times on each side. In comparison to the servers that had worked for the restaurant in years past, she stood in stark contrast.

"Good evening. My name is Rae and I'll be taking care of you this evening," she said as she handed out the menus. As she reached out to hand the single laminated page to Gabi, the edge of a tattoo peeked out from the cuff of her long-sleeve shirt.

"Nice ink," Gabi said. "Is that a sleeve?"

"It is," the server said. "Got in done in Florida before I got dragged here last year against my will." She pulled her sleeve toward the elbow and revealed more of the artwork.

Their orders were placed quickly and Rae disappeared into the kitchen. Gabi stared at Nick until he broke the silence.

"What?"

"Would you like to explain yourself?" Gabi asked.

"Concerning?"

"All these years and you never told me that you speak Italian."

"It never came up," he said, averting his eyes, waiting. When she offered only silence, he said, "*Io parlo l'Italiano un po.*" Then he repeated, in English, "I speak Italian a little."

"You infuriate me sometimes," she said. "Do you speak anything else? Maybe some Mandarin or a little Arabic?"

"Don't be ridiculous, Gabi," he said after a drink of water. "Just English, Italian, Spanish, French, and some conversational modern Hebrew. That's all."

"*That's all?*" she asked in a voice louder than she intended. Heads turned at the table next to the entrance. "You speak five languages and this is the first time you've shared this with me?"

"*Oui,*" he said in French. Yes.

"I will never understand you, Nick."

Think again. You're the only one who does.

"I wouldn't go that far," he said. "Unless I start throwing some Hebrew at you."

Without speaking, Rae slid a basket of sliced Italian bread and a small bowl of seasoned olive oil into the center of the table and disappeared.

"Spanish I get. Italian, French, they all have a similar source so they should be easy to learn in succession. But why Hebrew?"

"I get bored easily and I like a challenge."

She balled up her cloth napkin and tossed it at his face. "You're the weirdest person I have ever known but I love you anyway."

"You better," Nick said, and tossed it back into her lap.

"Okay, so you speak the language. I have to ask you something I've never asked you before."

This should be good.

"Fire away, Doctor McLane."

"*Peccato di Gola.* We've gotten takeout from here forever. We eat in here together, like, once or twice a month. What does the name mean?"

"Do you really want to know?" he asked with a sly grin that made her second guess her question.

"Yes."

"It means 'sin of gluttony'."

"You're kidding me," she said.

"Why in the world would I make that up?"

The restaurant's business hours ended at 10 p.m. on weeknights and the Burke party of two was the last table to vacate the premises. They'd each nursed an entrée, a shared dessert, and a glass of the house red wine, a cabernet sauvignon, for more than three hours. Marco and Gianna, the elderly owners who served primarily as hosts while their oldest son oversaw the daily operation of the restaurant, stood at the table and chatted for twenty minutes before leaving themselves an hour before closing.

"Those two are amazing," Nick had said to Gabi, watching them walk out the door and toward their car, holding hands. "They've been married for over sixty years. Can you imagine?"

"No," she said flatly. "I can't. They always come to talk to you. How do you know them so well?"

"Family friends," Nick said. He watched their car exit the tiny parking lot and said, "My parents knew them well. From the time we moved here, this was our spot. Every time we watched a show over at the Barter, we came here either before or afterward. I don't remember a single time that it didn't happen."

"You've been coming here that long? Since you were…" She paused as her tired mind tried to remember the exact year that Nick and his family had moved to Virginia.

Nick finished her sentence. "Since I was ten."

The subject was difficult. The area had been his home since the late 1990s. The math sparked a reminder of how long they had been gone: Twelve years. His hands transformed into fists, then released to a resting form, remnants of a stress-relieving technique taught to him by a counselor in years past. He pushed them into the front pouch of his black hooded sweatshirt, the most comfortable one he owned. Across the front, in gold letters outlined in white, was the homage to his place of birth, the world where he spent the first ten years of his life. The university was part of the fabric of the state. His father was a graduate, his mother grew into a fan, and Nick wore the name and the logo proudly in a place where his attire was considered entirely foreign. Although he mostly followed football and basketball, he was forever tied to the Iowa Hawkeyes and his home state in the heart of the Midwest.

"I know how much you miss them," Gabi had said, and reached to the middle of the table to touch his hand. "You still haven't been back have you?"

"No." To himself, he silently added, "Just once."

Gabi insisted on paying, as she almost always did but only succeeded half of the time. The tip was generous: twenty-five percent on a nearly seventy-dollar bill. Rae deserved it and probably needed it, Gabi could do it, and the decision was simple.

One glass of wine and the hour of time that had passed since consumption meant that driving home was not a concern for either of them. Nick was facing a ride more than twice as long as his dinner date. The long, winding drive through the valley and back up the side of the mountain was the only part of the evening that he dreaded.

At five after ten, Rae held open the front door, looked to their table and said, "I hate to do it but we're past ten already," and waved her hand through the doorway as if she were attempting to herd cattle. By the time Nick and Gabi stood and began their walk in her direction, she has already turned the corner and was walking toward the Main Street intersection.

Rae was at the crosswalk, standing in front of Nick's Honda, when they turned the corner, and she activated the keyless entry system on her green Toyota Prius that was parked, pointed headfirst toward a building on the westbound side of the road. Halfway down the block, the lights blinked twice and the locks opened and she stepped into the road without looking in either direction. At 10 p.m. on a Monday night, there was little traffic to be seen on the east end of town.

To the right, Nick spotted a set of headlights moving in their direction but still several blocks away. The light at the intersection turned to green just as Rae turned left and fumbled her keys onto the concrete and illuminated a human outline standing in the entrance of a locked building.

Dark shirt, dark sweats.

The headlights were now only two blocks away and moving closer. It was an SUV, he saw; a recent design, not a compact, tinted windows. Once Rae retrieved her keys and began moving again, the unknown figure stepped out of the shadows and onto the sidewalk, looking over his shoulder in the direction of the approaching vehicle.

What are you doing?

Nick reached for the back pocket of his jeans and said to Gabi, "I think I left my wallet in the booth. Will you run back and check for me?"

"Seriously?" she stopped and asked.

Get out of here, Gabi.

"I'll owe you one," he said with his eyes still fixed on Rae, who was still a hundred feet ahead of the man was who was now watching her but had yet to move.

"You owe me two," she said and started back toward the restaurant.

A block from the intersection, the lights on the SUV switched off and the vehicle reduced its speed while the man from the shadows began walking in the direction of the Prius.

Nick was almost to the corner. Despite a noticeable limp favoring his left foot, the man increased his pace and was gaining ground on Rae, who was unaware of his presence. The SUV was moving again, approaching the intersection, but slowed to remain behind the action.

The man closed the distance to less than thirty feet before Nick stepped into the westbound lane of Main Street, with a car headed toward him to his left. "Rae!" he shouted and jogged toward her car, angling across the road from right to left in order to place himself between the woman and the man behind her.

Startled by hearing her name, she looked up and said, "What?"

Reaching the sidewalk, his eyes locked with the man whose face was otherwise obscured by the darkness.

White, forties, 5-11, left leg injury.

Looking back to Rae but stepping into a position to her left, shielding her from a person whose presence she had not yet noticed, Nick pulled a twenty-dollar bill from his pocket and said, "I think we forgot to tip you. Your service was excellent tonight."

"No, your friend already..."

"Thank you," he said, and handed her the bill before he looked back toward the man who had reversed course and was moving toward a side street. The lights on the SUV powered on again, illuminating the man's outline. His arms were down, his hands below his waist, and he signaled to the driver to move.

Where are you going?

The color drained from her face. "What just happened?" Rae asked.

"I don't know that anything *has* happened but you should get home, wherever that is."

Rae opened the door to her car, started the engine, and pulled away as Nick crossed back to the corner where his Honda sat in front of Gabi's BMW. Seeing Gabi walking toward him, he opened the driver side door and feigned a search for the lost wallet before turning to look for the man, the SUV, or both, but failing to locate either of the two.

Thin air.

"No luck," Gabi said as she emerged from the darkness and into the light from the street lamp.

Nick patted the front pocket on his hoodie, then reached in, pulled out his wallet and said, "You've got to be kidding me."

Gabi looked skyward and groaned. "Nick!" she shouted.

"I'm sorry!" he exclaimed, then closed his eyes, blew out his breath, and said, "Okay, I owe you three."

Gabi yawned, stretched and arched her back, and said, "I'm running on fumes. I'm going home." She embraced him and said, "You drive me crazy."

"Thank you for tonight."

"We both needed it," she said. Nick opened his mouth to speak but was cut off before he could muster a word. "I know. Let you know when I get home. I will."

"You better."

She sneered, then smiled, and said, "I'll talk to you tomorrow," and opened the driver door to her X5.

After watching Gabi's taillights fade into the night, he reached into the car and grabbed his phone, pulled up his contact list, and selected Micah Bruce.

Micah was in the same time zone but could be active in any number of projects in any number of locations at any given time. To avoid security concerns, in a non-emergency situation the ice would be broken by text message, then the subject would be addressed later by voice. Protocol never changed.

The text to Micah read: *Call tomorrow, 9 a.m., on the secure VoIP. Registry check.*

The time on the clock was a quarter after midnight when Nick opened the center drawer of the desk in his office and extracted his short-form journal. The computer monitor was off, the desk lamp was on, and the blinds were closed. Light was minimal. Appropriate, he thought, both internally and externally, but the sun would soon rise.

The thought had to be expressed onto a canvas. To allow it to remain unsaid, unwritten, casting a shadow on his days and nights without escape, was unfair to himself and to the others who crossed his path regardless of frequency. Pen to paper was one of God's greatest therapies.

He dated the upper right hand corner of the page and wrote:

> *The lie of narcissistic sociopathy says that you are responsible for everything but guilty of nothing. That's also not reality. The truth always comes out and things always come back. They believe that they are invincible and that we will forever endure and embrace them, along with their manipulation, by choice. This is why we must find ourselves thankful when we are providentially rescued from everything we wanted.*

4

It was known in professional circles as the ego wall, even though this particular example existed in the office of a rural, private home that rarely hosted visitors.

Nick compiled his personal ego wall on the exterior wall of the office, to the left of the window and immediately visible from the doorway upon entry. There were five college degrees in all, three undergraduates and two graduates, from three alma maters in three states – Radford, Southern Illinois, and Wake Forest – and an assortment of certificates from professional organizations and honor societies. Five rows of three columns, fifteen frames displayed the culmination of decades of work.

Sitting behind his dark oak executive desk, the clock still three minutes away from 9 a.m., he examined the frames on the wall, the surfaces obscured by the glare of the morning sun peering through the front window, and wondered if there would be additions in his future, not out of necessity but of pleasure, the challenge, the construction of an entirely unique skill set. Such things could wait. Backburners existed for a reason.

On the monitor for his computer, the window for the encrypted VoIP phone system appeared promptly at the appointed time. Nick donned his USB headset and answered the call.

"Micah, it's been too long," he said. They were his first spoken words of the day and his throat was in need of clearing. "How is everything, my friend? How was the getaway?"

"Until yesterday, I never knew I needed the satisfaction of having my beard complimented by Chewbacca at Disney World but here I am," Micah said. His voice was midrange, his cadence fast and staccato, lending him the ability to relay a lot of information in very little time and requiring the listener to remain on their proverbial toes. The words always mattered.

When information was the need, Micah Bruce was the source. He was an information technology specialist by trade, operating a remote help desk in Florida from an office with a view of the Atlantic Ocean. It was mostly a mundane 9-to-5 occupation, answering questions that he believed to have simple answers, rarely dealing with issues that required an explanation that lasted more than five minutes with even the most technologically ignorant employee in the corporation. In those cases, the Level 2 help desk would step in. Micah struggled to understand how the chemists who developed lifesaving medications for a major pharmaceutical corporation could manage to screw up their email.

At five feet and seven inches tall, he considered himself somewhat vertically challenged despite standing just shy of the average for an American male. His black beard was thick and a source of pride, even legendary, if he was asked, and he both spoke and behaved with energy that soon spread to those nearby. A one-man research department, on the clock or off, Micah was on call and available 24/7 to research, to dig, to learn, and to assist. His digital eyes and ears were open in almost any location, by design or request, and security was merely a speed bump, a low hurdle rather than a brick wall.

Nick had met Micah only a single time in person, two years earlier at a company retreat, but the two spoke weekly regarding professional matters. Micah was younger than Nick and not in the field. His time was spent primarily in logistical support but often colored outside the lines of his job description. Nick was on the receiving end of his work, often succeeding, in part, because of it. The unit was the sum of its parts, visible and concealed, local and remote.

For ten minutes, Nick relayed the events of the night before in detail. From the personal details of the dinner with Gabi, who was a frequent subject of discussion, to what appeared to be an attempted abduction of their server, Rae, after the restaurant closed, nothing was omitted regardless of the perceived significance.

"Thoughts?" Nick asked upon reaching the conclusion.

"I don't know, brother," Micah said. "Could be random but it doesn't seem that way. The guy on foot is one thing..."

"But the trailing SUV is another," Nick interrupted. "We're on the same page. Multiple levels in play and an unseen someone or something calling shots."

"Did you get a plate, or a make and model? A look at the guy on foot?"

"Nothing that important. He had an injury that he was nursing. He was limping on his left foot. All of his identifying features were obscured. He was average height and build so nothing stands out there. He didn't speak. He's a dead end. Can you look into any web-based security systems with exterior cameras that might be running in the area?"

"Gotcha. I'll be looking and I'll let you know. Anything else?"

Nick paused and said, "Yes. Look at the sex offender registry. See if we have anyone out there that has escaped or failed to register in the area, and then dig a little deeper and check on recent releases. Let's see if anyone stands out as a major concern, with this or in general. If so, find out who they are, where they are, and what they are doing. Full workup."

"On it, my man. Rush?"

"The latter more so than the former. Get back to me as soon as you can. Thank you, Micah."

"Eyes and ears, bro. I'll talk to you," Micah said before the call ended.

At noon, with a freshly prepared lunch of grilled salmon and steamed broccoli sitting on the desk in place of the keyboard, the VoIP phone system window appeared and Nick answered.

"Anything good?" he said.

"That depends on your definition of the word," Micah said. "Still working on the cameras, if there are any, but we've got a hit on the registry. One absconder, another that failed to register, but they're tied together."

"How?" Nick asked with a mouthful.

"According to what I accessed, they were locked up together, cellmates for at least a couple of years."

"I like how you use the word 'accessed' and we all just generally accept it for what we know it really means."

Micah laughed and said, "It's part of my charm. "

"How close are we talking?"

"One of them is probably shacked up with his girl in Hansonville. She's got a rap sheet longer than his but mostly petit stuff and drugs. Typical pillhead with a mattress strapped to her back. Once I see her credit card records I'll know if she's got him there, or at least I'll have a better idea. I don't know about the other one but he hasn't been seen in a while and he could only have a few people to reach out to. It wouldn't be a shock if he's there or headed that way."

"Put it together, separate files but the same report, and get it to me when you feel like it's got enough to move on."

"That all?" Micah asked.

"Call Bret," Nick said. "Tell him to get down here when he can. In the mean time, keep looking."

A crosswind was blowing at twenty miles per hour across Interstate 81 and directly into the terminal at Mountain Empire Airport in Smyth County, Virginia. The runway of just over 5200 feet was sufficient for Bret Stevenson to land the Cessna 421C Golden Eagle but he preferred more than the recommended space, not less. MKJ was his airport of choice for the flights to Virginia. The Virginia Highlands Airport in Abingdon was closer but failed to meet his personal requirements. An hour drive to the farmhouse was an easy trade for his peace of mind.

The pilot moved through his pre-landing checklist item by item. Fuel mixture fully rich, brakes checked, the setting on the flaps correct, he had done this a thousand times. Inside a mile to the airport, he reduced his airspeed. The Cessna veered slightly off course to the left on approach but Bret corrected, adjusting the aileron to control his lateral balance along with increased back pressure on the yoke, pulling the nose of the aircraft up, and slowly touched down.

After a short taxi to the hangar, uninterrupted with no other activity at the facility, Bret exited the terminal to find that the rental car was waiting in the parking lot just as expected, the same as every other trip from Cleveland, Ohio to Virginia. The solo flights in the Cessna, registered to a corporate entity rather than himself, lacked the excitement of his time in the United States Air Force but the events that followed his landing often exceeded expectations. Being asked to arrive on 72 hours notice was assuredly a sign of action in the near future.

Before backing out of the parking space, he connected his phone to the stereo using a Bluetooth connection. The hour-long drive to the farmhouse was scenic but uneventful and silence was unacceptable. Music, loud music, lots of it, was appropriate. As the first drops of rain fell onto the windshield from an approaching shower, he shifted in his seat and looked at the backpack in the passenger side floorboard. He'd brought enough clothing to last a week. Surely that would be more than enough. Nick wasn't one to waste time.

Some people hated to run in the rain but Nick didn't understand why. In the dog days of August when heat and humidity were the most miserable and draining of the year, the rain was refreshing, even revitalizing, in the homestretch of a three-mile run up and down the country roads. There was no need for music, no cell phone to distract, because the run was therapeutic, a chance to think, to reflect, to work.

Nick crossed the bridge on the way back to the house and stopped just past the fork in the road that split Moccasin Valley Road with Route 679, the same place where he paused on every run to peer down to the creek bed.

After a moment, he turned and resumed his run headed east back to the house. At the unpaved driveway, he slowed to a walk and stepped into the yard. His guest was early and that, too, was expected. The military stressed attention to detail and punctuality was near the top of the list.

"You look different every time I see you," Nick said as he approached the front steps to the porch.

"I try to keep it fresh," Bret said.

"Fresh? Try nondescript. You look like the default character on a video game that lets you make your own guy. Just open the editor and hit finish."

The banter was standard issue.

Stevenson was 5-9, naturally strong without the kind of physicality that drew attention, and was hypersensitive to the details of his surroundings. For the time being his head was shaved, his face clean-shaven. He maintained the ability to be both emotionally driven and passé at the same time, with the ability to flip a switch whenever necessary that Nick envied in his friend and associate.

"It's been three months. How's life treating you?" Nick asked. He sat at the top of the stone steps and leaned back against the post.

Bret was sitting in the wooden swing at the end of the porch opposite the side entrance to the house. "Like it caught me breaking into its house unarmed," he said.

"Ex-wife?"

"Still trash, I'm sure. She's spent more time on her knees than a priest and more time on her back than a Brazilian Jiu-Jitsu black belt. But it's whatever. She's someone else's problem now."

"Brutal," Nick said. "So do you want to know why you're here or not?"

"Why are any of us here?"

"I don't think we have the time to get into all that at the moment," Nick said. "We've had some action down here in the last week or so."

For the next fifteen minutes, Nick relayed the same story, in full detail, as he had to Micah on the previous Tuesday morning.

"Any leads since then? It's been four days," Bret asked.

"Nothing yet. But hope springs eternal on a Saturday."

Nick pushed himself to his feet, opened the screen door in the center of the house, and said, "Let's call Micah. He texted an hour ago and said he has an update and a full rundown."

In the office, Nick sat behind his desk while Bret took one of the two chairs facing him. The USB headset was unplugged, replaced by an external omnidirectional microphone and standard speakers. After two rings on the secure VoIP line, Micah answered.

"Good afternoon, gentlemen," he said.

"What's the word, Micah?" Nick asked.

"Is Bret there?"

"I'm here, man," Bret said.

"Still rocking the beard this time or bald as a cue ball?" Micah asked and then laughed. "Probably not just the 'stache. You haven't worked your way back around to that yet."

"Not bad considering we're not on camera," Nick said.

"Just get to it, little guy," Bret said and leaned back with his hands interlaced behind his neck.

"I got a look at what went down a few days ago from a security cam at a gun shop of all places. They always have the best security systems outside of a bank or a hospital. It's pretty easy to see what was going on that night. I guess you could say that you got there in the nick of time."

Bret laughed. With his fingers pinching the bridge of his nose, Nick said, "I hate you. Just keep going."

Micah continued, "No clear view of a plate. The windows on the SUV were tinted and it was barely more than a glance before it turned off anyway. The guy with the limp covered his tracks and his face. There's not much to go on, bro."

"Keep looking for patterns. Spread out if you need to," Nick said. "What else?"

"We have a couple of bad *hombres* on the loose that we might be interested in."

"What kind?"

"You asked me to run the registry check and I did. Two on the run and it's suspected that they're probably close by."

The sex offender registry.

"Micah, is it possible that they are involved in what happened with the abduction attempt?"

"I don't know how else to say this, Nick, but I think your waitress is a little old for them."

Nick tapped his index finger on the desk.

Bret leaned forward in his chair and rested his elbows on his knees as he listened. He rubbed his face where a beard sometimes existed. "Let's hear it, Micah. Who are these guys?"

"First guy is Victor Lane. Biracial male, early thirties, originally from Blacksburg, Virginia but spent the last few years locked up. Statutory rape was the charge, multiple cases. Two were fifteen but one was thirteen. How far is that from you, Nick?"

"Couple of hours east. What else?"

"Ian Henry. White male in his late twenties, hometown listed as Norfolk but he was shacked up with a girl in Hansonville when he was arrested four years ago. He was locked up with Lane for three years. They shared a cell. Some kind of illness broke out in the prison and inmates were being treated offsite. The transport van was involved in an accident on the return trip, both of them managed to get out, and they were out of the area before anyone could do anything about it."

"You just can't beat prison for networking," Nick said.

"How far away?" Bret asked.

"They were both being held at Marion. This happened about ten days ago but the Virginia State Police haven't managed to grab them so far."

"What was Henry in for?" Nick asked.

Micah's end of the call went silent.

"Talk to me, kid," Nick said.

"Same thing as his cellmate but worse. He was convicted of everything from sexual assault to child porn, and supposed to be locked up for more than fifty years. His youngest victim was an eight-year-old little girl, Nick. These people are the cancer of our society; the kind that our world is better off without."

Bret stood from his chair and paced the length of the office.

Nick stood but remained behind his desk and spoke into the microphone. "Where are they, Micah?"

"I couldn't even tell you why but it looks like the girl has them both hanging around for now. Her debit card started getting active a couple of days ago. Grocery store, gas station, and multiple fast food joints but that's not the issue."

"What is?" Bret asked.

"They're high dollar amounts being spent for someone who is supposedly living alone and it only started within our time window."

Nick muted the microphone and said to Bret, "I'm sure his access to these things is perfectly legal." Then to Micah: "I assume you have the location."

"Everything you need is waiting in a PDF file in the secure email box, right down to the GPS coordinates that will take you straight to their front door and the mug shots that will let you pick them out of a lineup of a hundred."

"Tell D.T. I'll call him, okay?"

"You got it."

"Thanks, Micah," Nick said before ending the call. He turned to the weapons safe that stood in the back right corner of the office behind his desk, typed in the seven-digit combination, 6354772, opened the door, and motioned for Bret to join him. Each selected what was needed and preferred before the door was shut.

"Let's go for a ride."

Manufactured housing was often spoken as a pejorative term by elitists but modern versions of the mobile homes took on the appearance of buildings with far more positive reputations, far different than the simple, white metal trailers of the 1970s. The accommodations for

Victor Lane and Ian Henry were far better than they deserved, Nick thought, and likely felt like a multimillion-dollar mansion by comparison to the standard eight-by-eight cell to which they had been banished until ten days earlier. The choice of food, the space, even this version of freedom, after a fashion, would have grown foreign in the confines of the Marion Correctional Center.

The home was a double wide, light brown with a basic black roof and four windows across the front. An aftermarket wooden deck attached to the back of the structure but the wood was left untreated and had been badly damaged by the elements. A single five hundred gallon propane tank was situated at the corner of the house next to the deck, which led into the kitchen through a sliding glass door.

Visually, the house was out of place. It sat on the incorporated limits of Hansonville, in sight of Route 58 Alternate but in the middle of a lot that was only accessible from an unpaved dirt road. This portion of the state route was a four lane highway that ran through the valley on mostly flat ground. With mountains on either side, the scenery was plentiful but the tactical situation was troublesome for anyone who approached. The line of sight was clear for anyone in the home who may be watching, including paranoid absconders with no desire to return to their cellblock.

With the sun setting behind the mountains and the temperature dropping into the low sixties, the cover of darkness was approaching. In open space, with limited light sources nearby, the need for dressing in solid black was gone but tradition was held. Comfort and agility were non-negotiable; speed, a luxury. The pickup truck that the company had rented at Micah's direction was parked on the side of the road a half-mile away, close enough for access but far enough away to avoid the suspicion of curious eyes.

Twenty minutes after arrival, while still sitting in the truck, examining the property through binoculars, and running through their stratagem point-by-point, the girl whose activity had led them to their targets left the property. They watched her pull onto the highway and pass by their location and wondered how she would react upon seeing the scene when she returned.

When the blue hour had passed, the purple sky having transitioned fully into black with only the occasional cloud obscuring the stars and partial moon, the nearest light source came from the highway. First there would be something to draw their attention, followed by a diversion to draw them out. The strategy was straight out of their playbook, cut and dried, and used more than once in the past.

"I'm left, you're right," Nick said.

Bret replied without looking. "Copy."

Nick stayed in a crouch, his nine-millimeter semi-automatic pistol drawn but not raised, and stepped toward the back of the house. Bret was upright, moving slowly and carrying a flat cardboard pizza box as he walked up the steps to the front door, which was near the left end of the home. He knocked three times and backed away far enough to peer around the corner where Nick was waiting for the next step. When the door opened, Victor Lane appeared. His dark black hair was cut to a quarter-inch in length with an electric trimmer. He was shirtless and his dark grey sweatpants revealed no sign of concealed weapons. His eyes caught Bret's attention. The pupils were dilated, redness setting in around the iris.

Seeing Bret, he scratched his head and muttered, "What?"

"That'll be $17.00 even," Bret said. He smiled and added, "Before the tip."

He turned back into the house and shouted "Ian!" With no answer, he turned his back to Bret and said, "Ian! Did you order anything from town?"

Henry emerged from the bathroom, wiping his hands on his pants, and walked toward the door. "What are you talking about? I didn't order nothin'." His stained a-shirt failed to cover the developing gut that was beginning to obscure the beltline of his jeans. "Get this guy outta here."

Henry walked to the window at the end of the house and peered into the empty space where both his estranged girlfriend and any visitors typically parked. Seeing no one, he backed away from the window and toward the kitchen table where a snubnose revolver was laying in a chair. Looking past Victor and through the door at Bret, he stepped forward and asked, "Who are you, buddy?"

Before Bret could answer, a police car sped by on the four-lane, sirens blaring and lights flashing. "Cops! He's a cop!" Henry screamed.

"Not exactly," Bret said as he grabbed Victor by the arm, pulling him through the doorway and into the front yard. He swept Victor's right leg with his own and took him to the ground. Bret changed positions immediately with a pass to his right, swung his legs across Victor's neck, and pulled back on his arm, applying an armbar. Victor screamed while Bret pulled back with one explosive move, hyperextending the elbow until he heard an audible snap.

As Bret took Victor to the ground, Henry scrambled toward his gun under the kitchen table. He looked outside but knew that he did not have a clear shot to free Victor from his attacker. As he started toward the front door, hoping to get into the yard and assist his former cellmate, Nick fired a single shot through the window and Ian froze for a moment before turning and firing three shots in return.

Do it.

In the front yard, still one-on-one, Bret stood and dragged Victor away from the house. Tears ran down Victor's face as he held the elbow on the arm that was not being used to pull him along the ground. "How's it feel?" Bret asked without caring about the answer.

His gun raised, Nick sidestepped toward the back of the house after losing sight of Henry moving inside.

It's like watching a movie. They always go out the back.

Bret had pulled Victor a hundred feet from the house and scanned the area to find where Nick was standing. Thick, black plastic zip ties bound Victor Lane's wrists in front of him and he groaned each time his feet made contact with the ground. Nick motioned toward him, then toward the truck, and Bret began walking his new detainee off of the property.

The glass door flew open and Ian ran onto the deck but stopped when he saw Nick standing in front of him. The red dot from Nick's laser sight appeared center mass in his chest. Ian raised his hands and Nick commanded him to drop to his knees. The snubnose revolver was stuffed in the front of Ian's pants.

"How do you want to play this, Ian?" Nick asked.

"I'm not going back," Ian responded. His voice combined a shout and a whimper.

Fear.

Nick smiled and began to back away from the house, gaining distance and angling into a perfect line of sight. Ian dropped his hands and pulled the revolver from his pants, letting out a scream of frustration and anger as he rushed to take aim. With his hand still rising, Nick fired a single shot into his right shoulder. The impact and damage from the pre-fragmented hollow point round caused Ian to drop the gun as he spun down to the ground, holding the wound as the blood began to move through his fingers. He cursed at Nick, who admired his own accuracy with a shrug and a nod.

"I can't see you, Ian," Nick taunted. "Where'd you go?"

More profanity flew from the mouth of the wounded criminal but Nick continued to move away.

Nick reached into the front pocket of his hooded sweatshirt and removed a road flare, then activated it, and tossed it onto the porch at Ian's feet. The sparks from the flare popped in the face of the escapee, causing him to shield his eyes and push himself away.

An eight-year-old girl. Prison is too good for you.

Nick removed a second flare, removed the cap, lit the flame, and threw it end over end to the back corner of the house. He backed away to a safer distance before setting his feet, then locked eyes with the sexual predator that had already destroyed an unknown number of lives and fired a quick burst of three shots into the propane tank.

A split second after a brief, audible *whoosh*, the explosion blew the house apart just as Nick dove to the ground, away from the blast, and covered his head. Bret saw the flames and watched the debris fly in every direction but felt the shockwave on a delay inside the truck. Panic-stricken, Victor began to thrash in the bed of the truck.

Bret jumped out, moved to the back, opened the tailgate, and grabbed the injured arm directly at the elbow. Victor screamed until Bret released the grip. "Don't do that," Bret said. "Be grateful. That could have been you."

Nick was jogging away from the scene, estimating a five-minute response time from the local volunteer fire department but knowing that there was little work for them to do. He stopped at the side of the truck on the passenger side, looked at Victor long enough to make eye contact, and got into the cab.

"Let's get to town."

The Food City supermarket in Lebanon, a ten-minute drive from Hansonville, was an ideal drop point for Victor Lane: easy access to the Route 19 Bypass, the clutter and potential bottleneck of downtown easily avoided, far enough away from the police station to ensure a quick getaway with limited visibility, a large parking lot with no video coverage away from the store proper. Bret drove the pickup truck into the parking lot, at the edge furthest away from the building and nearest the main entrance.

Bret opened the tailgate and said, "Give me your feet." Victor pushed himself backward into the corner of the truck bed. "That wasn't a request, kiddo. Stop trying to delay the inevitable," Bret added. Defeated, Victor complied and Bret bound his feet with two more zip ties, immobilization complete.

Nick pulled Victor out of the back of the truck, pointed him toward the trees that stood beside the access road, and knocked him to the ground when he reached the right spot.

Victor began to speak but Bret put a finger to his mouth, shook his head, and shushed him. "I wouldn't," he said.

His eyes wide with genuine fear, Victor remained silent.

Nick reached into the truck and took a cell phone from the glove compartment, a prepaid flip phone that had been activated that day. He dialed the only contact that was entered into the phone's memory, the non-emergency number for the Lebanon Police Department. A female voice answered the call.

"Everyone has been looking for Victor Lane and Ian Henry. I can tell you where they are."

"Sir, could I please have your name?" she asked. "Do you have information on their whereabouts? Do not attempt to make contact with these men. They are considered to be armed and dangerous. Let me connect you with...."

Nick interrupted her script without acknowledging the request. "Ian Henry is dead. Victor Lane is resting uncomfortably under the trees in the Food City parking lot."

The voice was silent, and then asked sardonically, "Will you be bringing him in?"

"We only gift-wrap. We don't deliver," Nick said and ended the call.

5

He missed the controlled but functional chaos of New York, the weather of San Diego, and the endless supply of model-quality women in Miami. Texas, the land of cowboys and football, was of little interest. Chicago featured some of the finest cuisine in the United States but nothing else that managed to cast a lasting spell on him. Boston was too cold for too long. Amsterdam had been his favorite place to live, work, exist, but it was inevitably transient. Hedonism was an escape from reality but having every appetite fed at will, without limitation or question, was destructive to his work ethic. It also permanently altered his perception of red lights.

This town in the hills of Virginia, one of the original thirteen colonies of which his education was scant, was scenic but offered little else to a man who had lived a life such as his. Such peasants, he thought. The lack of imagination bored him. Life here was lived in a slow-motion vacuum when compared to most of his adult existence. It was no wonder that its citizenry rarely escaped the green acres to what he would consider to be greener pastures. He was uninterested in his surroundings but his input was discouraged, as is always the case when working for a man who fancied himself a benevolent dictator rather than a leader of a group with a common goal. He craved intrigue, action, something both exciting and lucrative, not the sleepy life of a place that he would forget the moment that his plane lifted off from the runway for the last time.

It was the girl that occupied his thoughts: the young blonde, Shelby. She was so naïve, so innocent when she first started, so unlike any of the others in both appearance and personality. She was hesitant at first, then enthusiastic, but never weak, and that was part of the appeal. He admired her, imagined a scenario with different circumstances, and then chastised himself for fawning over a woman that he barely knew.

Technically, he had gotten what he wanted two weeks before. It was her first time shooting a video and he had volunteered to serve as her co-star, knowing that the familiarity would alleviate tensions. She was tense in the opening moments but, with his expert guidance, quickly acclimated. The girl was a natural and he wanted more, needed more, and found himself fixated on more. When a second scene was set to be produced five days later, he volunteered again. The director insisted on a different male partner but, after a reminder of his place in the pecking order, relented.

This was the breaking of new ground for Lucien Murdoc. In every past venture, the women were mere placeholders, means to an end. They were disposable, easily cast aside in favor of the next flavor of the week. In every city there was a coalition of the willing ranging from the desperate to the adventurous and all points in between. There was just something about this girl and her journey from innocence to experience that left him craving more intimate personal knowledge and longing for contact. He yearned for the conversation as much as the touch.

Eyes closed and lying on his back, he was ten minutes into another Shelby fantasy when his cell phone startled him back into reality. He turned and lunged for the bedside table before the second play through the ringtone, hoping to see the name and number and then hear the voice from his dreams. He swore aloud in French when he saw the name of his boss.

"Yes, *patron*," Lucien said with a roll of his eyes. He ran his hand through his hair and sat up on the edge of the bed, facing the window in the hotel room that faced the parking lot. The same scenery, day after day, was becoming mentally and emotionally tiresome.

"Status?" the man said. The other end of the call was loud and nearly overpowering, voices and dance music that sounded like a nightclub made up the ambient noise that would have been appropriate at 2 a.m. but seemed out of place just before noon.

"Three of five," Lucien said, speaking loudly to cut through the sounds in the background. "Perhaps four but it is uncertain at the moment."

"Be certain," the man said. The connection was terminated before Lucien could respond.

Lucien stood and walked a slow lap around the room, the largest suite available in the building, before returning to the bed, picking up the phone, and scrolling through the list of contacts. First, a touch on the only name on the list that he cared to see, then a tap of the phone icon that produced the sound of ringing in the speaker.

"Please answer," he whispered into the empty space that seemed to grow a foot tighter with each passing day.

He heard her voice, felt the heaviness in his chest fade, and spoke as quickly as he could without sounding too forward, forgoing so much as a greeting. "It's Lucien," he said, forgetting that caller ID was now a standard item rather than a luxury. She knew who was calling. "Would you join me for lunch?" Touching his wrist with his thumb, he felt his pulse racing and shuddered at his immaturity.

The wait for her response felt like an eternity but, in reality, was less than a second. He felt like a teenager, his hands shaking, walking back and forth in front of the window and changing directions every three steps.

"Sure," she said. He clinched his fist and closed his eyes when she spoke the words.

"You choose," he said. "We can go anywhere you like. My only desire is for you to join me today."

It was the first completely honest statement that he had made in nearly eight weeks.

"What?" Shelby smiled and asked.

"I'm sorry," Lucien said. "I didn't mean to stare. That smile is enchanting."

"You're forgiven," she replied with a wink and picked at the last quarter of her lasagna.

Her lunch date was more than attractive. He was charming, intelligent, successful, and persuasive. There was depth and charisma. He had experienced indescribable things in parts of the world that barely seemed real to her, more so as she remembered that her most exotic vacation consisted of a week-long cruise with her parents. When he spoke, Lucien radiated a mysterious worldly charm that contrasted with the college boys and working class young men who now seemed boring, juvenile, and painfully shallow. Saying no to him was not option, as she had already discovered but without complaint. She was learning about Lucien in reverse order, the personal details followed the intimate. It was uncharted territory. The wisdom of social interaction with her coworker, her employer, whatever he could be called, was debatable but the allure was an irresistible force.

Across the table, his cell phone vibrated before the ringtone sounded. She saw him flinch after looking at the screen. He managed a nervous smile, said, "*Excusez-moi, magnifique,*" and slid out of the booth. Hearing his native French was an instant turn-on. She understood an occasional word, never a phrase, and missed that he had referred to her as gorgeous just as he exited.

Shelby scrolled through her various social media apps while she waited, looking up every few seconds in hopes that his business call was nearing its end and sneaking a look behind the counter at the server whose face seemed familiar. The slim brunette had been tasked with other tables during the lunch rush and was entering orders into the point of sale system, separating the bills from the coins in her tips, and sneaking a drink from her water bottle before hurrying back out onto the floor to check for empty glasses and plates waiting to be cleared.

"The hotel," she murmured.

She had seen the server at the hotel on the very first day. It was the tattoo that jogged her memory, a full sleeve from shoulder to wrist that popped with reds and yellows in addition to the traditional green. The unmistakable gauges in the ears served as confirmation. "Why would anyone do that?" she whispered to herself, raising her eyebrows as she looked back down to the phone. It was the girl who absconded before the test shots, Shelby thought, and then chuckled at her usage of the word *absconded* in her own internal dialogue. "She sure has strange ideas for what is acceptable for her body and what isn't," she mumbled to herself.

She looked around once more for Lucien, spotted him pacing in the parking lot through the window, still on his call and visibly frustrated, then looked back down to the screen and swiped away unwanted text messages and worthless coupons from her notifications.

When she looked up, the server was at the table.

"More water? Anything else?" Rae asked.

"No, thanks," Shelby said. She leaned forward and lowered her voice. "You look so familiar. What's your name?"

"Rae," the server responded and sat down in the empty booth. "I was thinking the same thing. I swear I know you from somewhere. Your friend, too."

With a quick scan of their surroundings, Shelby said, "It was a couple of months ago. I think we were in a conference room together over at Wyndale."

Rae's face morphed from curiosity to shock and she fumbled with the pen clipped to her order pad. "Oh, right. I, uh..." she stuttered but didn't finish and began to slide out of the booth.

Shelby placed her hand on top of Rae's and smiled. "It's okay. It's not like anyone else here knows, girl. Hang on a second."

"The guy that was here?" Rae asked. The intent of the question was unspoken but unavoidable.

"Uh-huh. That's Lucien," Shelby answered, feeling the redness rush to her face and hoping that Rae was too distracted and flustered to notice.

"Are you two, you know…" Her question trailed off without adding the obvious ending.

"I don't know. I guess. I'm not sure." Her answer, or the attempted avoidance, hung in the air as an awkward silence, the necessity to break it growing exponentially with each second. Neither wanted to speak but Shelby took a deep breath and asked, "Why did you leave?"

The door to the restaurant opened and Lucien entered, walking toward the entrance and returning the phone to his pocket.

"It just didn't feel right," Rae said quietly, left the bill on the edge of the table, and stood up from the booth as Lucien approached. "It was so good to see you again," she added, louder, audible to Shelby and Lucien, as well as the diners at the adjacent tables.

The Frenchman offered a dutiful but polite smile to the server when she turned to walk away and sighed as he slid into his seat. "Apologies," he said. "Do you two know one another?"

"Only in passing. That's what we were trying to figure out actually." She sipped her water and looked away in hopes that he had overlooked her attempted dodge.

"Pity that," Lucien said. "She looks like fun," he added, raised his eyebrows and smiled. "You think?"

Shelby's face flushed. She smiled and turned away from the man whose power to convince her of anything, to lead her into new worlds, to alter reality and eliminate barriers, was mounting. "Lucien…" she said in a bashful whisper.

He wiped his mouth, despite not having eaten in twenty minutes, and dropped the cloth napkin onto the table. "Shall we go?" He extended his hand, which Shelby took, and stood. Their eyes remained connected.

"Where are we going?" she asked.

"Anywhere you wish, as long as you permit me to follow."

She tucked her blonde hair behind her ears, on the right, then the left, and retrieved her clutch bag from the table. "I've missed the view from your suite."

Lucien touched the small of her back and kissed her cheek, lingering there an extra beat to mentally record the sensory response to every touch, every scent, and every taste. "Meet me outside," he whispered into her ear.

Shelby walked toward the exit, glancing over her shoulder and smiling as she pushed the door open, and Lucien handed his credit card to Marco behind the counter.

"Everything good?" Marco asked through his marked Italian accent.

"Perhaps my finest Italian experience since I was last on holiday in Venice." Lucien feigned sudden recall and said, "The gratuity. My mistake." He returned to the cluttered table, and then turned in the direction of the table nearby where Rae was taking the drink order for the newly seated party and waited for her to notice his attention. She slid the order pad into her back pocket and stopped when she saw him.

He closed his eyes, nodded his head in recognition, and dropped a fifty-dollar bill onto the table. Attached to it with a paper clip was a single business card. Printed in black ink above an out-of-state phone number was the name Lucien Murdoc. "*Merci beaucoup,*" he said as he passed her on his way out the door.

"Welcome back, Rae," he thought, then immediately removed her from his thoughts upon the sight of Shelby waiting for him on the passenger side of his sedan.

He hated the sticky feeling of sweat, no matter how enjoyable the process of creating the necessary conditions, but he had encouraged Shelby to use the shower first. Laying shirtless on the bed, his pulse rate was still above normal, his breathing rapid, and his mind racing, all of which were tied to the new object of his affection. He heard the water falling off of her body and onto the floor of the tub and longed to join her, to feel her skin pressed against his, but knew that there would be plenty of time to come for such things. His affection was more than a casual interest. The combination of business and pleasure was long considered problematic at best and toxic at worst but his was a life of calculated risk and reward. The faces and bodies and experiences of the past were superficial, quickly discarded, and easily replaced. The connection he had sought, and for which he long ago had lost hope, appeared suddenly and unexpectedly but would not be relinquished in like manner. Finally, there was a personal to run parallel with the professional.

Still, the necessity of the professional remained and could not be avoided. There was work, responsibility, and a living to be earned. She knew what she needed to know and nothing more. He would do only what was required and nothing more. Soon, he hoped, there would be no more, only a walk into the sunset with a healthy bank account and a rebooted life full of normality and serenity.

His vision of the future was changing and the greatest threat to the next chapter of his epic tale was the untold reality from which Shelby was shielded with great care and purpose. A year earlier, the prospective journey was going to be made alone. Now, he hoped, there would be a companion, another suitcase packed and loaded onto the plane, another set of footprints in the sand.

He rubbed his eyes and shook his head when he considered the outlandishness of considering these things after such a relatively short time with the stereotypical ordinary small-town college girl who, in the eyes of his associates, would pale in comparison to the high-end professionals in their line of work but had captivated him since their first encounter.

His phone vibrated, and then sounded the tone of a bell to indicate the arrival a new text message. The sounds of the shower had ceased in the bathroom, meaning his window of time to view and respond to whatever business was awaiting him in his inbox was short. He unlocked his screen just as the door opened and Shelby emerged surrounded by a cloud of steam. She was wrapped in a thick white towel. Her hair was still damp but had been brushed and beads of water sat on her shoulders.

"Hey there," she said.

Lucien opened the text message and saw that it had been sent from a number that was not included in his contact list.

The message read:

> *This is Rae, from the restaurant. I think you remember me. Call or text.*

"Lucien?" she asked but watched as he typed a quick sentence to whoever had made contact.

"Lucien..." This time her voice trailed off but the pitch rose, then lowered, all with a playful lilt, teasing him in an effort to draw his focus away from the screen.

He looked up in time to see her loosen the towel and watched it fall to the floor. She ran her hands through her hair, then shook her head, and playfully posed in front of him. He held the phone up to his face, opened the camera on his phone, snapped a photo, and then tossed the phone onto the desk and pulled her onto the bed.

6

The calls were always scheduled late at night, midnight or 1 a.m., sometimes as late as 2 o'clock in the morning, but a corporate life full of worldwide travel required freedom from the bonds of Eastern Standard Time, the most recognized name of UTC-5. Both the caller and the recipient understood the nature of the business, the strains of a schedule that prioritized flexibility and adaptability over rigid plans and textbook definitions of what should be said and done at all times. The caller also knew that the man who was waiting on his call maintained an irregular sleep schedule at best and battled insomnia at worst.

The farmhouse was sufficiently heated by the coal furnace but drafts of cold air managed to sweep through certain rooms at random times without warning or reason. One such place was the area behind the desk in Nick's office but the coolness was appreciated in contrast to the heat of late October when autumn began its gradual fade into early winter. Now, with Thanksgiving a week away, the weather was unseasonably warm and the breeze was welcome. Nick appreciated the late-night calls. The conversation broke the silence. The methodical discussion of business focused his brain on the matters of the present rather than remaining fixated on the sights and sounds of the past or needlessly filling in the blanks of an unknown future.

This call, arranged via text message by the man's personal assistant and originally on the books for 1 a.m., was nearly an hour overdue. There was business in Scotland for the man who had built his company from the ground up without the aid of old family money or the need for investors. In his four decades of operation, he had purchased controlling interest or outright ownership of the competitors who once offered to do the same at less than fifty cents on the dollar of what he knew to be the value.

He had first reached out to Nick Burke, then a teaching assistant at Radford University, to inquire about his interest in an entry-level position with his company. Nick knew the name from cable news broadcasts and press clippings but little else. The first letter, authenticated by the company logo at the top, a handwritten signature at the bottom, and a cell phone number to a personal and private line, asked only for an email or a phone call in return. When Nick, out of nothing more than morbid curiosity, dialed the number, the man answered on the second ring and knew with whom he was speaking. His employer would soon assume another role, a surrogate father to the young man who lost his own only weeks later.

Nick held his watch under the lamp on his desk and saw the time. The next waft of cold air brushed by and he tugged at the plain black long-sleeved shirt that matched the black and gold plaid fleece lounge pants with an embroidered University of Iowa logo on one leg. In tense moments, he found himself running his fingers around the edge of the Tigerhawk.

It's almost 7 a.m. over there. I know he's awake.

In the silence, he wondered where she was, who she was with, if he crossed her mind or if his name so much as passed her lips. The initial destruction was sudden but weeks soon became months and the shock turned to silence and rebuilding. Gabi was there for him, battling alongside him, and others joined, but it was in the middle of the night, amidst the battle for sleep and rest, which were not always the same, when the past snaked its way back into the present and an unbridled imagination ripped the scab from what had been a healing wound. Memories thought to be locked away in boxes were of no threat but it was the abstract that remained inescapable. Shadows of actions and reverberations of spoken words lingered in the corners of every room and he knew that his mental and emotional freedom would only be granted when old was finally and fully displaced by new, no longer forced by his mind and heart to distinguish in hindsight between truth and lies. Every room needed a change or an addition, something attached to a different person or event or somehow creating a space and time of emotionless neutrality.

One person was capable of bringing these things to pass, and she had done so with tireless effort, but there was more to be done. Gabi lived a fast-paced life of her own and had a business to run, lives to save, a legacy to build, without the obligation to play lifeguard to save him from drowning in the memories of Mia.

Five minutes shy of 2 a.m., the electronic ring of the videoconferencing software burst through the speakers on the computer in his office and Nick fell into the chair before answering. He smiled briefly when the video feed connected. The man was in his late sixties. He sported a Van Dyke beard, now fully gray in contrast to the black that it had been when they first met and shook hands at a time and place so long ago and so far away that Nick shuddered at the recollection. His hair was dark gray on top, significantly lighter on the sides above his ears, combed straight back and never out of place, and now matched his gray eyes, a characteristic shared by only three percent of the world's population. He was tan, no matter the time of year or his location, willing to find a tanning bed or a warm place in the sun to maintain his appearance. The cold, rainy November climate in Scotland was sure to be no different.

"Good morning," Nick said with a flat affect and monotone deliver without waiting for the other man to open the proceedings.

"Always good to see the highest paid pharmaceutical rep in the country," the man said. "You look tired." Their familiarity and practically familial relationship meant the forgoing of pleasantries and, during most times, professional courtesy. He spoke as a baritone, with a bit of rasp, free of a discernible accent with the exception of a hint of southern California that remained from his childhood that appeared when he relaxed enough to turn off his CEO persona.

"2 a.m. meetings will disturb even the healthiest sleep patterns. Not to mention the fact that this is a little out of nowhere. What's going on?"

The man on the screen was located in a luxury hotel suite. He was leaning forward on the desk but then reclined back in the rolling chair and tapped a ballpoint pen on the case of his open laptop. The sound was amplified by the internal microphone. "How are you doing, son? The truth."

"You ask as if you already know. Some things never change. Purpose is what drives the machine. Little victories build into bigger ones. Win today and build hope for tomorrow, as trite as it might sound."

The man nodded, waited, and asked, "Have you heard from her?"

Nick answered quickly. "No. But it wouldn't make a difference anyway."

"Because?"

"Because the one that comes back is never the same as the one who left, just like the one that she left is not the same as the one who now exists. Those people may look the same, sound the same, and even act the same, but they're both forever changed."

"Not at the core," the man said. "Please never forget that. Time will reveal that much, on both sides."

"I'll take your word for it. But that's not why you called. We could have had that exchange in the middle of the day while you were stateside. What's going on?"

"Ian Henry and Victor Lane."

"I think we can refer to at least one of those in the past tense. What about them?"

"Henry's in the ground so let's talk about Victor Lane for a moment."

Nick nodded without responding.

"Would you believe that no one has made so much as an official inquiry into anything that took place?"

"You mean the authorities didn't pay any attention to the ramblings of a violent pervert? You're kidding."

"We know that he claimed to have been attacked by two men, neither of whom he could describe aside from the fact that one of them was bald. He claims to have been beaten, abducted, drugged, and then whisked away before being abandoned in a parking lot before he was taken into custody. The police are saying that they were cooking methamphetamines and there was an accident that caused the house to explode but he claims that the two mystery men were responsible. What do you know about that?"

"No one was drugged."

"Nick, no one believes a word that he said." He paused, and then started to continue. "But..."

Nick pinched the bridge of his nose with one hand and held up the other, the palm facing up. "But what? You know what you know. Why don't you just ask the question that you called me to ask?"

"If you know the question, I'd like for you to answer it," the man said, leaning toward the camera once more.

"No."

"No?"

"No, I don't have some kind of death wish. Yes, I know what happened but I felt like it was the best course of action given the circumstances, the settings, and the people in question. I was already at a safe distance when I fired the first shot into the propane tank."

"I just need to know that your judgment and perspective haven't been clouded by recent events."

Nick closed his eyes, blew his breath out of his nose, and rolled the tension out of his neck. "They're not, and I have the right people around me to keep those things in check. I assure you. Gabi has that covered."

Satisfied, the man's tone and posture relaxed. "Speaking of whom, how is Gabi?"

"Overworked, stressed out, and searching for answers without always knowing the questions. Some things never change." Nick yawned as he asked, "Anything else?"

"What happened last month, the incident outside the restaurant. Did anything ever come of that?"

"Nothing. Micah has been monitoring reports on a local level but nothing suspicious. Everything says that it was an isolated incident."

The man watched as Nick looked away from the camera for the last sentence. "But?"

Twice, he started to speak, then stopped, and reconsidered his assessment. Finally, he said, "It was too organized, even for a failed abduction. You had a lookout on the perimeter before the car was within sight. The target was specific because they left once she was in the car and gone. We've been to the restaurant twice since then and she is still there, still working, and perfectly normal. It makes no sense but there's always the possibility that they got what they wanted because it was an intimidation tactic with a motivation that we don't know, or they got what they wanted elsewhere. For all we know, they'll take another shot but it's out of our hands."

The man nodded affirmatively and said, "Tell Micah to stay on it. As for you, rest is calling."

"Yes, sir. I hear you. I'll be in touch. Thank you." He paused before finishing. "For everything."

The man smiled, said, "Goodnight, son," and ended the call.

Nick turned off the lamp, closed the door to the office, and walked out onto the porch and into the very definition of quiet. The half-request, half-order to rest was appreciated but not realistic for the moment. With one glance at his phone, intending only to check the time, his mental centrifuge spun to life.

First, he thought of the call he desperately wanted to make. He highlighted her contact and saw her face, a picture of the two of them together that had been taken years earlier. Gabi would answer purely out of concern for him, without a hint of anger or annoyance, but her own rest and rebuilding and healing were paramount. It was her voice that he needed but her words were always with him. He could often predict her point of view and response to a given topic or question or concern. Their connection saw to that. For the moment, the comfort of her presence in that regard would suffice. He touched the back button on the screen and returned to the contact list.

He stopped scrolling when he saw the next name. This time it was the call that he simultaneously awaited and feared. It was either inevitable or impossible but would not be in his control in either instance. He looked into the nighttime sky and rebuked himself for not removing Mia's entry. Their history of text messages was archived but not deleted. Standing on the porch in the middle of the night, he thought of the times when he was unable to sleep, leaving him to walk through the yard or walk to the bridge and focus on the sounds of the slow-moving creek, when the phone would vibrate. The message, sent from inside the house, would ask him to come back to bed, sometimes using seduction as motivation. The absence of the text notification seemed magnified in the present.

He touched the trash can icon beneath her contact information and the dialog box asked him to confirm the deletion of her number. His thumb hovered over yes before finally selecting no, and then pressed the power button and the screen went dark.

"One more day," he muttered, and walked back into the house.

Halfway up the steps, en route to the bedroom, he stopped, descended the staircase, and returned to his office. He flicked the switch on the desk lamp, pulled open the desk drawer, and took out his journal. The format was static: the date in the upper right hand corner, a blank line, and then the projection of the contents of his mind onto the canvas.

Is an excellent memory a blessing or a curse? Most would argue the former, some the latter, but the reality is that both are true. We cling to the best of times in the past because they provide motivation in the present and spring eternal hope for the future. This is our common ground but it is both short-sighted and short-lived. For those of us who seemingly exist in a never-ending mental and emotional war unseen to the casual observer and hidden to all but the closest confidants, the scar tissue, while tough, occupies more and more territory with the turn of each page of the calendar. The excitement of accomplishment and pleasure tends to fade, eroded by the sands of time and consumed by the fiery trials from which none of us can escape, but we remember the worst, the most painful and hurtful things that were ever said and done to us by every person in our lives because that is what depression does. It is the world in which we live, every day and every night, regardless of the view from the outside looking in. So is memory a blessing or a curse? The plus side is that you always remember. The destruction comes because you never forget.

7

When asked for a description of his work, he would smile and deflect with the broad stroke generalization that he worked in acquisitions for a private organization. His colleagues spoke of him as a recruiter. Others, usually those in competition or direct opposition, saw him as a bounty hunter that preyed on the innocent and vulnerable with no personal interest in, or regard for, either the karma of this world or the eternal consequence in an afterlife that he considered to be little more than the collective delusion of the uneducated masses. No civilized nation deemed his behavior to be kosher but their approval was insignificant.

His occupation was wholly unrelated to finance, aside from the bi-annual deposit wired securely and quietly into to one of his four accounts in Switzerland whenever his fees were paid or the payment he demanded when special requests were made or additional measures were needed was rendered. There was no stock market, no skyscraper on Wall Street or luxury sedans with salaried drivers who understood the need for privacy, loyalty, and a limited memory. Working as what some would call an independent contractor but others would call a mercenary meant sharing none of the blame and accepting the entirety of both the accolades and the compensation, but blame could be passed more easily than lost income could be recovered. The trade-off was worth it.

The mere sight of the Mississippi River captured a part of his soul the first time he laid eyes on it in person. Such a powerful force of nature, a beautiful creation of evolution, which some thought to be an oxymoronic term, and unmatched in most of the world. Traveling for work and leisure had allowed him to experience the Nile, the Amazon, the Murray, even the renowned and storied Jordan, but only the Mighty Mississippi, from Minnesota's Lake Itasca in the north to the Gulf of Mexico in the south, regardless of the port of call, inspired him. It was one of the few things that had managed to remain somewhat uncorrupted by mankind and the pollution that results from the unchecked avarice of those who manage to grant themselves personal absolution for their own sins of the past and tender only an uncaring nod of acknowledgement to the generations to come. He was a man that lived his fullest life in the present but did not simply ignore the reality of a world that was still to come. In fact, he cared more for the generations to come than for those whom he encountered in the present.

The tourist season in Memphis, Tennessee had passed for the year, having slowed dramatically from the hottest days of summer, spiking briefly for the celebration of the New Year before falling again until the arrival of spring, but the buzz of Beale Street was a mainstay. Bargain-seeking stragglers found their way to the city during the early winter, riding the riverboats at half-price fares and grumbling about the cost of parking on their way to the buffet for the Early Bird special. He felt surrounded by them, socially claustrophobic in a sense, even in the most open of spaces.

Standing on the grass of the bank that descended to the surface of the river, he lifted the brim of his Panama hat and closed his eyes, drew a deep breath through his nose, and listened. The serenity, the grace, the underappreciated might, the life that it sustained, all would be within view when he opened his eyes. Clear and cloudless days such as this one added to the mystique for reasons that escaped him. To his left, he heard the waters churning. The white, three-level riverboat with its handful of passengers was finishing its half-hour circuit. Even this eighteenth-century relic somehow added to the charm of the setting.

"Hey there, buddy," a whining voice accented by the South said from behind him. "How ya doin'?"

He rolled his eyes before turning to find the source of the annoyance. The man was stocky, balding in the male pattern with white hair on each side, and wearing a white t-shirt with a pocket on the chest and blue denim jeans that had seen better days. The bare skin on his head was red from sunburn that belied of the temperature in the forties.

"Hello," Spencer St. Clair said. "Bugger off, mouth-breather," he mumbled low enough to remain unheard.

"You just payin' us a visit or what?" The man left his mouth agape as he awaited Spencer's response.

"Here for business," said Spencer, without making eye contact.

The bald man laughed and said, "That's quite an accent there, guy. You must be from *across the pond*, as they say," adding a generic British accent.

"Australia, but I was born in the States."

"I should have known from the hat." Hands in his pockets, jingling the ring of keys, the native said, "I'm from Proctor, just over the bridge in Arkansas." He slapped Spencer on the back with force that knocked him off-balance and said, "You kindly enjoy your stay now."

Spencer pulled one final, long drag from his cigarette, offered a dismissive smirk, and said, "I'll do that," before tossing the butt into the water and walking back toward his automobile parked at the state-operated Welcome Center.

"Bogans," he said to himself and reached into his pocket for his pack of Marlboro Reds.

For three days, Spencer had watched her every move. This day was the coldest of the three but without the rain of the first two, and neither the temperature nor the weather had impacted her choice of attire. He was impressed with her ability and desire to work through such adverse conditions, a character trait that would grow in importance should his offer be accepted, although he knew that she had to be freezing. Wearing so little in the midst of a downpour and twenty mile per hour gusts of cool air was a recipe for disaster, he thought, or perhaps pneumonia, but her present method of earning a living was far more dangerous than even the harshest conditions.

A day earlier, he had purposely exited his vehicle and scaled the hill to the legendary Beale Street, following her east for two blocks before reaching what he assumed to be her apartment building, the only door she had walked through alone during the time he had spent watching her. Spencer watched while she fumbled with her keys and dropped them, only for a passerby to pick them up and hand them to her. She thanked him quietly and looked away before unlocking the door and hurrying into the stairwell.

"She's so unsure of herself when she's not playing the role," he had whispered to himself. "She couldn't even look him in the eye." He wondered which apartment was hers. Did she live alone? Was there a roommate, or a partner, perhaps? A roommate could be package deal in order to provide a sense of security. He hoped there wasn't a consistent male presence in her world, one with any kind of emotional investment or financial power. The boyfriends were always a stumbling block, normally hangers-on with addictions and believers in the fallacy that cologne was an acceptable substitute for bathing and general hygiene. The memory of one such case, a young man in his mid-twenties and in a state of arrested development from a suburb of Chicago, prompted him to stick out his tongue and fake a gag.

He shook off the recollection of the day before and focused on the present. She stood in the doorway of a liquor and tobacco outlet, stepping into the rain only when a passing car slowed or stopped but retreating when a window failed to roll down. Was she experienced enough to have regulars? Possibly, he thought, but he also knew that women of her kind were unfamiliar with the concept of strangers.

Strangers, much like the inability to remain discreet or keep a secret, were bad for business.

For the first time in his nearly 72 hours of observation, she had yet to leave for a period of time and return. A slow day, perhaps, but an opportunity awaited her, a fork in the road that allowed for a radical change of both direction and destination. Unknown to her, at least for the time being, Spencer St. Clair held the key that could unlock the door to a new life. "We are nothing more than a product of the choices we make," Spencer often said as part of his sales pitch and this girl, whose name he did not yet know, was moments away from being presented with a golden ticket to enter a world of experience and enlightenment, should she so choose.

He believed that she would.

From his curbside parking space nearly a block away, he watched as the girl hurried into the alley adjacent to the storefront, disappearing for more than two minutes before reemerging.

Spencer lifted the brim of his hat and scratched the three-day growth that darkened his face. "Love is in the air," he said with a laugh and turned the key to start the engine.

He had always been a sucker for freckles, especially on redheads. It was such a simple, common fetish for a man with a history of diversity, he admitted to himself. This girl was a perfect picture of what he always kept tucked away in his personal fantasies – one of them, at least. Now, she was mere steps away.

Spencer shifted into park and rolled down the passenger window, looking in her direction and waiting to make eye contact. In certain areas of commerce, nonverbal communication is universal and he was simply following protocol. She turned in the direction of his idling car after a few seconds, caught his eyes, and moved toward him.

"Good afternoon, my dear," he said just before she reached the curb.

"Hey there," she said, and looked around the interior of the vehicle before returning her attention to the driver.

"You look like you could use a lift somewhere. Am I right?"

With a playful roll of her eyes, she said, "How'd you know?"

"I'm a bit psychic but it comes and goes. Must be a good day. Hop in," Spencer said, and unlocked the door. They were moving the moment the door closed.

"Where're you from, mister?" she asked from the passenger seat, now shaking her hair loose with one hand.

"Australia now but I'm a mutt. I'm from a little bit of everywhere and I've left a little of me everywhere, too." They rolled to a stop at the first traffic light and Spencer extended his hand to his guest. "What's your name, love?"

"Allison. Call me Allie. What's yours?"

"You can call me..." He paused for effect before saying, "Anytime." She laughed, giving him his desired ice-breaking reaction. "But my name is Spencer."

She bit her lower lip, smirking, looking at the dashboard and into the backseat, then back to Spencer and said, "With a ride like this, I might be doing that."

He laughed, both with visual and auditory approval of her remark and the knowledge that the bait had already been taken. More than business, this was a personal conquest. He felt his own physical reaction building and shifted in his seat. That time would come, he knew, and sooner rather than later, just not yet.

"Tell me about yourself, Allie," Spencer said.

"Not much to tell, really. What do you want to know?"

Spencer turned onto the on-ramp for Interstate 40 and entered the traffic on the Hernando de Soto Bridge, crossing the Mississippi out of Tennessee and into Arkansas. "Everyone has a story, my dear. You never know who may find yours completely enthralling, even if you do not."

For the first time in his three days of closely watching the girl whose name he now knew to be Allison, or Allie, whether that was true or not, she appeared thoughtful, processing the depth of what she had just heard. Someone, albeit a well-off stranger, was looking beyond her temporary usefulness, her status as a fix for an addiction that emanates purely from the raw, hyperactive male libido, detached from love and accented by disposable income, the thrill of illicit activity in the face of the law and social mores, and the lack of willingness to put in the work for anything meaningful.

Spencer struggled to limit his focus to the task. He was mesmerized by her. Surely she was not yet of age, a ridiculous notion in the first place according to most of the rest of the world, but managed to pass the eye test for the general public. She certainly had the body of a nine-teen-year-old coed, he thought and shifted in his seat again, even if she wasn't there yet. The black, cropped t-shirt he could take or leave but the denim miniskirt, so short that virtually nothing underneath was left to the imagination, was the image that drew his eye. Resisting the urge to move his hand from the gearshift to her thigh was becoming more difficult by the minute.

"Well, I've been here for a few years now but I was born in Michigan. Ended up here because it's warmer."

"Most places are warmer than Michigan," Spencer said. Interstates 40 and 55 briefly merged in West Memphis, Arkansas, creating a throughway that featured a litany of hotels and chain restaurants on each side, before splitting again, each road leading away from the lights and sounds of Memphis and into hundreds of miles of seemingly end-less farmland interspersed with small communities. "You look hungry. Let's get some lunch. Business can wait."

She groaned and said, "I'm starving!"

"I know just the place," he said. "The best Memphis barbecue I've ever had and you'd never know from looking at it. It looks like a bloody wreck but the food is to die for."

"Best ones are usually like that."

"A girl after my own heart, Allie," Spencer said.

Six miles of monotonous scenery led to their destination and Spencer slid to a stop in the gravel parking lot. The barbecue joint was a hidden gem, the kind of place only known to insiders and fully ap-preciated by those with an educated palate, and its humble external ap-pearance belied the incredible reality that would soon be presented on their plates. With only a produce stand and a small gas station in the adjacent property, all of which sat at the crossroads of Arkansas-147 and US-70, which ran parallel to I-40 and served as a frontage road, the restaurant was the last viable attraction, without turning back in the direction of Memphis, for thirty miles. The building was a rectangular wooden shack with a reasonably new black tile roof, painted red and covered with six-pane windows, framed in white, all across the front. Beneath each window sat a white vinyl sign with a single menu item boldly printed in red, and a red neon "OPEN" sign flickered in the one nearest the entrance, although only the "E" was functional at the time.

Allie looked in both directions of the crossroads and watched the road fade into the surrounding farmland in the distance. "This is it?" she asked.

"This is it. Don't let the area fool you. Come on."

She shielded her eyes and peered into the field on the other side of the road, watching a crow soar through the sky and hearing its call, something that was never done in the city. Spencer touched the small of her back and guided her toward the entrance. She flinched at the initial contact, then relaxed and turned toward him.

"Don't be shy," he said. "But I don't believe you to be the type. We have each other for the day. Let's have lunch."

One step through the door, which slammed shut behind them, and the visuals overwhelmed. Allie looked to the left, then the right, then to the ceiling, only to see every inch of every surface covered in graffiti. Names, cities and states, and dates, hand-drawn logos of sports teams and military organizations, untold thousands of guests had recorded the details of their visit. Behind the counter, license plates from states all around the country were hung on the wall, with more setting on a shelf below. The local, border states, Tennessee, Arkansas, and Mississippi, were accounted for multiple times, but others had been donated by guests from far greater distances.

"California, Texas, Maine, West Virginia," Allie said as she read each one aloud. "Michigan!" Her voice climbed an octave when she read the name of her home state and she touched Spencer's arm. He returned a grin. "This is so cool."

A middle-aged black woman, bent over and leaning forward, emerged from the kitchen and limped to the counter, smiling in spite of whatever condition visibly slowed her. "What can I get for y'all?" she asked.

"Ladies first," Spencer said, and gestured in her direction to step toward the menu taped to the counter.

An order of a pulled pork dinner with baked beans and coleslaw, a grilled burger, and a smoked turkey leg later, the perplexed owner turned to Spencer and said, "And for *you*, sir?"

"Just a half rack of ribs and slaw, please," he said to the owner, who turned without acknowledgement and moved back to the kitchen. Then to Allie: "You just ordered half of your body weight, Allison. Where's it all going to go?"

"You'd be surprised," she said.

"Let's have a seat."

The two sat at a plain wooden table just to the right of the entrance, underneath one of two overworked and barely effective ceiling fans in the dining area. Two old Coca-Cola coolers stood against the wall, packed with cans of every variety but non-functional. A roll of paper towels sat on each table in lieu of napkins, and the only cold spot in the building was the chest freezer packed with ice next to the counter.

Spencer removed his hat and sat it on the table beside him. "So why don't you regale me with the story of Allie?"

She leaned forward on her elbows, resting her head in her hands and asked with a wry smile, "What do you wanna know?"

"We'll start simple. Does Allie have a last name?"

"She does. It's Kendall. I like your hat. Is that a fedora?"

"It's a Panama. I'm a rugged gentleman from the Outback, not a twenty-year-old socialist from Portland."

Allie slid the hat toward herself and eased it onto her head, then lifted her chin just enough to catch Spencer's eye and smile. "What do you think?"

"Perfect fit, Allison Kendall. How long have you been here, doing what you're doing?"

She broke eye contact and said, "I don't know, a while. I love your accent."

"Listen, Allie..." he started to say but was interrupted by the sound of the owner dipping Styrofoam cups into the ice in the freezer. The cups were dropped in front of Spencer and Allie as she said, "Drinks are over there in the cooler. Help yourselves."

He lowered his voice and continued, "You don't have to be so guarded here. We're just having a conversation. It's safe, and so are you."

She scoffed and, without looking at her guest, said, "I haven't been safe in a long time."

"You're young and you're scared. You've lived a lot of years in a very short time, I'm sure, and you don't know exactly what to think or do, much less believe in. Am I getting warm?" He kept his eyes on the young girl as he spoke, waiting for her to look back at him. "How old are you, Allison?"

"I'm eighteen," she said, reading the graffiti on the walls. Her left leg was shaking.

"Fifteen, if you're a day," Spencer whispered.

Her leg continued to shake but she looked back at Spencer and whispered back, "Sixteen, but I'll be seventeen in a few months. Why are you doing this?"

"I'd like to ask you the same thing," he said.

"I do whatever I have to survive, man. This isn't how I saw life working out for me but things change pretty quick," she said. "The money's decent. I keep living every day and it hasn't caught up with me yet."

"You can't be doing this on your own. Is someone controlling you?"

"Someone helps me when I need it."

"For a percentage?"

"Nothing is free, dude. A guy that's been all over the world like you should know that."

The owner returned to the table, sliding a single plate in front of Spencer and three in front of Allison. Before Spencer could speak, she bit into the giant smoked turkey leg and tore a chunk free with her teeth.

"Where are your parents?"

"I split last year. My stepdad is a dick and my mom worships him. Not much more to say. That's how I ended up here with some friends. I can take care of myself."

"There's a distinct difference between surviving and living, Allison. The world traveler in me had to figure that out a long time ago. What would you do if you had the chance to live?" he asked.

"What are you talking about?"

Spencer went to work on his rack of ribs, pulling the meat from the bones with his fork and avoiding the immediate need to reach for the roll of paper towels. "I'm talking about the fact that there is a whole world out there that does not involve Allie in alleys in Memphis, Tennessee. Do you enjoy what you do?"

Without looking up from her plate, she said, "It pays the bills."

"That's not what I asked." Spencer knew not to let her off of the hook. If there was a time to gain, hold, and keep her attention, this was it. "Do you like what you do, or do you dread the thought of life being the same in five years, or ten, or twenty?"

"I guess I hadn't thought about it."

"So think about it. What if you had a chance to see the world, to meet people, to experience new places and things that would otherwise remain a mystery to you? Would you do it?"

The turkey leg was stripped to the bone. She dropped it onto the empty plate and swapped it out with the grilled burger. The pulled pork and sides were still to come.

"Anything to get me out of here," she said. "I hate it here."

For ten minutes, while she ate and he picked, Spencer explained the baseline details of his work, his business, and the opportunities available for a bright, young girl like Allison Kendall. He had been watching her for days, he said, and he just knew that there was something about her, something magnetic and beautiful, charismatic and playful. Others were sure to see the same thing. There would be male suitors, those with money, power, and prestige who required discretion and silence but would reward those around them richly for their trouble. The work would be similar but different. Names, faces, and locales would change. Instead of being used, she would be worshipped and pampered. She could see new places in the world, ride in private jets, stay in fine hotels, and eat from the finest tables. There was a marginal commitment. In a few years, should she so choose, she could walk away free and clear with a sizeable percentage of her earnings, her experiences, and her freedom.

"How long do I have to decide?"

"The offer expires at the end of our evening together. For every girl that says 'no', there are a hundred that will say 'yes'," Spencer lied.

"What am I supposed to tell...?"

"I'll take care of him," Spencer said. Small-time handlers of working girls were mostly bark and little bite in his experience. He found their temporary resistance to be entertaining, a last source of amusement before leaving an area and moving on to the next.

"When would I have to leave?"

"You will be in the air tomorrow afternoon, a private flight to one of our locations. You can pack some of your personal effects that you wish to keep but every need you have will be met, from lodging to clothing and everything in between."

She tapped her fingers on the table and swallowed the last mouthful of burger. For the first time in almost twenty minutes, she locked eyes with Spencer St. Clair. "Why me?" she asked.

"Why not you? Believe it or not, women like you are greatly in demand. The world runs on a continuous cycle of supply and demand. The clients we serve will be head over heels for you, Allison Kendall. Your future is brighter than any star in that afternoon sky," he said, pointing out the window behind her.

She closed her eyes, inhaled deeply, slowly, and exhaled, opening her eyes and looking at Spencer as she said, "Okay. I'll do it under one condition."

A smile formed at the corner of Spencer's mouth. "What's that?"

"I get to keep your hat."

He blew out his breath and said, "Done. I've got a dozen of them in my flat."

Another one acquired, another spot taken, another income source identified. How many of the girls had ever successfully left the program of their own volition, in good health and with their faculties and finances in tact? Three, he thought, and those had been years ago now. They were beyond their usefulness by the time of their exit and their loss was of no great consequence. This one could be valuable for years to come, personally and professionally. She may not ever make it to the screen, he knew. Instead, she may begin and remain on the first page of the digital catalog viewed by the bigwigs with digital currency ready for transfer and energy to burn. She would see the world. She would meet exciting, high-profile, powerful people. She would get paid. None of what he'd told her was a lie. The sales pitch was dripping with incomplete truths. The costs were also great but, just as no car salesman speaks of depreciation during the closing of a sale, that topic was best left uncovered in the present.

Most importantly, he thought, his conversion rate remained perfect.

Spencer reached across the table and touched her hand, prompting her to lift her head from her plate of pulled pork and look into his eyes. He smiled, winked, and said, "Allison Kendall, welcome to the world of possibilities."

She smiled in return, bit her lower lip, and slipped into her first daydream of the exciting life that was sure to come.

Spencer promised that he would see her soon, and indeed he would. Their next time together would be somewhere on the East coast, likely in the South. Florida was most probable. Others would be joining her, although the exact number was unknown. The others in acquisitions were still recruiting from their happy hunting grounds, wherever and whatever they were, and the profits and losses of the current roster were in a state of perpetual analysis.

He had helped her carry her two bags into the Cessna Citation CJ3+ private jet that was idling on the runway at the West Memphis Municipal Airport. His boss had sent the aircraft to town overnight at Spencer's request. She was wearing the same clothes from the day before, having stayed with Spencer at his hotel through the night.

"I'll see you soon?" she had asked, slouched in the leather seat.

"You will," he replied. "Let's get you in the air and on your way. If you need anything, your pilot will take care of you. Once you're on the ground, there will be people waiting for you. This is the first day of the rest of your life." He lifted her arm from the arm rest, kissed the back of her hand, and replaced it.

Without speaking again, he exited the plane and closed the door, slapping the side of the aircraft and jogging back toward the terminal. By the time he reached the private lounge, the aircraft began to taxi and prepare for takeoff. Spencer stood next to the window and watched the Citation move, thinking of the redheaded passenger and the events of the last twenty-four hours. He felt a connection to each girl he recruited, some more than others.

His boss would require an update, although the phone call was a formality for the operation's cleanup hitter that was still batting a thousand. He reached for his pack of Marlboro Reds but remembered that smoking indoors was illegal in the States, leaving him to shake his head in disgust. He would be off the grounds, and free, soon enough. His eyes shifted focus from distance to near and he caught a look at his reflection in the glass. It was bizarre, he thought. To be caught without his Panama was strange but it was in good hands and would soon be airborne. This was a first. None of the girls had ever stolen his hat but his prized brown Panama with the black band was in the right place and he had another one waiting.

Hands in his pockets, he paced the perimeter of the lounge, then moved back to the window in time to see the jet lift from the ground and into the morning sky over the Mississippi River. He stretched his leg taut, feeling the pop in his left knee that momentarily relieved some pressure, and then shook out the tension again. Lesser men would be self-conscious about always walking with a limp, he thought, but those men were not he.

"Best wishes, Allison Kendall," he said and reached into his pocket for his business phone. He selected one of the five contacts in the list and waited for the answer.

"Spencer?" the voice said.

"Yes, sir. We have another one on the way."

"Is this the young one you've had your eyes on?"

"It is," Spencer said. "She's a prime candidate, sir."

"You're my All-Star," the man said, and ended the call.

"What a sweetheart."

8

Every takeoff and landing was an assault on the senses, no matter how much unquestionable trust he placed in the pilot. The speed and convenience failed to override the feeling that it was all so unnatural. Aside from air conditioning, he considered sustained flight to be the single greatest accomplishment of mankind. With air travel, nearly anything was possible.

In spite of the positives, Nick Burke hated to fly.

His rules were steadfast. Commercial was preferable to private for comfort but private flights avoided the hassles of airport security, luggage searches, and pointless delays. Engines: No fewer than two. By his math, flying in a single-engine prop and losing an engine meant your total dropping to zero and your aircraft dropping to the ground. Bret's twin-engine Cessna 421C Golden Eagle was the smallest airplane he cared to board, having done so dozens of times throughout the years. With that in mind, a spacious commute in the first-class section of a 757 was virtually unbeatable, if for no other reason than the leg room.

The late-night flight from Mountain Empire (MKJ) where Bret had landed just long enough to refuel and allow Nick to board, to ZZV in Muskingum County, Ohio, their next destination, took less than fifty minutes. One guest was waiting to join, another associate who specialized in logistics and would offer assistance planning and a watchful eye from the perimeter, and they would be off to their next destination in minutes. Pending drastic changes or unforeseen circumstances, each of the three men would be back in their respective homes after less than twenty-four hours round-trip.

Bret tossed a half-full bottle of water over his shoulder toward Nick in the second set of leather passenger seats in the cabin, the first set that faced toward the cockpit, and said, "We're about to drop. You ready?"

"Am I ever?" Nick moved into the copilot seat, as he did during every flight for takeoffs and landings. The visuals, from the controls to the ever-changing environment, calmed his nerves. He put on the headset and microphone and placed his hands on the yoke.

"What are you doing?" Bret asked.

"Just pretending I have any business up here in the first place. Do you mind?"

"It's whatever. Just remember which buttons not to push and switches not to flip and we'll be fine. I don't feel like ending up in the water like a Kennedy later tonight."

The gradual descent of final approach took three minutes through cloud cover and gusts of crosswind.

"Is he here yet?" Bret asked as the wheels touched down.

"He better be. A guy that makes his bones in logistics should probably be punctual."

The aircraft slowed and Bret turned to taxi toward the apron for a brief moment of rest and refueling. "Get me out of this thing," Nick said.

"You realize the next flight is twice as long and we get to do the whole thing again tomorrow, don't you?"

"And over water, let's not forget that." Nick opened the door and stepped out of the Cessna and onto the concrete with a combination groan, yell, and stretch, followed by Bret, who made his way to the refueling area. "Right on time," he said as the man with a single bag, dressed in a red and black flannel shirt and tattered jeans, stepped from the doorway of the terminal.

"I hope you all bought a bigger plane," the man said to Nick. He tossed the bag toward Nick, who caught it and returned the favor. "You've gotta accommodate the big guy."

"We didn't buy this one," Nick said. The two shook hands and Nick smacked their associate on the back. "Good to see you, Oso." His real first name was rarely used, as he was known almost exclusively by his nickname, Oso, the Spanish word for bear.

Oso, at six feet tall, nearly 300 pounds, and sporting a red beard that extended down to his chest, wedged himself through the door of the Cessna and backed into one of the leather seats at an angle, letting out a groan as he settled.

"That never gets any easier," he said.

"I thought you'd lost some weight," Bret said as he returned to the aircraft. Then to Nick: "I paid one of the maintenance guys to handle it. Shouldn't take long to top us off."

"Come on, man. Don't say that. It'll make the ladies cry," Oso said to Bret and rubbed his stomach through his shirt.

"Just leave the dancing for the postgame celebration. Okay? You don't spike until you score," Bret said.

"Deal."

"Speaking of scoring, how are the wife and the slew of kids? Working on the next team member?" Nick asked.

Oso scoffed and said, "What are you talking about? I get less action than a quadriplegic's running shoes."

"That's horrible," Bret said through a laugh.

"Hey, it's the truth. I've got five kids and all that proves is that I've had sex five times."

"It really is a stellar conversion rate," Nick said. "But that's what happens when you insist on pulling the goalie."

Nick's phone buzzed. He opened it to find a text message from Gabi:

> *Stopped by the house but you weren't home. Half the time you're a hermit that only leaves to go to work, then you just disappear without warning other times. Some of us were expecting dinner and conversation! Let me know what's going on.*

He responded with a vague explanation involving a two-day trip out of town for a seminar related to his work as a pharmaceutical sales representative and dropped the phone back into his backpack, satisfied with the amount of time he had bought.

"Wheels up, gentlemen," Bret said.

"Not a moment too soon. Let's get this over with," Nick replied.

The flight from Ohio to Kenosha, Wisconsin (ENW) was scheduled for just over an hour and a half and the flight plan included crossing Lake Michigan from east to west.

Micah had prepared a briefing on the mission, the target, and the cover.

Nick planned to be asleep.

Fifteen minutes from the Kenosha airport, Oso shook Nick to wake him. "Welcome back to the world, Captain," he said.

Nick rubbed his eyes and then stared at Oso.

"It's an unofficial title. You're not a military guy."

"Get a chance to look at the file?" Nick asked.

"I did. Sounds like a real winner. Child abuse, domestic violence, a stint upstate for armed robbery and attempted murder, you name it. How in the world did he get off on a technicality?"

"Smooth-talking lawyers in one instance and recanted charges in another. In the one case there was physical evidence, it was deemed inadmissible because it was improperly collected. Guilty as sin, free as a bird."

"'Justice system' is an oxymoron, my man," Bret said over his shoulder from the cockpit.

"The concept of justice is not exclusive to the justice system," Nick said. "It predates the police and the courts."

"And it's most efficient when served outside of them," Oso added.

"How far out?" Nick asked Bret.

"Few more minutes."

Darkness had set in during the flight, drastically reducing the scenery and resulting in the kind of rural, nighttime landing that Bret would handle much easier than his passengers.

"What's this guy's name again?"

Nick took the paper copy of Micah's report from the empty seat next to him. "Raul Ibarra. Lives in…"

"A van down by the river," Oso interrupted.

Bret laughed from the cockpit.

"No, but you're close. He's in a small lot on the side of the road, in what amounts to an old camper straight out of the 1960s. The ex-girl-friend has the restraining order in place and moved with the little boy to New Hampshire."

"Sounds like a good place to hide," Oso said.

"By all accounts he'll be there alone but everything is close knit in those places so keep your eyes up and your ears open." The other men nodded without answering audibly.

"Time to set her down," Bret said.

The landing was uneventful and relatively smooth, which was always a relief to Nick, and the taxi to the hangar was brief. Each man exited the aircraft dressed in a long-sleeved black shirt and black polyester athletic pants, carrying a black backpack and moving with confident efficiency toward the terminal.

The weather was unseasonably warm for the middle of winter in Wisconsin but hooded sweatshirts, also black, were tucked into the backpacks in case they were required.

"Three white guys dressed in solid black leaving an airport with backpacks after ten o'clock at night. This doesn't look conspicuous at all," Oso said as they walked through the front door of the terminal and into the parking lot.

"If anyone asks, we're here for a ninja competition," Bret said.

"I don't think ninjas use the gear we're packing, gentlemen," Nick said. He pointed to a midnight blue SUV that was tucked away in the far corner of the lot and said, "There's our ride."

"Think you can start it?" Bret asked.

"I hope so. The keys are in it, courtesy of our fearless financier. I hope he arranged for the supplemental insurance just in case things go sideways."

"With us? Never," Oso said.

"Perish the thought," Nick said.

With the GPS coordinates entered into the navigation system, the estimated time of travel from the airport to the site was eight minutes. Nick was driving, with Oso riding shotgun and Bret in the backseat.

"What's the plan?" Oso asked.

"This isn't even a real mobile home park. It's a wide spot in the road on the back side of the garbage dump, next to the river, with a camper and a rusted out single wide trailer on it. Take a close look at the shot that was taken from the street view. They're both there but spaced out more than you'd think and I can't imagine anyone living in that trailer."

Bret rubbed his shaved head and said, "So this is our guy. When are we getting started?"

"When the clock strikes midnight, so does his," Nick said.

"What does this thing look like anyway?" Oso asked, scratching his beard.

"Micah says it's an old Shasta from the '60s or '70s. There's never a car beside it so he's relatively sedentary."

"The guy lives in a pull-behind with nothing to pull it. Sweet," Oso said.

"He's also a genetic disaster that gets off on hurting people and, instead of being in prison, he's living free and prowling for his next victim because of prosecutorial incompetence and hiring the right defense attorney," Bret said.

Nick passed the camper and said, "There it is," slowing briefly to allow for a closer look.

"There's a light on inside but nothing in the trailer. He's all alone," Oso said.

"We've got a cluster of houses here but not much within earshot, even in the middle of the night. Probably a half-mile."

Bret nodded in agreement and Nick continued past the houses and to the intersection where he pulled onto the edge of the road and turned off the lights and ignition, leaving the accessories on.

Nick handed Oso his backpack and said, "Need you to do something for me. Take those boxes of strike anywhere matches and start breaking off the heads. Get as many as you can."

"You got it. What for?"

"You'll see," Nick said with a grin.

"I know that look," Bret said.

"Hand me a tennis ball and the pocket knife from the front pouch." Oso did so and Nick used the knife to cut a hole in the top of the ball. "Pack as many of those match heads in there as you can and then tape over the hole. See if we can make two out of what we have."

"You're not..." Bret said, looking over Oso's shoulder and into Nick's backpack.

"I am."

The process took fifteen minutes and yielded two full tennis balls, as requested, both of which were placed carefully into Bret's bag.

Nick took a deep breath and asked, "We ready?"

"Ready," both men said.

The interior clock read 11:45 p.m. Without being given a cue, each man took a cell phone from their bag, activated the Bluetooth, and placed a single in-ear headset into their left ears.

"Starting the conference call now. We'll mute until we get there," Nick said. He dialed the first number and Bret's phone began to vibrate. The call was answered, the microphone muted, and the same process was repeated for Oso's phone.

The nearly mile-long walk to the target area would take ten minutes at a slow pace, under lowlight conditions with the exception of the homes with exterior lighting that aimed toward the road.

"Oso, you're on the perimeter. We're a few miles from civilization but there are always stragglers. Bret, you're with me, on the door. I'll go in," Nick whispered, just loud enough for them to hear.

"One of these days I'm going to be somewhere other than the perimeter and working logistics," Oso said.

"Those kids need their dad to come home and your wife needs her husband. This is an in-and-out, single target operation. You've been in the middle of the action before and you will be again."

"I know." Oso grabbed Nick's shoulder and said, "Just make sure to put your phone on vibrate in case your girlfriend texts you."

"I'm not getting into this again."

"Love the focus," Bret said.

With eyes on the camper, which remained a quarter-mile away, Oso stopped, nodded, and backed underneath a tree, leaving him invisible without the screen of his phone activated. He unmuted his sound, as did Nick, and placed the phone in his pocket.

"You got me?" Oso asked.

"Copy. Bret?"

"Copy," Bret said.

Oso looked in each direction, seeing empty roads and no headlights, and said, "We're all clear for now."

Nick and Bret broke into a light jog to cover the remaining ground, stopping at the edge of the wide circle of dirt that surrounded the camper. A rumbling buzz was heard nearby.

"Generator," Nick said. "When I get inside, disconnect those propane tanks and get them as far away as you can."

"You got it," Bret said.

"Still good, Oso?"

Oso checked both directions. "Affirmative."

Nick knelt at the edge of the road and took a stun gun from his bag. "Here we go."

"Good luck, brothers," Oso said in the headset.

"How are you going to approach?" Bret asked Nick.

"We'll find out at the same time."

The camper was solid white with spots of rust appearing in random places, a single window on each side that rolled outward, and a large vent on the roof. The lone entrance, on the right side, faced the road. Nick pounded his open hand on the door, then spun away and knelt under the window out of sight. He heard movement inside the trailer and felt it shake.

"He's looking out the window toward the door, Nick," Bret said from the road, waiting to approach once Nick gained entry. "He didn't look down."

The door opened and Raul Ibarra, shirtless and wearing sweatpants, grabbed his crotch and leaned through the doorway in search for the source of the disturbance that interrupted his television show. Nick stood and stepped toward him.

"Who the..." the man started to say.

Nick brought the stun gun up to the Ibarra's exposed stomach and pressed the trigger. The man's body went rigid and he groaned as Nick moved closer, pushing him into the camper. Ibarra fell backward and crashed into the wooden door of the closet. Nick stepped inside and pulled the door closed behind him.

"Very subtle, Nick," Bret said. "I'm headed that way. Taking care of the tanks now."

"You've got some time," Nick said. "I have some work to do."

Is this what he considers freedom? Prison has to be nicer than this.

The grand tour of the space involved turning in a circle. A small LCD television sat on the counter in the small space between the three-burner stove and the sink, neither of which appeared to have had much use. The interior was draped in drab green with bright yellow curtains, with dark wooden doors and cabinets. The table, held up by a metal pole, converted into a bed.

Raul started to stir and attempted to push himself upward. Nick used the stun gun a second time and the man went limp, slumped into the corner between the closet and the sink.

Poor guy.

Raul Ibarra was short at 5-7 and stocky. His skin was dark brown but his naturally hazel eyes were obscured by contacts that made them appear black. His facial features were chiseled, taking on the appearance of a sculpture, and his hair was jet black.

The look matches the man. Life would be much simpler if we could read everyone this easily.

Nick pulled the man to his feet and allowed him to fall into the bench seat on the far side of the table. He then extracted a pair of two-foot plastic zip ties from his bag and tightly bound Raul's wrists and ankles, turned his legs so they rested under the table, and sat on the opposite side to face him.

It took four minutes for Raul to regain coherence, during which Nick closed each window in the camper.

"Hi there," Nick said.

Raul started to scramble and felt the restriction on his hands and feet.

Nick shook his head and said, "I don't think that's going to work. Let's have a chat." Raul stopped moving and glared at the stranger that had invaded his modest living quarters. "You have quite a history, Raul."

Raul leaned back in the seat. "Who are you?"

"Not important right now. You don't have enough time for questions, only answers."

"Tanks are disconnected, Nick," Bret said. "We good, Oso?"

"Got a truck coming from the east but it's moving fast. Looks like a semi. Just slide around back." Bret moved to the back of the camper. "Clear," Oso said, and Bret walked back to the front.

Inside, Nick said, "Let's cover the highlights. Domestic violence, child abuse, both of which were racked up on the same night. Restraining order filed by your ex. Pressured her into backing off of the charges. The others didn't stick but we both know what happened. The pictures were telling."

"I didn't..."

Nick held up the stun gun and pulled the trigger. Raul stopped speaking. "We have to be honest with each other, Raul. Lies destroy relationships. We need to be better than that."

Raul cursed at Nick in Portuguese.

"That's not very polite," Nick said. "You really should be more courteous to your visitors."

Raul began gathering saliva in his mouth and leaned into the table. He lurched forward and spit toward Nick, who, in anticipation of Raul's action, moved his head to the right and allowed it to pass by him and onto the wall. As he moved back to a centralized position, he grabbed Raul by the back of the head and slammed him into the table face-first, then slid out from the bench and cracked the back of Raul's head against the wall.

Nick leaned forward and whispered into Raul's ear. "I would suggest not doing that again. Come here." He pulled Raul out of the seat and into the floor.

The beginnings of hyperventilation setting in, Raul asked, "Why are you doing this?"

"Let's take a run through your history and I could ask you the same thing about almost all of it. You're a terrorist and there's not a redeeming quality in your existence. If you can't control something, you destroy it."

Nick opened the first drawer beneath the sink and dumped the contents into the floor. He did the same with the second drawer and a syringe dropped onto the top of the pile. He rested on one knee and picked up the needle, holding it up to Raul's face. "Still looking for your chemical escape from reality, I see. Where's the rest?"

Raul looked away, refusing to answer.

"Don't make me ask again."

Raul made eye contact, cursed at him in Portuguese again, and looked away.

"You really aren't in a position to determine terms and conditions, Raul."

"That *puta* put you up to this?" Raul said.

"And who would that be?"

Raul scoffed and said, "If you know anything about her, you know she needed put in her place. Little brat did, too."

Nick stood and laughed. "You see? Honesty matters, Raul. Now we're getting somewhere."

"Hard to deny that," Oso said through the headset.

"Who knows what he's done that no one knows about," Bret said.

"Where are you from, Raul?" Nick asked.

"Miami. I was born in Brazil." He spit a mouthful of blood onto the floor, careful to avoid Nick's shoes.

There's a win.

"What difference does that make?" Raul asked.

"Just making conversation. Are you familiar with the term 'sociopath', Raul?"

"Yeah. Why?"

Nick dropped to one knee again and said, "Because I'm looking at one, Raul. I'm looking at one that has hurt people, broken people, who has no regard for anyone but themselves and will gratify their own selfish desires at any cost. Do you know what a sociopath is?"

Silence.

"A sociopath is what happens when malice meets hubris." Nick stood and opened a third drawer. "What else do you have in here, Raul?"

Raul looked up but did not speak.

"Tell me now, save some time. I know you're not working clean."

Raul let out a breath and said, "Oven. Taped to the top."

Nick opened the door to the oven and pulled a one-gallon plastic bag free. "See? That was easy." He dumped the contents of the bag onto the table. The television continued to play in the background.

Unlabeled prescription bottles filled with pills were scattered across the surface, with glass vials interspersed among them. Nick picked up a vial and held it up to the light. "You don't work small-time do you, Raul? Fentanyl is serious business. Do I even want to know what the rest of this is?"

"Just take it, man," Raul said. "All of it."

"Take it? This is the last thing I want. I have no need for any of it. I'm going to bet you're a drinking man, Raul. Am I right?"

"Closet. Bottle of tequila on the top shelf."

"You're kind of in my way," Nick said. "What else do you have?"

"Beer in the fridge."

"Now we're talking." Nick opened the refrigerator and took out two bottles of beer, twisted the caps off, and set them on the counter in front of the television.

Nick took the prescription bottles from the table and opened them one-by-one, looking at each pill until finding one that was recognizable. He held the pill in his hand, showing it to Raul, and said, "You sure don't seem like the anxious type. Why so many anxiety meds, Raul?"

Raul glared forward toward the door and said, "Street value. Little white college girls will pay whatever you want for them."

"Ah, so you're a businessman, too? Makes sense. You're just providing a service to those girls." Nick leaned down to Raul's ear and whispered, "And maybe they provide services to you, too. Am I right?" before standing up again.

"How we doing?" Oso said in the headset.

"Good here," Bret replied.

Nick picked up a spoon from the sink, placed ten tablets of the assorted benzodiazepines onto the counter, and ground them into a powder.

"What are you doing, man?" Raul asked.

Nick put his index finger across his mouth and shushed him. "Watch TV. I apologize for blocking your view."

Bret chuckled in the headset.

Nick swept the powder into his hand and began depositing it into one of the bottles of beer. "You know what's funny, Raul?"

The man on the floor did not respond.

"Maybe it's more interesting or ironic than funny." Nick swirled the beer in the bottle, careful not to allow any spillage, and turned to Raul. "She never saw you coming. No one can play basically good people for a fool like a narcissist. You said the right things. You did the right things, and then..." – Nick snapped his fingers – "everything changed and you were transformed from man into beast." Nick held the bottle out to the man and said, "Have a beer with me, Raul. You look thirsty."

Raul looked up at Nick but still would not speak.

"What do you have to lose, Mr. Ibarra?" Nick asked.

Raul held up his bound hands.

"I knew I forgot something," Nick said and held the bottle to Raul's lips. Raul opened his mouth and Nick tilted the bottle upward, giving him a mouthful. "I hope that's your favorite brand."

"Thank you," Raul said.

"Don't thank me," Nick said, slapping Raul on the shoulder. "It's a common courtesy." Nick gave the man another drink, this one larger, then waited and did so a third time, draining more than half of the twelve ounce bottle.

"What do you mean?"

"People on death row get a last meal. A free man should, at least, have a last beer."

Raul's eyes opened wide.

"People who prey on the powerless represent the worst kind of evil. You hide under a cloak of charisma and fun, waiting for your chance to strike. When your pleasure ends or your boredom begins, you move to the next source, and the next, and the next, until your behavior finally catches up with you or you die of old age with a smile on your face that is a diametrical polar opposite of the sadness that you induced in your victims. Would you like to finish this off? Last chance."

"Yeah," Raul said. Nick touched the bottle to his lips and turned it upward, draining the remaining contents. "Now what?" he added.

"Now we wait," Nick said, sliding into the bench seat and moving back to the wall with his feet propped up. "I hope you can pick up more than one channel with this thing. I hate this show."

For fifteen minutes they sat in silence, looking at the television screen. Raul's eyes became glassy after ten and the effects of the drugs were increasing. Nick moved out of the seat, stood up, and then knelt on one knee in front of Raul. "I think it's time for me to go," he said. "You be good. Stay away from your ex-girl and her boy."

Drowsy and mumbling, Raul said, "If I don't?"

Nick whispered, "My second impression isn't quite as pleasant as my first."

"Maybe I'll see you in New Hampshire," Raul said, laughing.

"Unbelievable," Oso said on the phone.

"Maybe you will, Raul," Nick said. He stood, picked up his bag, and pushed open the door, stepping out of the camper and onto the ground.

"Hey..." Raul muttered as the door closed.

"Did you get the tanks away from here?" Nick asked Bret.

"Other side of the road in the ditch, covered in water. That thing is like a moat."

"Be ready to roll in five, Oso," Nick said.

"Gotcha," Oso replied.

Nick reached into his gear bag, took out two bottles of lighter fluid, and began circling the camper, dousing the sides with as much coverage as possible. The first bottle emptied after two slow-paced laps. A second bottle was dedicated solely to the roof, some of which entered the vent and dripped inside. The empty bottles were collected and placed back into the bag.

"Oso, head toward the SUV. Get it fired up and headed this way," Nick said.

"On my way," Oso said.

"I'll take one. You take one," Nick said to Bret, who took the tennis balls from his own backpack and handed one to Nick. "Count of three. Let's get some distance first."

Inside, Raul fell unconscious. The combination of benzodiazepines and alcohol depressed his respiratory system to a degree that would soon require resuscitation.

"Oso, what was the estimated response time from fire?" Bret asked.

"Ten minutes but I don't see anyone that would call immediately."

"All I needed to hear," Nick said. They moved to thirty feet away, the camper centered in their vision, and Nick began to count. "One, two, three." On the third count, both men threw the tennis balls and made contact at different points. The surface of the ball compressed from the pressure of impact, causing the match heads inside to strike upon one another. The resulting ball of fire ignited the lighter fluid and flames engulfed the structure, spreading around the four walls and onto the roof, where the supply of oxygen inside would be drawn into the flames above.

Without speaking, Nick and Bret threw a strap of their backpacks over one shoulder and began walking east on the empty two-lane road, away from the direction where Oso was retrieving their vehicle. After a quarter-mile, Nick said, "Where are you, big guy?"

"Thirty seconds," Oso said. "I'll flash the lights." All three men disconnected from the phone call.

Ten seconds early, the lights flashed and the SUV passed them and slowed to a stop in the right lane. "Right on time," Nick said.

Oso exited and circled around to the passenger seat, allowing Nick to jump into the driver side and Bret to enter the back along with the backpacks.

They were moving again within seconds. Nick looked into the side mirror and saw the orange glow of the fire fading into the distance. "Oso, I need a favor."

"Name it," he said.

"Find us a 24-hour diner close by. I could use a nice hearty meal."

9

"Here's to another successful run, my friend," Spencer St. Clair said. He held his glass of scotch, always need, and waited for his guest to toast him. The glasses clinked together. "*Salud.*"

"Hear, hear," Lucien said. "New hat?"

"New hat, same style. My new girl fancied the old one. We all make sacrifices, mate. I've got a stockpile of them, yeah. Always keep an extra about." Spencer looked around the room and said, "I can't believe I can't smoke in here now. It's a pub not a bloody health club."

"Relax, Spencer," Lucien said. "I must say that it is good to see you clean-shaven and well groomed for a change. You almost look as if you're somewhat cultured."

"Me relax? You're the only one in the place wearing a tie, friend."

"You seem more enamored with this girl than any of the others. Why?" Lucien signaled to the bartender for another drink.

Spencer leaned forward onto the bar, looked to his right at Lucien and said, "She's exquisite." He lifted the brim of his Panama hat and pulled it back down. "The kind you see when you close your eyes at night and decide what show is playing."

"The girl is sixteen years of age, Spencer. Let's not forget that."

"Oh, bollocks. Most nations in the world would be amused by your disapproval. What rich, white man in this country pulled eighteen out of a hat and encouraged a friend to pass a law? Fine wines are aged but not overly so." He scoffed and swirled the ice in his empty glass. "How old is your new star, the blonde? Shelby, is it?"

"She is of age, I assure you. In any country."

"Then why isn't she here having a drink with us?" He allowed a moment of silence and said, "She's a prime piece, that. You have excellent taste, Murdoc."

Lucien repositioned on his stool and said, "Let's talk about other things."

"Ooh," Spencer replied, then chuckled, and said, "You fancy this one, yeah? I understand but don't throw stones, mate."

The bartender approached and asked, "Can I get you gentlemen anything?"

"Another scotch, love," Spencer replied. "And whatever my friend is having."

Lucien tapped his glass and held up a finger.

Spencer watched the bartender walk away and said, "I always was a lover of fine chocolate."

"You're incorrigible."

The bartender was tall and slender. She wore a shirt that bared her midriff and jeans that rode low and clung to every inch of the lower half of her body. Spencer was drawn to her skin tone, a dark caramel that contrasted with her smooth and straight black hair and unexpected bright green eyes. She leaned forward slightly to reach for a rag and Spencer leaned with her on his stool to maintain his view.

He allowed a vibration to pass through his lips. "Mmm…"

She returned, slid a glass to Spencer and Lucien and asked, "Anything else?"

"I think we're covered for now. What do they call this place again?"

"Anvil Forge Tavern. It's Abingdon's finest," she said.

"And what do they call you, darling?"

"They call me Sienna. How about you?"

"Spencer St. Clair," he said and extended his hand, which she shook. "From what I can see, even with soft lighting, *you* are Abingdon's finest."

"Oh, you're a charmer," she said. "What's the accent?"

"Australia, at present, but mixed with a little of everywhere else."

She bit her lower lip, smiled, leaned forward on the bar and said, "Voice is a little rough. You sick?"

"Only in the fun ways. You only get a voice like this from a life of experience, love," Spencer said, taking the time to add a little extra rasp.

"You'll have to excuse my friend, ma'am. We haven't yet taken him to the veterinarian," Lucien said with his eyes looking straight ahead.

"He's fine," she said, and moved down the bar to the next customer.

Spencer waited until she was out of earshot and said to Lucien, "I want her. She has the kind of hips that are a perfect fit for my hands," which he held up to examine.

"She is working you for a tip, Spencer. Don't be a fool."

Spencer said nothing but returned his gaze to the bartender.

"I wonder what key unlocks your world," he thought but didn't say.

"How long should we expect to be here?" Spencer asked Lucien.

"As long as it is profitable and until the *patron* says otherwise. Why?"

"It's not quite my speed, you know?"

"Few things are, St. Clair."

Lucien's phone buzzed and he opened it to find a text from Shelby, asking where he was and when she would see him. He smiled as he read it.

"And you call me enamored," Spencer said.

"About another month. Two at the most," Lucien said, ignoring Spencer's remark.

"The kid always keeps the machine running longer than expected. This will be no different, Murdoc."

"Perhaps but the time will come when warmer climates and new landscapes await us. After all, expansion and exploration *is* the American way. We're building enough material for the next six months and arrangements are already being made overseas. These digital currencies are untraceable when handled properly and we appear to be ahead of the curve, as they say. Only a fool would conduct the auctions in person. It's a virtual world now, Spencer."

"Do these plans include Shelby?"

Lucien looked away from Spencer and out the front window of the tavern. "I suppose," he said.

"Perhaps you could place a bid yourself."

The phone vibrated on the bar and Lucien opened another text from Shelby saying that she had something to tell him. His heart rate increased. His hands began to shake. The physical panic response matched the one in his brain.

She found someone, he thought.

How should he respond? Waiting until later to speak with her was not an option. He would consider and feel every possibility between now and then.

"Are you listening, Lucien?" Spencer asked, this time speaking seriously.

Another buzz.

"Excuse me," he said to Spencer. He walked outside and onto the sidewalk before opening the next message. It read:

> *I dropped out of my classes this morning. It was early enough that I could still withdraw. You said I have a bright future and I believe you so I took a chance. I hope you're proud of me. We're going to do this together!* ♥

He responded as simply as he could:

> *I am. I'll see you tonight. – L*

His heart sunk in his chest. All the things she thought she knew, her newfound understanding of the world and all that it has to offer, and she was entirely unaware of what lay ahead. He shivered when a gust of cold February air caught him off guard and he stepped back into the restaurant.

Spencer started to speak but Lucien held up his hand and sat down on his stool.

Hundreds of similar conversations had taken place through the years but each one was difficult. Speaking to a family in the aftermath a procedure meant the relay of information, good news or bad, and the plan for the immediate future. Beforehand, the idea of balance was at a premium. She would explain exactly what would happen, the ideal results and the possible complications, impart confidence and hope but allowing them to retain the understanding that nothing is certain, no one is perfect, and there were absolutely no promises aside from her best effort and judgment.

For Gabi, there was as much pressure in the waiting room as there was in the operating room.

She leaned against the wall in the hallway outside the waiting room and reviewed her patient's file and the associated notes one last time. Knowing as much as possible about those in her care was a priority. She would talk about their family, their work, their interests, all the things that were important to them. Should tragedy strike, these were the things that would make up their legacy, things that should be regarded with just as much importance in the present.

Her patient was Gary Wellman, 46 years old with a wife and two adult children, a son and a daughter, and a lifelong resident of the Commonwealth. He was an electrician and served in the Virginia National Guard. He spent his time away from work playing golf and rebuilding classic cars, a hobby he picked up from his father. On the first visit to his primary care physician, he had indicated a family history of both high blood pressure and high cholesterol. After a battery of tests, he was referred to Commonwealth Cardiology Associates. Two years earlier, he lost his father to an aortic aneurysm that was later found to be a result of the same undiagnosed condition for which Gary was being treated.

Gabi drew a deep breath upon reading the last sentence of her notes, having been reminded of the striking detail that she had forgotten until that moment.

"Wow," she whispered to herself.

She closed her eyes and prayed, asking for guidance, wisdom, and a safe, successful procedure, clarity when speaking with the family before and after, and that her hands would be guided by a hand stronger than her own. No procedure took place without first doing so. The family was gathered just around the corner. Another life could be hanging in the balance and the moment of truth was drawing nearer by the second.

"Good afternoon, Mrs. Wellman," Gabi said. She smiled to offer immediate reassurance and sat beside her patient's wife. The two adult children stood nearby.

"Hello," the woman said. Her voice shook with the single word.

She's scared to death, Gabi thought.

"I'm just going to give you a rundown of what we are doing today. I know we went through this in the office but I wanted to cover it one more time. Okay?"

"Good," the son said. He stood with his arms folded.

"The chest pains, the shortness of breath, they're being caused by a condition called aortic stenosis. We see it a lot in older patients but Gary has a family history of high blood pressure, high cholesterol, and things like that, so an early onset isn't really a surprise. Your heart has what is called the aortic valve that controls the flow of blood that leads to the rest of your body." She turned a page of her notes to the blank side and began to illustrate the valve. "What generally happens is calcium deposits form which cause the opening to narrow and the valve just can't function as it should. There isn't a medication that can reverse the issue so the only option is to replace the valve. Considering Gary's medical history, I just didn't feel that he was a candidate for open heart surgery. He's just too high-risk."

"Okay," Mrs. Wellman said, waiting for Gabi to continue.

"Don't let that worry you. A lot of people are high-risk for open heart surgery. Thankfully, we have the option of performing the procedure we are here for today. It's called a Transcatheter Aortic Valve Replacement. It's a fancy way to say that we are replacing the valve in his heart with one that was taken from a cow or a pig." She placed her hand on top of Mrs. Wellman's and continued, "Nothing is ever one-hundred percent certain but this is the best option for Gary. We'll go in with a catheter and place the new valve directly over top of the old one." Gabi looked up to make eye contact with the son and daughter and said, "I'm sure I made it sound a lot simpler than it is," then smiled, which was returned by both. "Pending any complications, this should take no more than 90 minutes. Open-heart surgery would be hours."

"Assuming everything goes well, how long will Dad be here," the daughter asked.

"As long as everything goes as planned, just a few days. It's a much longer stay after open heart. Some say three days but I'd like to keep him a couple of days longer just to be sure." Then speaking to Mrs. Wellman again: "There are always risks but this has to be done. Do you have any questions for me?"

Without speaking, all three family members shook their heads to indicate that they did not.

"Okay," Gabi said. "I'll be out to speak with you as soon as we're finished."

While preparation of the patient was being completed, Gabi finished her own. She was dressed in navy blue surgical scrubs, cap included, and a white mask. Working in the catheterization lab instead of a standard operating room, forgoing a standard greeting, she said, "Here we go, everyone."

She closed her eyes, drew in a deep breath, and let it out slowly, finally releasing the tension that had built during the 82 minute procedure. The explanation of the results to the family would come next. The news was good. These were the easy conversations, the moments that made her profession of choice so rewarding. She knew that they were waiting, anxious and scared, some pacing and others unable to move from their seat, but they would have to wait, if only for a moment. Mental and emotional decompression was non-negotiable.

She waited for the word that her patient was in recovery then, after doing her best to look as presentable as possible, made her way to the waiting room.

Gabi made sure to approach them smiling, allowing for them to feel instant relief before a word was spoken. Before she spoke, they stood. "Gary is in recovery. Everything went exactly as planned," she said.

"Oh, thank God," Mrs. Wellman said. Her eyes welled up with tears and she hugged each of her children.

"Sit down with me," Gabi said. All three complied. "The new valve is in place. I'm going to recommend that we keep him here for about five days, so just think about him being released on Sunday. Okay?" Each person nodded along but remained silent. "I wanted to talk to you about this, and I will be sure to speak with Gary as well. Replacing the valve is absolutely the best thing to do at this point but his blood pressure is still high, even though it is being managed, and the family history of high cholesterol can sometimes be more than medication alone can deal with. His recovery period is going to be as much as two months but he will need all of your support when it comes to making lifestyle changes."

"Whatever we need to do," his wife said.

"That's what I like to hear. That also means regular checkups, some exercise a few days a week, and laying off the bacon cheeseburgers."

The three family members shared a laugh at Gabi's advice, their first lighthearted moment of the day.

"They'll let you know when you can see him," Gabi said.

"Thank you, Dr. McLane," Mrs. Wellman said. Gabi shared a hug with the wife and daughter, a handshake with the son, and made her way to the physicians' lounge for her last piece of business in a day that she had anticipated for months.

Inside her personal locker was a sealed envelope containing the official letter to declare, not request, a leave of absence from her position at the hospital. Administration was aware of, although not excited about, the decision. Arrangements for time away had already been made with her partners at Commonwealth Cardiology Associates. The last year had turned the concept of physician burnout from a possibility to a near certainty, something she was desperate to avoid for the well-being of her patients as well as her own sanity. Three months was the time frame she had in mind, although six months would be ideal. The move would be unannounced until after her departure, thus avoiding the painful, obligatory goodbyes. After all, she would return.

She changed into her civilian clothes, such as they were, and reached inside the locker for the piece of paper that would forever change her path. Holding the envelope in her hand, she took a moment to consider where she had been, where she was, and where she was headed.

For the first time since the summer before her junior year of high school, her upcoming calendar was gloriously empty.

She took the time to take in every sight and sound on her way out the door. What if this was her last day in this place?

Places change, plans change, people change, she thought. In three months, or six or twelve, opportunities could be different. Goals, hopes, and dreams could be either closer or farther away. For all of the positive possibilities that her newfound freedom brought, some uncertainty remained.

Those things could wait.

In the physicians' parking lot, she turned for one more look at the hospital, the place of healing and hope where she had spent countless hours.

"Until we meet again," she said to herself and walked to her car, optimistic and enthusiastic about the immediate future for the first time that she could remember.

It was not the way the day was supposed to end.

She pounded both fists on the steering wheel and muttered, "Come on."

She pressed the button to start the engine on her BMW X5 SUV for the fifth time. The lights activated on the dashboard, the display screen lit up as normal, but the engine failed to respond.

Her head on the steering wheel, centered between her hands at ten and two, she let out a frustrated scream, then reached for her cell phone for the first of two calls. The first would be placed to the towing company. The second would be to her ride.

"How soon can you get here?" she asked when he answered the call.

"Half an hour, if I leave now," Nick replied. "I'll try for 20 minutes but it would be a new record."

"The wrecker will be here at 5:00. No rush."

"Of course not," Nick said. "Where exactly would you go?"

"Very funny. I started my leave of absence when I walked out the door today, by the way."

Nick let the statement hang in the air and said, "It's about time, Gabrielle. I'm glad. I'll see you in a few."

An accident on Interstate 81 resulted in a traffic backup that detained Nick until 5:15, which meant navigating the traffic of the hospital shift change. The SUV was nearly loaded when he arrived, mouthing "I'm sorry" as he closed the door on his Honda. The driver of the tow truck was still completing the paperwork.

"I can't believe I have to get this thing towed all the way to Kingsport to get it serviced," Gabi said. She held out her hand, looked up into an overcast sky and said, "Is it sprinkling? This day keeps getting better."

"First world problems, Dr. McLane," Nick said. "This is no way to start your vacation."

She gave him a playful shove on the shoulder and said, "Shut up," with a smile.

Nick gestured toward the Civic and said, "My queen, your chariot awaits. Let's get you home." He opened and closed the passenger side door for Gabi, then walked around to the driver side. "You're certainly dressed up today."

"I'm not going home. Can you just take me to Roundhouse Grill? I have dinner at 6:00."

Nick turned out of the hospital complex and onto Lee Highway. "Dinner? Dr. McLane has a date tonight?"

"It's no big deal, Nick. His name is Noah. He works in accounting for the hospital. We went out a couple of weeks ago and he asked me to go to dinner tonight."

"You don't seem all that excited."

She scrolled through the texts on her phone and said, "I don't know. There's just no…"

"No what?"

"Spark. I don't know. He's a nice enough guy but I just don't feel it."

"At least dinner at Roundhouse means a perfectly cooked medium rare filet. He could have taken you to Peccato di Gola."

"Never!" Gabi said. "That's our spot. You know better."

Nick turned into the parking lot of the restaurant and coasted to the front door, rolling to a stop with the passenger side opening directly toward the door. "I have the worst looking car in the area for miles," he said. "Do you need me to pick you up or…"

"No. I'll just have him run me home," Gabi said. She gathered her bag and got out of the car, then leaned back in the open door and, with a grin, said, "He's going to drive me home. He's not going home with me. There's a difference. Don't worry."

"Call me tomorrow," Nick said, and Gabi closed the door.

The drive back home would take place in the dark, meaning a slower commute over the twists and turns of Moccasin Valley Road. Silence and boredom were pure torture to someone with an analytical mind. The farmhouse was not an ideal destination for the time being.

Entering the city limits of Hansonville, he drove into the parking lot of Value King, the only grocery store on the route between his home and Abingdon and site of the largest, mostly empty parking lot around. He pulled into a space in the center row, away from the cluster of cars closest to the building but near enough to keep from drawing unnecessary attention, and turned off the engine. To a casual observer, he was waiting for someone inside. In reality, he was seeking a quiet environment for introspection without wandering his own property after sunset.

His mind was on Gabi. It was a second date with someone for whom she had already admitted she felt no spark.

What was his name?

He thought back to their conversation on the way to the restaurant. "Noah the accountant," he muttered aloud.

He knew where she was and who she was with. His protective nature was heightened for her. He was also preoccupied by it without an understanding of why.

The guy's an accountant, for God's sake.

Letting out a sigh, he reclined the seat and stared at the plain gray felt on the roof.

I can't believe it. I'm jealous. I'm actually jealous. That's why you end up in the parking lot of supermarket thinking about what two other people are doing. Jealous that my best friend is out with someone, that she has someone.

He returned his seat to an upright position.

No. I'm not jealous of Gabi.

He shook his head and said aloud, "I'm jealous of *him*. Unbelievable."

Directly in front of the car in the next row, a middle-aged man in tattered jeans and an untucked white button-down shirt was pacing back and forth on the driver side of his Ford Bronco and speaking with increasing intensity to whomever was on the other end of the call. He was six feet tall at most and carried extra weight around his midsection. His brown hair was thinning on top, his hairline receding in the front, with gray patches over each ear.

He looked Middle Eastern, Nick thought, a demographic departure for Hansonville.

When the call ended, he threw the phone through the open window and bounced it off of the passenger window with an audible *thud*.

"Anger issues," Nick said to himself. "A man facing internal crisis that stays mad at the world."

He turned on the CD player in the Civic, advanced to the second track, increased the volume, and slouched in his seat as he waited for the song to play.

First the drums, then the vocals.

"Only you can save me..."

The guitar began to play, and Nick mouthed the words.

"Only you can save me..."

He picked up his cell phone from the cup holder and scrolled through the contacts until he found her.

Mia.

With a swipe, he could call her. With the touch of a button, he could text her. With the touch of a different button, he could delete her. In the background, the song continued to play.

Instead, he touched the power button, turning off the screen and ending the temporary insanity.

If Gabi asks tomorrow, I went straight home.

In the car that was parked in the next aisle, the man was on the phone again. This time he was noticeably calmer, Nick thought. He kept his eyes on the entrance of the supermarket, craning his neck for a better view each time someone exited the store.

Who are you so interested in?

He unlocked the doors and sat up straight, now focused on the man in the red Ford Bronco. The automatic doors to the supermarket slid open again and a young woman, in her early twenties by Nick's estimation, walked through pushing a cart that was half full of plastic bags. In the row between them, the man in the Bronco ended his call and began watching the woman as she approached.

Nick relaxed.

Probably her dad. He's just waiting for her to help her unload the cart.

The man opened the driver door and stood, pushed the seat forward, reached into the back to extract a set of silver aluminum crutches that he leaned against the side of his vehicle, then hurried to the rear and opened the tailgate. He emptied the contents of a plastic bag from the supermarket onto the ground behind the Bronco, looked toward the woman, and retrieved the crutches.

He's not hurt. It's a distraction.

Nick opened the glove compartment and took out a Taurus TH9 9mm pistol, a serviceable but budget-friendly clone of his Glock 19 that was reliable to use but could be sacrificed if disposed of or confiscated. He chambered a round, one of 17 in the magazine.

Don't do this.

The woman pressed the lock button on the remote control for her security system. On the Hyundai Genesis coupe beside the Bronco, the headlights flashed and the horn sounded. Realizing that she was a row away, she turned and repeated the process, moving toward the lights and sounds with her cart. She was a brunette, her hair cut to shoulder length with a single blue streak to satisfy a trend that Nick failed to understand. She wore a long-sleeve black t-shirt and blue jeans. He took time to make a mental note of every detail.

Careful to avoid unnecessary noise and movement that would draw attention, Nick deactivated the overhead light in the Civic, eased open the driver door, and slid out onto the pavement. He inched forward to the front wheel and peered across the hood.

Don't talk to him. Just get out of here.

Nick settled onto the ground with his back against the door and heard the trunk lid on the Hyundai pop open.

If this is nothing and I run in with a gun raised, demanding action, I'm the criminal.

He heard one bag fall into the trunk, then another.

"Excuse me, ma'am," the man in the Bronco said.

Oh, no.

Nick turned and saw him emerge from an unseen angle, moving awkwardly with the crutches.

"I'm sorry. Could you help me with this stuff? The bag busted and I dropped everything and can't seem to get it together. I've been waiting here for ten minutes to see somebody."

"Sure!" she said while she placed the last of her bags in the trunk and closed the lid.

Nick raised himself up to a crouch, looking for any movement from other angles.

Where are you? There had to be someone on that call.

In the fire lane in front of the market, the engine started in a four-door sedan with tinted windows. She was on her third separate effort to collect all of strategically selected small items from the ground behind the Bronco.

The sedan rolled into the far end of the aisle and began moving in their collective direction. As it passed under one of the lights that illuminated the parking lot, Nick looked through the windshield to assess the targets.

One driver, no passenger. He'll try to throw her in the back and be gone in ten seconds.

With each hand full of candy bars, she stood and reached into the back of the Bronco to leave them in another bag and the man threw the crutches to the ground. Hearing the sound of metal meeting asphalt, she turned to see the miraculously healed man standing upright without assistance. She took a step backward, then turned to rush to the driver door of her car but dropped the keys. The man lunged forward and grabbed her from behind. She let out a shriek that was left unheard by anyone but Nick and her assailant.

No weapon. They're vulnerable on the transfer.

The sedan suddenly accelerated, closing the distance to the back of the Bronco. Nick stood to his feet as the woman struggled to gain traction with her feet, attempting to break free. The man lifted her off the ground with his right arm, using his left to cover her mouth with his hand. "Shut up!" he groaned through his exertion. "Shut up! Let's go!"

Nick raised the gun and began moving forward. He fired a single shot into the windshield of the approaching sedan and the driver swerved to the right and into a parked car. He fired again, this time into the left front tire, which popped with a *bang* and began to deflate.

The man was startled by the sudden gunfire and the woman broke free, running toward Nick. Behind her, the man reached toward the back of his pants.

Gun.

"Get down!" Nick shouted, and the woman dropped to the ground.

His first shot struck the man in the left shoulder, thrusting him backward. He regained his balance and started to reach behind his back a second time.

Nick's second shot struck the man center mass, in his upper chest and millimeters from his heart. He dropped the ground with no resistance and began gasping for air.

The driver of the sedan shifted into reverse and spun the tires, retreating with limited control until he reached the end of the aisle where he turned and sped away with the sound of the flat tire flapping against the pavement.

"Stay there," Nick said to the woman, who rolled into a seated position but remained on the ground.

Nick dropped to his knees, set the pistol on the ground, and assessed the man's wounds. Blood began to saturate the fabric of the shirt and Nick knew that his chances of survival were nonexistent.

Nick pinned his shoulders to prevent whatever struggle might come and said, "Who are you? Who do you work for?"

The man's eyes were opened wide and he continued to gasp. He made eye contact but failed to speak. Shock was setting in. The reality of the end of his time on Earth was undeniable and unavoidable. Nick could hear the gurgling sound in his chest as blood blocked his airway.

"Listen to me. Courage is for those who are still alive. Everyone is scared at the end," Nick said, keeping his eyes locked on those of his target. "I don't know you but I bet you've already got enough points on your license and could use a little good karma on your way out the door. Give me a name."

The man's gasps were getting shallower and increasing in frequency.

He's fading.

"Give me a name," Nick emphasized again.

The man coughed, then drew in the deepest breath he could manage and said, "Lucien Murdoc."

"Who is he? What does he do?" Nick asked.

The man began to panic, trying in vain to breathe through the obstruction in his chest.

Nick stood and watched the man whose name he never learned give into his fate. There was one last gasp followed by an exhale and his lifeless head fell to the side.

Turning his attention to the woman, he knelt on one knee beside her and asked, "Are you okay? Are you hurt?"

"Uh, no," she stuttered, still looking straight ahead. Then, looking at Nick, she asked, "What just happened to me?"

"I think you already know," he said. "But it's over now. Do you have your cell phone?"

"Yeah. It's in the car."

"Okay. Get it, call 911, and tell them everything that happened from start to finish."

"Everything?" she asked as she rose to her feet.

"Everything, in detail. What's your name?"

"Makenzie," she said.

"My name's Nick," he said, offering his hand which she shook.

She quickly embraced him and said, "Thank you, Nick," and opened the door to her car. "I'm calling right now. Okay?"

"I'll be right here. I have a call to make as well."

He ran to the Civic, grabbed his phone, and dialed the number for Micah.

"What's up, Nick?" Micah said.

"Red flag," Nick said.

Hundreds of miles away, Micah sat up in his chair. "What happened?"

"Another abduction attempt. Remember a few months ago with Gabi and the server?"

"I got you. How bad? Where are you?"

"Hansonville. One dead. The driver got away but the woman is okay."

"Right place, right time."

"For her, yes. For me, we'll see. Hansonville PD is on the way and you know what that means."

Knowing there was no need to respond, Micah asked, "What do you need, bro?"

"This guy was a hired gun. Mid-forties, Middle Eastern..."

"That's strange," Micah interjected.

"Yeah, but on his way into the dark night he gave me a name. Lucien Murdoc. Run it through every system, every database, every source you have." He heard the sirens first, then looked toward the main road and saw the lights of the approaching patrol cars, two by his count and likely more on the way.

"One more thing. Look everywhere you can and find out how many abductions or attempted abductions have taken place around here in the last few months. The thing with Gabi seemed like a one-off until now."

"What's my radius?" Micah asked.

"Let's say 50 miles," Nick said. "See what you can do and I'll get with you tomorrow. My eventful evening has just begun."

"I'm on it," Micah said and ended the call.

Returning to Makenzie, Nick said, "I'm sure they are going to take you to the station and have you give them a statement. Just tell them everything that happened that you remember."

"Will you be there, too?" she asked.

"Oh, yeah," Nick said. "They'll talk to me longer than they talk to you."

"But you didn't do anything wrong. You..."

"That doesn't always matter. It'll be okay."

The two patrol cars rushed into the parking lot and four officers exited, all of whom approached Makenzie first.

Nick rested on the hood of the Civic.

Lucien Murdoc. Who are you and where are you?

He smiled and looked skyward.

"Now I'm actually glad Gabi had dinner plans," he said to himself.

10

It was a combination of federal grants, low-interest loans, and private fundraising that brought the multimillion dollar complex into existence in Hansonville, a series of buildings that stood in stark contrast to their primitive, dilapidated predecessors. The concept worked for the smallest incorporated city in the area. The fire department, the police department, and city hall were housed in separate but neighboring buildings. Offices were of a clean, modern design in city hall. The fire and police departments were granted every amenity, from private fitness centers to showers and lodging.

While outer appearance and office spaces have changed with time, interrogation spaces have largely remained unchanged. There was no single, uncovered light bulb under an aluminum dome or hanging from a chain in the center of the room, no overwhelming heat and denial of sustenance, in spite of the commonly held beliefs perpetuated by films and television. The spaces were, however, generally well-lit with fluorescent lights overhead but otherwise barren, with a single table accompanied by several standard uncomfortable metal chairs, one door in which to go in and out, no clock on the wall, and occasional two-way mirrors. Physical contact was rare and confrontational conversations even more so, at least at the beginning.

The room occupied by Nick Burke had no such mirror and the discussion was expected to be less than friendly. In most instances, his statement would be given to an officer while sitting at a desk in an area accessible to the general public. Someone would provide a bottle of water, even a can of soda, and simple questions would produce simple answers.

In most instances, the man who prevented a kidnapping and potential assault was not identified and regarded as a perpetual person of interest by the local chief of police.

Seated at the table in the chair facing the door, Nick waited inside the room for 45 minutes after his arrival before Hansonville police chief John Pratt finally entered the room, pretending to read the front page of a collection of papers on a clipboard.

"Mr. Burke, I didn't expect to see you again," Pratt said.

Without moving his head, Nick looked up at Pratt and, deadpan, said, "It must be fate."

Pratt was in his mid-fifties, tall and barrel-chested with a belly that added to his overall size. White with close-cropped buzz cut gray hair and a matching mustache, his exposed head came to a phallic point at the top that would have been better concealed with more follicular coverage. His eyes maintained a beady look, although Nick wondered if that was a personal interpretation that was influenced by past experiences with the man. What stood out most to Nick was the voice. Pratt intentionally projected every sentence in an effort to exert authority and presence but his tone was whiny, almost nasally, leaving his efforts unsuccessful.

"We're still working out exactly what all happened tonight but I'm not surprised that you're somehow involved. Why is it that we have to deal with you every now and again?"

"Deal with *me*?" Nick asked. "What exactly are you dealing with, Chief?"

Pratt sat in the chair on the opposite side of the table. "One of my other men is talking to McKinley..."

"Makenzie," Nick interrupted. He shook his head at the lack of attention to detail.

Agitated, Pratt said, "Excuse me?"

"Her name is Makenzie. I'm glad you have your finger on the pulse of the situation, John."

Pratt hesitated and said, "Why don't you tell me what happened then?"

Maybe the gut is where he stores all that extra ego.

Nick recounted the events from earlier in the evening in lurid detail. He included a description of the sedan that escaped with damage, although the driver was unseen. He also intentionally omitted the name that was given to him by the man now dead.

Pratt tapped a pen against the table and asked, "Why didn't you call 911, or even our non-emergency line, when you thought things looked suspicious?"

"Everything progressed so quickly that it clearly was not an option. I could intervene or be a spectator. Even your best response time would have gotten you there too late."

"So you believe you *had* to intervene?"

"Absolutely."

"And you just happened to be there at the right time, sitting in the right place?"

"That puts it all in a nice little package, yes."

"No," Pratt said, leaning back in the chair. "Something isn't adding up here, Burke."

Mirroring the man on the other side of the table, Nick leaned back and said, "I'm sorry that math isn't your strong suit, John."

"You can call me 'Chief'."

Nick shrugged. "That's correct. I could."

"You're awfully supercilious, aren't you, Burke?"

"I could say the same for you, Chief," Nick answered, deliberately emphasizing the last word.

Pratt stood to his feet and said, "It would behoove you to take this seriously."

Behoove?

Nick leaned onto the table with his arms folded and said, "Those vocabulary builder tapes from the library truly can work wonders."

Pratt dropped the clipboard on the table and said, "Even if everything happened the way you claim it did and, believe me, we'll verify everything with the young lady and whatever security footage we have, we might have had a lot more to work with if it wasn't for you."

"You'll have to explain that one to me."

"Don't you think it would have been nice to speak with the man responsible for this?"

"Obviously."

"Well, he's in a bag, Burke. You could have stopped with the shot in the shoulder but you had to take another one."

"My first priority, sir, was to neutralize the threat to that girl. I did that. What would you have preferred me to do? Politely ask him to let her go and invite him to an early dinner so we can play 20 Questions? Spare me. She's alive and he's not. Those details are a direct result of his decision-making, not mine."

"That doesn't change the fact that we don't know a thing about what really happened out there. The only thing we know is that you were there and this isn't the first time we've had to speak to one another."

"And it's always such a pleasure. We really should do this more often."

Pratt pushed the metal chair from the table to the wall. Its legs scraped across the floor with a screech before it crashed and toppled over. "What's your problem, buddy? What's with the attitude?"

"It's called contempt."

He walked around the table to the side where Nick was seated. "Oh, is that right?" Pratt said. He stood over Nick, waiting for a response.

Still looking toward the door, Nick said, "You have grossly overestimated your ability to intimidate."

Pratt returned to the other side of the table and sat down. "I don't see a problem with being suspicious of a guy that's always around when bad things happen. Have you ever heard of a conspiracy?"

His eyes locked with Pratt's, Nick said, "Sure I have. I've also heard of incompetence, paranoia, an overactive imagination, all kinds of new and exciting concepts."

Pratt exhaled sharply, puffing out his cheeks, and said, "Let me tell you somethin', buddy. That girl in the other room is safe and that's a good thing you did. But there's a man who's dead that I don't think had to be and you're the one responsible for that."

"Am I supposed to shed tears over an evil man that dies as a result of his own actions?"

"I think you like that the man is dead and I don't believe that needed to happen. I don't believe I would have done the same thing."

"When the part-time cop and full-time porn shop owner tries to lecture me on ethics and morality, I can assure you that it will not be taken seriously," Nick said, referencing the chief's secondary income stream that was considered classified knowledge, and was rarely discussed by the few who knew and never to his face. "Why are you here, John? We're well-passed regular business hours."

"I wanted to speak with you personally," Pratt said.

"Special treatment is flattering but you have a business to run." Nick shook his finger and said, "Priorities, John."

Pratt's breathing grew rapid and his face was flushed with red.

There it is.

"That young lady should have completed giving her preliminary statement. You had better hope that there are no inconsistencies," he said.

Nick showed a solemn look, clasped his hands in feigned prayer, and smiled.

Pratt exited and pulled the door closed with twice the necessary force.

Fifteen minutes later, Pratt returned.

There's no substitute for confidence.

"So what did we find out?" Nick asked.

Pratt walked two circuits around the area of the room between the table and the door, his hands on his hips and rolling his neck to force it to crack. He slid a clear plastic bag containing Nick's pistol, with the ammunition removed, across the table and said, "You can take this with you."

"That's it?" Nick asked with his eyebrows raised, wrinkling his forehead.

"That's it. You're free to go."

"Would you mind telling me what all you just found out? What changed, John?"

"Burke, I don't have to discuss this with you. I said you can leave, so leave," Pratt snapped, turned his back, and opened the door.

He knows something. What are you hiding? If he cracks, he'll spill.

Nick stood, took two steps toward the door, and stopped. "Do you have any plans to retire soon? Focus on other projects, perhaps?"

"What kind of a question is that?"

"Forget it. The thought of you in charge of law enforcement is just a ghastly thought."

Pratt scoffed, smiled, and said, "Who uses the word 'ghastly' in a sentence?"

"I don't know. Someone who's read a book since middle school?"

His face red, Pratt stepped in Nick's direction and said, "Excuse me?"

Nick raised his hands and said, "A man who throws around the word 'behoove' might not want to cast stones."

Pratt pushed the door closed and said, "Have a seat, Burke."

Nick complied and Pratt took the opposite chair for himself.

"Value King has a good security system with several perimeter cameras and we were able to verify the details of your account of what took place."

"You seem disappointed."

Pratt ignored the statement and continued. "You saved her life but you're all very fortunate." He sighed, held the bridge of his nose, and continued, "There have been multiple abductions and abduction attempts across the border in Tennessee in the last couple of months. Two of them were children. This is the first one that was thwarted."

Multiple?

Nick shifted in his seat. "Organized effort," he said.

"We're going to do our best to keep names out of the press. There'll be enough attention just because of what happened. The girl wanted to make sure that we knew what all you did out there."

"I appreciate that," Nick said. "I hope it carries some weight."

"It does but you're out of your league, Burke. Stay clear of this thing."

Nick stood and said, "My league? Chief, we don't play the same sport but it sure is nice of you to worry," and walked toward the door.

Pratt pointed to him as he passed and said, "I don't want to see you back in here."

Without turning on his way out, Nick said, "You and me both."

At the farmhouse, Nick sat at the desk in his office and contacted Micah using the secure videoconferencing program.

He chose to forgo the standard greetings when Micah answered and said, "Tell me you have something."

"Some, but I'll keep looking. How did it go with the authorities? Did you have to deal with Pratt?"

"He's the same charmer as always. He did, however, offer some interesting details. Tell me your news first."

"It took a few tries to get the spelling right but I think we've found the right guy," he said. Two files appeared on the left side of the window, one a high-resolution picture and the other a PDF document. "Lucien Murdoc. A world traveler, a producer in the world of erotic cinema, and a part-time performer himself."

"Before I click on that picture, promise me that it's not an action shot."

"You've got my word, bro. But check out the PDF."

Nick opened the document and found five pages of Micah's notes.

"Murdoc is listed as a producer and performer for Brann Cinema. 'Brann', apparently, is the Norwegian word for 'fire'."

"Subtle," Nick said. "What else?"

"Once I located Murdoc, I was able to gain access to his credit card records."

"By 'gain access', I'm assuming that means unauthorized access."

"Possibly. But what I found is several months' worth of transactions within an hour of where you are with occasional expenses that are either automatic charges or times that he traveled elsewhere and returned. When he's local, most of his actions repeat. He is active on the same days, doing the same things. If we need to pin him down, we will have a time window."

"Go on."

"Even his personal expenses are extreme for one man so I did some digging into a few places in the area and found a connection to the company. Brann Cinema has been renting a block of rooms at Wyndale Hotel and Conference Center for the last few months, as well as a couple of luxury rental cabins outside of town."

"So Murdoc is here?"

"For now, anyway. Go to the third page."

Nick did and the data was startling.

"That is a record of the unsolved abductions or attempted abductions in the last six months within a fifty-mile radius of your humble abode."

Nick counted the entries and said, "Ten separate records and that doesn't include the one with Rae downtown."

"That area covers a lot of ground and some large cities but it definitely suggests a pattern."

Nick sat up in his chair and said, "It also confirms something Pratt told me. He said there had been multiple abductions across the border in Tennessee recently and that two of them were children."

"Uh-huh," Micah said, waiting for the rest.

"He also said that I was out of my league and I needed to stay away from things."

Micah laughed and said, "The man has no idea." Nick remained quiet. Breaking the silence, Micah asked, "What next?"

After a long pause, Nick said, "Next, we find out if Lucien Murdoc is still gracing the area with his presence. If he is, I think we should meet and talk business. As for the rest of his work, I'll leave that research entirely up to you as well."

"How much of a hand do you think he has in all this?"

"Until he proves otherwise, or we do, his fingerprints are all over it. Right now, he's the trailhead. It's a matter of following it from there. Be in touch."

"Got it," Micah said and disconnected.

It was certain that Lucien Murdoc was involved to some degree with one abduction attempt. What remained unknown was the fullness of his role, if any, with the others. The film company could be legitimate. The dead man in the parking lot could be a former associate with a grudge.

Nick also knew to trust patterns, not words, and that little could be accomplished in the immediate.

He reached for the journal in the desk drawer, turned to the next blank page, and wrote the date in the corner. Even in the midst of the chaos, memories lingered, reminders appeared and then vanished as quickly as they had arrived. Gabi's second date with Noah had served as an unexpected trigger for unknown concerns and feelings. In silence, he wondered where she was, who she was with, and if he crossed her mind after so much time had passed. He wondered if she regretted her actions or her decisions, or if she was capable of doing so in an honest manner. For all that he did not miss, there were things that he did and, for that, there was the empty page in front of him for projection.

He turned the desk lamp to provide the best illumination possible and wrote:

> *She already knows what she's done, and the price that has been paid. Lies can't cover reality forever, the reality that lives in the darkness and the silence, the private world where no smartphone screens, no concerts, no*

noise, no distractions, no other minds and souls can exist. It is in the quiet, lonesome darkness that conscience screams loudest. That is where it seems, at times, that I will live with her forever and her with me. How is it possible that we can share everything and nothing, all at once?

11

Two days of research and aptly named unauthorized access led to Micah's production of a digital portfolio of the immediately available material concerning Lucien Murdoc.

"Just an everyday, run-of-the-mill pornstar-slash-producer," Nick said on the videoconference with Bret and Micah. He turned on the desk lamp and flipped through the hard copy of the file that he had printed upon delivery.

"How did he pull off that gig?" Bret asked. "He gets to produce the film, be on screen with whoever he wants, and fly first class around the world. Does he own the company, too?"

"He exploits women all over the world, too. Don't forget that, my man," Micah said. "But he doesn't own the company. I still can't figure out who does though."

Still reading through one of the pages, Nick said, "Here's one thing to remember. The porn industry doesn't exploit women. It exploits everyone. They objectify women on camera, take away their identity and their humanity, and discard them once they are considered worthless or their lives have been entirely derailed. They take advantage of men by appealing to their loneliness, their so-called primal instincts, boredom, perversion, the lust for power, or any combination of those. It breeds insecurity in the viewers. It ruins their brains. It creates a fantasy world that could never be duplicated in real life. It crushes relationships. That's why their viewers are called consumers. They consume it, and it consumes them without their knowledge or consent."

He dropped the papers onto the desk, looked into the camera, and said, "And that's how we get to this point, where people like this are buying, selling, and using women like currency." He held the papers up to the camera and added, "That's how we get *here*. If people considered that more often, maybe certain sites would get fewer clicks."

"These guys are still around?" Bret asked Micah.

"For now, yeah, but they have already been around here for longer than their patterns suggest. Not to mention this." A notification flashed on the screen, indicating the arrival of a new file. "Look at the numbers. There's a pattern. Everywhere this group goes, there's a rash of crimes like the ones we've seen within a couple of hours of their sites. When they need a change, or someone starts to ask questions, they move on. It's a machine. They have multiple crews operating at once and lots of stuff being cranked out internationally. The travel budget alone is unbelievable, from Europe to Asia to the Middle East."

Nick leaned back in his chair and said, "And that's how we know it's more than just pictures and videos. It's lucrative but not to that degree."

Bret, looking at the digital version of the file on his laptop said, "This guy's passport picture looks like a headshot for an actor."

Micah scratched his beard and said, "I've seen much more of him than I ever intended to when I was putting that file together," drawing a laugh from the other two.

"So now what?" Nick asked to the virtual room.

After a minute of silence, Bret spoke. "We go simple. We don't overanalyze it. Approach him, talk to him, see what he has to say."

"And we approach him as who exactly?" Nick asked.

"Create an alias or use an old one. Go vague, throw the appearance of money and influence around, and hint at what we know. If it gets his attention, he'll move on it. If not, we find another way."

"You better sell it, Nick," Micah said.

"It's a two-man job. Bret, can you get here?" Nick asked.

"I'll head down tomorrow. We'll plan it, sleep on it, and then run it."

"Let me know what you need, gentlemen," Micah said.

"Copy that," Bret said.

"Resources, Micah. It's not going to be cheap to make it look authentic."

"I'll move some around tonight and you'll have it tomorrow. Anything else?"

"Actually, yes," Nick said. "I need a new suit."

"That's all you, bro," Micah said and disconnected from the call.

"We need to isolate him, Bret."

"The hotel is the best bet. Do some recon and then pick the right spot."

"Right, but we need to know exactly where he'll be in case we have to go back."

After a moment of dead air, Bret asked, "Any ideas?"

"How do you feel about some smoke and mirrors?"

"It's our specialty, isn't it?"

"Among other things," Nick said.

Inside the expansive lobby of the Wyndale Hotel and Conference Center, Bret chose the most strategic location available: a seat at the end of a back-to-back double row of chairs, the bank of elevators and the front entrance in view, no blind spots for surprise guests to enter his frame of view, and a television, with the closed captioning displayed, mounted on the opposite wall, albeit at a distance, to prevent death by boredom. He was dressed to blend in, wearing khaki cargo shorts and a t-shirt to match, browsing a complimentary print copy of the Wall Street Journal in which he had little interest.

The Bluetooth headset in his ear was connected a phone call with Nick, who was waiting outside in the parking lot inside a luxury rental car pointed to the sliding doors that led to the front desk and waiting area. His battered Honda failed to live up to the necessary projected image.

"We've been here for three hours," Bret said. "I snaked my way into a plate from their continental breakfast but that wasn't worth much. They need to pick a continent with better food."

"When we finish up here, lunch is on me. Okay?" Nick said from the car.

"Bill the company. Just be glad Oso isn't here. The bill would be triple."

"I'm telling him you said that." After a pause, Nick said, "The first day I have to wear a suit all year and it has to be the warmest day since fall. I'm running the A/C out here."

"Oh, stop grumbling."

"Are you talking to me or your stomach?" Before Bret could fire off a retort, Nick broke in and said, "Eyes up. Here comes the mail truck. I'm muting." Nick muted his microphone but remained on the line.

A USPS mail truck rolled to a stop in front of the doorway, partially obscuring Nick's view. The postal worker, a young black man dressed in the traditional light blue shirt and dark blue shorts, stepped out and walked to the back to lift the door.

Nick activated his microphone and said, "This is it. I'm partially blocked until he leaves."

"If the room is booked by the company and we don't know the number, do you think they'll get it to him?"

"He's been here for months and has paid them untold thousands of dollars. They'll know him. If the desk clerk doesn't, I guarantee you the manager will."

Shelby sat on the bed with her legs crossed and scrolled on the home page until she found the search box, then entered her screen name and browsed the results. She touched the thumbnail image that also served as a link to the video, then waited for the next page to load.

She let out a screech with excitement and said, "Lucien!"

Typing on his laptop, he stopped and spun in a half circle in the desk chair toward her. "What is it?" he asked and stretched his arms over his head.

"270,000 views, Lucien. 270,000!"

"I'm sorry. For what?"

"For our scene at the cabin!" Shelby said. She pushed herself forward and bounced toward the edge of the bed, then leaned toward him with the phone.

He hated watching himself on camera but took note of the view count. To have nearly 300,000 views in six weeks since its release was unheard-of. In a career of less than a year, Shelby had gained a supportive, almost obsessed, following. It was her natural look, Lucien thought. Her so-called girl next door quality that left the viewer wondering, but not caring, if she truly was of legal age, the implied but soon-to-be shattered innocence was invaluable and lucrative in their industry.

"It's remarkable, isn't it?" he said.

"I sure thought so," Shelby whispered, then reached and ran her hand to his inner thigh. "The video views are, too."

"You make it impossible to do my work," he said with a smirk.

Feigning being taken aback, she said, "I don't remember you ever complaining."

Lucien leaned forward to kiss the girl for whom he had fallen but was interrupted by the ring of the hotel phone on the nightstand.

"Perfect," she whined and fell onto her back, rolling her eyes.

"Yes?" Lucien answered.

"Mr. Murdoc, you have a package that has been delivered to the front desk. It is here whenever you wish to pick it up," the desk clerk said.

"I am not expecting a delivery of any kind. Who is the sender?"

"There is only a return address but no name, sir."

Lucien shook his head, said, "I'll be right there," and slammed the handset down. To Shelby, he said, "I've had something delivered downstairs," and kissed her on the cheek.

In the lobby, the elevator door opened and Lucien stepped out.

Bret sat up straight and said, "Got him. I wish I could see the look on his face." Even with the television playing and activity flowing toward an event in the conference center, Bret was within earshot of the front desk. He dropped the newspaper onto the adjacent empty chair and turned his attention to the television that was mounted on the wall to the right of where Lucien would be standing.

"Mr. Murdoc, good afternoon. Just a moment, sir," the desk clerk said when Lucien approached.

The clerk disappeared into an office behind the desk and returned with a box four feet by four feet in size, covered in sparkling red wrapping paper and topped with a blue and white bow. A shipping label with a nameless return address, which led to an abandoned building in a city several hours away, was affixed to the top. The clerk walked around the desk and sat the box on the floor at Lucien's feet.

"Nick, that box is almost as big as he is," Bret said into the headset. "What all's in there?"

"Bubble wrap, foam packing peanuts, cardboard scraps, and a plastic bag with a note and a number suspended from a string taped to the top," Nick said and muted the microphone again.

"You have a style that's all your own."

"Would you like some help, sir? I can have someone..." the desk clerk said to Lucien.

"Thank you, no," Lucien replied. It took two attempts to wrangle the box but he lifted it with a groan, taking a step backward, off-balance, before righting himself and moving toward the elevator.

Bret stood from his seat and arrived at the elevator before Lucien. "Let me get that for you, man. Looks like you've got your hands full," he said. He pushed the call button and waited along side. "Need some help?"

Straining, Lucien said, "I believe I have it." He nearly dropped the box but regained his grip.

When the door opened, both men stepped inside. Bret moved into the corner and Lucien was straightaway with the door.

"What floor?" Bret asked.

"Three, please."

With Lucien watching, Bret pushed the buttons for the third and fourth floors and waited for the door to close. They both adhered to the unspoken social contract of silence in the elevator, watching the digital display as the movement upward began. The box slowly slipped from Lucien's grasp and Bret reached down to catch the bottom.

Lucien swore in French and pushed the box upward with his knee.

The door slid open at the third floor and Lucien stepped out, followed by Bret. "Hang on a minute," Bret said. "Let me get that for you and you just worry about the door. Call it southern hospitality." Bret took the box from Lucien and experienced the challenge of transporting it for himself.

At the door to the room, Lucien opened the lock with his key card, cracked the door, held it with his foot, and took the box from Bret. Shelby pulled the door the rest of the way open, then stepped aside as Lucien slowly wedged himself inside.

"*Merci beaucoup*," Lucien said without turning around.

"You're welcome. Have a good day." Walking away, Bret heard the door to Lucien's room close and said into the headset, "He's in room 312 with a blonde that may or may not be 18, wearing a white dress shirt, black dress pants, and thousand-dollar shoes with nowhere to go. He's hard to miss, unless you look right over top of his head."

"He has to come out and play eventually," Nick said.

"What did you write on the note?"

"Just enough to pique his interest and to ensure he'll make the connection when we speak. Initials, a number to a VoIP service that forwards to one of the burner phones, and a box full of garbage that will give the housekeeper a coronary. I should probably find a way to tip her."

"I'm headed down to the bench outside the entrance," Bret said. "I need some sunlight and fresh air."

"Is there another special lady in your life?" Shelby asked. She walked around each side of the bed and back again, looking at the box and wondering what was inside.

"Never," Lucien said and then realized that he was speaking honestly.

"Who's it from?"

He tilted the box toward himself and squinted to read the small print on the label. "There is only an address here." He looked at Shelby and said, "Perhaps you should leave the room."

"It's not a bomb, Lucien. I don't hear anything ticking." Her grin disappeared, replaced by a tinge of sadness and concern. "What's going on? There's something you're not telling me."

Lucien placed his hands on her shoulders and said, "There is not. If you'd like to open it, go ahead. It's all right."

Shelby used a fingernail to slice the paper along the edge of the lid of the oversized gift box until it was free. She lifted the top and the string that Nick had taped in place pulled the plastic bag into view.

"I think this is for you," she said and handed the bag to Lucien. She sat the box on the ground sorted through the contents, finding nothing of importance or value. Foam peanuts scattered onto the floor with every movement. "What's it say?"

Lucien read the handwritten note aloud:

> *Looking forward to discussing business with you. I'll be in touch.*

■ *SM*

She walked behind him and looked over his shoulder at the index card. "Who is 'S.M.'?"

He turned the card over, finding the phone number on the back side, and then looked again at the address label. "I have no idea, *mon amour.*" He looked at his watch and said, "I'm famished. Shall we have a late lunch?"

She took his hand and led him to his feet, then hooked her arm inside his and said, "It's a date."

"He's late," Nick said from the car. He could see Bret sitting on the bench, sprawled out as if he was dozing off in the sun. "He's usually doing something by 4 p.m. according to his patterns and it's already 3:00." He combed his beard, which was still longer than he preferred but not unkempt, and looked in the mirror to check his work.

Look the part.

"Don't get impatient. He'll be here."

"Maybe the box rattled him more than I intended."

"Relax. I know exactly where he is and why he's late."

"Enlighten me."

"I saw the blonde he was with and she wasn't there to clean the room."

"I hate doing this," Nick said. "Being me is enough work. I have no desire to be an actor, too. The aliases, the fake accents, the details, it's all so tiresome."

"It's the only way to attack this one though."

"I hate it, but I know."

"Where did you get the name for this one?"

"Random name generator online."

Bret laughed and said, "Perfect."

"Work smarter not harder."

The automatic doors opened at the front of the building and Lucien emerged, dressed just as Bret had described, now holding hands with the woman at his side. Bret looked toward Nick in the car and said, "You're up." It was his turn to mute his microphone.

Nick opened the door and stepped out, put on a pair of black wrap-around sunglasses, and began moving toward Lucien, who was walking toward his own car with Shelby. He fastened the button on his suit coat as he approached. "Lucien Murdoc?" he asked.

"Yes?"

"Sean McCormick. It's nice to finally meet you in person."

Lucien shook his hand and, puzzled, said, "I don't believe we know one another."

"You're 'S.M.'," Shelby said.

"Very good," Nick said to Shelby. Then to Lucien: "You might not know me but I know you. I'd like to speak with you for a moment." Again, to Shelby: "It's just business." Each sentence was spoken clearly, with a smile, projecting confidence and power.

"We were actually about to have a late lunch. So if you'll excuse me..."

"Five minutes. A man of your great success already knows that both victory and disaster can come about in a matter of minutes. It's something in which you'll be interested."

Lucien turned to Shelby, said, "Wait for me in the car, please. I'll be there in a moment," and handed her his key ring.

They walked to Nick's sedan and Lucien said, "All right, Mr. Mc-Cormick. You have my attention. What is this about? Who are you?"

Deliberately looking away from Lucien and into the distance, Nick said, "Brann Cinema, the Norwegian word for 'fire'. A multimillion dollar company that's a leader in a multibillion dollar industry and you are one of the point men. Operational and filming locations all over the globe..." He stopped, then turned and looked at Lucien and said, "And you are the constant presence."

"You said this was business, Mr. McCormick."

Refusing to surrender control of the dialogue, and then intentionally leering at Shelby, Nick asked, "Is she one of your starlets, Lucien?"

This time it was Lucien who looked away. "She is a performer under an exclusive contract, among other things. Let us talk business, Mr. McCormick."

I know exactly what and who she is under. We just found his weakness.

"Call me Sean," Nick said.

"'Mr. McCormick' will do until we are comfortable enough to be less formal."

He's trying to retain whatever power he can.

"Very well." Nick leaned against the driver door and said, "You wanted to know who I am so it's only polite to tell you. I unofficially manage a hedge fund based in New York but we have offices in Chicago and Los Angeles." Lucien took his phone out of his pocket and Nick said, "I'll save you some time. We have presidents and CEOs and board members who exist in order to serve as the other two cards in the shell game. No one ever finds the king. Invisibility is a rare but remarkable superpower in the financial world. You'll never find my name attached to anything."

Lucien replaced the phone in his pocket and said, "And why is that?"

"Because I'm good at what I do, especially in the way that I do it. Discretion is my specialty."

"I can appreciate that. What does it have to do with me?"

"People talk, Lucien. Nothing is truly a secret if more than one person knows."

"Either say what you are trying to say or let us enjoy our evening, Mr. McCormick." He looked to his car and saw Shelby looking back. He smiled at her and then looked back at Nick.

"Adult cinema and fundamentalist Islamic nations mix like oil and water, Lucien. So how do you explain your presence in the region on such a regular basis?"

Regaining confidence, Lucien said. "I was unaware that international travel was against the law, sir. I rather enjoy vacationing in

Dubai. You claim to be a wealthy man. You should visit there yourself some time. I need to be going."

Lucien took two steps away before Nick said, "Dubai is not located in Saudi Arabia, Lucien."

He turned and walked back to Nick and said, "Excuse me? How do you know about the Saudis?"

Without anyone nearby but doing so for effect, Nick lowered his voice and said, "I know that because, as I told you, I'm good at what I do. No one else knows because, as I also told you, discretion is my specialty." Nick turned, stepped away, sighed loudly enough for Lucien to hear him then returned and said, "We can act as if neither of us knows what is going on behind the scenes, so to speak, but I don't have time for games. I'm assuming you don't either. Do I need to spell it out for you?"

"What does that mean?" Lucien asked.

"I have clients, investors, with tastes that are both exotic and expensive and tend to require a great deal of travel, effort, and secrecy to satisfy. Considering your time spent in Riyadh, not to mention virtually every major city in Western Europe over the last decade, combined with the overall nature of your so-called business, further discussion seems unnecessary."

Stone-faced, Lucien said, "You could not possibly know these things."

Returning the expression and intonation, Nick asked, "I found you, didn't I?" and waited for a response. When one failed to come, he said, "Lucien, I'm not unfamiliar with how the real world works. You're a successful man but you're middle management."

"Excuse me?"

Power.

A grin turned up at one corner of Nick's mouth. "It's not intended to be a slight, Mr. Murdoc," Nick said, making a point to address him in the same manner that Lucien had insisted on using. "It's reality. You answer to someone, a seemingly nameless and faceless entity that exists either at the head of a table in a board room or is sitting at a desk somewhere in a dark office. Either way, I found you in order to speak to them. Someone in middle management should be accustomed to his role as an intermediary."

The man knew things, Lucien thought. He knew things that were supposed to be impossible to know. Only someone who was truly connected could have access to such information. McCormick's authenticity was not in question. Concerns regarding his motives remained, regardless if he was law enforcement, a vengeful former client, or competition.

"You'll be compensated for your trouble, provided we can reach an agreement. You have my number. Make a call, have a talk, let your boss know everything that we've discussed. If it's his desire to leave that much money on the table, that's his decision. Either way, let me know," Nick said.

"One question: Why did you send the box?" Lucien asked.

"There's nothing wrong with a little panache. I'm an entertainer at heart. I enjoy knowing that I will forever live on in the memory of those I meet. So tell me, will *you* ever forget this encounter?"

Without answering Nick's question, Lucien said, "I'll contact him this evening. You will have your answer tomorrow. He does not leave business on the table unresolved."

Nick handed Lucien two fifty-dollar bills and said, "Dinner is on me. Have a good evening."

Lucien walked at a hurried pace to his automobile where Shelby was waiting. His back was to Nick, who opened the door, sat in the sedan, and started the engine.

Bret, who was still watching Lucien from his vantage point, activated his headset and said, "That's the look of a man experiencing absolute fear."

After dinner, Shelby returned to the room in advance of Lucien, who remained in the car to place the phone call to his boss. The possibilities of this call were endless. The man in power could dismiss the issue and end the call abruptly, he could demand every detail of information that Lucien could provide, or he could terminate Lucien from his position simply for entertaining the man who tracked him down at a supposedly secure recruiting and production site and failed to quench his thirst for knowledge.

The call was answered on the second ring. "What do you need, Lucien?" the man said.

"You said no work stuff tonight," a woman's voice said in the background.

"Two seconds, baby," he replied to his guest.

"We have an issue, *patron*," Lucien said.

"I'll be right back," the man said to the woman in the room. Lucien heard the bed creak as the man rolled out. "Why do I employ you, Lucien?"

"Because..."

"Because you are able to handle anything that happens in our business without involving me," the man interrupted. "Anything."

"This may be beyond me."

The man let out his breath into the phone, overwhelming the microphone and causing Lucien to pull the speaker away from his ear until it ended. "What is it?"

"A man approached me at the hotel today. He was waiting in the parking lot for me. Before that, he sent a package to the hotel with a message inside. After it was opened, he was waiting for me outside."

On the call, he heard a door close followed by ambient noise of traffic and the organized chaos of the busy streets of a large city at night. "Tell me everything," the man said sternly.

"He knew things he should not know, *patron*; things that no one could possibly know. "

"What things, Lucien?" the man said. His frustration was growing at an equal pace with Lucien's anxiety. He activated the speakerphone and opened the notepad app.

"He knew that we have been active in the Middle East. He alluded to other areas in which we operate and indicated a desire to be a part of it."

"His name?"

"He says that his name is Sean McCormick and claims to be a hedge fund manager from New York that operates covertly. He said that there would be no trace of him tied to Wall Street and I was unable to find anything on my own."

The man was making a record of every detail that was relayed by Lucien. "What did he look like, Lucien?"

"What does...?"

"Because I am going to have our chief of security look into him and turn over whatever stone he resides under."

"He was 6-2 in my estimation, around 200 pounds, athletic, lean muscle but average build. Nothing extraordinary. It was difficult to discern very much beyond these things because he was wearing a suit. Brown hair parted and combed back, and a beard that was not long. He was wearing sunglasses. That is all I remember."

There was a delay as the man entered the details into his phone, then he said, "Very good, Lucien. That's impressive recall."

"I will not forget him," Lucien said. "There is something else."

"Go ahead."

"He wishes to meet you. He does not know who you are, where you are, or what you do, but he found me in order to speak with you. He believes that the two of you could conduct business. If he is who he says he is, he could be a client, a partner, an opportunity to enter an entirely new market. If he's not..."

"If he's not who he says he is, we will know," the man says. "A man of such tastes and financial means can easily defend his identity and position. An impostor will be exposed in short order. Our security is impeccable." He sat down in a chair on his balcony, reclined, propped his feet up on a table, and said, "If he would like to meet, we will meet. We have a game scheduled for next Monday in Boston and one of our regulars is unable to attend. Relay the details to him and extend an invitation with the standard terms but continue to seek as much information as possible."

"Yes, *patron*," Lucien said. "Anything else?"

"Make sure he has a game piece."

"I will. Thank you, sir."

The man ended the call without formally signing off.

Lucien pondered his next encounter with Sean McCormick, one that would begin with a phone call to the number on the card.

The phone call placed to the number on the card connected with a server somewhere in the continental United States and was redirected to the device that Nick planned to keep with him until Murdoc made contact, which took place promptly at 8 a.m. the next morning.

"Yes?" Nick answered, despite knowing who was on the line.

"Mr. McCormick, this is Lucien Murdoc. Can you meet me in the hotel lobby in, say, thirty minutes?"

"Make it an hour. I'll see you then," Nick said, and ended the call.

Power.

Using his personal phone, Nick called Bret, who was staying in a room at the hotel until Lucien made contact again, and updated him on the plans.

Bret was waiting in the lobby, still connected to the call, when Lucien arrived a full ten minutes early for his meeting with Nick, dressed differently but still recognizable as the helpful man from the day before.

Having recognized him from the day before, Lucien took the seat beside him and said, "Hello again."

"Hey, what's going on?" Bret said. "Your hands are less full today."

"Yes, indeed. Thank you for the assistance yesterday. That box was getting the better of me in the elevator."

"I was glad to help. I didn't catch your name."

Lucien extended his hand and said, "I'm Lucien. And yours?"

Bret shook it and said, "Steve."

Knowing he could not respond, Nick said into his earpiece, "You help him with a box and you're on a first-name basis. I give him money and I'm still 'Mr. McCormick'."

"I'm about to go grab some breakfast in the dining area if you want to join me and chat," Bret said.

"Thank you, no. I'm afraid I have a meeting at 9 a.m. but thank you for your offer," Lucien replied. He looked to the door each time it opened. He watched as Nick parked in the only vacant spot on the front row and walked through the doors and said, "There is my guest now. Thank you again for your assistance yesterday, Steve."

"No problem," Bret said.

Approaching Nick, Lucien said, "Good morning, Mr. McCormick. Why don't we sit down over here for a moment?"

"Good to see you again, Lucien. You weren't kidding, were you? You said I would have an answer today and I ended up waking up to one. You're a man of your word. That's good to know going forward. I assume we *are* moving forward."

"The man for whom I work does not operate in an orthodox manner, Mr. McCormick. If you are to meet with him it will not be under, as they say, normal circumstances."

"Care to explain that?"

"Do you like to gamble, Mr. McCormick?"

Nick raised his eyebrows, smiled, and said, "I've been drawing to an inside straight all my life, Lucien. It's what made me who I am. Why?"

A fake name but a true statement.

"A keen analogy, my friend. You say that you are a wealthy man. You claim to be cultured and experienced, well traveled, so this, while unorthodox, should be of interest to you. Yes, he would like to meet with you, speak with you. Several times per year he enjoys a friendly game of poker with others of similar means and interests. The next such event takes place in Boston on Monday evening next week and there is an open seat at the table. It is a black tie event so please plan accordingly. If you are interested, you have been formally invited."

Now I'm his friend?

"I formally accept," Nick said.

"Excellent. There are, however, some terms and conditions."

"I assumed as much."

"The buy-in for the game is $200,000. The game will consist of five players and will be played for the entire $1 million. I assume that amount will not be a problem."

"Not at all. Continue."

"You may bring your personal stake to the venue in cash, if you choose, or you may wire it to this account in advance." He handed Nick a white business card with account and routing numbers printed on the front. An address was scrawled on the back. "It is perfectly secure, I assure you. The victor will be cashed out with physical currency at the end of the evening. The game will begin promptly at 8 p.m. so please arrive early."

Wire 200 grand to an account so it can be traced back to the source? I think not.

"Cash will be just fine. I like to watch my money move, especially as it moves in my direction."

"Very well. You will also need this." Lucien handed Nick a coin, minted in Canada with a maple leaf on the front, a profile of Queen Elizabeth II on the opposite side, and consisting of one ounce of pure silver. "That is your game piece. Provide it to security upon your arrival to gain admission."

"Will I need anything else? My birth certificate and driver's license, perhaps?"

"Absolutely not, Mr. McCormick. Those items can be easily forged. That is why you have your game piece. Without possession of that coin, it makes no difference who you are. You are nothing more than an intruder."

"Fair enough."

"You will find the address for the event on the back of the card, Mr. McCormick. Be advised, however, that this friendly game can easily become quite intense."

"Most things do with a million dollars at stake."

"That is true." Lucien shook his hand and said, "Good luck, Sean."

Nick chuckled and said, "Thank you, Lucien. I appreciate it."

Lucien turned to walk away and stopped. He turned back to Nick and said, "One last detail. If you are able, bring a date with you to the event. The others at the table will do so. Daniel fancies pleasant scenery around the table."

"I'll do my best," Nick said. "I'm sure we'll meet again."

Lucien nodded without speaking and walked to the elevator. Nick looked to Bret and tapped his headset before walking into the parking lot.

Bret waited for Lucien to step into the elevator and said to Nick, "You just bought into a poker game worth a million dollars to learn the identity of one man, Nick."

"Let's get even more specific. I just paid $200,000 to sit at a table to find out someone's last name and it may not even be real."

"That's fair. We didn't have a first name until today. Daniel, was it?"

"It was. It's not much for Micah to look into but it fills in a blank space in the file. Monday should fill in the rest."

There was a pause, then, "Do you think that game is rigged?"

"Not if the high rollers are regulars. They wouldn't stick around long if something seemed amiss."

"What are you going to do?"

"Me?" Bret asked. "I'm going to check out and then lift off."

"Your work is easy. I have to find a date that looks good in a dress and won't ask a million questions," Nick said.

"The first part will be way easier than the second, brother."

"That makes me feel better. I'm out," Nick said and ended the call.

Merging the rented luxury sedan onto the interstate to begin the half-hour drive back to the farmhouse, Nick groaned aloud at the thought of the next call he would have to make. He hated breaking plans. He hated breaking plans with certain people more than others.

Maybe she can just go to dinner with Noah instead.

He silently chastised himself and then, audibly, said, "Don't start that again."

Gabi answered on the third ring.

"I didn't wake you, did I?"

"Of course not," she said. "Even without driving to work, my internal clock still tells me to wake up early. What's up?" She turned down the volume on the music that played in the background.

"I'm going to need a rain check on Monday night."

"Nick..." Gabi said, drawing out the sound of his name to indicate her disappointment.

"I know. I'm sorry. I have to go out of town."

"Where to?" she asked.

"Boston, and I have a million things to do before I leave."

"This is for work?"

"Right," Nick said.

She's doing the work for me.

Skeptical, she asked, "Why does a drug rep have to go to Boston on short notice?"

Maybe not.

"It's a charity thing, black tie formal. I've apparently been chosen to be the representative."

"Black tie formal, you say?" Gabi paused and added, "When do we leave?"

"We?"

"Well, we had plans anyway. Let's just move them. Besides, a girl doesn't get to dress up for a formal event every day in southwest Virginia. Unless..."

How am I supposed to explain this one?

"Unless what?"

"Unless you already have a guest lined up."

"Actually…"

"Good. Is the flight already booked?"

"That's one of the million things I have to do."

"Leave it to me. I have tons of miles." Nick could hear the excitement building in her voice as she spoke. "Now, when do we leave?"

"Monday. The earlier, the better."

"It's a date."

I wish.

"Are you sure you want to do this, Gabrielle? It's a quick trip there and back. Twenty-four hours at the most."

"Nick, for the next couple of months I'm a jobless slacker with time to kill and there is only so much time I can spend on the couch eating snacks and watching television without feeling like my brain is melting. Mundane is not for the insane."

"Okay," he said. "Book it."

"I want all the details later," she demanded.

"Count on it." Nick made sure that his fingers were crossed.

"Oh, I'll get my answers. Love you, bye."

Yes, you will.

12

"Isn't this great?" Gabi asked as she looked out the window and snapped a picture of the wings and cloud cover with her phone.

She was nursing a glass of white wine but chose to forgo the in-flight meal. Nick was on his second bottle of water, struggling to appreciate the allure of the environment.

"Even first class isn't built for people like me," Nick said. He moved in his seat, failing to find an accommodating position.

"It's a two-hour flight, you big baby," Gabi said. She kicked his foot as she said it and he faked an injured moan.

"It's been so long since I've flown somewhere first class," she said. "Then I get to go somewhere first class when we land."

This should be fun to explain.

"You said this event was formal and black tie but you didn't tell me what it's for. Is it a charity benefit or a convention or what?"

"About that..." His sentence fragment trailed off and he squinted at the thought of what to say next.

"Nick..." she said sharply and waited for something to be said.

"It's not a convention."

"Okay."

"It's not a charity benefit, at least not in the traditional sense."

"Spill it, Nick."

He locked his eyes on the front of the plane and said, "Have you ever watched a poker tournament on TV?"

161

Gabi kept her eyes fixed on the side of Nick's head and said, "Not on purpose."

"You're going to be seeing one in person. I'm one of the five players tonight."

"You brought me here to gamble?" she asked with a high-pitched inflection at the end.

Nick turned to look at her and said, "Technically, you asked to come here to watch me gamble."

She shook her head and said, "This is too much. So why is it a formal thing?"

"It's a charity tournament. The winnings go to a nonprofit, winner takes all, and my boss is paying for my buy-in."

"That's impressive," she said. "Have you played in games like this before?"

"I've dabbled," he lied. His heart rate increased.

I hate not telling her the truth.

"How much did your boss pay for you to get into this thing?"

Nick looked away, to the other side of the plane, gritted his teeth, then looked back to her and said, "$200,000."

"And there are five players," she muttered.

"Correct."

"A million dollars?" she exclaimed louder than she intended. She lowered her voice and asked, "Nick, are you serious?"

"I'm serious."

Gabi looked straight ahead and said, "Okay. That explains why it's formal. Are people going to be watching this?"

"Just the people in the room. It's sort of an unofficial event."

"That sounds like code for 'illegal'."

"Considering we're gambling for seven figures and keeping it quiet, you would be right."

She lowered her voice, leaned closer to Nick and said, "That's exciting."

"It'll be more exciting if I win," Nick whispered in return.

"It's not like you get to keep the money, Nick."

"No, but I get bragging rights."

And a cool million, if all goes right.

Gabi finished her glass, tapped the side with her nails, and asked, "Is there anything else I need to know about tonight?"

Nick took a deep breath and exhaled.

In the pause, Gabi said, "Nick?"

"Like I said, this is an unofficial event. So there may or may not be pseudonyms being used when we get there. For tonight, I'm Sean Mc-Cormick, hedge fund manager from New York with a seven-digit bank account and a gorgeous date."

"Oh, really?" Gabi said. "When does she get here?"

"I wouldn't let anyone else disparage you, so I won't let you do it either."

"Well, thank you," she said as a hint of red flushed in her face.

Nick waited a beat and said, "That really is a lovely shade."

"Stop!" she replied and added a playful slap on his shoulder. "So if you are Sean McCormick, who am I for the evening?"

Having failed to consider her alias, Nick said, "It's up to you. Think about it and we'll talk about it after we get ready.

"Consider yourself lucky. You get to witness something far rarer than Halley's Comet tonight."

"And what's that?"

"Nick Burke voluntarily wearing a tux."

Despite a physical distance of only four and a half miles, the mid-afternoon drive via taxi from Boston's Logan International Airport to the Boston Park Plaza hotel took nearly twenty minutes, including the accident-induced backup on the portion of I-90 that stretched across Boston Main Channel. Fifteen stories high and nearly a century old, the building housed more than a thousand rooms and four restaurants, including the one located in conjunction with the lobby where Nick and Gabi sat at a table while waiting for the unexpectedly long line at the front desk to thin before being told that their room was not yet ready upon checking in. A complimentary drink had been supplied as a result of their perceived inconvenience.

"When does this thing start anyway?" Gabi asked. She sipped from her glass of Moscato and removed the foil from a piece of white chocolate.

"Promptly at 8:00 is what I was told by one of the organizers," Nick said. "And you still need a name for the evening."

She took another sip and said, "I'm working on it."

The general manager of the hotel approached their table and said, "Mr. Burke, your room is ready." He handed Nick a paper folder with two electronic keycards inside and added, "Eleventh floor. We're sorry for your wait. You may take your bags and belongings to your room at once."

"Thank you very much," Nick said. Adding a manufactured air of sophistication, he said to Gabi, "Our suite awaits, my dear," and took her hand as she stood to her feet.

She tilted her head back and replied, "Off we go."

They shared a laugh at their private attempt at humor and walked onto the elevator, pushing the gold luggage cart packed with garment bags and suitcases sufficient for a week-long vacation.

"You're loving this, aren't you?" Nick asked on the ride to the eleventh floor.

"What's not to love?" Gabi said, watching the floor display change. "First class flights, amazing meals, luxury hotels…" She looked at Nick and said, "Getting dressed up, assuming a fake identity, and watching someone gamble for an absurd amount of money in a mysterious game of poker with wealthy people who either remain anonymous or are too rich and powerful to care."

Nick, refusing to look back at her, said, "It sounds sketchy when you say it that way."

She looked to the door as the elevator slowed to a stop and said, "It's exciting and new. I can handle that."

Their room was adorned in white, contrasted with brown earth tones in the carpet. The sunlight shone through the window and reflected off of every colorless surface, prompting Nick to shield his eyes when he followed Gabi through the door that he had held open for her.

"I feel like I need to put my shades back on," he said.

Gabi walked to the window and stretched her arms as she looked out at the Boston skyline. "What a view," she said. "Come look."

Nick stood beside her as they both took in the midday scenery, the blue sky reflecting off of the mirrored glass of nearby skyscrapers. "I'm glad you're here," he said without looking. "Exciting or not, flying solo is never a good time."

She hugged him around the waist with one arm and said, "I wasn't going to miss this," then looked up at him and added, "You better win."

"You better start getting ready," Nick said and walked to the other side of the room where he began to unpack his suitcase.

Gabi checked the time on her iPhone and said, "We have four hours until the game starts, Nick. What's the rush?"

Still unpacking, he said, "First of all, we might have a stop to make before the game. Second, I've waited for you to get ready before and there's a good chance we're already behind schedule."

"You know..." Gabi started to say.

Nick smiled, still looking into his suitcase, and said, "I tease because I love." He looked up, waited for her to look back at him, and said, "We have plenty of time. I'll go first, as soon as my tux is delivered, and you'll still have plenty of time." Nick closed the lid and heard the knock on the door. "Perfect timing," he said on his way to the door.

The deliveryman was white, tall, and overweight, although the extra pounds were hidden behind a winter coat. His cheeks were puffy and he sported a double chin that would have been concealed had he not been clean-shaven. Dark brown sideburns were visible underneath his blue Dodgers hat, the bill of which he touched and tipped the moment Nick opened the door. Nick nodded silently in return. The signal had been sent and received.

"Good afternoon," Nick said.

"Your rental, sir," the man replied. "Everything is included."

"Pickup tomorrow morning?" Nick said loud enough to ensure that he was overheard by Gabi.

"Yes, sir. Just as you requested."

"Thank you," Nick said. The man handed him two garment bags and a shoebox. Nick rewarded him with a $20 bill, and closed the door. "Give me half an hour and you can do as you please," he said to Gabi.

She squinted, feigning intimidation and said, "I'll be timing you."

Nick carried the bags into the bathroom and, as he closed the door, said, "I'll have time to spare."

Inside the bathroom, he hung the clothes from the back of the door, removed the plastic coverings from the garments, and turned on the water in the shower. He reached inside the jacket pocket of the tuxedo and checked the contents: a Glock 26 subcompact pistol loaded with ten rounds of nine-millimeter ammunition and a round in the chamber, two additional fully loaded magazines, and a cellular flip phone that was capable of voice calls and texts but little more.

He replaced the items in the jacket pocket for the time being and said aloud, "It even matches the jacket."

Twenty-eight minutes later, by his calculation, he emerged from the bathroom fully dressed and prepared to surrender the space to his traveling partner. His beard was trimmed short, courtesy of the electric trimmer, and his hair was slicked back with pomade and slightly parted on the left side. Only the bowtie was missing from the tuxedo, which he held in his hand on the walk back into the room. "I hate these things," he said to Gabi. "Would you mind?"

She laughed as she pushed herself off of the bed and said, "I'll get it before we go. It wouldn't be the first time."

"You're the best."

"I know," Gabi said as she grabbed her garment bags from the leather chair that sat in the corner of the room and started toward the bathroom, pulling the suitcase behind her.

"We have plenty of time. Don't feel like you're in a rush," he said, then stood and checked his suitcase to confirm the presence of the silver game piece.

As Nick sat back down at the edge of his bed, Gabi left her suitcase just inside the bathroom door, then turned back to him, said, "You look really nice. You should dress up more often," and disappeared before he could answer.

He anticipated at least an hour of prep time for Gabi and turned on the television to add background noise to the sounds of the shower running and the analysis of the litany of activities that would soon follow. The game was means to an end, a chance to lay eyes on Daniel, the person to whom Lucien Murdoc answered. Standing to his feet, he paced the perimeter of the room twice before settling at the window, admiring the skyline that earlier caught Gabi's eye and considering his strategy. The game was supposed to be an afterthought but victory would indeed be sweet. Many things could be accomplished with an $800,000 profit, once the initial investment was returned to the source.

The other players were almost certainly known commodities, at least semi-regulars, at the table. Their tendencies and styles would be known to each other. Bluffs would be called, playful jabs and insults would be traded, drinks shared, and money won and lost. For men, and possibly women, for whom pocket change would be considered a fortune to the common man, this would be a fortress of freedom and enjoyment, free of the concerns of business, family, and the daily aggravations of those in their employ. They would, in fact, be shedding their respective Jungian personas and revealing their true selves to their compatriots, the select few of whom they felt worthy of such honesty and respect.

They would do so entirely unaware that their guest for the evening was a fictional character.

He would wear sunglasses without mirrored lenses while playing, a tradition among serious players. He would not tinker with the stacks of chips. He preferred controlled chaos over established patterns or a specific strategy early in games. Patterns are easily exploited, no matter how successful they appear. These were professional men – or women, he silently corrected himself – but they were not professional players. Each game would have holes, weaknesses that were presumably tied to a personality trait or faulty belief structure, and that is where he would enter with a competitive advantage. There was no book, so to speak, on Sean McCormick, either for the players at the table or anywhere else. For that reason, the others may play tight in the early going. The environment may be more tense than usual with a mystery man sitting nearby. But as the night wore on, conversation and spirits would allow them to unwind and the game would change.

I need a tell. They see a pattern, I allow them to buy into their suspicion, they prepare to exploit, and it's all a setup.

He smirked and nodded along with the rhythm of his thoughts.

Handoff, handoff, handoff, same formation every time and, then, a play-action pass.

He walked to the suitcase, took out the silver game piece, and flipped it into the air, then caught it, and turned it onto his wrist. "Tails," he whispered into the empty room. He uncovered the coin to see the head of Queen Elizabeth, dropped the coin into his pocket, and sat down in the leather chair. "I'm gonna need better luck tonight," he said.

After forty minutes of mind-numbing cable news and commercials, the latter of which somehow seemed more believable, the bathroom door opened and Nick stood when Gabi appeared.

She wore a dark blue strapless evening gown that clung to her form until it flared outward just below her hips in the classic mermaid style. Her hair was down, touching her shoulders and with an almost imperceptible wave, but styled in a way that he had not seen in recent memory, and a simple silver chain was draped around her neck just above the notch in the neckline. She smiled when he stood and Nick found himself unable to speak.

Gabi waited for the silence to break before Nick managed to draw a deep breath and say, "Wow."

"Thank you," she said.

Nick approached her, then took her hand, lifted it up, and led her in a slow, full spin. When she faced him again, he said, "Gabrielle, you are absolutely breathtaking."

She responded with a kiss on his cheek and asked, "Are we ready?"

She always deflects. Skeptical of every compliment but believes every criticism.

"Almost," he said. "I'll call the town car service and let them know we're ready."

Incredulous, she asked, "Town car? How far are we going?"

"A mile or so." He made a show of straightening his jacket and said, "But we have to maintain the image for the evening."

"Speaking of which, Mr. McCormick, you're missing your tie." She took the tie from the marble desktop and said, "Sit down." As she wrapped the tie around his neck, carefully twisting and turning it into its proper form, Nick took advantage of the moment to look into her eyes as she worked. She smiled when she finished, stood, and stepped back. "What would you ever do without me?" she asked.

Looking up at her from the foot of the bed, he said, "Let's make sure we never find out. Okay?"

"What's this?" she asked, picking up a metal box from Nick's suitcase.

"That is our entry fee." He took the laptop safe from Gabi's hands, entered a four-digit code into the digital keypad, and lifted the lid. Inside were twenty paper-wrapped stacks of $100 bills, accounting for the $200,000 buy-in for the game.

She held a stack and said, "I don't think I've ever seen this much cash at once," then dropped it back inside. "Isn't the box a little big?"

"The rest is for my winnings."

She shook her head and rolled her eyes. "Let me get my shoes."

When she turned away, Nick grabbed an ankle holster from his suitcase and placed it into his pocket.

"I'll call for the car."

"Isn't it a little early?" she asked as she slipped into one of her shoes.

"We have a stop to make."

The town car rolled to a stop at the corner of Huntington and Belvedere, in front of the entrance to the Prudential Center complex in the Back Bay district of Boston. Dusk was approaching and the shadows cast by the nearby towers seemed to evolve by the minute. Gabi slid across the seat and opened the door, carefully stepping out onto the sidewalk.

"Find a spot somewhere close. I'll be back down in a half-hour or so. I'll call you when I'm close," Nick said to the driver. He handed the man a $20 bill, looked outside and saw that Gabi was distracted by the bustling surroundings, and dropped the pistol, ankle holster, and spare magazines on top of the safe in the rear floorboard before stepping out of the car and watching it move into the flow of traffic.

"I can't wait to find out what this is about," Gabi said. "Look at this place," she added while looking up to the peak of the tower.

"This is where the game will be. We're on the seventh floor. But we're headed over to the Prudential Tower first."

Passersby allowed their looks to linger at the two people dressed in formal wear strolling through the shopping complex. "I think we're drawing attention, Nick," Gabi said. "I can feel people leering at me."

"You? For sure. Me? Not so much."

"How much farther do we have? I'm not dressed for this."

"Just be glad you didn't wear heels."

They left the mall through the doorway near St. Francis Chapel, entered the ground level of the Prudential Tower, and stepped onto the first available elevator.

"Where in the world are you taking me?" Gabi asked as the car began its ascent.

"All the way to the top of the world."

The Skywalk Observatory sets atop the Prudential Tower, the highest point accessible to the public among the fifty-two floors. The door opened and Gabi gasped as they walked into the observatory. She took Nick's hand and pulled him toward the nearest window.

"You love things like this," he said.

"Thank you," Gabi replied and hugged him around the waist again, then grabbed him by the arm and pulled him across the room, locating a different vantage point which overlooked the Charles River. Her eyes scanning every inch of the visual landscape, she said, "This view is spectacular. Don't you think so?"

Ignoring the scenery and admiring his companion while her attention was focused elsewhere, Nick said, "The view is positively stunning." When she turned to look at him, he averted his eyes out the window.

For half an hour, Gabi walked to each window, peered through the tower viewers that were mounted throughout the room, and borrowed Nick's phone to snap photos of every scene, including a selfie of the two of them at the window that featured the river view. He texted the driver to alert him to their return and, to Gabi, said, "We need to go. It's almost game time." She faked a pout and he said, "We'll come back sometime. Don't worry."

"There are lots of places to go and things to do," she said. "I'll make a list."

On the elevator ride to the ground floor, Nick said, "Have you decided on an alias for the evening?"

She looked to the upper corner of the car, pondering the question, then back to Nick and said, "I like the name Alexandra."

"Ooh, that's rather sultry," Nick said. "It suits you. I like it."

The doors opened and they moved back toward the main entrance to meet the town car, this time opting for the short walk through the outdoor park area despite a temperature that had cooled considerably since their arrival. The decision would save her from the eyes of onlookers, Nick knew.

Outside the entrance, Nick spotted the town car and said, "Wait here. I won't be a minute."

He opened the rear door, slid inside, and deliberately turned to his left, away from Gabi. To the driver he said, "I don't know how long this evening's festivities are going to last but we'll need you back here when it's over. I'll see to it that it's worth your while." He handed the driver a $100 bill.

"Thank you, sir. I'll be available," the driver said.

Nick lifted the leg of his dress pants and strapped the holster to his ankle, securing the pistol first and then adding the two magazines behind Velcro straps.

Only I would have to lock and load at a poker game. Am I in the Old West? What year is this?

He pulled the pants leg over the weapon and picked up the safe.

"Have a good evening, sir," the driver said.

"You, too. I'll be in touch," Nick answered and stepped onto the sidewalk as the town car drove away into a city whose nightlife was growing as the sun was setting.

Gabi met him outside the door and asked, "Where to?"

Nick backed up and Gabi moved with him. He looked skyward, pointed, and said, "This tower is called 111 Huntington Avenue. We're headed to the seventh floor for a no-pressure game of high stakes Texas Hold'Em. Are you ready, Alexandra?"

Gabi looked away from the building and up to Nick and said, "I'm ready, Sean."

Her arm hooked inside Nick's, Gabi led him through the automatic doors and into the lobby. Looking at the bank of elevators, she said, "You better win tonight."

Nick tightened his arm to hers and said, "Not to worry. I already have."

Wearing a black suit, white shirt, and black tie, the first security guard they encountered stood with his hands folded below his waist when the elevator door opened on the seventh floor of the 111 Huntington Avenue tower. A light-skinned black man, his dark hair was cut short and faded on the sides. The shoulders and arms of his suit jacket were under pressure from the size of his deltoids and biceps. His legs were less sizable, Nick noticed, an important tactical detail should the necessity of combat arise.

If he's not ex-military, he should have enlisted.

Gabi stepped off of the elevator first and Nick followed. The guard offered a long look at Gabi before turning his attention to Nick.

"Good evening," Nick said.

The guard did not respond.

Nick handed the safe to Gabi, took the silver game piece from his pocket and held it in his palm, showing to the guard. "I'm assuming you need to see this."

The man dialed a number on his cell phone. When the call was answered, he said, with a French accent, "Mr. McCormick and his guest have arrived." When the call ended, he said to Nick, "This way, please," and led them through an open, unused area of the floor and into a hallway.

Nick looked to Gabi and raised his eyebrows without speaking. She shrugged in response.

The floor of the building was uninhabited, likely rented quietly, privately, and specifically for the festivities of the evening by the host, a man named Daniel who served as the person in charge of a well-paid minion named Lucien Murdoc. Office spaces had been constructed at some point in the recent past, used by a former tenant that had since vacated. Two spaces were illuminated, Nick saw. The guard led them past the first closed door that allowed light to escape from the crack at the floor and gestured to the door on the opposite side of the hallway, which was secured by two additional guards of virtually identical appearance.

Nick made a show of holding out both arms, then opening each side of his jacket and turning in a circle. "Are you sure you don't want to frisk me?"

Expressionless, the guard said, "Good luck, sir," and disappeared down the corridor.

"He's no fun," Gabi said.

When Nick opened the door and walked inside, Gabi in tow, the four men who sat around the table stood to their feet. Their respective companions remained still. The table, designed for ten players, was nearly ten feet long and brand new; a high-dollar oval variety constructed from mahogany with a green felt playing surface devoid of graphics, a cushioned vinyl armrest, stainless steel cup holder, and foot rest was provided for each seat, allowing the occupant to gamble in comfort and style. Each player was dressed in a manner similar to Nick. Their female companions were already standing alongside each man, showing far more skin than Gabi, and turned to look at the two new figures that had entered the room.

"Sean McCormick, I presume," the man on the opposite side of the table said. Substantially younger than the other men and flanked by two women rather than one, his hair was thin and bright blonde, similar in color to that of Lucien Murdoc, and slicked straight back, the ends touching the back of his neck, but his skin appeared to have a hint of a naturally copper hue, one that was more heavily influenced by genetics than a tanning bed. He walked halfway around the table where he was met by Nick and extended his hand, which Nick shook firmly. "Thank you for coming. Welcome."

"Thank you for having me," Nick said. He looked around the room to the other men and said, "Be gentle," which drew a laugh from the men and women alike. Turning toward Gabi, he said, "This is Alexandra."

"She's lovely," the young man said to Nick. To Gabi, he said, "Welcome. Enjoy your evening."

Portly and balding, the remaining white strands combed over in a vain attempt to retain the remnants of former follicular glory, the man to Nick's left approached Gabi and held out his hand. When she placed her hand in his, he lifted it, kissed the back and said, "Roger Cavanagh. How do you do?"

"Very well. Thank you," Gabi said with a polite smile.

"Gentlemen, be seated," the young man said to the room. To Nick, he said, "It's customary for the female guests to stand throughout the game."

Nick started to speak but Gabi touched his shoulder and said into his ear, "It's fine. I've spent most of the day on my feet."

The young man nodded to her and said, "Very well." Looking around, he said, "You've all met Mr. McCormick, our new player for the evening. Sean, allow me to introduce everyone to you." He looked to the white-haired man to Nick's left and said, "Your guest, Alexandra, has already encountered Roger Cavanagh." Cavanagh leaned to the right and offered his hand to Nick, which was shaken.

"Pleasure to have you, Sean," he said.

"Thank you, sir. I'm hearing a Southern accent."

"Alabama," Cavanagh said. "You have a good ear, son." He chuckled when he spoke through his overbite and his double chin jiggled.

"I'm just well traveled," Nick said.

And I'm most definitely not your son, old man. Perversion is not my style.

Speaking to Nick, the host said, "To your right is Foster Mason, our most recently added regular."

"Welcome," Mason said. He closed his hand into a fist, which Nick bumped with his own.

"Thank you," Nick said.

Foster Mason was white, his skin nearly giving the appearance of alabaster. The top of his head was mostly smooth but a long flow of hair that gradually faded from black to light gray and began on the sides before being pulled back and braided, extending to the middle of his back, tucked behind him and pressed into the chair. Tall and spindly, clean-shaven aside from a gray soul patch on his chin, he tried in vain to recapture the youth that had expired two decades before and slouched in his seat, sprawled throughout enough space at the table for two players.

The host looked to his right, which was Nick's left, and said, "This is Musad Khan, our international player from the Middle East. His first name means 'lucky' in Arabic, hence his penchant for gambling."

Khan raised his glass to Nick but did not speak. Nick returned the gesture in kind.

Musad Khan was the oldest player in the room. His complexion was medium brown. His head was shaved and his face appeared weathered and showed a three-day growth of white stubble. A wooden cane was leaned against the table beside him.

Looking back to the host, Nick asked, "And you?"

The host stood and said, "My name is Daniel Staal."

"A-L or H-L?" Nick stood and asked.

"Two As, no H." Staal reached across the table and shook Nick's hand. "Are you ready?"

"I am," Nick said as he returned to his chair.

Staal looked to the door and waved. A young green-eyed blonde in a short red dress and matching high heels entered the room, stepped between the two brunettes who hovered over each of his shoulders and sat down beside him at the table. "Gentlemen, meet Lacey, our dealer for the evening," he said. She took a moment to meet the eyes of each player before turning her attention to the decks of cards that were stacked before her, placing them into the shuffler.

"The rules for the evening will be as follows," Daniel said. He scanned the room as he spoke. "Per usual, we will be playing traditional Texas Hold'em, aces high, no jokers, no limits, and nothing wild. The blinds will be $1,000 small and $2,000 big. As you can see, we will be playing with six decks and using an automatic shuffler. No dealer tricks in this room, only an honest game. We will break after each set of fifteen hands. Winner takes all."

"An honest game played among honest men, I presume," Nick said with a smile. He was the only player without a glass of scotch on the table in front of him.

"Mr. McCormick, your opposition tonight represents a collection of high-class individuals from the worlds of energy, entertainment, and criminal defense law."

"You seem to fall more in line with entertainment than the others, Daniel," Nick said.

The other three men laughed under their breath and Daniel smiled at the implied jab. "In a manner of speaking, yes, but I am a man who relishes diversity in all that I do and that includes business."

"Fair enough."

"Do you have your buy-in? Lucien informed me that you preferred to work in cash."

Without offering an answer, Nick entered his four-digit code into the safe and opened the lid. He removed the cash and tossed the stacks across the table, which were collected and counted by Lacey, the dealer with the long blonde hair, before being exchanged for the appropriate amount of chips.

Nick arranged the chips in front of him, took his black sunglasses from his jacket pocket, slid them onto his face and said, "*Now* we're ready."

"We are," Daniel replied. "Lacey, let's begin."

Daniel had the privilege of the dealer button, leaving him immune to the small and big blind bets for the first hand. Mason, seated between Daniel and Nick, added $1,000 to the pot before Nick added $2,000.

New guy starts the game with the big blind. I would expect no less.

The first hand was dealt, with two pocket cards given to each player before the three community cards, known as the flop, were dropped in the center of the table: The 5 of clubs, 10 of spades, and 8 of hearts. Nick checked his hand and held an offsuit 3 and 7. Being the first player to the left of Nick, the big blind for the hand, Cavanagh remained in the hand and bet $2,000 before Khan folded, Staal bet his own $2,000, and Foster added $1,000 to his small blind. Nick folded and tossed his cards to the center of the table. The queen of hearts was dealt in the turn, the fourth of the five community cards, prompting Foster to bet $5,000. Cavanagh folded and Staal called before Lacey turned the river card, a 4 of spades, onto the table. Both Foster and Staal checked. At the showdown, Foster's pair of tens trumped Daniel's jack and 8, winning an $11,000 pot and giving the aging child of the seventies an early lead.

As Lacey collected the cards from the table, Nick scanned the perimeter of the room. He leaned back in the chair and stretched, allowing him the visual range to take in 180 degrees of sight without raising suspicion, and found four cameras mounted on the wall opposite his side of the table. The two cameras in the corners pointed at Khan and Foster respectively, while the two at the one-quarter and three-quarter points of the wall were positioned to watch himself and Roger Cavanagh.

Four cameras at a poker game that can see the players and not the cards. Staal has an angle.

Nick was assigned the small blind bet and tossed $1,000 worth of chips into the pot. Cavanagh, the big blind, added his $2,000. The cards for the second hand were being distributed when he broke the silence.

"Staal is a Scandinavian name, isn't it?" Nick asked.

"It is," Daniel said sternly and without looking up from the table.

It's never too early to shake the tree.

"I don't hear much of an accent."

Staal looked up and said, "Sean, we normally reserve the conversation for before and after our games."

Nick checked his cards and found a 5 and 9 of clubs. He leaned back from the table and said, "Everyone else is well-acquainted, Daniel. I'm just trying to catch up."

Staal sighed, checked his own cards, and fiddled with a stack of his chips. "My father is an Asian man with an insatiable hunger for Swedish blondes with questionable morals and personality disorders but no personality. There was a brief moment in time when my mother fit the bill perfectly for him. My homeland provided a sheltered, idealistic childhood and the kind of boredom to motivate me to explore what the rest of the world had to offer a man in his twenties who remains free of the burden of a wife and children. What else would you like to know?"

"The night's still young," Nick said.

Lacey revealed the flop, a king of hearts surrounded by a 6 and 8 of clubs, which left Nick a single card shy of a straight, and a suited 7 from a straight flush. Khan matched the $2,000 big blind, then Daniel raised to $4,000 and the remaining players called.

To Khan, Nick asked, "Would I be wrong to assume you are the one involved in energy?"

His voice deep, and heard by Nick for the first time, Khan said, "Oil."

Cavanagh spoke without being addressed and offered, "I own four television and six radio stations."

Nick turned his chair to the right and said to Mason, "So Mr. Foster is the defense attorney?"

Foster drank from his glass and said, "I'll leave my card in case you need it, Sean."

The turn card was the 4 of spades, useless to Nick. Khan folded, Daniel wagered $30,000, and Foster paused before exiting the hand.

Nick tapped his fingers on the armrest.

The intel matters more than the investment.

"Raise to $50,000," he said.

"Absolutely not," Cavanagh said and slid his cards to the dealer.

Daniel rested his arms on the armrest and said, "I'll call," and tossed an additional $20,000 into the pot.

Lacey dealt the river card, a 7 of spades, and Nick felt a burst of adrenaline in his stomach. The card gave him a straight flush, a hand beaten only by the ace-high royal flush. He adjusted his sunglasses and wagered another $50,000.

Staal glared at Nick, then leaned back in his chair and said, "Fold."

Gabi squeezed Nick's shoulder before he reached to the center of the table and dragged the chips toward him.

"Beginner's luck, McCormick," Cavanagh said. He held his empty glass into the air and said to his female guest, "A refill, if you will." She took the glass to the makeshift bar on the wall next to the doorway.

"We'll call it newcomer's luck, Mr. Cavanagh. I'm far from a beginner but thank you all the same."

In the next four hands, Nick folded twice, fell in the showdown with two pair that lost to three of a kind, and lost $75,000 on a bluff, a necessary setup to further establish his pattern of only adjusting his sunglasses with a winning hand.

Before the seventh round, Cavanagh leaned toward Nick and, loud enough for Gabi to hear, said, "Your companion is absolutely stunning, Sean. What was her name again?"

"Alexandra," Gabi whispered back.

Cavanagh sat back up, turned to Gabi, and said, "I would trade twenty of this lady for one of you." His sufficiently scorned guest stormed away to the bar.

"I think you've offended her," Nick said.

"It's not a crisis, McCormick. She's a rental for the evening."

"That's quite a line item to have on a budget, Mr. Cavanagh. Your accountant must think the world of you."

Cavanagh lowered his voice and said, "Speaking of which, is your Alexandra..."

Nick raised his hand and interrupted him. "She is exactly that: *My* Alexandra."

That'll shut him down.

Cavanagh again raised his glass to the new player and said, "My compliments."

Nick turned to Gabi, who looked back with her mouth agape. He mouthed, "Wow," and turned back to the table.

The outlandish wagers in rounds seven through ten allowed Nick to play conservatively while Daniel Staal and Musad Khan seized the lion's share of chips from both Mason and Cavanagh, both of whom overplayed weak hands against Daniel's consecutive flushes and Khan's full house. Going into the eleventh round, Daniel had amassed more than $400,000 of the available million, Khan $235,000, while Nick sat quietly in third place with $206,000. The field was narrowing as Nick allowed the game to come to him. The overconfidence of the defense attorney and carelessness of the media mogul had proved damaging to their respective games, although neither appeared to be concerned. The loss of pocket change was worth an evening of entertainment with those who shared their social class and other appetites.

With all five players still in the game, the dealer button rotation returned to its original order for the hand. Daniel possessed the button for the third time, with Foster and Nick placing the small and big blind bets. Nick was dealt offsuit pocket cards, a 3 of clubs and queen of hearts. The three-card flop contained an ace of clubs, 3 of spades, and queen of clubs. Cavanagh and Khan matched the $2,000 blind to remain active in the hand.

Before Daniel announced his play, Nick again lifted his pocket cards, calculating the strength of his hand with two pair, and adjusted his sunglasses.

Without hesitation, Daniel said, "Fold," and slid his cards to Lacey in the next seat.

Bait taken. He and Khan are the only seasoned players at the table.

Mason added another $1,000 to the pot and the turn card was added to the table: the 3 of hearts.

Cavanagh picked up his remaining balance of chips, $69,000, and tossed them into the pot. "I'll go all-in." The action drew a whistle from Mason and a curious stare from the otherwise stern Khan, who then folded and passed the action to Mason.

"Call," Mason said. He moved his last $48,000 worth of chips to the pot and turned to Nick, who needed only to call Roger's $69,000.

"Call," Nick said.

Lacey dealt the river card, a king of diamonds, and Nick saw the top of Roger's head flush with redness.

You're done.

With his two opponents in the hand having gone all-in, they would forgo the wagering after the river card and advance to the showdown.

"Let see 'em, Foster," Cavanagh said.

Mason sat up straight in his chair and said, "Two pair, aces high."

Foster turned the cards to reveal an ace and king of spades.

Roger displayed his pocket cards, a 3 and 4 of diamonds. "Three-of-a-kind."

Mason grumbled and stood.

"That's one down," Cavanagh said. "Sean?"

Nick flipped over his first card, the three of clubs, which gave him three-of-a-kind and a tie with Roger in the pot.

Roger clapped his hands and said, "Ah well."

With a sideways grin, Nick then revealed the second card, the queen of hearts, giving him a full house and the win. "Full house."

"Premature as always, Cavanagh," Khan grumbled through a stifled chortle.

"You suckered me, McCormick," Cavanagh said. He stood and slapped Nick on the back.

Nick stood and shook Cavanagh's hand. "You're still lively for your age. I'll give you that."

Mason sauntered up beside them and said, "Don't pay attention to his birth certificate. He might be the youngest man in the room." He was next to shake Nick's hand and said, "You play well, like a snake in the grass."

"That's high praise coming from a criminal defense attorney," Nick said.

Mason chuckled, showing signs of levity for the first time in the evening, then said, "We know our own," and walked to the bar.

"Let's break a little early, shall we?" Daniel said from across the table. "We'll take a half-hour to relax and then come back and finish."

Away from the crowd, Gabi stood next to Nick and watched the interactions of the other players amongst themselves. The women with them were treated as accessories and spoke only to each other.

"Would you believe that not one of these pretty girls has bothered to speak all night?" Gabi said to Nick.

"You're not missing out on anything. I don't think you speak their language."

"How so?"

"You're a high-class professional woman, Gabrielle. They're professionals of a far different kind."

Disgusted, Gabi said, "I need to take a shower."

"That makes two of us."

Gabi saw Cavanagh approaching and said, "The creeper's back."

Before the eliminated player was within earshot, Nick said, "At least you have a rich benefactor to serve as president of your fan club." The remark earned him an elbow in the ribs.

"Those beady little eyes freak me out."

"You're a worthy opponent, young man," Cavanagh said to Nick. "You may very well be the one leaving here with my money." Then to Gabi, he said, "I don't believe I caught your last name, Miss Alexandra."

Nick leaned down to the man and quietly said, "It's McCormick."

The confident smirk faded from his face and Cavanagh said, "Very well." He squeezed Nick's shoulder as he passed. The bar was his destination, another drink his new desire.

From behind, unseen to Nick, Khan said, "You'll have to excuse Roger. His primal urges dominate his mental processes to a fault."

"Mr. Khan, it's a pleasure to finally converse with you."

Khan shook Nick's hand and said, "Make no mistake. You are still the enemy until the winner is determined."

"At least I know I'm leaving here with no worse than bronze."

Cavanagh reappeared in the group with a full glass. "That first hand you won was quite a gamble, no pun intended."

"If you must know, it was a bluff that turned into a brilliant move. Dumb luck, at best. Cheers." He held his bottle of water up to the men's two glasses.

"It certainly paid off," Khan said. "Roger, would you be so kind as to bring me a scotch, neat?"

"I'll top myself off, too," Cavanagh said and headed back to the bar.

Khan watched Cavanagh leave his audible range and said to Nick, "I know many people in the financial district, even in the United States. Why is it that I've never heard of you, Mr. McCormick?"

"That speaks volumes of my discretion, don't you think?"

"And how did you manage to locate Daniel Staal, if I may ask?"

"That's speaks highly of my resources."

"I suppose so." Khan waited for Cavanagh to return with his glass and said, "Thank you, Roger."

"You know what they say," Roger said. "I'd rather have a bottle in front of me than a frontal lobotomy."

"Wouldn't we all?" Nick said. "Please excuse me."

Nick took Gabi's hand and guided her away from the groups that had formed. "Have you noticed anything about this room?" he asked.

"I've noticed a lot of things about this room and the people in it. Anything in particular?"

He checked for the presence or attention of anyone who might be eavesdropping and said, "To your right, at the top of the wall. Four cameras."

Gabi turned her head and glanced upward.

"Turn with me and act like we're still talking," Nick said. He touched her elbow and moved her in a semicircle.

"What's going on, Nick?"

He stopped their movement and said, "Now look at the other wall."

She did, and then said, "No cameras. Why?"

"Those cameras can see the other four players but not the host. They can also see the faces but not their cards. On the other wall, no camera pointed at Daniel. Doesn't that strike you as strange?"

"Everything and everyone in this place strikes me as strange." Nick started to object but she smiled and added, "Present company included, Sean," emphasizing his pseudonym.

Daniel noticed their detachment from the group and waved to catch Nick's attention.

"Are you enjoying yourself, Sean?"

"Very much so."

"And you as well," he said to Gabi.

"What girl doesn't love to dress up for a night on the town?" she said.

"You've found yourself a gem, my friend."

"That's an understatement but thank you."

Daniel looked to Gabi and said, "Would you excuse us for a moment?"

Nick nodded with affirmation and Gabi stepped away.

"You went to great lengths to make contact with me, Mr. McCormick. What's on your mind?" Nick looked around the room and Daniel said, "Rest assured you are in good company. It's a secure location with discreet people."

"You have, let's say, international contacts that are different from my own, access to things that a restrained, frustrated society fails to comprehend. I have friends with resources and plenty of time on their hands."

Daniel looked toward an oblivious Gabi and then back to Nick. "You seem to be doing well for yourself."

"Maybe I have some proclivities of my own. What's the harm? International travel for purposes other than business is always in vogue."

"What are you proposing, Mr. McCormick?"

"I direct clients to you, you redirect a commission to me, everyone wins and the world keeps turning."

"Mr. McCormick, you are surrounded by men who gamble with empires, not mere currency. What can you offer that they cannot?"

"More of the same. You don't strike me as a man who would needlessly turn down the chance at more."

"More what?"

"More anything. More everything. Excess is subjective, Daniel."

Staal laughed and said, "That's very true."

"Lucien has my number. The next time it rings, I'd like it to be you, not him, on the line."

"It will be. But we have a game to finish. I have a lead to protect."

"Do I at least get to keep the game piece? I'm a sentimental fool that loves memorabilia."

"With my compliments. Good luck," Daniel said before returning to his seat at the table.

With Daniel gone, Gabi returned to Nick and asked, "What was that about?"

"When I find out, you'll be the first to know."

Before Gabi could respond, Daniel said, loud enough for the room to hear, "Are you ready, gentlemen?"

Nick touched her side and returned to the table, walking beside her until he reached the chair.

"How are you feeling tonight, Musad," Daniel asked Khan.

Khan toppled a stack of chips, then stood them back up and, without looking, said, "I'm feeling rather heavy, Daniel."

"Oh?" Staal asked.

"I am significantly heavier, weighed down by the sudden windfall of legal tender that you so generously donated at the conclusion of our last meeting."

Cavanagh, who was now sitting in his chair without participating in the game, cackled at the remark.

"I wouldn't laugh so hard, Roger. Part of that currency belonged to you and I," Mason said from his chair.

Rivalry. Let it play out.

"Lacey, we're ready," Daniel said.

With three players remaining and Mason, in the chair to his right, no longer alive, Nick possessed the dealer button when the game resumed. He would do so every three hands until the field was reduced to two, at which point the remaining players would alternate small and big blinds. He folded pre-flop with the dealer button on the first hand, and continued to do so for the next six that followed, two of which included the immunity from blind bets. The other players would enjoy that privilege only twice each and his passive strategy would force Daniel and Khan to engage each other exclusively, likely leaving one of them considerably weaker and vulnerable to elimination.

His strategy was proven effective as Daniel won five of the seven hands, with another ending in a tie, although three of the wins netted only marginal profits. Nick's balance dropped only $6,000 by way of blind bets, while Khan had lost $60,000 and was forced to change his style of play with dwindling funds. Nick reentered the fray on the eighth hand of the second segment, the nineteenth hand overall.

His big blind bet was $2,000, while Daniel was in for $1,000 and Khan was given the button. He was dealt a suited 3 and 10 but the flop, a 7 of diamonds, 5 of hearts, and ace of spades, yielded no assistance. Nick considered folding again but his established bluff pattern urged him to reconsider. Khan and Daniel were in for $2,000, matching Nick's big blind bet, but when Lacey dealt a 10 of spades for the turn card, Khan raised to $30,000 and was called by Daniel and Nick. The river card, a queen of spades, was revealed, and Nick folded in order to avoid another loss of chips. Khan wagered another $50,000 and Daniel called.

Confident, Daniel said, "Let's see it."

Khan flipped his pocket cards. "Two pair, aces and tens."

Daniel fell back in his chair, slid his cards to Lacey and said, "Two pair, queen high. You win."

The $114,000 profit for Khan propelled him into a near tie with Nick, only $4,000 behind, but was not enough to supplant him. The gap widened again through the next three hands, with Khan losing $70,000, of which $30,000 went to Nick. But the dynamics changed course again when Khan won $100,000 back from Daniel on a single hand, an almost unthinkable gamble on pocket aces that became three-of-a-kind with the river card and won out over Daniel's queen-high two pair, a questionable play on its own, leading to another dead heat for second place. Nick had folded before the flop with the benefit of the dealer button.

Khan was energetic, feeling the rush of a sudden change and momentum shifting in his favor, and sent his professional companion to the bar for another drink. Gabi leaned down to Nick's ear and said, "Do you need anything?"

He looked back enough to see her and said, "A suited ace and king would be nice."

"You're doing fine. Let them drink."

Despite being burdened with the big blind, Nick's patience was rewarded with a spade-suited king and jack. The flop offered a 2 of diamonds plus a jack and queen of spades, prompting Daniel to fold and

Khan to wager $60,000, which Nick, after a moment of contemplation, raised to $100,000 and was called by Khan.

Lacey added the turn card to the table, a king of hearts, and Gabi squeezed Nick's shoulder. Nick felt the squeeze and adjusted his sunglasses.

"$50,000," Nick said and tossed the chips into the pot.

"Call," Khan said.

Nick felt his breathing grow shallow as his pulse increased and resisted the urge to loosen the bowtie that, for the moment, felt like a noose around his neck. He forced himself to breathe evenly and show no signs of distress or concern.

The river card, a 3 of diamonds, was dealt and attention turned to Nick.

Already $152,000 deep into the pot, Nick said, "All-in," and slid his remaining $169,000 forward. He heard a gasp from Cavanagh in the seat next to him and Mason snickered on the other side.

Khan drew in a deep breath and exhaled slowly. "Call. All-in."

Nick felt as if time slowed. With the reveal of the hands at the showdown, one of them would be eliminated while the other would take first place in chips and hold a sizable edge over Daniel. He examined the community cards again.

No flush. Pocket face cards will beat me but he hesitated. He's played straight all night.

Staring straight ahead, Khan said, "The moment of truth, Sean. Who should reveal first?"

"I'll flip you for it. Winner reveals last," Nick said. He took the silver game piece from his pocket said, "Call it," and tossed it into the air.

"Tails," Khan said.

Nick caught the coin and turned it onto his wrist. "Heads. Let's see them."

Khan revealed his suited jack and ace of diamonds, one card away from an ace-high flush that would have been nearly unbeatable. Instead, he was left with a pair of jacks and an unpaired ace as his high card.

Behind the dark lenses, Nick closed his eyes and awaited the audible response that was sure to come. He used the card in his right hand to turn the card on the left, then dropped it face up and said, "Two pair, kings and jacks."

Khan closed his eyes and tucked his chin to his chest. Cavanagh applauded and guffawed as Nick collected the chips from the pot and began arranging them in front of him.

Nick stood when Khan approached him and Khan shook his hand. "Congratulations, young man," he said.

"Thank you, sir. I look forward to matching up with you again sometime."

"Likewise," Khan said, then leaned in and said, "You can beat Daniel. Desperation fuels him to go big. Best of luck," and gestured for Foster to join him at the bar.

You're better than this. Play smarter. Any other time you would have folded at the flop.

While Nick silently chastised himself, Daniel counted his chips and said, "Let's break for a moment and have a drink. Is that okay with you, Sean?"

"Whatever you like," Nick said.

Daniel and his two escorts poured drinks from the bar and Gabi gestured for Nick to stand.

"This is unbelievable. I have chills," she said.

Nick looked around the room and said, "I can't believe they don't have a chair for you."

"None of the others have one either, Nick. I'm fine. Focus. How much do you have?"

"$639,000. That leaves him with $361,000. I'm up almost two-to-one."

"How much longer do you think?" she asked. "My feet are killing me."

"I can play aggressive and get us out of here fast or I can play conservative and try to win."

She checked to see where Daniel was standing and said, "Beat him and buy me dinner."

"Deal."

Staal removed his jacket and draped it over the back of his chair. "You've played well in your first appearance."

"I appreciate that, Daniel but we've got a long way to go," Nick said.

Both men took their seats and Daniel said, "Lacey, if you will." She held up her hand and waited for Cavanagh, Mason, and Khan to return from the bar.

"Sorry," Cavanagh said. "Proceed," he added with a wave of his hand.

"How kind of you to grant us permission, Roger," Daniel said. "Go ahead, Lacey."

For the twenty-sixth hand of the game, Nick was assigned the $1,000 small blind with Staal surrendering the $2,000 big blind. After the flop was revealed, an ace of spades, 4 of diamonds, and 9 of spades, Daniel raised his bet to $100,000, nearly a third of his remaining balance.

Khan wasn't kidding. He's trying to close the gap fast.

Nick called and raised to $200,000, which was called by Daniel, leaving the host with only $161,000 for the remainder of the game.

He's going for a flush.

The turn card was the ace of clubs, resulting in a pair of aces in the community cards but only two spades, leaving Daniel one card shy of a theoretical flush.

How confident are you, Daniel? Reckless youth and extreme privilege breeds the kind of bravado that tends to backfire.

Lacey set the river card, the king of spades, onto the table and Nick's heart raced.

There's the flush.

Daniel glared at him from across the table, waiting for the moment when his opponent's tell would appear. Nick drummed his fingers on the armrest but took care to avoid adjusting his sunglasses. "$25,000," Nick said.

Immediately, Daniel said, "All-in," and the men in the room sat up in their chairs and rolled forward.

No glasses.

"Call," Nick said and pushed $96,000 worth of chips into the pile with what Daniel had deposited.

"What are you doin', kid?" Cavanagh said. Daniel stared at him from across the table and Cavanagh said, "What?"

Unseen to Nick, Gabi paced back and forth, three steps at a time, waiting for the showdown.

"Are you going to keep us waiting all night, Daniel?" Mason asked. "Some of us have to work tomorrow."

Cavanagh drained his glass and said, "He's bluffing."

"Says the drunk with the early exit," Khan muttered.

Daniel turned his first card, the queen of spades, and left the second card face down.

"Come on, man," a frustrated Mason said.

Daniel turned the second card and revealed the jack of spades, giving him the ace-high flush that Nick anticipated. Even with pocket spades, a statistical improbability, the highest flush Nick could muster was a high of ten and Daniel would have reversed his fortunes in a single hand.

"Sean?" Daniel asked.

"Two pair," Nick said flatly.

The three eliminated players groaned aloud and Daniel stood, shouted, and pumped his fist into the air. "Yes!" he exclaimed. He reached toward the pile of chips and began to pull them toward his position when Nick spoke.

"Just a minute," he said.

"Yes?" Daniel asked.

"I have two pair."

Daniel laughed, looked around the table to Khan, Cavanagh, and Foster, and said, "Surely you understand the ranking of hands in Texas Hold'Em, Sean. A flush beats two pair."

"Not necessarily."

The smile disappeared from Staal's face. "Excuse me? A flush beats two pair, Mr. McCormick."

Nick slid his pocket cards to the center of the table and said, "Not when both pairs are aces," revealing the four-of-a-kind that won the hand and secured his victory in the game.

Cavanagh leapt to his feet, spilling the ice from his glass onto the table, and said, "What a hand!"

"Not bad, kid," Mason said.

Daniel was speechless, his hands interlocked behind his head as he stared at the pile of cards and chips on the table.

Gabi hugged Nick from behind, squeezing him around the neck as he remained seated and letting out a high-pitched squeal into his ear. "That was amazing!" she said in an excited whisper.

He turned and kissed her on the cheek, then whispered back, "You're a cardiologist. What does a heart attack feel like?"

Daniel walked slowly around the table and said, "It takes some serious stones to walk into a room full of strangers and play like that."

"I appreciate that, Daniel."

He extended his hand and said, "I look forward to the rematch."

"Likewise," Khan said from the end of the table.

"Lacey will cash out your winnings in just a moment. If you'll please excuse me," he said, allowing his unfinished sentence to trail off. He picked up his empty glass and accompanied his escorts to the bar.

Nick stood and fully embraced Gabi for the first time of the night. He picked her up and turned in a circle, then set her down, and said, "Did you see what just happened?"

"Oh my gosh," she whispered. "How long have you been doing this kind of thing?"

"I've been playing poker since high school, just not with seven digits on the line."

Lacey finished arranging the stacks of cash and said, "Mr. McCormick, your winnings. Would you like them transferred to your safe?"

"Please."

Halfway through the transfer, she said, "Your safe might not be large enough to accommodate everything. Would you like to have it transferred electronically?"

"I think it'll fit," Nick said, then wrapped his arm around Gabi's waist, pulled her close, and said, "If not, I know someone who wouldn't mind helping me get it home."

After two rounds of rearrangement and compression, she closed the lid on the safe and handed it to Nick. "Congratulations, Mr. McCormick."

Nick shared a final word and handshake with Mason and Cavanagh before making his way to Khan, who was gathering his belongings and discussing late-night plans with his escort.

"That was impressive," Khan said.

"I don't think I'm going to be invited back for round two," Nick said.

"Ultracompetitive spoiled little brat, that one," Khan said. "He won't rest until he secures at least two victories over you. Your phone will ring, rest assured. But cherish this in the meantime and invest wisely."

"That much I can guarantee. Thank you for the tip. You were absolutely right."

Khan lowered his voice and said, "He could use some humility now and again." He then looked to his escort, a dark-skinned Middle Eastern woman in her early twenties and said, "The car is downstairs."

Daniel paced at the bar, unwilling to speak to the players or the women who remained at his side. As Nick took Gabi's hand, he looked to the bar. Daniel offered an obligatory wave goodbye and reached into the front pocket of his pants for his cell phone.

"Sore loser," Gabi mumbled so only Nick could hear.

"What now?" Nick asked. "We have an enormous budget and one of the most exciting cities in the world just outside the door."

"I want to get out of these shoes, out of this dress, and into a t-shirt and sweatpants, then have something deliciously unhealthy delivered so we can sleep and hit the airport on time in the morning. How's that?"

Nick held her hand in the air and twirled her as he had done in the hotel room, then stopped her and said, "Let's go home."

After the departure of Cavanagh, Mason, and Khan, along with their respective guests, Daniel left the room and entered the second occupied room across the hallway. He slammed the door behind him and stormed toward the desk on the opposite wall. He ran his hand through his hair, then stood with his hands on his hips, and said, "What just happened?"

"I don't know, sir," the man said.

The room was illuminated by six color monitors, two of which displayed the feed from a camera that was pointed at the elevator and another hidden somewhere in the main lobby. The remaining four were dedicated to the cameras from the game room, one allocated to the seat of any player that was not Daniel Staal.

"He deliberately embarrassed me," Daniel said. "Did you see that?"

The man sat silently, allowing his boss to vent.

Daniel pointed his index finger toward the face of the other man in the room and said, "I want to know everything there is to know about this Sean McCormick. Do you understand me? He's this mystery man that manages billions of dollars but hides in the shadows. Musad Khan doesn't even know who he is but someone does. I want to know all there is to know about him. Where he lives, where he works, how he spends his money and his time, skeletons, trophies, all of it."

"That won't be necessary, sir," the man said.

"You misunderstand the employer-employee relationship. I determine what is necessary. You do not."

"I understand perfectly, sir. But if you employ me for my services, you have to trust me to do what I do best."

"You were hired as my chief of security because your history speaks for itself but I trust you to do as you are told. Are we clear?"

The man remained silent.

Daniel closed his eyes and calmed himself. "Go ahead."

"His name is not Sean McCormick. His name is Nick."

Daniel ran both hands down his face and asked, "And how do you know this?"

"Let's just say that we were acquaintances in another life," the man said.

"Sean, Nick, whoever he is, is he going to be a problem for us?"

The man lifted the brim of his hat and pulled it back down, then removed a cigarette from his soft pack and lit the end.

"No, sir," Spencer St. Clair said. "Absolutely not. Consider him a hurdle, not a barrier, and one that will soon be cleared."

13

"Cut! Beautiful!" the director shouted to the room. "Let's break for lunch. Lucien, can I talk to you?" The director stood in the doorway and spoke Lucien's name twice more with increasing intensity before a response came.

"Yes?" Lucien said from the next room. He was peering out the window into the woods that surrounded the cabin and ignoring a buzzing phone on the table nearby.

"Do you need to get that?"

Without looking at the screen, Lucien said, "No. What do you want?"

The director stood beside Lucien, choosing to look at him rather than out the window. "You want to tell me what this is all about, man? Two days of filming and you've barely said a word. Three years of nit-picking and requirements for every little detail for every shot, every scene, every site, and for two months you've either had your head in the clouds or in the sand." He placed his hand on Lucien's shoulder and Lucien flinched. "Whoa. Calm down."

"Is production complete?"

"We're wrapped for the day." He walked to the other side of Lucien, further from the door, and said, "Did you think she would only be filming with you? She's turning into a star, my friend, not a retread."

Lucien looked to him for the first time and started to speak but stopped and turned back to the window.

"You aren't the first producer to get involved with a co-star, Mr. Murdoc, much less fall for one."

Lucien brushed back his blonde hair at the part, then stood with his hands on his hips and snapped, "What is it that you want?"

"There's someone here to speak with you. He's waiting outside."

"We don't allow guests on set. You know that. What is this person doing here?"

The director held up his hands and said, "Don't blame me. Mr. Staal gave the okay. He was watching off and on from the back today but you weren't..."

Lucien held up his own hand and interrupted. "Enough. Tell him I'll be with him in a moment."

Guests were never permitted on the set of domestic filming locations. The rules set forth by Daniel Staal had been both clear and unwavering since the inception of the production company. Closed sets, private records, high quality, and discretion were integral components of success in the world in which they worked. Outside access exponentially jeopardized the security of the operation. In the months leading up to the first productions and ensuing overseas tours, the talking points, including those regarding guest policy, were repeated ad infinitum. For Lucien, it was ad nauseam.

The wooden deck stretched across the front of the cabin with steps in the center, a concrete pathway leading to the asphalt driveway. The brown-skinned man was sitting in a wooden rocking chair. He wore silver sunglasses that contrasted with his black suit with silver pinstripes. As the front door opened, he wiped the sweat from the top of his bald head with a white handkerchief.

When the door closed, the man looked but did not stand. Instead, he removed his sunglasses and asked, "Lucien Murdoc?"

"Yes, sir. You are?"

"My name is Musad Khan. I arrived earlier this morning. Daniel sends his regards. Is there somewhere that we can talk?"

"I thought we were talking now," Lucien said.

"Privately," Khan said. He pointed his sunglasses toward Lucien and said, "This is not a conversation for uninvited ears."

Lucien entered the second-floor bedroom that had been converted into a makeshift office space shortly following the signing of the six-month lease agreement and sat in the chair behind the desk. "Close the door behind you," he said to Khan, who acquiesced.

Khan sat in the chair opposite the desk. "I assume you know why I am here."

"Mr. Khan, I was only made aware that you were here moments ago. So no, I do not. Please enlighten me."

"Have I offended you in some way, Mr. Murdoc? You have been nothing but curt and dismissive to me and, as one of the primary financial supporters of this organization, I would think some respect would be in order."

Unfazed, Lucien said, "State your business, Mr. Khan."

"I have come here today to do some scouting, as those in sports would say."

"And that means?"

"Two months from now there will be a gathering of those in my industry and others in my homeland. They expect, as do I, many forms of entertainment. Certain desires are more easily fulfilled than others, Mr. Murdoc, and I do not disappoint."

"Speak your mind, Mr. Khan."

"Very well. The women who were filming today, what were their names?" He leaned forward and, with a knowing smile said, "We have no need for the man."

"There were multiple scenes filmed today. To whom are you referring?"

"We would like to employ the services of these lovely performers of yours for, shall we say, a more private affair."

Leaning back, Khan continued, "Nothing different than prior arrangements."

"I have no prior arrangements, sir," Lucien said, knowing that his forceful statement was false. "This is best discussed with Mr. Staal. If you would, please excuse me."

Lucien was in the act of standing when Khan said, "He has delegated this to you, Mr. Murdoc. Acting as if you are ignorant of the nature of this transaction, or those in the past, is both dishonest and insulting."

Returning to his seat, Lucien said, "Go on."

"I am willing to pay as much as $100,000 American," Khan said. He waited a beat and added, "Each."

Lucien felt his hands grow clammy and cold as his heart raced. Four female performers had filmed in the course of the morning and afternoon. Three were fair game but one was off limits.

"For how many?"

Khan grimaced and said, "I have no interest in the petite woman. My visitors find the tattoos and other – what do they call them – body modifications rather revolting. But if it is, as they say, a package deal, I understand. The young blonde girl has been requested. Her popularity is growing online. Shelby, I believe, is her legal name."

Lucien, in a stern whisper, demanded, "How do you know that?"

His volume increasing with each sentence, Khan said, "I did not come here to negotiate, Mr. Murdoc, but to stake a claim and inform you of the transaction. Daniel assured me that this would not be an issue."

Lucien rubbed his eyes and attempted to focus on the business portion of the conversation while avoiding the swell of personal turmoil that Khan's demands were creating. The Brann Cinema roster of performers was littered with possibilities for their purposes. Of all of them, why Shelby?

"Who else?" Lucien asked.

Khan looked toward the closed door and back to Lucien. "The other girl with red hair and freckles, that performed in the scene with Shelby today..."

"Please refrain from using her legal name, Mr. Khan," Lucien interrupted.

"As you wish. Tell me about her."

"What do you want to know?"

"Her performances are not, shall we say, legal. She is just a girl."

"Mr. Khan, all of our contracted performers..."

"$150,000 for her, $100,000 for the other, and an additional $50,000 for another one of your choosing."

"I cannot simply demand that each of them comply with your desires or those of your associates."

"Has your business model changed, Mr. Murdoc?"

"Certainly not."

"Might I suggest that you consult with Daniel concerning this matter?"

Rather than responding, Lucien dialed the number for Daniel's cell phone and activated the speaker.

"Yes?" Daniel answered.

"Sir, this is Lucien."

"I have Caller ID. What is it?"

"I have a Musad Khan here."

"Give him whatever he wants, no questions asked."

"But, sir..."

"Musad Khan has been one of the primary investors in this company since it was founded. He is the reason you are employed and are paid a generous sum of money for what little work you do. You are expendable. His generosity is not. Are we clear?"

"We are, sir."

Daniel disconnected the call and Khan smiled at Lucien. "Satisfied?" Khan asked.

"I will make the arrangements as you requested but I cannot guarantee that any of them will be eager to comply."

"There are many men who find the resistance to be rather appealing." Khan laid a business card in front of Lucien and said, "Contact me at this number with any updates. Travel arrangements will be finalized by the end of the month."

Lucien stood, slid his office chair underneath the desk, and extended his hand toward Khan, who ignored the gesture and moved to the door. With his back turned, Khan said, "Thank you for your assistance," and opened the door to find a showered and dressed Shelby standing outside, her hair still wet, scrolling through a social media page on her phone.

Smiling, she looked around Khan and said to Lucien, "Hey, I was just about to knock."

"Come in," Lucien said.

"You were magnificent today," Khan said to Shelby, then turned to Lucien and raised his eyebrows before making his way down the steps.

"What was that about?" Shelby asked. She sat on the desk in front of Lucien and dangled her legs.

Lucien walked to the door, watched Khan step onto the first floor and exit the building, and closed it softly.

"There is a matter we need to discuss, *mon amour*," he said.

She listened intently for fifteen minutes. The explanation was detailed, often rehearsed, and mostly false. The hypothetical event was eight weeks and several thousand miles away. First-class private travel would be arranged, an experience that was truly once-in-a-lifetime. Once she was on-site, she and the others would have access to every amenity imaginable. Their performances would be professionally produced but privately subsidized by the wealthy one-time co-stars, resulting, in Lucien's words, in the world's most expensive homemade video that would never be viewable by the public eye.

In spite of his best efforts, Lucien watched as Shelby's reservations and frustrations mounted. When each bullet point of the sales pitch was relayed, Shelby would nod, break eye contact, mumble a single word response, and allow him to continue. At various points, she moved from her seat on the desk to the chair where Khan had been seated earlier, then to the window behind the desk and a short visit to the hallway before returning to the desk.

"I can't keep doing this, Lucien," she said when Lucien finished. "This is crossing a line."

For the first time since they met, Lucien felt as though she was a million miles away while in the same room. "What do you mean, Shelby?"

"My parents think I work in public relations for a movie company, Lucien!" she shouted.

Even with the door closed, Lucien looked around the room and said, "Please lower your voice."

She complied and said, "My life has been nothing but lies for months. I lie about where I go. I lie about what I do and who I'm with. I disappear for two weeks for work and come back with money I can't explain." Her voice broke but she continued. "People look at me like they recognize me. I look in the mirror and the girl that looks back isn't someone I even know anymore."

"You are a young, beautiful, successful woman. You are the fantasy of men around the world." He stood in front of her and brushed the hair from her eyes, waiting for her to look back at him. "And you are the woman that I have been searching for."

"What's real, Lucien?" She stood in front of a floor-length mirror on the opposite side of the room. "The fake hair, fake tan, fake name, the makeup, none of it's real." She began to sob and Lucien hurried to her side.

He wrapped his arms around her, resting his head on her shoulder, and whispered into her ear, "Look into the mirror." He asked twice more before she opened her eyes and did so. "This is real."

"I don't want to go," she said. "Can't someone else go? I know they asked for me but I'm not ready for this, going to some other godforsaken country and working in front of a bunch of folks I don't know."

"They will be paying…"

"I don't care about the money anymore, Lucien!" she said, shouting again.

Lucien whispered in an effort to calm her. "I know. I know. Perhaps this can be your last performance before you move on."

She took in a deep breath, exhaled, and wiped the tears from her cheeks but the dark residue of her eyeliner remained. "If I go, will you be there with me?"

"Of course I will. I will not leave your side," he lied.

"Who else is going?"

"Allison will be going along with you. I'm unsure of the third but that will be decided soon."

She placed both of her hands on Lucien's face and said, "As long as you are going with me, I'll go, but no more after this."

"I understand."

"You won't leave my side? Promise me."

"I promise," he lied again, knowing that their time together was reaching its necessary conclusion. He would travel with her to the Middle East as promised. Then at an unexpected moment, he would excuse himself to a nearby café for a meeting or would rush to the location to address an emergent situation. He would kiss her softly and assure her that he would return in less than an hour before boarding a commercial airliner that would carry him to another location that had not yet been determined. Amsterdam was a short-term possibility. There he had access to a full menu of opportunities for distraction and pleasure, his only chance of distancing himself from voices that were almost certain to echo through the caverns of his mind during every waking hour of his immediate future.

"What am I supposed to tell my parents?"

"There will be plenty of time for that."

Her voice was stable, her eyes dry. "And you will be with me the whole time?"

"I will."

She embraced him, pulling him tight and closing her eyes as she tried to block out the ambient noise from the first floor. "Then we can get away from all of this, just like you said."

He kissed the side of her head and said, "Just like I said."

Through the force of habit, just as he had done as a child, he crossed his fingers.

14

The sign that stood at each of the two entrances to the housing development read "The Ridge", a title that she considered insipid and entirely devoid of both creativity and inspiration.

"People ask me where I live all the time. When I tell them that I live at The Ridge, they look at me like I have three heads. It sounds like an apartment complex or a white collar prison, not an upper-class housing community," Gabi had said to Nick when the construction on her home was completed.

"I live in a place where I can honestly say that I have neighbors who live in Lick Skillet Hollow. You're doing just fine," Nick had replied at the time.

Her home was located in the first lot past the western entrance to the development, set in the center of a spacious one-acre corner lot that formed a triangle. A manmade pond had been constructed in the adjacent lot on the other side of the property line while dense forest stood on the border of the backyard.

The size of the home was excessive by her personal estimation. She had told her father as much as he financed the construction two years before but he would hear nothing of it. Surely she would have the need for the space and amenities in years to come, he said. Two floors, five bedrooms, four bathrooms, a finished basement, a two-car garage; the square footage was unreasonable for a family of three, much less a single woman with no husband or children but she and her lifestyle would grow into it whenever the time was right and the opportunity arose.

The exterior was sand dune brown with a matching roof, white frames and black shutters framing each window. Weathered stone steps led to the wooden porch that was stained the color of pewter and spanned the entirety of the front of the house, bordered by white pillars and vinyl Victorian railing. The roof was built with a steep pitch and three dormer windows were featured on the second floor, facing the road, the middle of which was a double.

The road that wove through the community was a flat, one-mile oval circuit that, technically, began in front of her house and ended at the intersection across the street. It was her intention to run at least three laps, no more than five, every other day. The aptly named runner's high was therapeutic and the stresses that ultimately led to her leave of absence from her medical practice were washed away by the rush of adrenaline, eliminated by sweat along with the physical toxins that reside in even the healthiest of bodies.

She was halfway through her second lap when the sky darkened. A severe thunderstorm blowing in from the west prompted a severe weather warning notification from the app on her phone and she felt the temperature drop at least ten degrees from the time she left the driveway and started the first song on her playlist. Knowing that time was limited, she adjusted her headband and double-checked the tension in the armband that secured her iPhone, increased the volume in her headphones, and picked up her pace.

The gust was cold against her face when she paused at the stop sign across from her house and watched the dark gray storm clouds moving in quickly, progressively overtaking the sunset as the sounds of rain in the trees grew closer.

"One more," she muttered and turned to begin her third and final lap.

A quarter-mile in, she felt the first sprinkling of raindrops and looked over her shoulder into the sky. "Five more minutes. Come on."

She rounded the turn at the end of the road opposite her home and a woman sitting on her porch waved, which Gabi returned. The remainder of the run would take place against the wind, rapidly drying the sweat on her skin and saturating her clothes, reminding her that her t-shirt and shorts would not provide sufficient cover and protection for the approaching downpour that was coupled with the sudden plunge into the low fifties.

With a quarter-mile remaining, the sun was setting and the front porch was within view. Her music was blaring and she felt, but did not hear, a rumble of thunder. A cloud burst opened overhead and, as if God Himself had turned on a faucet, the rain began to fall all around her with drops that were the size of dimes and momentarily stung when they struck her bare skin. She gritted her teeth and groaned, sprinting at the fastest speed she could manage, looking both ways before ignoring and blowing through the intersection and cruising to a stop in the driveway outside of her garage, closing the door, and reactivating the security system.

Gabi stepped inside the door and stripped off her shirt, which she tossed into the laundry room and heard it land in front of the washing machine with a splat. Her headband was removed next, then the socks and shoes. She loved the workout but hated the feel of the sweat-laden clothing that remained afterward. Her legs were burning after the unexpected quarter-mile sprint at the end of the run but she jogged up the steps and into the upstairs bathroom that she frequently used.

She looked into the mirror over the sink, then splashed a double-handed scoop of cold water onto her face and took a deep breath before checking her phone, hoping for a text or voicemail message that was not there.

"I need a shower," she said to the empty room and closed the door.

She remained inside for a half-hour but only washed for ten minutes, spending the balance of the time allowing the heat to soothe her muscles while she rested against the wall, and pulled on an oversized t-shirt that was stolen long ago from Nick and her favorite gray sweatpants. Downstairs, dinner was next on the agenda but she felt herself being drawn to the comfort of the couch and away from the kitchen, the work, and the inevitable cleanup. The sizeable investment into the appliances and cookware and the granite countertops was no match for the convenience of delivery and streaming a television show or a movie.

She picked up the phone and started to text Nick an invitation for dinner and a night in but deleted the message before pressing send when her attention was drawn to the sound of rain slamming against the window, followed by a flash of lightning that illuminated the living room as though a flood light had been switched on and off and a clap of thunder that shook the walls. She hated the thought of asking him to make the drive off of the mountain and into town through such a storm, knowing he would do so without hesitation.

Surely there was something to watch to pass the time.

She switched on the lamp, located the remote for her streaming media device, and was scrolling aimlessly through the main menu when the screen went dark along with the lights in the kitchen. "Great," she said, and tossed the remote onto the coffee table and fell onto her side and into a pile of pillows.

He flinched with each flash of lightning, increasingly aware of the fact that he was surrounded by trees and fearing the remote possibility of becoming a news headline. The wind, the rain, the thunder, the climate, these could be dealt with. Lightning, on the other hand, was one of nature's most violent and unpredictable forces and he was standing in a location that rendered him without shelter and extremely vulnerable, albeit temporarily.

For reasons of which he was not immediately concerned, he took care to match the chocolate brown rain slicker with his brown Panama hat and boots. The inclement weather had forced him out of his suede jacket, a look that he greatly preferred, and his attention to detail mandated that the changes were in line with his original vision. The jacket was buttoned up the chest all the way to his neck and hung to the top of his boots, nearly dragging the ground.

Two other men accompanied him, familiar associates, trusted within reason, who would obey orders, keep secrets, and not ask questions. Standing at the edge of the canopy of trees, he waited for nightfall to completely set in and quietly motioned for the other two to join him.

"Give me your satchel," Spencer said to the man to his left. The man complied and Spencer sifted through the contents that had been sealed in plastic bags. He momentarily lifted his head, subjecting it to the rain, and said, "I can't even smoke in this mess. Is this everything?"

"Yeah," the man said. He wiped the rain from his face and shook the water from his hand before placing it back in his pocket.

"The back door is my point of entry," Spencer said. Directing the attention of the man to the garage, he said, "You will be there, awaiting my entry." To the second man, he said, "You will be there," indicating the side of the front porch. "If she is in the front room, her escape route will be the front entrance or one of the windows. Remain alert."

"I understand," the second man said.

For an hour, they watched. There were no lights turned on, no movement that could be seen. The power outage was in its second hour, leaving every residence in sight encased in darkness.

"The weather appears to be clearing soon," Spencer said. Another clap of thunder sounded and Spencer jolted, instinctively ducking his head. "Perhaps not. Into position, please." He removed a plastic bag from the leather satchel, pointed to the man assigned to the front of the house, and said, "Place the device and activate it."

"Yes, sir, right away," he said and moved in a crouch around the side of the house, below the view of the side windows, to the back rear corner of the porch.

Watching the second man approach his position, Spencer dialed a number on his phone and said, "We are ready to breach." He checked the time on the phone and said, "Have the automobile in the driveway in precisely seven minutes," and ended the call.

Inside the clear plastic bag, protected from the rainfall without hampering performance, was a black metal box topped with ten antennas and containing a built-in rechargeable battery that would be used in lieu of a conventional power supply. Technically illegal for civilian use in the United States, the military-grade device was capable of jamming every band of cellular phone signal along with in-home Wi-Fi, GPS, and even portable radio frequencies. The sign in the front yard indicated that the alarm system in Gabi's home was one that operated by way of a cellular signal rather than a traditional landline, a detail that was used as a selling point by the parent company but remained vulnerable to the tactic that Spencer employed. Boasting an effective range of nearly fifty yards, no signal would be sent to a monitoring center and no police would be dispatched.

Sitting on the ground and looking back to the edge of the woods, the man activated the jammer and took an LED flashlight from his pocket, which he pointed toward Spencer and flicked the power switch on and off a single time to indicate that he was in his assigned position.

Spencer jogged to the back door and retrieved a cotton towel and a roll of duct tape from the satchel. He wiped the pane of glass closest to the handle until it was dry, shielding it from the wind and falling rain with his body, then began covering the surface with strips of tape to prevent a complete shatter when it was broken. Wearing leather gloves, he pressed it firmly with his thumbs, smoothing it to maximize contact. He pounded the three times, increasing the force each time until he felt the glass crack without hearing a single piece fall to the ground on the other side of the door. It was a sensation that he had felt hundreds of times in his life.

He eased pressure on the tape, making certain that the shards of glass remained fastened to the adhesive, and reached inside, unlocked the door, and turned the knob. When the door slid open, he stepped inside onto the black and white tile floor and the wet surface of his shoes created an audible squeak. He froze and peered through the unlit kitchen and into the rooms of the home that lay beyond but detected no movement. There was another step forward, then a look behind him to check for the man who was instructed to follow him inside if the so-called coast was clear, when a gust of wind slammed into the door, pulling the knob from his hand and causing it to slam against the back wall.

The sudden crash awakened a sleeping Gabi on the living room couch. She sat up, then stood, and craned her neck to look into the kitchen where she saw the back door that led from the kitchen and into the backyard standing open as the wind blew rain inside. She started to move forward but stopped and gasped when the silhouette of an intruder stepped in front of the door. Her eyes wide, she stepped backward and toward the front door. Spencer rushed forward, closing the gap and forcing Gabi into the space between the couch and the exterior wall where the television was mounted and blocked her path to the front door.

Her breath was short and she felt beads of sweat forming at her hairline. A pain shot into her chest and fell into her stomach. "Don't hurt me," she said.

"You won't be harmed if you do as we ask," Spencer said.

"We?"

Spencer ignored the question and said, "You need to come with us."

She shook her head and said, "I'm not going anywhere with you. Who are you?"

Spencer stepped toward her and was within arm's-length when the power was restored. The lamp on the table behind Gabi was fitted with a three-way bulb, switched to the highest setting. Having spent more than two hours in lowlight conditions, the sudden flash caused Spencer to shield his eyes and turn away. She drove a kick into Spencer's groin, causing him to double over, then landed a right cross to the bridge of his nose and drove her shoulder into his chest, toppling him onto the ground. She started to run into the kitchen but another figure stepped into the doorway. Looking back, she saw Spencer struggling to his feet.

Gabi turned and scrambled up the stairs. The two intruders followed, Spencer in the lead with his pistol drawn. She ran into the master bedroom, closed and locked the door behind her in an effort to buy time, and opened the drawer on the nightstand. She grabbed the panic button for her alarm system and pressed it once, then again, and a third time, but heard no response.

Outside, Spencer crashed his foot into the door and heard the wood crack. Gabi opened the door to her walk-in closet, pushed the hanging clothes away, and found the pistol-grip 12-gauge shotgun that her father had insisted she keep nearby for self-defense. She fumbled for the box of shells on the shelf, then chambered a round and fired toward the doorway, leaving a pattern of buckshot in the door. Spencer and his associate spun away from the door, one to each side.

Gabi tried the panic button again with no success, then looked out the bedroom window and contemplated a leap into the darkness before ejecting the spent shell and chambering a fresh round of buckshot. "We," she said to herself, remembering the words of the intruder and wondering how many of them could be waiting outside. She stepped closer and fired again, this time to the side of the door and into the wall where the man with Spencer stood with his shoulder and biceps flat against the surface, then quickly reloaded and fired into the same area again and heard the main scream as the pellets pierced the skin on his arm.

She ejected the shell and loaded another, moving back toward the closet and reaching for the box of ammunition. One round was ready to fire, she held another in her hand, and felt one more in the box. In the hall, Spencer crashed his foot into the door a second time, nearly breaking through and into the room before spinning away in anticipation of another round. Another flash of lightning shined through the window and reflected off of the white walls of the room.

"I'm almost inside," Spencer said to the wounded man. "Are you all right, Calvin?"

"Fine," he groaned. He lifted his hand from his arm, where he checked for and saw blood.

"After the next shot is fired, we go into the room before she can reload."

Calvin nodded affirmatively but did not speak.

Without moving from his position, Spencer pounded his fist on the door and Gabi fired in response. Spencer turned and kicked the door just above the handle. The wood splintered and the door jamb broke from its position, allowing Spencer to push through the door and into the room as Gabi attempted to reload. The round in her hand dropped onto the ground and Spencer took advantage, marching into range and striking her cheekbone with the back of his hand. He squeezed her throat with his right hand and pushed her flat against the wall.

"Quiet," he said.

She furrowed her brow and breathed through her nose, looking up at her attacker. "What do you want?" she rasped.

"Not what, love," he said. "Who."

"What are you talking about?" she asked.

"Let's go," Spencer said. He kept his hand on Gabi's throat and walked her backward toward the door where Calvin locked onto her arm with his left hand, the strength in his right compromised from the gunshot wound, as they approached the staircase.

Spencer stopped at the top of the stairs and said, "Not a sound when we step outside. Understood?"

Through labored breathing, Gabi said, "Yes."

"Good," Spencer said to Gabi. Then to Calvin, he said, "Let her go. I have her," and walked her methodically step-by-step.

Four steps from the bottom, he swept Gabi's feet from beneath her, causing her to bounce off of the bottom step and onto the landing. She landed shoulder first and cracked the side of her head against the floor, leaving her momentarily dazed and moaning from the sudden jolt. He took a handful of her t-shirt at the neck and pulled her to her feet, then spun her to face him. "That's for the kick in the balls, love."

Standing behind her, Spencer pushed the barrel of his pistol into Gabi's back and tightened his other arm around her neck, pulling her tight to his body. "I don't need you to get what I want. Never forget that."

"Then why are you doing this?" she mumbled.

He rested his chin on her shoulder, touching his unshaven cheek to hers and rubbing the stubble against the smoothness of her face until it began to redden with irritation. She could smell the residue of smoke in his mouth and turned away. "Because I want to, Dr. McLane," he said, mocking her title and family name as he said them. He grabbed a handful of her hair and pulled her head backward. "Now be a good girl, come with me, and wait."

She turned her face back to his and asked, "Wait for what?"

He smiled and whispered, "You'll see." To Calvin, he said, "Run outside and tell your friend to fetch our little toy and come to the driveway."

The driver of the SUV in the driveway sounded the horn to indicate both his presence and impatience. "Bloody moron," Spencer muttered. To Gabi, he said, "The transmitter for your security system. Where is it?" Gabi refused to answer and Spencer snapped her head back by the hair. "Don't make me find it myself," he growled.

"Living room," she said quietly.

Spencer stifled a laugh and said, "Why are you whispering? There's no one here to hear you." He pushed her from the kitchen and into the living room. "Where?"

"The table by the window."

He moved her to the table and said, "Pick it up." When she complied, he started back in the direction of the kitchen. She stumbled as he dragged her but stopped in front of the sink. He inserted the plug for the drain, turned on the faucet, and said, "Toss it in." Water slowly overtook the transmitter and Spencer said, "We're moving."

Calvin and the man who had been guarding the front of the house appeared at the back door. Spencer said, "Get to your sedan. We reconvene in an hour. Understood?"

"Yes, sir," Calvin said.

"This was a sight better than your last assignment at the market, yeah? Bloody shambles that was."

"Thank you, sir."

"It was a statement, not a compliment. Off you go."

The men ran through the backyard and disappeared into the trees. Gabi began to hyperventilate as Spencer forced her through the kitchen and toward the door that led into the garage. "The garage door. Open it now," he said. She touched a button on the wall and the garage doors lifted from the ground.

Spencer removed the gun from her back and placed it into the front pocket of his rain slicker, and momentarily released the tension from his hold around her neck. Gabi felt the change of position, thrust herself backward and created space that allowed her to break free from his grasp. She reached the back corner of the SUV but slipped on the rain-covered pavement when she attempted to change directions, allowing Spencer to reach her and regain his hold. "Don't do that again," he said as he opened the rear driver's side door.

Covered by a roar of thunder that sent shockwaves into her body, although he was nearly thirty miles away, she screamed his name into the night. "Nick!" The sound ceased instantly as Spencer pushed her inside and slammed the door closed.

Nick sat on the front porch of the farmhouse, slouched in a black rocking chair that been repainted more times than he could count and dated back to the 1940s, ignoring the blustering cold air, intermittently sipping from a mug of citrus green tea that sat growing cold on the nearby table and listening to the pellets of rain strike the metal over-hang, when he felt the burn of an adrenaline rush in his stomach. His hands tingled as though an electrical current was connected to the base of his neck and was running into his arms.

He stood and looked into the late-night sky that covered the open field across the road, the moon obscured by moving cloud cover, following the movement with his eyes as they passed over the mountain tops that were barely visible in the distance.

Into the silence, his eyes wide, he said, "Gabrielle."

15

"This is Gabi. Leave me a message..."

Nick disconnected the fourth call to her cell phone, all of which were routed to voicemail after a series of rings, and dropped his phone onto the empty passenger seat. "It's almost nine o'clock at night in the middle of a storm. Where are you, Gabrielle?" he said.

The intensity of the rain had increased since the moment he turned the key in the ignition. Headlights lighting the way, the windshield wipers switched on high, his foot pressing the accelerator to the nearly to the floor, the engine in the Civic whined as Nick sped across the two-lane road, with alternating segments shadowed by tree cover and bordered by rugged farmland, for five miles, braking hard and skidding to a crawl to navigate the sharp button hook turn that wound down the mountain and into the valley before turning onto the four-lane Route 58.

Gabi found security and comfort in her routine. Reliability was among her most prominent traits. A sudden disappearing act was antithetical to her profile. He racked his brain for rational explanations without success. It was the feeling on the porch that served as the spark that kindled a fire that was consuming his stomach. That, he knew, was the origin of the panic response to an unknown crisis.

A tractor-trailer in the left lane, a rusting minivan puttering in the right, Nick crossed the rumble strips and turned onto the shoulder, blowing past and crossing in front of the minivan, reentering the left lane. The disapproving drivers of both vehicles sounded their horns.

The road ahead both straight and momentarily free of traffic, he dialed her phone for a fifth time but was sent to voicemail again.

"This is Gabi. Leave me a message..."

He ended the call once more and stuffed the phone between his legs on the seat.

That can't be the last time I hear her voice.

Another thought crossed his mind and he laughed under his breath.

If I get there and she's asleep on the couch, I'll never hear the end of this.

He felt another rush of acid in his stomach and knew better.

Where are you, Gabrielle?

He slowed when he entered downtown and exited Route 19 for the secondary road that led to her community. He reduced his speed, looking for the entrance to The Ridge through the haze of rain and fog, and slowly rolled past the stone sign toward the entry of the driveway at the side of the house.

Black shirt, black sweatpants, black car, late-night arrival with a slow approach. This doesn't look suspicious at all.

Nick exited the Civic but left the engine running, having seen the right garage door lifted and Gabi's BMW SUV still inside. He looked around her vehicle to the interior wall and saw the door leading into the kitchen standing open, lights on throughout the first floor, but heard no sounds coming from inside. Halfway into the garage, he stopped.

A sound: air, water, something.

Then, at the doorway, he saw the faucet running into a sink overflowing onto the floor below. Instinctively, he jogged to the car, sat in the driver seat, and extracted his Taurus TH9 nine-millimeter semi-automatic from the glove compartment, which had been cleaned and reloaded since the thwarted abduction attempt at Value King in Hansonville.

He deactivated the safety, closed the door on the Civic, and moved back into the garage.

Never leave home without it.

His first action was to shut off the faucet, doing so while holding a paper towel in order to preserve any fingerprints or other forensic evidence that could possibly exist and was not subject to contamination due to his mere presence. As he stepped away from the sink, his feet sloshing through the water that stood on the floor, his foot struck an object with an audible *clack,* which bounced away before coming to a rest.

Nick bent down and picked up the gray plastic cylinder and set it down on the floor again.

"The alarm transmitter," he said aloud. "She's gone."

A wave of nausea washed over him. His first thought was the police. A call to 911 would summon a wave of law enforcement officers asking questions with no answers, not the least of which was to inquire as to what led him to drive to her home, unannounced, at such a late hour. To do so without assessing the rest of the house was unacceptable and potentially dangerous.

What if this was a misunderstanding and there was an explanation for the alarm transmitter in the sink, the running water, the open door?

What if she was upstairs, asleep, having taken a heavy dose of cold medicine, unaware of the condition of her home?

What if she had heard an intrusion and was standing at the top of the stairs with a firearm?

Nick worked through the questions, the possibilities, the concerns, and crept out of the kitchen and into the living room, sloshing water onto every nearby surface with each step.

She would kill me if I wore wet, muddy shoes this far into her house.

With the lamp on its highest setting in the living room, his field of vision was clear. On his cell, he dialed Gabi's number for the sixth time of the night. The phone's vibration rattled on the table, drawing his eye, before he heard the ringtone that she had set for his contact and saw the screen light up, his contact set to display a picture of the two of them that had been taken years before as they leaned against the railing in front of the fountain at Radford University's Jefferson Hall.

Where are you, Gabrielle?

Having switched off the power, Nick pocketed her iPhone and dialed Micah on his own.

"What's good, brother?" Micah answered.

Monotone, Nick replied, "Black flag," indicating a developing dangerous emergency situation involving a friend or member of the family.

There was a pause before Micah said, "We're recording. Who is it?"

"It's Gabi." He held the phone in his left hand, the pistol in his right, and started slowly toward the steps.

"Where are you? What happened?"

"I don't know. I just got to her house. The garage doors were open. Her car is here, her phone is here, and she's gone." He touched his back to the rear wall, sliding slowly and silently against the surface as he ascended the staircase, alternating both his attention and his aim between the two floors until the upper floor was fully in view. "I'm headed upstairs. Stay on the line with me."

"You got it."

Nick lowered his voice and asked, "Do you have the address here?"

"You put it in her file, yeah."

"If you hear shots fired, if you hear voices other than mine, get the police en route but keep the line active so it's still recording."

He looked through the railing that bordered the floor where the upstairs hallway wrapped around the staircase and led to the rooms that were set above the kitchen and away from the master bedroom. The smell of copper and spent gunpowder hung in the air and Nick froze at the sight of the exterior wall of the bedroom.

"Blood," he said. The spray pattern of holes in the wall was unmistakable. He felt his feet grind on pellets that had landed on the carpet and he said, "She used her shotgun. I've got pellets on the ground and blood on the wall."

"Inside or outside?" Micah asked.

"Outside wall, which means she fired from inside, at least twice to get it to penetrate, and she hit her target." Moving toward the doorway, he said, "The door's been kicked in. Shotgun is on the ground between the bed and the closet."

"Tell me she's not in there, Nick."

He lowered the gun and said, "She's not here."

"Thank God," Micah said. "At least you didn't just walk in and find her on the ground."

"Yeah." Nick look through the bedroom window, peering into the backyard and watching as the wind and rain bent the trees. "But where is she?"

"What do you want to do?"

"Get Bret and Oso here ASAP," Nick said. "I want both of them in the air first thing in the morning."

"Already texted them. Anything else?"

He descended the staircase and returned to the ground floor, stepping into the kitchen. Wind was pushing the back door open further, scraping across the rug that Gabi had placed on the floor. The sound caught his attention and two shards of glass that shone with reflected light turned Nick's eyes to the ground. "Well, we know how they got in."

"What is it?"

He knelt to examine the glass and then looked up to the door. "One of the panes of glass in the back door was covered with duct tape before it was broken. They pushed it right in, the broken pieces landed on the rug and never made a sound."

"Which means the glass break sensor for the alarm wasn't triggered either," Micah said.

"Right."

He stood and pushed the door closed, then left the kitchen and walked into the living room. "This is where she was," Nick said. He moved with each event in the sequence. "Blankets are on the couch. Her phone was on the table. The garage door was open. She took off upstairs to get the shotgun and fight them off. It's not hard to see. If I had someone outside, this is how I'd do it."

"Nick…" Micah said.

Nick ignored the attempt to sway his attention and, scanning the area, speaking as if he were alone, said, "Front door was locked and whoever it is came in behind her and blocked her way out. Somehow she got upstairs." He followed each step with his eyes and grimaced at the thought of Gabi in fear, fleeing an attacker, finding herself pinned down like an outnumbered soldier on a battlefield. "Who did this to you?" he said aloud to himself.

"Nick…" Micah said again.

"Yeah?"

"Are you even going to consider calling…"

"Absolutely not," he interjected. "Not yet. There's nothing missing. She's not dead. If she was, I'd know. This had a purpose. The only thing a police presence will do right now is muck it up, slow us down, and give whoever is responsible for this another reason to put a premature end to it."

"I had to ask," Micah said.

"You already knew better. Get them in the air as soon as you can. Tell D.T. that I need every resource possible. Wake him up, if you have to. He'll understand."

Nick heard the audible *clacks* of fingers pressing keys on a keyboard and Micah said, "Roger that. Where are you headed now?"

Silent, he looked around the room and sat on the arm of the couch, sensing the emotional gravity of the moment for the first time.

Helpless.

That was the feeling. It was foreign, uncomfortable, and unacceptable.

He set the gun on top of the couch and tightened his hand into a fist, squeezing the blood from his fingers and palm, turning them white, and feeling his fingernails digging into the skin, then opened his hand and repeated the process again.

There was something else: A void, a vacuum, an empty space where she should be, where she belonged, on the plane of existence that seemed exclusive to them and them alone.

Where are you, Gabrielle? You're not gone but you're not here. Where are you?

"Nick?" Micah asked.

His voice broke as he said, "I don't know," and he wiped a tear from his eye. He cleared his throat, closed his eyes, and slowed his breathing to an even rhythm, then opened them again, said, "I'll be in touch," and disconnected the call.

The Civic was parked outside the entrance to the housing community on the end opposite of Gabrielle's home, one that offered less visibility to curious neighbors and the availability of a quick getaway should the need arise.

He touched the home button on Gabi's iPhone and activated the lock screen to check the time.

12:03 a.m.

Each check of the time meant that the screen would remain active for fifteen seconds before going dark; fifteen seconds to look at the picture of Gabi with two of her co-workers, fifteen seconds to look at another notification from an app, another text message from a friend or co-worker that would not be answered, fifteen seconds to watch another minute pass on the clock from the present to the past.

"Where are you, Gabrielle?" he asked into the silence.

In operational time, hours seemed to pass like minutes, Nick thought, but there was no mission at hand. There were no warnings issued, no threats of violence, no demands, no contact. Gabrielle seemed to be the target, not a ransom. Despite the complexity of their relationship, there were no secrets. If there was danger, if she had an enemy, he would have known.

At 1 a.m., having been agreed upon during an earlier check-in, Nick's phone buzzed with a call from Micah.

"Yeah?" Nick answered.

"Anything?"

"Nothing." He activated Gabi's phone and watched the clock move from 1:00 to 1:01 a.m. and pushed the power button to darken the screen.

"This makes no sense, bro," Micah said. "One of us, maybe. But Gabi? You think it's a ransom thing? Her folks are well-off."

Nick reclined in the driver seat, his arm raised and folded behind his head, his eyes closed. "I don't know, Micah." The rain had stopped before midnight and the gusts of wind were now sporadic. The window was down, drawing cool but humid air into the cabin of the car.

"Do I hear crickets? Where are you, man?"

"Parked outside of her development."

"Nick, they're not just going to show back up tonight. You need to rest."

"I don't see myself getting a solid eight tonight, Micah."

Micah breathed into the phone and spoke calmly. "And what if her folks call at you at noon tomorrow and tell you someone has made contact about their daughter and they need to talk to you? You look like you've been up all night on a booze bender and feel worse than you look. How's that going to work?"

Nick opened his eyes and looked through the moon roof and into the sky. "I know," he said through an exhale. "I just can't bring myself to leave yet."

"Then sleep there. You're not going to be much good to her if you're not tip-top, bro."

"I hear you," Nick said and closed his eyes again.

"Bret and Oso are headed your way in a few hours. Buzz me if you hear anything."

"I will. Thank you."

"For what?" Micah answered and disconnected the call before Nick could respond.

At 7:30 a.m., the aggressive tapping of a flashlight on the roof startled Nick awake. He shielded his eyes from the light and looked through the window to see the police officer; average height, white, a bulky frame, a blond buzz cut, and an unwavering void of emotion.

"How are we doing this morning?" the officer asked into the open window.

Still reclined and covering his eyes from the brightness of the morning sun, Nick said, "Good morning, sir. We are doing fine."

The officer looked away and said, "Do you mind telling me what you're doing here?"

Nick inclined the seat and said, "Getting a little much-needed sleep."

Resting his hand on the roof, he leaned down, looked inside the car without looking at Nick, and said, "And you think this is the place to do that?"

Is there some obscure federal law that requires every cop to have that haircut?

"It was a long night," Nick said, then put his thumb to his mouth, extended his pinky, and tipped his head back before placing his hands on the steering wheel. "Driving home seemed unwise. Just trying to be a responsible citizen."

"Step out of the car, please."

Nick shook his head and said, "I don't think so."

"That wasn't a request," the officer said sternly.

"But you said 'please'. Do you ever smile? Laugh? Anything?"

"Get out of the car now."

"First of all, for my own protection, I'm going to stay in the car because I've done nothing that would warrant such aggressive action. Secondly, even the loosest interpretation of the Fourth Amendment would consider a search of me or my car unreasonable. You've not met the threshold for reasonable suspicion, much less probable cause."

"Are you a lawyer?"

Today is not the day for this.

Nick moved his hands to the bottom of the steering wheel but maintained contact and visibility. "No, but we can hang out here until my attorney arrives, if you'd like. He has less of a sense of humor than I do, especially at a time like this. He's not a morning person." He made a show of screening his mouth with his hand, curved toward the man outside his window, and said, "Just imagine all the paperwork," then shrugged his shoulders and smirked. "Am I free to go now?"

The man tapped his fingers on the roof and said, "Is all this attitude really necessary?"

"Probably not," Nick said. "Consider it a bonus, kind of like the prize at the bottom of a box of Cracker Jack. It's never worth much but you're still kind of excited to get it."

"Go home, sir. Wherever home is," the officer said.

"Aye aye, captain," Nick said, offering a sarcastic salute from his forehead, then squinted and leaned forward for a closer look at the name tag, and added, "Never mind, you're not a captain. Have a nice day," and started the engine.

In the side mirror, Nick watched the officer return to his cruiser, shaking his head and mumbling what he was certain were unflattering thoughts.

Picking up breakfast in a fast-food drive-thru occupied half an hour, eating in the parking lot an additional fifteen minutes, before the dreaded commute back to the farmhouse where he would be surrounded by empty space, racing thoughts, and passing time. In an adult life characterized by proactive action without apology, forced reactivity was more than uncomfortable or working against preference. It was unacceptable, almost painful. With Gabrielle, her well-being, her life, and her future all hanging in the balance, it was excruciating.

Then there was the silence.

No phone call, no text, no pop-in visit.

The void. The empty space. The vacuum. So foreign and unwelcome.

Notifications and the occasional text message continued to buzz and ring on her iPhone and he checked them each time, disappointed when none of them offered so much as a crumb of useful information, with the exception of the good morning text from her father that arrived while he was stalled in the drive-thru lane. Whatever had happened, her parents were unaware but would grow concerned by the radio silence in the hours, if not days, to come.

Winding up the mountain and in the direction of the farmhouse, he drove at a speed that was half of that from the night before. Large branches and leaves were strewn about the roadway from the wind and rain produced by the storm but the roads were dry courtesy of the morning sun that had risen in spite of the circumstances at hand. He fought the urge to check his own phone for a text, a missed call, any contact from Gabrielle from which he had grown so accustomed, reminding himself that her only means of doing so was resting in the passenger seat, sliding with each turn.

He exited the portion of the two-lane road that was bordered on each side by trees and grey stones that seemed to emerge from the ground by force, covered by branches and foliage that left the pathway striped with alternating sequences of light and dark as if the sun was peering through a picket fence. No longer obscured by the canopy of brown and green above, his field of vision opened and he saw sunlight touching every surface, momentarily instilling the hope that the sudden transformation of the landscape around him was somehow a divine sign of a swift and positive resolution.

He crossed the bridge, the decades-old wooden boards rumbling against the bolts and gently shaking the car, and slowed to a stop at the mailbox at the edge of the road beside the steps that led into the front yard. Standing on the porch with his back to the road was a man, pacing to and fro in the space between the two doorways, deliberately sliding his shoes across the ground and kicking dust into the air while smoking a cigarette. The physicality and attire were nondescript, common and basic, but the sight of the headwear caused Nick to sit up straight, his eyes wide with focused intensity rather than shock, awe, or fear.

The brown Panama was the signature choice of a single individual with whom he had crossed paths, one who was an uninvited, unwelcome guest in his presence, much less at his home.

In a flash, his vision turned white, then red. The pieces of the puzzle snapped into place. His vision darkened, then lightened again, mimicking the lens of a camera, and he began grinding his back teeth, feeling pressure in his eardrums that brought on the high-pitched whine of temporary tinnitus. He turned the Civic into the driveway, behind the SUV that the man had parked ahead of him. As if he were experiencing an apparition, he found himself standing in the kitchen of Gabi's house, watching her retreat in fear, then scramble up the stairs, barricading herself in her bedroom, desperately firing her shotgun into the door and the walls while facing a fate that was uncertain at best.

The man awaiting his approach was responsible for the night before, Nick knew. The why and the how were irrelevant when viewed through the lens of who and what.

Nick walked up the dirt and gravel driveway and into the front yard. He stopped before reaching the stone steps and said, "I thought you were dead."

His back turned, Spencer said, "Not yet." He spun to face Nick, tossed the spent cigarette into the yard, and said, "Been a long time, Burke. How've you been, mate?"

Nick refused eye contact and ignored his question, looking instead in the direction of the bridge. "I thought the bad guys were supposed to wear black hats. What are you doing here, Spencer?"

"I like earth tones." Spencer raised his hands, showing both to be empty and said, "I just want to talk."

"So talk."

Without moving from his place on the porch, Spencer said, "You have a piece?"

"Not on me, no. Why? Is this about to get hostile?"

Spencer tilted his head and said, "I've not survived this long without being careful. Care for some show-and-tell?"

Nick lifted his shirt, baring his stomach as well as the waistline of his sweatpants, and slowly turned in a circle, then lifted each leg of the pants to reveal his ankles. "Satisfied?"

"I am," Spencer said. A black soft-sided cooler sat atop the table beside the rocking chair and Spencer withdrew a dark brown glass bottle of beer. "Care to join me for a coldie?" he asked, looking at Nick.

"I'm not thirsty," Nick said.

Spencer popped the lid on the bottle with an opener on his keychain and scanned the area, looking first through the yard and then into the property across the road that ran to the mountains in the distance. "Do you like it out here?" he asked.

"Sure. Why?" Nick asked. The answer was as immaterial as the question.

"Where you see tranquility, I see boredom. I'd go mad out here in this wasteland," Spencer said and shook his head in disgust. He pulled a drink from the bottle, faked a gag, then held it up, examined the label, and said, "American beers are god-awful. It's no wonder imports are so popular, yeah?"

"I'll take your word for it."

"Still straight-edge and all that, Burke? That's an Irish surname, no?" He pointed the mouth of the bottle at Nick and said, "That's where we differ. Where is your flare, your excitement? Such a no-hoper when it comes to fun. It's like watching every movie in black and white with you."

"I could fill up a spreadsheet with all the ways that we differ, Spencer. What are you doing at my house?"

With outstretched arms, Spencer asked, "Can't an old friend stop by to catch up?"

Nick raised his eyebrows and responded, "We're friends, are we? I don't recall exchanging cards this past Christmas."

Spencer sat down on the top step. "What would you call us then?"

"What I would call you and what I would call us are two different things."

"I can respect that." He squinted as he looked up at Nick from his seat on the steps. "Late night out?" Spencer asked and drank from the bottle again.

"You could say that."

Spencer narrowed his eyes, smiled, and groaned as he pushed himself to his feet. "It's been a while but some things never change." He turned his back to Nick, walked to the chair, and unzipped the top of the cooler. "I'd be willing to bet every last one of my chips that you spent the night with your friend, the good doctor. Prime piece, that. No wonder you fancy her so."

Nick stepped onto the first step but stopped when Spencer pulled a matte black pistol from the cooler and aimed it at his chest.

"Tsk-tsk," Spencer said with the gun raised.

Nick stepped backward onto the ground but kept his gaze fixed on Spencer, breathing through his nose and feeling numbness in his hands.

"Let's talk," Spencer said and used the barrel of the gun to wave Nick closer. Nick walked onto the porch as Spencer eased himself into the wooden swing at the end nearest the driveway. He raised the pistol again and said, "That's close enough."

"Talk fast."

"A million dollars is a successful night, Nick. Or what was it again? Sean McCormick?" He kept the gun trained on Nick but leaned forward and lifted the cooler from the chair with his other hand. "How did it feel to have the lovely Alexandra alongside you like that?" He held the bottle between his legs and popped the lid with the opener.

Nick felt the color drain from his face, leaving his skin cold. His chest was heavy and dull pain was setting in. He felt himself suffocating, unable to breathe or speak or move. After a moment of silence, wide-eyed and in a voice just above a whisper, he said, "You were there." His words were spoken as a statement rather than a question.

"For as brash and irreverent as the rich little scamp can be, he still demands the kind of security that folks like me can provide." Nick stepped slowly in Spencer's direction. Spencer motioned toward him with the gun and said, "Hold it."

Nick ignored the directive and moved another step closer. "That's what this is about? Daniel Staal lost a poker game and sent his mercenary to come seize his expected plunder and make it right?"

Spencer stood up from the swing and said, "Stop right there." He looked away, laughing to himself and, through a toothy grin, said, "That's rather disingenuous, don't you think? This isn't about poker any more than your presence in Boston." Another drink from the bottle, then he circled behind Nick and said, "Let's not forget that I know you, I know what you do, and for whom," and poked the barrel of the gun into Nick's back, pushing him off-balance. "And you know what I am capable of all the same."

With Spencer standing nearby, maintaining his position of power, Nick sat down in the rocking chair. "Wherever you go, mayhem follows," he said, then ran his hand along the bottom of the table when Spencer drank again from the bottle.

Spencer drained the remaining contents into his mouth and set the bottle on the ground at the edge of the steps, allowing it to clink against the side of the one he had previously finished. He rested on the wall beside the side entrance and took a cigarette from the pack in the pocket on the front of his shirt, lighting it with a lighter from his pants pocket, all with one hand while keeping the pistol trained on Nick in the rocking chair.

After all these years, he never flinches.

"What do you want, Spencer?"

"I don't make rules or give orders, Nick. I do as I'm told and cash checks. You know that."

Nick slouched in the rocking chair and said, "Fine. What does Daniel Staal want?"

"Do you always wear black, Burke?" He used the gun as a pointer. "The shirt, the pants, always so dark."

"Out with it, Spencer."

"You embarrassed my boss, Burke. Made him look like an overemotional fool at the table in front of his friends."

"I had a winning hand and beat him."

"You walked out of there with $800,000 that was supposed to belong to him."

"He should have played better. Tell me what you want."

"A million and one dollars. American."

"I'll…"

"Get me a cashier's check?" Spencer interrupted. "I don't think so. You want to get into the open, go to a bank, and control the environment. No, you can make the arrangements to wire it from here."

"Why the extra dollar?"

Spencer exhaled a lungful of smoke and said, "You took a million from him. He takes a dollar more from you." Then a shrug and, "He wins."

"All this over money and a bruised ego."

Spencer moved from the wall and toward Nick in the chair. For the first time, he affected a serious tone and said, "No, all this to remind you to leave well enough alone and keep your distance from things you do not understand and those for whom you are unwelcome."

He's got her.

Nick stood from the chair with his hands in his pockets. "There's something to be said for consistency, Spencer. You've not changed a bit and you're as sharp as ever."

"My lifestyle keeps me young at heart," Spencer said and tossed the next smoldering cigarette butt into the yard. He lowered the gun and held out both hands. "You haven't even tried to make a move."

Not yet.

"You know I can't and you know why I can't."

"Indeed."

"So what next? What guarantee do I have that this is all settled and over with?"

"Absolutely none, which is why your best bet is to comply," Spencer said. "He has no desire for this to go any further. The power of money does crazy things to people, Burke. Look at me." He walked back toward the wall beside the side entrance, grimacing and limping with the first few steps. He shook his leg and said, "Rain gets me every time. Old war wounds and all."

Nick spotted the limp and said, "How long have you been in town, Spencer?"

"Oh, I come and go. I've been a drifter as long as you've known me." He groaned and shook his leg again.

The man in the shadows. He was watching Rae.

Looking at the ground, Nick said, "It was you."

"I'm sorry?" Spencer said.

"Correct me if I'm wrong but I believe you had your eyes on a waitress at an Italian restaurant a few months ago."

Spencer tapped the tip of the pistol against the wall and smiled. He wrinkled his nose and said, "Cute little thing, isn't she? I saw your work that night. Always a step ahead, yeah? You even managed to get Dr. McLane out of the way that time."

"I didn't ruin your evening, did I?"

"Briefly," Spencer said.

Nick lifted his head and said, "The old Spencer wouldn't have just let that go. What gives?"

"Maybe I've gotten soft with age. Hand me another coldie, will you?"

Nick handed the third and last bottle to Spencer and said, "You, soft? That seems unlikely considering the current circumstances."

"We all lose our edge, Burke. You will one day."

Nick walked to the steps, maintaining eye contact and showing his empty hands to Spencer, and picked up the empty bottles. "Let's see if you're right. Are you game?"

Spencer drank from the third bottle and said, "I'm not here for games, Burke."

"Humor me. I'll throw in another dollar," Nick said. He strolled slowly past the center of the porch and stopped in front of the rocking chair. "My hands are tied here, Spencer. What do you think I'm going to do?"

"All right," Spencer said and pushed himself away from the wall. He stood beside Nick and said, "It's been a while, huh? What are we playing for?"

"Pride should be enough. You're the away team but I'll let you go last." Spencer smiled and nodded. Nick held out his hand and asked, "Shall we?"

Looking at Nick through the side of his eye, Spencer handed him the pistol and said, "Good luck, Nick."

Nick handed him the first of the two bottles and said, "Whenever you're ready."

Spencer stepped to the edge of the porch and tossed the bottle high into the air, the neck first facing upward but then turning toward the ground. Nick raised the gun and followed the path with his eyes, then aimed and fired a single shot. The bullet struck the body of the bottle, which shattered and showered the ground with its pieces.

As Nick lowered the gun, Spencer said, "Nice shot."

"Thank you. You even gave me a fair toss." He handed the pistol to Spencer and said, "You're up."

Holding the second bottle in his hand, he slid back a step without lifting his feet from the ground. "Ready?" he asked.

"Ready," Spencer said and raised the gun, pointing it across the front yard and into the field on the other side of the road.

Nick held the bottle by the neck and tossed it to the same height as the one he had been given but with one less rotation. Spencer followed the target with the gun and Nick took another step backward. He reached underneath the table and pulled the Sig Sauer P228 pistol free from the Velcro strap around the barrel that held the gun in place and watched Spencer fire a single shot that splintered the bottle and sent the remains to the ground.

Spencer grinned and admired his work. "It's a tie," he said and turned to see the barrel of the Sig Sauer pointed between his eyes.

"Where's Gabi?" Nick said. His eyes were wide. When he spoke, his voice was emitted as a low rumble.

"You know better than this, Burke," Spencer said with their eyes locked. His pistol was pointed to the ground and he remained motionless.

"You get one chance, Spencer. Take your finger off of the trigger. Let the gun spin on your index finger, then reach over and hand it to me by the barrel. You know the drill. Move slowly and deliberately." Spencer complied and Nick took the pistol with his left hand, his right hand still pointing the Sig Sauer at the bridge of Spencer's nose. He tossed Spencer's firearm behind him and heard it land in the porch swing.

Nick moved a step closer to Spencer and asked, "Where's Gabi?"

"I didn't even have to say it, did I?"

Nick drove his foot into Spencer's knee then struck the base of his neck with the fist that held grip of pistol. Spencer cried out and crashed to the ground, wincing and holding his leg in the vain attempt to lessen the pain. "You expect me to believe that a rich kid in his twenties is going to do all of this over losing pocket change in a poker game?"

Spencer rolled onto his side and groaned. "It's just business, Burke," he said.

Nick stood over Spencer with the gun pointed at the side of his head and said, "This stopped being about business the second you involved Gabrielle. Where is she?"

"Just wire Daniel his money and she will be set free," Spencer said. He turned to look up at Nick and said, "I'm a man of my word."

Nick struck the injured knee with his heel and Spencer wailed, clutching his leg and rocking, his eyes closed.

"A man overrun with avarice knows no bounds, Spencer. You've been making your thinly veiled references to poker and chips and gambling from the moment I got here. I'd be willing to bet that the account you wanted me to wire those funds to is yours, not Daniel Staal's." He knelt on one knee and placed the gun under Spencer's chin. "Staal has his hands in all kinds of things. But this has Spencer St. Clair written all over it. The world is full of men like Daniel Staal and Lucien Murdoc. You, on the other hand, are barely human. You don't do any of this for the money. You never have. You do it because there's a place in whatever soul you have that feeds on it."

The worst of the pain subsiding, Spencer said, "The thrill of the hunt."

"Gabrielle is not fair game," Nick said. He switched the gun to his left hand and locked his grip on Spencer's leg, squeezing and twisting with all the force he could muster. Spencer shrieked then began coughing as Nick released his grasp and returned the gun to his dominant hand.

"My phone," Spencer said. "In my back pocket. There is no security. Look in the gallery."

Nick took the iPhone from Spencer's pocket and opened the photo gallery. The first image showed Gabrielle seated in a chair, her wrists bound but her eyes and mouth unrestricted. He zoomed in on the red welt that was visible on her cheekbone and turned off the screen.

"This morning," Spencer said. "She's fine."

"You always have a failsafe, Spencer."

Spencer rested on his back. His face was covered with sweat and tears. "They are waiting to hear from me."

"Voice or text?"

"Either," Spencer said.

"If they don't?"

Spencer moved his eyes to look at Nick but did not answer. Nick reached toward the injured leg and Spencer shouted, "Wait!"

"You're going to dial the number and put it on speaker. You're going to tell them that I've yet to arrive and you are still waiting. No panic codes, no hidden messages, just a quick check-in and hang up."

"If I don't, you'll kill me?"

"If you don't, I'll remind you that death is not the worst thing that can happen to you, and I'll spend ungodly amounts of money to keep you alive just to prove my point."

"Wire me the money and I will take you to her."

"Make the call, Spencer."

"Redial the last number." Nick dialed the most recent number in the contact list and activated the speaker.

"Yeah?" Calvin said when he answered.

"It's me," Spencer said. He looked up at Nick when he asked, "How is she?"

"She's fine, quiet. But she's tempting."

Nick moved the gun to Spencer's temple. Spencer raised his voice and said, "Don't touch her, you drongo! Burke isn't here yet. Leave her be."

"Whatever you say, boss man."

"I'll contact you soon." Spencer ended the call and handed the phone back to Nick. "Satisfied?"

"For now," Nick said. He grabbed the front of Spencer's shirt and pulled him to a seated position. "Get up." Spencer held out his hand, asking for assistance, but Nick backed away. "You can manage."

Spencer struggled to his feet and held his balance on one leg. Nick followed Spencer with his aim and said, "In the house."

The screen door to the side entrance banged shut and Nick pushed Spencer in the back, causing him to fall onto the couch. He pulled a bag of two-foot plastic cable ties from the table in front of the window and tore it open, then extracted a tie, inserted two inches into the locking head to form a loose loop, and pitched it into Spencer's lap.

"Hands first. Do it," Nick said.

Spencer complied, tightening the cable tie around his wrists by pulling the plastic through the locking head with his teeth.

Nick examined his work and said, "Tighter."

Spencer held up his bound wrists and asked, "You want me to cut off the circulation, Burke?"

"Sure. Why not? It's going to be the least of your concerns."

Nick took his cell phone from his pocket and dialed the number for Bret. He pointed the gun at Spencer and said, "You be good."

Bret answered before the call went to voicemail. "Yeah, man. What's the word? You hear from Gabi?"

"No, but I have some answers. How far out are you guys?"

"Two hours or so, counting the drive. Why?

"You're never going to believe who was waiting for me on my porch this morning," Nick said, looking at Spencer.

"Who?"

"Spencer St. Clair."

A moment of silence, then, "I thought he..."

"Was dead. Yeah, no kidding," Nick interjected. "I assure you he's not."

Without Nick's knowledge, Bret had answered the call on speakerphone.

"Is he dead *now*?" Oso shouted from the second row of seats.

"Make it 90 minutes, guys," Nick said.

"Copy that," Bret said and ended the call.

Nick smiled at Spencer and said, "It's a beautiful day outside, isn't it? Let's go for a walk."

The untended land behind the farmhouse stretched out for two-tenths of a mile before a mix of brush, weed, and rocks covered the descent to the banks of the Big Moccasin Creek. Limping and wincing with every other step, a silent Spencer walked ahead of Nick, who kept his distance in anticipation of an attempted escape or attack.

There was a clearing in the brush that created a path to creek bank and Spencer stopped before easing his way down, his injured leg on the back side and absorbing none of his weight. He felt his endurance fading as a result of the pain response in his body.

"You okay up there, Spencer?" Nick shouted.

"I got it," Spencer said. Breathing heavily, he paused to rest for several seconds between steps.

During one of his rest periods, Nick closed the gap and pushed Spencer's foot with his shoulder. Spencer pitched forward and barrel rolled down the path and onto the sandbar.

Nick jogged down the path, stood over Spencer, and said, "How about now?" Spencer glared at his captor without speaking.

He pulled Spencer to his feet by the collar of his shirt and pointed toward a space in the side of the hill where the sunlight seemed to momentarily disappear.

Spencer craned his neck and said, "What is that?"

"All of your time in the Australian Outback and running around through Europe and the States, and you mean to tell me you've never wandered into a cave? They're really quite fascinating." He dropped the backpack from his shoulder and withdrew a battery-powered LED lantern. He switched it on and said, "What are you waiting for? I'm right behind you." Spencer turned to object but Nick held up his hand. "Yes, you are."

Tucked inside the mountain and away from the sunlight, the temperature inside the cave was considerably lower by comparison and Spencer shivered when he walked inside. "Could you shine that thing up here a bit more?" he asked.

"What's wrong, Spencer?" Nick asked. He turned off the light. Moving closer, he whispered, "Does this bother you?" He held out his hand and gently touched Spencer's back, causing him to jolt.

"Burke!" he cried. "Don't do this!"

Nick chuckled and said, "The bravado, the swagger, the superiority complex, and now little Spencer is left whimpering because he's still afraid of the dark." Nick moved quietly to his right and felt for the wall, establishing his boundary, then three steps forward, and one to the side, centering him in the cave. He held his breath and listened for the sound of Spencer's breath.

"Burke! Where are you?"

Nick held up the lantern and pressed the button. Light flooded the cave and revealed to Spencer that Nick was standing directly in front of him. Spencer gasped and attempted to shuffle backward but his knee buckled and he fell to the ground.

"Is this what you meant by the thrill of the hunt, Spencer?" He walked around his captive, stalking and standing behind him again, and said, "Keep going. Crawl if you have to."

Spencer turned to look at Nick and said, "How far?"

"I'm not sure yet. I don't know how far this thing goes."

Another fifty feet inside, Nick told Spencer to stop and sit down and set the lantern on the ground in front of him. He extracted another cable tie, formed the start of a loop, tossed it on Spencer's lap and said, "Now the ankles."

Spencer leaned against the wall, slowly drew his knees to his chest and pulled the tie over his shoes, then pulled it tight around his ankles and stretched out his legs.

Nick bent down to check the tension and, satisfied, turned and sat down on the ground beside the man who held Gabrielle's life in his hands. "Where is she, Spencer?"

Spencer rested his head against the stone wall, feeling the cold surface against his skin, and said, "It's a stalemate, Burke." He shifted his leg, moaning with the movement, and continued. "There's only so much you can do here. I may not be a threat at the moment but I'm also your only hope."

Nick pursed his lips and nodded. "So you think I'm out of moves?" he whispered.

Spencer looked to his left and saw a hint of light shining through the entrance that seemed miles away. "In a manner of speaking, yes."

Nick stood and then dropped his knee squarely onto the one that Spencer was favoring, resting his weight there as he leaned closer to Spencer's face, which contorted with a wail that echoed through the dark expanse. "How long do you want to do this?" he asked before he returned to his feet.

"Who are you kidding, Nick?" Spencer asked, citing the familiarity of a first name for the first time. "You know what they say. Torture only works in the movies. It's the threat of pain and suffering that gets answers." Looking away from Nick, he laughed again and said, "But I'm not afraid of you. As I said, it's a stalemate."

"You're probably right," Nick said. He fired a single shot into Spencer's shin, which broke upon impact. The sound of the gunshot inside the cave was deafening. Spencer let out a high-pitched scream and

Nick laughed in return. "It looks like we're about to find out together." For a moment, he thought that he heard Spencer St. Clair begin to cry.

Nick crouched in front of Spencer and asked, "Where's Gabi?"

Spencer was unable to speak, gritting his teeth and moaning as the pain pulsed into his leg.

"Let's go," Nick said. He picked up the lantern, gripped the collar of Spencer's shirt, and began to pull him deeper into the cave.

"What are you going to do to me?" Spencer asked in a panic as Nick pulled him along the ground. "You can't kill me, Burke. You do and my man is in the wind with your paramour."

Nick stopped and sat down on the ground opposite Spencer with his arms resting on his knees. "Killing you is easy, Spencer. It's so final. It lacks imagination." He pressed the button and turned off the light, then lowered his voice and said, "Look around you. I'm going to put you in a hole so deep that it will take sunlight a year to reach you. I'm going to take away your sights, your sounds, every sense that you have. Kill you? I'm going to make you wish you were dead, leave you in a place where the only sound you hear is your own voice begging me to end your misery. Your resilience will never outlast my patience. I will give you blood just to keep your heart pumping." He turned on the light again and waited for Spencer to make eye contact. "Everybody breaks. You *will* tell me where Gabrielle is. It's only a matter of how much pain you're willing to endure, how much suffering you are ready to undertake, before you finally come apart."

Nick swung around and moved on his knees to the side of the cave where Spencer lay. Spencer felt his hands begin to tremble as Nick approached and instinctively tried to back away only to feel the resistance of the stone wall behind him. Nick lowered his head and said, "The thrill of the hunt. Right, Spencer?" He emphasized the hiss at the start of his name.

The trembling intensified and beads of sweat formed on his forehead despite the coolness inside the cave. His eyes were wide, his mouth dry. He felt the desperate need for water, a beer, anything to quench the thirst, dull the pain, smooth the edge. "You've changed," he said. "You're not the Nick Burke I knew."

"No, Spencer," Nick said. He touched the tip of the pistol to Spencer's temple and said, "You just flipped a switch. The second you thought of Gabrielle, the moment you saw her, when you violated her space, when you stepped inside of her home, you changed the world forever." He stood with his feet between Spencer's legs and said, "I saw the picture, Spencer."

"Yes, and she's alive," Spencer pled.

"I saw her face," Nick said. He formed a fist and backhanded Spencer with full force across his cheekbone.

Spencer absorbed the blow and shook his head, trying to remove the cobwebs and regain what remained of his bearings. When he looked up, Nick struck him again and Spencer fell to the side.

"Whatever you or your men have said or done to her will be returned to you tenfold minimum. Do you hear me?" He yanked Spencer upright and repeated the question, emphasizing each word. "Do you hear me?"

"Yes," Spencer said.

Nick clutched his collar and pulled him deeper into the cave, twenty feet, then fifty, before stopping again. The sunlight at the entrance was no longer visible. He pushed Spencer against the wall and opened the backpack, then wrapped the cable ties on his wrists and ankles with three layers of duct tape and stood in front of him.

Nick grabbed a handful of his collar when Spencer shouted, "Stop! For God's sake, stop." He pulled for his breath and began to cough.

"Should you of all people bring God into this, or anything else for that matter?"

"Do you think you're God or something, Burke?"

"Of course not," Nick said. "But He returns my calls and I leave a ton of voicemails."

"Clever," Spencer scoffed. When Nick hovered his foot over the wound in Spencer's shin, Spencer cried out, "No, no, no!"

Nick placed his foot back on the ground, then grabbed Spencer's face and forced him to look upward. "Where's Gabrielle?"

"My phone," Spencer said. He wiped his brow with his arm and dropped his chin to his chest.

Nick turned on the phone and asked, "What about it?"

"The maps. Go to the last location where I dropped a pin."

He did so and held the phone toward Spencer's face. "Is this it?"

Spencer looked upward and laughed quietly through his nose. "I thought you might appreciate the irony, kid."

Nick felt the pressure building in his chest. Stone-faced, he fought the mounting emotions that crept into his throat and stared at Spencer, refusing to breathe, speak, or blink. Seconds elapsed into a full minute before Nick slowly bent down to Spencer, retrieved the plastic cigarette lighter and keychain from his shirt pocket and dropped them into the backpack.

Remaining silent, he picked up the lantern and began walking back toward the entrance.

"Burke! You can't leave me here to die!" Spencer cried out.

Nick slowly crept back to Spencer's position and stood before him.

"You can't do it," Spencer said.

"You're not going to die today, Spencer," Nick rumbled. Then with a smile, he said, "But, just so you know, when the time finally comes for you to get your ticket punched, I'll personally spring for the dance floor to be installed on top of your grave and the urinal to be mounted on your headstone."

Spencer lifted his hands, straightened his hat, and pulled it down on his forehead. He kept his eyes on the floor between his legs and asked, "Why not finish this now?"

"I want you to think about something. If Gabrielle isn't there, you need to tell me now."

"She's there, Burke."

"There is no limit to what I will do to you if any further harm has come to her. Do you understand me?"

"Yes," Spencer muttered. Nick reached for his leg and he shouted, "Yes!"

Nick stood again and said, "This is for Gabi." Aiming downward, he turned his hips and drove a right cross into the bridge of Spencer's nose, which fractured with an audible crack, driving the back of his head into the wall. Blood flowed from his nostrils and covered his mouth, cascading down his neck and saturating his shirt.

Spencer began to choke and coughed to clear his airway. "I can't breathe," he struggled to say.

"Good," Nick said and pushed the button to power off the lantern. He turned and began his walk toward the entrance, seeing the light grow larger with each step.

"Burke!" Spencer shouted following a cough. He repeated the cry twice more, drawing out the surname for effect, but the intended target heard the volume fade as the distance between them grew larger.

Nick stepped onto the creek bed and began scaling the hill, pushing through the brush and onto the level ground behind the house. He dialed Bret, who answered on the first ring.

"We've been calling for half an hour, man. What's going on?"

"How close are you?"

"We're almost there. Fifteen minutes, maybe ten."

"Be ready to leave within the hour."

16

"He's not answering!" Calvin shouted to the man standing outside the front entrance to the building. When the man failed to answer, he shouted, "Phil, get in here!"

"Come out here," Phil said. He was taller than his brother, skinny but sloppy without discernible muscle tone, and a sporting a beard, dark brown mixed with gray, scraggly but full. His drab green jacket smelled of residual tobacco smoke and the must of storage.

Calvin left the room and walked out to the concrete porch. "Spencer isn't answering. I've been calling for an hour. He's down." His black hair was thinning at the crown and he carried an extra twenty pounds in the belly that fell over his belt. His face was round and shaved with a prominent nose and a persistent frown.

"Is there even a signal out at that farm? Let's ask the chick."

Calvin turned to look back inside and took a deep breath of the outside air. "Gimme a minute, will you? I can't breathe in there. That place is probably full of black mold and mildew and God only knows what else."

"You oughta see the graffiti on the walls. It's everywhere. Can we open a window or something?"

"Spencer said not to mess with anything but I'll open one that's not broke or boarded shut already," Calvin said. "I'm gonna go see if I can get something out of her. Where are the other two?"

"One's around back and the other one's at the road. Who are these guys anyway?"

"St. Clair brought them in from somewhere else. They barely speak English. Can you ask one of them to try calling him?"

"They don't talk to me. Won't say a word. They just smile and walk away while I'm talking to them."

"Whatever," Calvin said. "You got some?"

Phil took a plastic bag from his pocket, then replaced it and said, "I'm fresh out of papers."

"Then what good are you?" Calvin asked. He jingled the keys in his pocket and said, "The girl won't say a word either. She asked for water, she wanted to go to the bathroom, and that's it. You talk to her and she just glares at you."

Phil moved closer and said, "Did you see that place under her eye?"

"Spencer put one on her in the house, dude," Calvin said. "Then he sent her down the stairs after she just about kicked his balls into his throat."

"Let me try," Phil said. "She'll talk to me."

"I'll stay here. Have at it." He dialed the number for Spencer and the phone rang five times before the same redirect to the same generic voicemail message.

Peering down the mountainside through the binoculars, Bret said, "At least he didn't use the old Presbyterian church," referencing the dilapidated and condemned white building on the opposite side of the dirt road. He handed them to Oso and said, "It's actually in better shape."

"You don't mess with a religious building, man. It's bad juju," Oso said.

Nick, Bret, and Oso stood atop the hill behind the target building, cloaked by the cover of trees and the resulting shade. The rear of the structure was in view, overgrown with weeds and brush and littered with debris that had broken free of the roof. Built at the base of the mountain, there were two floors, they saw, with a walkout basement to which a single open door on the back side allowed unfettered access.

"Pull up a map on your phone," Nick said to Oso. When he did, Nick asked, "Can we get a street view or not?" The archived image from the road illustrated the layout of the area from the primary access road.

"I'd love to have a drone with a camera right now," Bret said. "How far back around to the front from the backside of this hill?"

"Five minutes but you'll have to stop around the turn and get there on foot," Nick said. Looking at the street view image, he said, "The dirt road leaves the two-lane here; then it's, what, 500 feet to the front?" He zoomed out to the overhead satellite image. "It's mostly flat. The grass is overgrown but look at this." He zoomed in on an area of the field with large gray stones jutting out from the ground and said, "That'll provide some cover on the approach, if we need it."

"Nick, that's a lot of open space for you to get through on the right side. Like you said, I've got some cover coming in straight on but you've got nothing."

"That's not entirely true," Nick said. "I've got Oso with higher ground and good aim." To Oso, he asked, "Can you cover both sides from here and then get down there if you need to?"

"Count on it," Oso said. He stroked his beard and said, "Bears are right at home in the woods."

"There's not a grizzly in the world that's a better shot," Bret said.

"I'm more teddy than grizzly. I've been protecting people from monsters in the dark for years," Oso said.

"He's not wrong," Nick said to Bret.

"You said Spencer said you would appreciate the irony. What was he talking about?" Oso asked.

Nick looked away from the two men and focused on the roof of the building below. He breathed, blinked, took a deep breath and exhaled. "It's been abandoned for years. It closed in the '40s or '50s."

"It looks like it was built by the same people that built your house," Bret said. "But what was it?"

"It's the old Washington County Orphanage," Nick said.

Neither Bret nor Oso spoke. Instead, they looked to the roof of the building with Nick.

After a moment, Bret said, "He's going to burn for that one."

"Count on it," Oso added.

"Where is he, Nick?" Bret asked.

"He's in the cave behind my house, hands and feet bound with zip ties and covered with duct tape. I've got his phone, his lighter, his keys, everything he had on him."

Following a moment of silence, Oso asked the question that Bret was thinking. "What are you going to do when we get back there?"

Nick took a deep breath and said, "He won't be there."

"What do you mean?" Oso asked.

"You've heard of Spencer St. Clair. I know the man. I'd bet my life that he'll find a way out of there."

"You should have iced him on the way out," Bret said.

"Maybe so but if he was lying about this location and had her stashed somewhere else, then what? I had to keep him around in case he had another play. Not anymore."

"I hope he's still there," Bret said.

"I hope he was attacked by a venomous duck while we've been here," Oso said.

Both men looked at Oso and Bret said, "A venomous duck? Only you, Oso."

"Gotta keep it light," Oso said.

Nick refocused on the task and scanned the area with the binoculars a second time, then set them down and said to Bret, "You're right. I'm going to be exposed for a long time coming in from the right side. If I don't..."

"Don't start talking like that, Nick," Oso interrupted.

"It needs to be said."

Bret turned to Nick and said, "I hear you. We'll get her out."

Still looking down the mountain, Nick said, "Listen, this isn't our first time around. We all know that. But, before we even get started, I just need to just say thank you."

"This is what we do, man," Bret said. Oso nodded in agreement.

Nick looked to Bret, then to Oso, and said, "No. This is Gabrielle. This one's different."

A set of fractured concrete steps led from the ground to the elevated first floor. Rusted iron railings lined the perimeter of the covered porch, a single door entrance set in the center with bay windows on either side. On the front of the building were four windows on the aboveground basement, five on the first floor, and three dormers on the second floor, all of which were boarded to restrict unauthorized access and animal infestation. The side windows were in like condition and the rear of the building was inaccessible due to the tangled mesh of brush, the fallen debris, and the proximity to the steep incline of the mountain into which it had been constructed.

Beyond the single door was a large foyer that extended to the back wall, bordered on one side by a row of small rooms that once housed the administrative offices and a classroom with cracked and mold-covered blackboards still in place. A narrow stairwell led to the now inaccessible second floor that once served as the living quarters for the children who had lost their parents and become wards of the state. On the opposite side were a kitchen, a nursery that still held four nondescript silver metal cribs, and a door tucked in the corner where the front and side walls met, behind which was the stairway that descended into the basement. Aside from the foyer, the walls of each room on both floors were covered with spray-painted graffiti courtesy of teenaged vandals, filled with junk, or ripped apart to expose the wooden studs and aging, carcinogenic yellow asbestos insulation inside.

Per the directive of Spencer, Calvin had cleared the lobby of virtually all foreign materials and crammed them into the nearby rooms. To do so was to remove potential makeshift weapons, he explained at the time, and meant freedom of movement for those who were not restricted. All that remained was a cheap, round lightweight metal end table next to the single wooden chair where Gabrielle was restrained. Each wrist was bound to an arm of the chair but her legs remained free. Still wearing the attire from the time of her abduction, the hours of captivity in the aging building with little ventilation and mounting heat had left her t-shirt clinging to her body with sweat, a feeling that disgusted her like few others.

When Phil entered the room, she pushed herself up from her slouch and sat up straight. "It won't kill you to talk to us," he said.

She flashed a wry smile but remained silent.

Phil stood in front of her and leaned forward with his hands on his knees. He lowered his voice and said, "We're still waiting to hear from Spencer so you could at least say something or other to pass the time."

Gabi cleared her throat and asked, "Who's Spencer?"

"The man in the hat that was here. He left to go find your friend, what's-his-name."

"Who are you?"

"I'm Phil," he said. "Tell me about your friend out on the farm that he went to see."

She tilted her head and smiled again.

"Fine. Have it your way." He stood upright and walked away before returning to her chair. "You won't talk to my brother. You won't talk to me."

"Is the fat, bald guy your brother?" she asked.

"Calvin," Phil said.

"We've met," she said. "I just didn't know his name." She looked down to the bruise that was forming on her cheek and said, "He was there when your friend Spencer gave me this. How's his arm feeling, by the way?"

He held his tongue on the roof of his mouth and blew a sharp breath out of his nose. "You did that, huh?"

She raised her eyebrows, smiled, and nodded. "Feeling left out?"

Phil growled and crashed the back of his hand onto Gabi's cheek and the audible *smack* echoed through the room.

Gabi closed her eyes, leaned back her head, and began to laugh. "You hit like a bitch," she said while looking to the ceiling. "My ex used to hit me harder than that."

"Is that right?"

"That's right," she said. "He's dead now. Maybe you and your friend Spencer and the rest of your knuckle-dragging troglodyte friends can give him my regards when you take a one-way trip south here soon."

Phil closed his hand and drove his fist into her mouth on the other side of her face. Gabi felt her lip begin to swell. Blood from a cut inside her mouth settled into her cheek. She turned her head to spit onto the ground beside her chair and began laughing through her nose with her eyes closed.

As he cocked his first for a third blow, Calvin reentered the room through the front door and shouted, "Phil! What are you doing?" He stood beside his brother and said, "What happened here?"

Phil looked at the crudely wrapped bandages and said, "She did this?"

"Yeah," Calvin said.

"If this is good cop and bad cop, which is which?" Gabi asked.

"I liked it better when she wasn't talking," Phil said. "Anything from Spencer?"

"Still no answer," Calvin said. To Gabi, he asked, "This friend of yours, where does he live?"

Gabi spit another mouthful of blood onto the ground between them and shook her head to say no.

Phil grabbed Gabi around her throat but Calvin pulled him away and pushed him in the chest. "Enough!" he said. He pointed to the door and said, "Go downstairs and cool down!"

Phil threw up his hands and said, "I'm gonna go take a leak," and opened the door in the front corner, mumbling a derogatory term toward Gabi as he disappeared down the stairwell.

Bret was lying supine at the bottom of a ditch on the side of the road, out of view from passing traffic, and looked through the binoculars. His position was directly opposite that of Oso, who remained stationed at the top of the mountain behind the orphanage to assemble his Heckler & Koch SL8-1 rifle, affix the scope, bipod, and suppressor, and load the ten-round magazine. Between them, at the point of the triangle, was Nick, who would have the most dangerous advance through open field with limited cover.

The conference call had connected as Bret drove the rented SUV from their staging area on the other side of the mountain to a vacant wide spot on the side of the two-lane road a quarter-mile from his current position.

"What are we looking at, guys?" Nick asked into his earpiece with his eyes on the building in the distance.

"I've got a sentry in a pickup truck at the dirt road entrance and he's by himself. There was a guy on the porch with a cell phone a few minutes ago but he disappeared inside," Bret said.

Nick looked at Spencer's iPhone and said, "I can tell you who he was calling. Spencer's phone has been going off every few minutes. Oso?"

"One guard on your side. The back of the place is so grown up that I can't see a thing. So we've got three creeps, minimum. I've got a clear line on the one in front of you, Nick, but we're flying blind once we get close without eyes inside," Oso said.

"We do have one thing working for us," Bret said. "Whoever is on the porch can't see the guard on the right side. The porch is tucked into the front of the building too far and no one is going to purposely lean out over the rail like that."

"I'll plow the road," Oso said.

"You wait until the last second to take the shot, Oso."

"Nick, if I miss him, if there's a gust of wind or I flinch or sneeze, you're going to be right on him in open space and he's got a MAC-10."

Nick flicked off the safety on his Beretta 92FS semi-automatic nine-millimeter pistol, patted his pocket to confirm the presence of the two extra magazines, and said, "He can only kill me once. Just make sure you get to Gabrielle. Bret, how quick can you neutralize the sentry?"

"Seconds, but I'm going to get the truck moving and use it to approach."

"Keep your mic live. When you're in the truck, I'll move in," Nick said. "Oso, take your shot before I close in, then disassemble and get down here. We have to get through all of this in rapid succession, no warning."

"Copy that," Oso said.

"Suppressors on, safeties off, gentlemen," Bret said.

"Move in 30 seconds," Nick said.

The plain white full-size pickup was parked horizontally at the edge of the dirt path, blocking unauthorized access from those who sought to enter the property on wheels. The man behind the steering wheel was tasked with identifying and impeding any intruders who appeared on foot. The sun overhead generated stifling heat inside the cabin of the vehicle, forcing the driver to keep the windows down, when the engine and air conditioning were not running, when he was not walking a route around the perimeter of the property and silently considering any and all options to quell the unavoidable boredom and unbearable monotony.

While the guard remained seated in the truck, Bret crawled through the ditch below the visual range of the side and rear view mirrors and unseen by the guard on the side of the building. He deactivated the safety on his pistol and whispered, "On your toes, everybody." He pulled himself onto the road, scraping his stomach against the pavement, and picked up a handful of gravel. "Do you have eyes on him, Oso?"

Looking through the scope of the rifle, Oso said, "I can see him. He's dozing off; windows down, no phone."

Bret flung the gravel into the air and drew his pistol as the rocks landed in the bed of the truck, rattling off of the metal and startling the driver. The man opened the door and turned toward the rear of the vehicle and Bret stood quickly, firing three shots into his chest, the suppressor reducing the sound to a dull *thwack* each time.

"Oh, come on," Bret said when the man clutched his chest without falling.

The guard pulled for his breath and raised his MAC-10, the same fully automatic firearm carried by his ally at the side of the building, but was unable to pull the trigger before Bret fired again and struck flesh, the bullet entering his right shoulder and causing him to drop the weapon. When he righted himself, Bret fired a fifth shot into his forehead and the guard dropped to the ground in a small cloud of blood.

"One down," Bret said. He dropped to a knee beside the body and tore open the shirt, exposing the Kevlar vest on the chest of the guard. "Kevlar vest. It stopped all three center mass shots. He had a MAC-10 that I'm grabbing. Be ready to move, Nick." Bret sifted through the guard's pockets, then jumped into the bench seat of the truck and found the keys in the ignition. He started the engine, pulled the door closed, and said, "I'm moving."

Nick moved quickly in a crouch, his suppressed Beretta drawn, partially obscured by the overgrown, unkempt grass and weeds in the surrounding field. Bret shifted the transmission into first gear and slowly rolled up the dirt path toward the orphanage. The guard on the right side of the building turned toward the approaching truck and reached for a walkie-talkie.

He moved faster, closing the distance to a hundred feet, and Oso watched as the guard spoke into his radio, holding the MAC-10 in his left hand with the muzzle pointed to the ground.

"Slow down, Nick," Oso said softly and Nick complied, inching forward with the pistol still aimed at the guard.

Oso breathed deeply, slowly, and steadied the rifle. He breathed once more and waited for the exhale to squeeze the trigger. The .223 Remington round fired and the bullet moved through the barrel, then exited the suppressor with a *whack*, striking the guard in the center of his back and sending fragments of the boat-tail hollow-point into his chest cavity.

"Two down," Oso said. "I'm coming down. Right behind you, Nick."

"Copy," Nick said. He stood and sprinted toward the front of the building but stopped at the sound of Bret's voice.

"Stop!" Bret said into the earpiece. "Third guy just came out."

Calvin walked onto the porch and removed the phone from his pocket. Spencer's iPhone buzzed and Nick allowed the call to be routed to voicemail.

Nick turned away from the corner and, with his head tucked toward his shoulder, said, "Bret, let me know if he goes back inside." He looked to the mountainside and saw Oso moving closer.

Calvin spotted the truck headed toward the building and started down the concrete steps, speaking into the portable radio. "Where are you going? Don't leave the road!" Calvin shouted.

"He's coming down the steps," Bret said. "I'm stopping. It'll draw him over here to see what's going on."

Bret rolled to a stop as Calvin reached the bottom of the steps and started walking through the grass toward the truck. He slouched in the seat and turned away from Calvin. "How do you want to play this, Nick?"

"Hang on," Nick said. He unlocked Spencer's iPhone and dialed the number for Calvin.

Calvin stopped and answered the call. "Yeah?"

Nick pressed the microphone to his chest and said, "Hey," leaving the sound muffled and virtually unintelligible.

"Spencer, I can't hardly hear you. Where are you? We've been calling for hours."

"How's the girl?" Nick asked, mimicking Spencer's accent and raspy voice.

"She's fine, last I saw. Where are you?"

"Go check," Nick said.

Calvin turned and jogged up the steps and back into the large open lobby. He looked in toward Gabi and said, "She's pissed off but she's fine. Fiery little thing."

"Good," Nick said. "Come out to the truck."

"I didn't know that was you. Where's your man?"

"Stay on the line," Nick said.

Calvin descended the steps and Nick turned to Oso, who was now behind him, and motioned for him to follow. Oso acknowledged the direction and Nick turned the corner, his gun up, moving quickly and unseen.

Nick slowed as he drew near and said into the phone, "Turn around."

Calvin spun around and Nick fired a single shot between his eyes.

Bret opened the door and jogged to the place where Calvin had fallen and tore open his shirt. "No vest," he said.

Nick replaced the magazine in his Beretta with a fresh one, removed the suppressor and handed it to Oso, and said, "Take care of these two. Collect their weapons, phones, whatever they have. I'm going in for Gabi."

"Watch your six," Bret said.

Nick scaled the steps, the Beretta in his hand, and stopped at the doorway. "Gabrielle?" he called out.

"Nick?" she responded. "Nick?" she repeated, this time louder.

Nick turned the corner and entered the room, dark, musty, and empty, with Gabrielle restrained in the chair against the opposite wall. He raced toward her and said, "Thank God."

"How did you find me?" she asked.

Nick dropped the Beretta on the table, pulled a multipurpose knife from his pocket and sliced the cable ties on each of her wrists, setting her free for the first time in nineteen hours. He pulled her to her feet and embraced her, holding her tighter as each thought of what might have been moved through his mind, then pulled back, kissed the top of her head, and said, "Tell me you're okay."

"I'm fine," she said. Then she added, "I think."

Nick pulled back and locked eyes with her, seeing the bruise on her cheek, her swollen lip, the tinge of red blood on her teeth. He tried to speak but felt his throat close and pulled her close again, nearly lifting her off the ground, his cheek touching hers. "You're safe now," he said.

"Nick, what did you just do?"

He looked around the room and said, "Let's just say I can do things other people can't."

"What's all this about?" Gabi asked. "The poker game?"

"That and a million other things," Nick said into her ear. He rested his forehead on hers and said, "I don't know everything yet but I will. I promise."

Phil emerged from the door at the front of the room that led to the basement, raising his revolver toward Nick's back. The movement caught Gabi's eye. She broke away, shoved Nick aside with her left arm, and picked up his Beretta from the table.

Her first shot hit Phil in the chest, throwing him backward a step and causing him to drop the gun. Nick turned to see the second shot miss wide and land in the wall but her third struck Phil in the throat. His eyes went wide and his mouth fell open as he dropped to the ground clutching his throat. Blood poured from the wound and ran through his fingers and down his arm, causing him to choke as he struggled for oxygen in his final seconds.

Nick took the gun from Gabi's shaking hand and set it on the table.

She looked up at Nick, managed a nervous smile, and said, "My daddy always made sure I knew how to shoot."

Nick looked back to the front of the room, then again to Gabi, tucked her hair behind her ear and said, "You just saved my life."

"Now we're even," she said, and embraced him again, placing her head on his chest.

Bret and Oso ran through the doorway and into the room.

Bret saw the body of the previously unknown fourth man, then saw Nick and Gabi at the back of the room. "You two okay, Hawk?"

"We're fine," Nick replied without turning around.

Gabi stepped back and looked to the front of the room. Squinting to see through the lowlight, she asked, "Is that Bret?"

Watching Bret go through Phil's pockets, Nick said, "Yeah. That's our friend Oso, too."

Oso waved from the doorway and said, "Nice to finally meet you, Gabi."

Puzzled, having processed Bret's question, Gabi looked up at Nick and asked, "Why did he call you 'Hawk'?"

Nick ignored the question and said, "We need to get out of here." He retrieved the Beretta from the table, took her by the hand, and led her toward the exit.

"I'll get the Suburban," Bret said. He was first down the steps and ran through the field to the dirt road, turning onto the two-lane and disappearing out of sight.

"So do you guys do this sort of thing often?" Gabi asked.

Nick looked at Oso and said, "She gets taken hostage, has to shoot one of her kidnappers, and she still has jokes. Unbelievable."

Oso looked past Nick to Gabi and said, "We've heard a lot about you over the years."

To Nick, Gabi asked, "We?"

"What all did they have on them?" Nick asked Oso.

"The two outside guys had Kevlar vests and MAC-10s. We got their phones and radios. What do you want to do about the truck?"

"Torch it," Nick said.

"You all are talking about this like it's nothing," Gabi said.

"It's not exactly new," Oso said. "It'll be fine though. We're just glad you're okay."

Bret sped onto the dirt road and turned into the field in front of the building. When he skidded to a stop, Nick said, "Let's get packed up and back to the house." To Oso, he asked, "You got the truck?"

"On it," Oso said. He opened the back lid of the Suburban and removed a red one-gallon can of gasoline and a Zippo lighter. He turned to Gabi and said, "This is the fun part."

Oso covered the exterior of the white truck with gasoline and emptied the can in the cabin.

"I'll be right back," Gabi said to Nick and walked up to Oso. She held out her hand and asked, "Do you mind?"

"Not at all," Oso said and handed her the lighter.

Gabi stepped away from the truck and spun the flint wheel. She watched the flame dance on the wick and tossed the lighter into the cabin. The fire roared to life and black smoke billowed out the windows, the shallow orange pool moving across the hood and onto the roof.

"I think that's our cue," Bret said out the window of the Suburban. "Let's roll. We need to go back around to the other side of the mountain and run up to grab Oso's gear."

Oso slid into the passenger seat and Gabi climbed into the backseat behind him. Nick stood outside the SUV and looked at the orphanage.

That's where you almost lost her. Never forget that.

"Nick, let's go, man," Bret said.

Nick opened the door and rested in the backseat beside Gabi, who slid to the center and pulled his right arm around her.

"Let's go home, everyone," Nick said.

"Can I stay with you tonight? My bedroom walls are full of bullet holes," Gabi said to Nick. Bret glanced at the rear view mirror and into the back seat. Nick saw him raise his eyebrows but did not verbally acknowledge it.

"You are going to be by my side until all of this is over. My home is always your home," Nick said.

My home is wherever you are.

"Bret, you're with me," Nick said. The four stood on the porch of the farmhouse, the spoils of battle still in the back of the Suburban waiting to be unpacked. "Oso, you mind sticking here with Gabi for a bit?"

"That's perfect," Gabi said. She looked at Oso and said, "It'll give me a chance to pick his brain."

"Good luck, sir," Nick said and slapped him on the shoulder.

"Where are you going?" Gabi asked.

Bret took a flashlight from his backpack and answered instead of Nick. "We need to go for a walk."

Gabi looked at Nick, said, "You'll fill me in later. I need a drink," and walked through the side entrance with Oso following.

Nick and Bret walked around the house and into the field, moving fast in the direction of the creek.

"What exactly do you plan on doing?" Bret asked.

"Your guess is as good as mine."

Bret pressed his hand into Nick's chest and momentarily stopped him. "Before we get down there, you need to know that I'm going in there with you. I'm not staying outside. There's no one to watch for. There's nothing to secure. You aren't dealing with him on your own again."

"Understood."

Moving again, Bret said, "I can't believe she took out the fourth guy."

"You should have seen her work. Two out of three from that distance. I couldn't believe it."

They moved sideways down the slope and onto the bank. Bret switched on the flashlight, held it in his left hand with his thumb at the bottom of the metal case, and drew his pistol with his right hand, stacking it on top of his left wrist in the classic tactical position, and led Nick into the cave. "How far inside are we going?" Bret asked.

"Far enough that the lantern will be the only source of light there is," Nick said with his own gun raised.

After ninety seconds of consistent movement, Nick turned back to the entrance and was unable locate a source of light. "We're getting close," he said.

Bret continued moving forward, scanning the ground and the path ahead with the flashlight. "Nick," he said. "You need to see this."

On the ground next to the cave wall amidst a smattering of dried blood sat a brown Panama hat with a black band. Nick picked up the hat and sorted through the contents left inside: a half-empty pack of Marlboro Reds, two broken cable ties, and a wad of crumpled duct tape.

"How?" Bret asked.

"Look at this," Nick said. He held the cable ties under the light and said, "The break is perfectly smooth. It was cut."

"It's impossible."

"Apparently not." Nick emptied the hat onto the floor and ran his hand around the sweatband, stopping when he felt a surface anomaly at the front. He pulled down the band and a single razor blade dropped into his hand.

Nick held up the blade and said, "Found his master key."

"Do we need to be preparing for a rematch?"

"He's long gone. For now, anyway," Nick said.

"You're sure about that?"

"Think about it. Would you want to stick around right now?"

Gabi eased herself into the porcelain tub and the hot bath that Nick had insisted on drawing for her started to work its magic on the soreness and fatigue throughout her body. Any effort, any finger lifted, would be considered unacceptable, he told her. She was to rest, relax, decompress, and heal. Everything else would come soon enough.

The antique tub was housed in a small room off the kitchen, one of the few salvaged artifacts from decades before. It had been used only a handful of times since the purchase and renovation of the farmhouse, mostly by Mia. Nick stood outside the door, his back against the wall, the tub out of view.

"How are you feeling?"

"Like all my troubles are melting away for the moment. Thank you," she said.

"We need to talk about all this," Nick said.

"We do," Gabi sighed. "But not tonight."

Nick touched the back of his head to the wall and mouthed, "Thank God."

"Do you need anything?" he asked.

"I think you've done more than enough for the day, Nick Burke."

He heard the water slosh in the tub. "I left my robe and some towels in there with you. I'll get the bedroom upstairs ready in a minute."

She drummed her fingers on the side of the tub and said, "Every time certain subjects arise, you always say that you'll tell me all about it someday."

"I know," he said softly.

"Just promise me it'll be someday soon."

"I promise," Nick said.

The bath that she intended to last for twenty minutes continued on for nearly an hour, warmed up twice with fresh hot water along the way. She stepped out of the tub and dried her body with the towels, wincing when she touched her swollen lip and the bruise on her cheek, and pulled on the soft cotton terry robe that was borrowed from Nick.

He was assembling the array of pillows on the queen bed in the guest bedroom when she entered and sat on the bed.

"Feeling a little better, I hope," Nick said.

"Much," she said. "Can I grab something to sleep in?"

"Of course," he said and motioned toward the master bedroom at the other end of the hall. "Just steal whatever you like out of the dresser."

She looked over her shoulder on her way out of the room and said, "Don't I always?"

"If there's anyone alive that doesn't have to ask, it's you," he said to her as she walked down the hall.

Gabi returned a moment later dressed in another of his t-shirts and a pair of gym shorts. Her skin still glistened from the heat of the bath and Nick found himself unable to prevent his gaze from lingering at the woman standing in the doorway.

She touched her lip and said, "Does this look as bad as it feels?"

"I don't even know where to begin, Gabrielle. What happened to you, what you saw, what you had to do, I just don't know what to say right now."

"You did what you had to do, Nick, and so did I. We can talk about the rest later." She walked into the room and sat on the side of the bed next to him. "Someday, right?"

"Someday," he said. He stood and turned down the corner of the sheets and said, "I know you're physically and emotionally and mentally exhausted. Get some sleep. When you wake up, today's nightmare will finally be over."

She touched her hand to his leg and said, "That sounds good to me."

He stopped at the door, turned to Gabi and said, "No one will ever touch you like that again."

"Let's say you got there right in the nick of time," she said and flashed a smile with intimate knowledge of how Nick loathed the use of his name in such ways.

"Only you." He smiled back, said, "Goodnight, Gabi," and closed the door behind him.

Two hours of silence, tossing and turning, pacing, a mental review of every action of the day, a detailed parsing of every word spoken by Spencer St. Clair, a glance at the bedroom door behind which Gabi was asleep. He left his own door open, an unnecessary and unwanted barrier between himself and her.

He picked up his cell phone, opened the music player, and pushed the earbud headphones into his ears. The song was a new age instrumental: "Three Bikes in the Sky" by Tangerine Dream, the song to which he listened when deep thought and reflection and analysis were needed. He pressed play and listened to the synthesized sounds fade in.

None of this happens if she doesn't get on the plane.

He felt responsible for the marks on her face, the pain that she had endured, and the nightmares and flashbacks that were sure to come. She had taken a human life, albeit far from an innocent one, in order to protect his, an unthinkable burden to bear for most people. He lamented taking her to the poker game in Boston. He flashed back to the moment at the orphanage when he first ran to her while she was strapped down to the chair. No matter how fast he moved, he remembered, it was not fast enough. Every second was too long.

The song was halfway through.

Spencer St. Clair was in the wind, tending to his wounds and likely hell-bent on revenge. Daniel Staal would soon be aware of Spencer's absence. In other words, Spencer and his status aside, nothing in the big picture had changed.

His phone buzzed with a notification, a text from Micah:

Talk ASAP. 911. Info on Staal.

The song ended and Nick rolled off of the bed and walked to the window. He removed the headphones and replied to Micah:

In the a.m. I'll be in touch.

Following the events of the previous two days, the information on Staal felt unimportant. It could wait.

No, he thought, it *would* wait.

What was truly important, most important, was asleep at the other end of the hall.

Gabi turned the knob and slowly pulled the door open. She looked down the hallway and saw Nick gazing out the window, his face illuminated by the moonlight. He appeared contemplative, even sad, she thought, and considered closing the door and lying down again but tip-toed down the hall toward his bedroom.

Nick turned from the window when she appeared.

"Hi," she said from the doorway.

"Hey. Are you okay?"

She leaned her shoulder, then her head, against the door jamb. "I can't sleep either. Would you mind if I stayed in here with you tonight?"

"Of course not. Come on in."

She walked to the right side of the bed, remembering that Nick always slept on the left, and slid underneath the sheets. "You, too."

Nick eased into the bed beside her and pulled the cover over his legs. "You're safe now," he said.

"Yes, I am," she answered. She yawned and repeated, "Yes, I am."

Gabrielle wrapped her arms around him and rested her head on his chest. As the minutes passed, he felt the tension in her body release. He listened as the rhythm of her breathing fell even and grew shallow, the first stage of sleep setting in as the dawn of a new day drew nearer.

Nick leaned down and gently kissed her forehead, then rested his head onto hers.

Into the night, he whispered, "Only you can save me."

17

Nick woke two hours before Gabi, still drowsy, roused by another text from Micah that was flagged as urgent. While she slept soundly, his night was restless. A morose mood courtesy of morbid thoughts waxed and waned, the detailed, if not obsessive, analysis of every word, event, and option interrupted only by momentary respites to pull her closer, kiss her forehead, and listen to her breathe, appreciating the grace and mercy and providence that allowed for such things.

Standing in the kitchen, he dialed the number for Micah. "Do you have any idea what time it is?" he asked when Micah answered.

"9 a.m. Eastern," a matter-of-fact Micah said. "I'm always on time."

"Did Bret and Oso fill you in on everything?"

"They did."

"The whole story?"

"Every bit of it."

Nick groaned and ran a hand through his hair. "Can this wait?"

Micah paused a bit and said, "Not for long."

He had moved from the kitchen, walking and talking and now leaning on the post at the bottom of the stairs and looking up to the door of the master bedroom where Gabi remained asleep. "I'll call you for a videoconference later and you can update me from start to finish," he lowered his voice and said.

Micah caught the change in volume. "How is she, Nick?"

"She's Gabi: Fierce, independent, strong, brilliant, sarcastic, un-breakable, and beautiful. An abduction and shots fired won't change any of that, even if it would change most people, myself included."

"I mean is she all right?"

Nick moved back into the kitchen and said, "She's alive and breath-ing. She's still too close to it to appreciate the gravity of it all. She's still in the blissful gray area where there are more questions than answers and doesn't know that filling in the blanks may bring more darkness than light. If you were on the other end of this, what would you think?"

There was a sharp thud on the other end of the line.

"What was that?"

"That was my head hitting the desk," said Micah. "You're going to tell her, aren't you? All of it."

In a stern whisper, Nick said, "She's neck-deep in it now and doesn't even know it." He took a breath and continued, "She's deserved to know all along, Micah. How she reacts is out of my hands."

"Do you think she can handle it?"

"There's nothing she can't handle. It's me I'm not so sure about."

"Good luck, bro."

"Just tell me one thing. On a scale from one to Chernobyl, how bad is what you have to tell me?"

"Grab your hazmat suit," Micah said.

Nick looked to the ceiling and shook his head. "I'll call in a couple of hours. I have breakfast to make."

Her reflection in the mirror over the sink in the remodeled master bathroom, a repurposed and overhauled room in the center of the sec-ond floor, was startling. The swelling on her lip was decreasing but the bruise on her cheek was substantially darker, the blood having settled after a night of sleep. She winced when she touched the trouble spot and turned her head to examine further. She rolled her wrists, which were still sore from the cable ties, and rubbed the back of her legs. The hours of restriction in the wooden chair had taken a toll.

Some leave of absence, she thought.

She wondered if the Dr. McLane that returned would bear any resemblance to the one who required leave in the first place, for better or worse, and if her time away was a break in the action or a new beginning.

One day ago, she was tied to a chair in an abandoned orphanage that resembled the set of a horror film.

One day prior, she was facing the uncertainty of tomorrow.

One day earlier, she had squeezed a trigger and taken the life of a man who had held her captive, stricken her with a closed fist, and was prepared to kill the man who was there to set her free.

At the moment, she thought, she needed a massage.

"You're as beautiful as ever," Nick said from the doorway, momentarily startling her.

She looked over to him and then back to the mirror. "Are you kidding? I look like I just went twelve rounds."

"But you won."

"*We* won," she corrected. She saw the darkness under his eyes, the fatigue within them, and asked, "You didn't sleep much, did you?"

"I got all the sleep I needed."

"Liar," she said with a crooked smile, still looking in the mirror and running a hand through her hair. "I woke up twice and you were still awake."

"You never looked up at me so how would you know that?"

She turned from the mirror and asked, "If you were asleep, how would you know I never looked up at you?" Looking forward again, she said, "Your heart wouldn't be racing like that if you were asleep either."

The real issue is why it was racing.

"You haven't eaten in two days. Let's have breakfast."

"I really don't think I need to go out looking like this," she said and motioned toward her eye.

"Just meet me in the kitchen. You never know what might be waiting for you there," Nick said and returned to the first floor.

A moment later, Gabi descended the staircase and turned the corner into the dining room. Nick was sitting in one of two chairs on the side of the table nearest the hallway entrance.

He looked over his shoulder toward the table and said, "Not a bad spread, right?"

Examining the options, she said, "Biscuits, gravy, bacon, sausage, stewed apples, eggs; this looks like a buffet."

"I try to be a generous host and this is technically a farmhouse. Grab a plate."

"It's not exactly heart-healthy, you know. I'm going to have to run for a week after this."

"That all depends on how you define what's good for the heart, Dr. McLane."

They dined for half an hour and cleared the table for another fifteen minutes before Nick's phone buzzed with another text from Micah, one that contained only a question mark.

Am I really about to do this?

Gabi was reclined on the couch, staring at the ceiling, when Nick found a sliver of space beside her and sat down.

"Do you think we're unshakeable?" he asked.

"Unshakeable, unbreakable, unbeatable," Gabi said.

"Do you trust me?"

"Completely." She propped herself up on her elbows and asked, "What are you about to tell me?"

Nick stood, held out his hand and said, "Come with me."

Gabi took his hand and stood. "Where are we going?"

"To a place with no more shadows," he said and led her into the dining room.

Standing between the table and the wall that divided the room from the hallway, Nick looked toward the polished wooden bookshelves that lined the wall that was shared with his office. The shelves were divided into four sections from left to right, five rows per section, packed with novels, biographies, a legal library, and a variety of reference volumes.

"Tell me what you see," he said to Gabi.

She looked at him out of the side of her eye, then forward again and, with the tone of a question, said, "Your library." Then she looked forward and added, "Although I've always wondered how many of these you've actually read."

"Almost all of them," Nick said. "But that's not the point. What if, like so many other things in life, there was more than meets the eye?"

There was a moment of silence and then Gabi said, "I'm waiting," almost singing the words in the process.

"I know. You've waited long enough."

He stood at the center of the four shelves and pulled a three-inch thick reference volume from the end of the third row in the third section. Rather than being removed, the book simply moved toward him on a track and slid on a right angle in front of the others. Pulled to the forefront in its place was a previously concealed ten-digit keypad and Nick typed in the pass code: 1351211495.

As he pressed the enter key, he turned to Gabi and said, "Welcome to someday."

First, there was a click, then the sound of a motor whirring to life.

"Nick?" Gabi said, allowing the rest of her thought to remain silent.

The shelves separated, the second and third moving apart from one another, stacking in front of the first and fourth that slid back to create the necessary space.

Gabi's eyes grew wide. Her mouth fell open. She looked at Nick and asked, "What is this?"

Nick turned to her and said, "This is Halcyon."

On the left side of the now-revealed space was a black wall adorned with an array of weaponry: pistols, semi-automatic and fully automatic rifles, ammunition, and an area reserved for flash grenades that needed to be restocked. The MAC-10s and Kevlar vests confiscated from the men outside the orphanage would soon be added. On the right side was a flat-screen monitor topped with a webcam, a desktop computer tower, laser printer, keyboard and mouse, all neatly arranged on a standing desk. On the monitor was a logo consisting of a silver shield, a black, bold-faced capital letter "H" bordered in white and emblazoned in the center, captioned with the word Halcyon. In the center of the room, a single red rose was suspended from the ceiling.

Nick stepped in front of the computer, double-clicked the icon for the encrypted videoconferencing program and the light on the webcam turned green. He selected the contact for Micah and connected the call.

When Micah appeared on-screen, he said, "It's about time, Nick." He then caught a glimpse of the human analog in the background and leaned in his chair to the left, as if he could see around Nick. "Is that Gabi?" he asked.

"That's Gabi," Nick confirmed.

Gabi looked at Nick and said, "Does *everyone* know who I am?"

"Pretty much. Come over here."

Gabi moved in front of the camera and Nick said, "Gabi, this is Micah, our researcher, ancillary support, and information guru extraordinaire. Micah, meet Gabi."

"Well, it's nice to finally meet you. You're all we've heard about for years," Micah said.

"Years?" Gabi asked and looked at Nick, who shrugged and turned back to the screen.

"You're a well-known commodity with us," Micah said to Gabi. Then to Nick: "Are you ready to get caught up?"

"You can stay and listen in to everything, if you want, or you can just pretend that this was all a dream and go chill on the couch. It's up to you," Nick said.

Still processing the scene before her, Gabi said, "I think I'll stay."

"Let's do it," Nick said. "What do you have?"

"You said you wanted everything I could get on our friend Daniel Staal and it doesn't disappoint."

"You make it sound like we're about to peel an onion."

"More like going down Lewis Carroll's proverbial rabbit hole. There's no going back from this, Nick."

"That's been the case for a while now."

"All right. Staal is everything that we knew he was from the outset. The money, the porn, the trafficking, it all ties together. He's got his fingerprints on everything and it's global, not just domestic. He burst onto the scene with legitimate, innocent companies, made a big splash with invisible investors and hasn't looked back but he has a way of staying almost invisible any time he wants to do so."

"He said he was Scandinavian so that makes sense. His little henchman, Murdoc, is a fair-haired Euro, too."

"And with loyal people like Lucien working for him, and a security pro to remove any roadblocks..."

"He never gets his hands dirty and treats the world as his playground," Nick said, finishing Micah's thought. "How does a kid in his twenties just hit the ground running like this?"

Out of sight behind Nick, Gabi moved closer.

"Are you ready for the bombshell?"

"As ready as I'm gonna be," Nick said.

"Daniel Staal isn't his real name. It was legally changed when he turned eighteen."

Nick leaned forward on the desk and said, "Go on."

"He was born Daniel Kisho Sato."

Nick stepped back from the screen, ashen-faced. "Sato," he repeated. "Is he..." Nick said and allowed the question to trail off unfinished.

"Yes," Micah answered.

Seeing that Nick was shaken, Gabi placed her hand on his shoulder and asked, "Nick, what's wrong? You look like you've just seen a ghost."

"You want to unpack all this for her?" Micah asked.

"Grab a chair," Nick said to Gabi. To Micah, he asked, "How much does the boss know?"

"I thought I'd let you handle that."

Nick nodded and sat in a chair next to Gabi and still within the visual frame of the webcam.

"It's been years ago. We were still in undergrad at Radford, if that gives you an idea. There's a businessman with ties to the Japanese mafia running drugs into the country and using a little town in southern West Virginia to do it. He had the local police running protection for them or just looking the other way, all the stereotypical stuff. One of them wants out of the deal and ends up dead."

"I remember that. It was all over the news for months," Gabi said.

"This was all before my time," Micah said on the screen.

"Long story short, there was a witness the night the cop was killed. They framed a homeless man for the murder. The witness and her boyfriend were almost killed in a car accident, one of their friends was shot by the police chief before the feds swooped in and barely made it, and the guy at the head of it all was Yoshiro Sato, the man behind Sato Electronics."

"And the father of Daniel Staal," Micah added.

"What was the name of that town?" Nick asked Micah.

Micah clicked onto another screen on his monitor and answered, "Spring Creek."

Gabi took a moment to digest the story and said, "So Staal's father was connected to a crime that long ago and now his son is headed down the same road. It's that simple?"

"No. It's that complicated. It's more than just rotten fruit from the same poisoned family tree," Nick said.

"How so?" Gabi asked.

"The witness to the shooting was Lisa Taylor. Her father is Dallas Taylor, the founder and CEO of Tayco Pharmaceuticals."

Stunned, Gabi asked, "Your boss?"

"Yes, and Dallas Taylor is also the creator and financier of Halcyon."

The room fell silent for a moment, then Gabi asked, "So where's Sato now?"

"To be honest, I don't even know. The cops that were involved are all in jail, the last I knew. Sato was going to be sent back to Japan but got loose and has been in the wind ever since. It's just not a name I thought I would ever hear again."

"None of us did," Micah said.

"Micah, dig up everything you can from the archives about what happened back then. News articles, video clips, all of it. Let me know when it's ready. I'll talk to Dallas tonight."

"Aye-aye," Micah said.

Nick rubbed his eyes and said, "I'll be in touch," then flashed a thumbs-up to the screen before Micah disconnected.

Gabi got up from her chair, stood behind Nick and rubbed his neck. "Where do we go from here?"

"I don't know but I do like the sound of that," Nick said.

"The sound of what?" she asked.

"We."

The shelves now closed and the Halcyon command center again concealed, Nick sat in the chair behind the desk in his office with Gabi seated on the opposite side. The window facing the front yard was open, a cool, nighttime breeze blowing in and moving the curtains.

"I have so many questions," Gabi said.

"You'll have all the answers you can handle."

"Okay. I'll start slow. Why 'Halcyon'?"

"Dual meaning. It's a bird from Greek legend. They believed that it could calm the wind and waves but it was only temporary. There's a genus of kingfisher birds with that name now."

"And the second?"

"It's a word that refers to a period of time when things were calm and peaceful. For the most part, it's a reference to better days and happier times without the chaos and confusion."

Momentarily satisfied, she reclined in her chair, then leaned forward again and, flashing a curious smile, said, "You've got to tell me about the rose."

"The rose has been the symbol of secrecy for centuries. In the Middle Ages, meetings were held with a rose hanging from the ceiling as a reminder to everyone that they were sworn to secrecy. It's why intelligence agencies frequently use one as their emblem; secret brotherhoods that steal secrets and all. Halcyon exists in shadows. I just like the symbolism."

"Where do you get this stuff?"

"Mostly from those books that you were wondering if I've read or not," Nick said with a playful sneer. The ring of the videoconference software sounded and he said, "Hold that thought."

Nick connected the video call and the man who founded the project now known as Halcyon appeared on-screen.

"Good evening, Nick," Dallas said.

"You know I have to ask. Where are you this time?"

Dallas looked around the room and said, "A picturesque little villa in Paris right down the road from the *Jarden des Plantes*."

Nick looked across the desk to Gabi and said, "Botanical gardens from the seventeenth century." To Dallas, he asked, "What time is it there?"

Dallas checked his timepiece and said, "Almost 4 a.m."

"I don't know how you do it."

"What's that?" Dallas chuckled.

"The travel, the corporate work, the breakneck pace, day after day, it's unbelievable."

Dallas waved off the compliment, then straightened his polo shirt and asked, "Are you finally going to introduce me?"

Gabi looked up when she heard the question. Nick motioned for her to join him and she did so, pulling her chair to his side of the desk and into view of the camera.

"Gabi, meet the one and only Dallas Taylor of Tayco Pharmaceuticals. Dallas, the oft-discussed but always unseen Gabrielle."

"It's a pleasure to finally meet you, Dr. McLane," said a smiling Dallas. "Your reputation precedes you."

Gabi returned the grin and asked, "Personal or professional?"

"Both, I assure you," Dallas said. "You've been doing special things, both at Commonwealth and at Johnston Memorial. You should be very proud."

A stunned Gabi looked to Nick, who held up his hands in surrender. "The man has connections. He knows your professional work better than anyone, including me and probably you." He lowered his voice and said, "If it's important to me, it's important to him. That's why."

"The others gave me an overview of what all has taken place in the last few days. I'm just glad you're all right," Dallas said to Gabi.

"Nothing a few days of rest won't take care of. Thank you," she said.

"I can promise you one thing: The young man beside you would have done anything to see to that."

Gabi turned to Nick and said to Dallas, "Believe me, I know." To Nick, she said, "I'm going to go upstairs and let you two talk. Okay?" and allowed her hand to linger on top of his for a moment as she stood.

Nick nodded in agreement and Dallas said, "Goodnight, Dr. McLane."

"Call me Gabi," she said on her way out of the room and closed the door behind her.

Nick listened for Gabi to reach the top of the steps before he continued. "How much do you know about what went down?"

"Micah relayed some of the operational details from Bret and Oso but I was hoping you would fill in the blanks."

For fifteen minutes, Nick recounted in minute detail the events of the previous two days, from the scene at Gabrielle's house to the relation to Daniel Staal to the interrogation of the man responsible and, finally, the operation at the orphanage.

Decidedly serious and unsatisfied, Dallas said, "What aren't you telling me?"

"How much do you want to know?"

"If you are going to such great lengths to shield me from it, I need to know whatever it is."

Nick looked away from the camera and then back again. "Daniel Staal changed his name the minute he reached legal adult status. His given name is Daniel Kisho Sato."

The color drained from Dallas's face upon the utterance of the Sato surname. There was no additional clarification necessary. "My God," he said. "Nick, does this involve my daughter in any way?"

"If there's a connection somewhere, we haven't found it. So far, it's just a son following in the footsteps of his father. As far as we know, old man Sato has been off the grid for over a decade and I'd just as soon keep it that way."

"I want to be informed of every detail from this point forward. You have absolute freedom and trust in regards to taking action but I need to be kept in the loop for my own sanity."

"Yes, sir."

Visibly rattled, Dallas rubbed his face in a vain attempt to gather himself. "Is that all?"

"There's one more thing, and I've tried for hours to find a way to say this, so I'll just come right out with it."

Dallas drank from a bottle of water and said, "Proceed."

"Dallas, the man who came to my house was Staal's hired gun chief of security."

Dallas furrowed his brow in anticipation of the full impact. "I figured as much."

"It was Spencer St. Clair."

A pensive Dallas Taylor was left speechless, looking away from his screen and lost in a place that was unreachable for Nick. The silence remained suspended in the air like a storm cloud while Dallas carefully constructed his response.

Finally, he spoke. "I'm going to ask you a question and I want a simple, direct and honest response. Could you have terminated Spencer and still managed to locate Gabrielle?"

"In a word, no," Nick said. "I don't care what he says. He didn't do this for Staal. He did it for himself, for the money, just like the Spencer of old. This was a way to pad his pockets and satisfy Daniel's demands all in one. If he sends us into a trap but he's already dead, we'd never have found her in time. It was a calculated risk but I had to err on the side of caution to make absolutely certain that we found her and got her out and I won't apologize for that."

"I understand and I agree with you. But if you get another opportunity..."

"With extreme prejudice," Nick interjected. "You have my word."

"Do we have any idea where he has been for all these years?"

"With the exception of his time with Staal, no. Nor do we know where he's going."

"I see," a resigned Dallas said. "I'll leave you with one thought and then I'm off to bed."

Nick rubbed the base of his neck and said, "I hope it's something positive."

"It certainly is. That young lady loves you, just as you love her. Take care of one another."

"We will. You have my word."

"Goodnight, son."

"Goodnight, Dallas."

When the call ended, Nick reached for a notepad and pen, then scribbled and underlined two words: Spring Creek. He stood and walked to the window and looked out into the front yard, listening for ambient sounds of the serene environment around him, a stark contrast to the chaos that so often resided both around and with him. He decided on a late-night walk to the bridge should insomnia set in, provided he could do so without disturbing or alarming Gabi.

Nick exited the office and closed the door, then looked up to see her standing at the railing on the second floor. "Is everything okay?" she asked.

"I'm not sure much of anything is okay," Nick said, his voice tired and dejected.

She leaned on the railing and said, "Listen, Nick. I'm okay, you're okay, and we're okay. The rest will be, too."

He stood next to the door that led to the center of the porch and leaned against the wall. "I hope you're right."

Gabi began to descend the stairs, walking toward him and keeping her eyes matched with his, and Nick stepped forward to meet her. She held his face in her hand and pulled him to her, then kissed his forehead and said, "Only *you* can save *me*."

Before Nick could respond, Gabi took his hand in hers, said, "Come on. Let's get some sleep," and led him up the staircase.

18

Early morning runs were most common in the spring and fall, free of the extreme cold of winter and the humid heat of summer that ran counter to his preference. The air was cool in the moments after sunrise, the grass in the front yard slick with dew. A dense fog hung at the top of the mountains at the edge of the field across the road, obscuring the rolling peaks and adding a haunting air of mystery to a life where, in the present, the supply far outweighed the demand.

After gently easing himself out of the bed to avoid disturbing Gabi, Nick dressed for both the temperate climate and the activity: black sweatpants, a black hooded sweatshirt, and his black Iowa Hawkeyes hat, his standard issue wardrobe and monochrome palette. He chose to walk through the front yard rather than jog, his destination only a quarter-mile away. At the end of the driveway, he turned right, away from the bridge, and chose to walk the upcoming route but jog on the return. Awaiting him was a visual, an existential alarm clock of sorts that served to refocus him in times of uncertainty, confusion, or distress, and reminded him not only of the reality of an ultimate purpose but also the necessity of the continued, unending search for the same.

He was not yet out of the front yard when Gabi awoke inside the farmhouse. She sensed the void beside her before she reached into the empty space and called out to him. With no response, she walked downstairs and peered out the door in the center of the porch in time to see him disappear from view, moving away from the house, his hands in his pockets, scanning the area around him with his head on the proverbial swivel.

She ran up the steps and into the bedroom, threw on a borrowed sweatshirt, and scrambled to find her shoes.

"I don't even get to stretch," she mumbled while pulling on the first sneaker.

Nick was nearly out of view when Gabi reached the end of the driveway and stepped out onto Moccasin Valley Road. Walking along the narrow berm, she watched him stay right at the fork in the road and stop to examine the space beyond the shoulder, as if searching for a particular location, before continuing forward.

When she lost sight of him, she increased her pace from leisurely and curious to brisk, then jogged to the fork and found him further along, nearing a bridge that crossed the Big Moccasin Creek downstream from the farmhouse. He stopped a second time and craned his neck in search of the desired visual, then stepped to the left and rested with his hands in his pockets, wholly unaware of her presence.

As she approached, she waited for him to notice, to see her, to smile, to speak, to invite her to join him, anything to acknowledge and address his sudden secret morning excursion but his attention was elsewhere, lost in a place that she was unable to identify, much less access. A minivan passed her, its driver offering a polite Southern wave on his way. When he accelerated to climb the slight incline, blue exhaust flew from the rusted muffler with a roar and a rattle but Nick stood stockstill.

Gabi closed the gap to twenty yards before slowing again to a walk while Nick remained at rest, silent, focused. She sidled up to him and edged into his field of vision.

"You're up early," Nick said without looking. "I didn't mean to wake you."

"You didn't," she said. "After two nights I'm already used to you being there. When I looked outside and saw you wandering off this way, I wanted to make sure you were okay."

Without moving his head, Nick looked at Gabi out of the corner of his eye and, with a smirk, said, "You were curious."

"Maybe a little," she said and then stood quietly beside him.

His gaze was fixed upon the strip of land that began at the shoulder of the road and sloped downward before flattening into the creek bed, cluttered with grass and weeds and brush that was in the process of being overwhelmed by lush green kudzu and trees that grew from the bank, their branches suspended over the water of Big Moccasin Creek. They listened to sound of the water flowing by, still high from the recent rainfall, sloshing over rocks and carrying the small fish and bullfrog tadpoles downstream in its gentle but persistent current.

Minutes later, she asked, "Where are we supposed to be looking anyway?"

Nick leaned close and pointed to direct her attention to a point on the slope, on an angle that allowed maximum visibility from their position, where a thin wire fence stood lopsided and tangled with thorns and bushes. The two headstones encased by the fence were little more than an unkempt afterthought to the surviving family, eroded by decades of neglect and exposure to the elements, the names of the decedents no longer discernible.

"I don't really know."

She squinted and stepped forward. "Are those headstones?"

"The last remnants of lives that passed into eternity, north or south, long ago," Nick said.

Gabi touched his arm and asked, "Who were they?"

"I have no idea. I was wandering around out here one day, just exploring, you might say, and spotted them on the bank." He turned to her for the first time and said, "I end up here fairly often."

She looked back to the gravestones and asked, "Have you ever tried to get down there to them?"

"Between the ticks, the snakes, and whatever else might be in the middle of all that, I'll just keep my distance. I took pictures with a zoom lens a couple of years ago but the names are gone. The headstone on the left is about to topple over. Too many years of erosion and bad weather and no one here to look after them."

Perplexed, Gabi asked, "And you don't know who they are?"

"No," Nick said and exhaled slowly. "That's the point, Gabrielle. I don't know who they are and it doesn't matter in the least. It makes no difference who they are, who they were, what they did, anything. They're more mystery than memory and a stark reminder than an inheritance means very little without a legacy." He turned to her and continued, "That's why I come here. These people, whoever they are, are a reminder."

Her confusion having turned into concern, looking up at him, Gabi asked, "A reminder of what, Nick?"

"It's a reminder to refuse to go quietly in life. Make your presence felt in the world. Defy the odds and the standards and the judicious expectations of a lazy and complacent world. Treat convention as a weakness and not a building block." He looked again to the headstones, then back to Gabi. "In other words, find it unacceptable to be easily forgotten and washed away by the sands of time."

Incredulous, Gabi said, "I don't think you have to worry about that."

"Maybe," Nick whispered, both to Gabi and to himself.

"Wherever they are, I'm sure they're glad that you think about them."

"I hope so."

"Come on," Gabi said and grabbed his arm, pulling him further down the road in the direction of the bridge.

"Where are we going?"

"I didn't even know this bridge was here. I've never gone further than your house on this road."

She turned and pushed herself up onto the concrete barrier and looked over her shoulder to the creek.

"What are you doing?" he asked with a smile.

She motioned for him to move closer. He stood positioned between her legs, her arms around his neck. "Why haven't you ever brought me here?"

He looked away, over her shoulder, and said, "I don't know," then looked back to her and added, "But you're here now."

"I'm here now," she repeated.

Nick closed his eyes and said, "I almost lost you." His leg began to tremble, burning through nervous tension.

Gabi pulled him closer, touching her forehead to his. "Look at me." When he did, she said, "I'm here."

He brushed her swollen lip with his thumb, then leaned in and kissed the bruise on her cheek. "What would I ever do without you?"

"You'll never have to find out," she said. "But I'm sure you'd get along just fine," she added with a lighthearted lilt.

Nick reached up and held her arm, then guided her hand to his own and placed her fingers on the base of his wrist, touching his radial artery. "Do you know what that is, Dr. McLane?"

"In my highly educated opinion as a cardiologist, that's your radial pulse."

"No," Nick said. "That's you. Since the very first day, sitting at the fountain outside Jefferson Hall, it's you. Us against the world."

"That's us," she said and hopped back to the ground from the railing. She reached for his hand and said, "Let's go home."

Standing on the back porch and looking into the field that was in desperate need of a mow, Nick sipped from a bottle of root beer and said, "How can everything look this calm in the middle of a life that is so chaotic?"

Gabi furrowed her brow and said, "Your secret is out, Nick. Don't act like this chaos is anything new."

"It's not new, just different. The regular chaos is manageable."

She looked away from him and said, "Do you hear that?"

Nick scanned the immediate area and took in the silence. "Hear what?"

Gabi arched her back, stretched, and yawned. "Exactly. After everything that's happened in the last week, it's nice to hear absolutely nothing."

"I won't argue with that."

She took in a deep breath, tasting the freshness in the air that comes only after night of rainfall. "You really should try to do something with all this. At least spruce it up a little."

"Gabrielle, I am many things in this world. Farmer Nick is not one of them. I'd have to hire that out."

"I think you could pull off the straw hat and overalls," she said, holding back a laugh.

"This is unbearable." His phone started to buzz and he looked at the contact before accepting the call. "Oh, this should be good," he said before he answered on the second time through the ringtone.

"Everything you wanted is headed to your inbox," Micah said without offering a greeting. "This was an eye-opener, bro. How much of this were you around for anyway?"

"I'll be back in a few," Nick said to Gabi before he walked inside. To Micah, he said, "Dallas decided to create Halcyon after Lisa recovered. I was still a TA at Radford when it all went down. He gave me all the basics but I never got deep into everything that happened. Why?"

"You won't believe it. But I sent you everything we had stored or that was accessible online: newspaper articles, video clips from the local and national news, all the criminal trial coverage from CourtTV that's still out there. It's bizarre. Sato's dad was mixed up with some vicious people, dude. The cops, Dallas's daughter, the others that got dragged into it, it looks made up until you realize it's not, and all this stuff in a tiny little place that's barely a blip on the map."

Nick walked into his office and sat down behind the desk. The file archive was already in the process of uploading to his folder on the cloud, displaying another four minutes of time remaining. "You just dropped three gigs of data on my virtual doorstep?"

"I'm a comprehensive kind of guy," Micah said. "Better to have too much than too little, am I right?"

Nick opened the folder and watched the files pile up. "I don't think we're in any danger of having too little," he said. "What do we have on the key players?"

"There's a folder labeled 'Profiles'. Up-to-date bios on everyone involved are in there."

"Perfect. Looks like I've got homework to do."

"I don't grade on a curve."

"The professors with the highest standards never do. Thank you, Micah," Nick said.

"Always, bro," Micah replied and disconnected the call.

He left the office and found Gabi in the kitchen, searching the cabinet for an acceptable snack but coming up empty-handed. She turned when she heard him enter the room. "Everything good?"

"I'm about to go back in time," he said.

Details were limited and sketchy in the initial news stories. Local outlets were the first to report that Ray Kessler, an officer with the Spring Creek Police Department, had been shot and killed. Television and radio stations interviewed the shocked and concerned citizens from the region. The front page of the newspaper featured photos of city hall and an official statement from the chief of police. A shocking tragedy in a small Southern town: That was the immediate general consensus.

An investigation was underway, the chief said to the media. The killer will be brought to justice. Our thoughts and prayers are with the family of the fallen. Our small town is tight-knit and resilient. The catchphrases were plentiful and unavoidable.

Days later, the national news vultures turned their attention to Spring Creek, West Virginia with the arrest of a suspect, a local homeless black man named Alvin Willis. His motive was unknown. A firearm that was supposedly a ballistic match was discovered in his be-longings. There were more interviews with residents of the town. That Alvin, the well-known, friendly, down on his luck and possibly schiz-ophrenic homeless man that was a Spring Creek staple could ever per-petuate such a heinous act was unfathomable and shook the community to its core. In spite of the shock, he would be charged and would most certainly pay for his crime.

Nick rubbed his eyes and stretched. He felt as if he had barely made a dent in the digital materials sent by Micah but an understanding of the events from nearly fifteen years before was vital to the overall pic-ture of the Sato father and son, surnames notwithstanding. The next video, an update from a television station in Charleston, the capital city of West Virginia, in which the governor expressed his deepest sympa-thy and promised that any and all requests for resources or assistance would be granted in this time of need, reached its conclusion and Nick made a note on his legal pad of the date and time.

Corrupt cops and politicians: an incestuous relationship as old as civiliza-tion.

Nick turned his attention back to the videos and articles.

In the weeks following the arrest of Alvin Willis, the national news stations disappeared as quickly as they had arrived. There were new events on which to feast and in locations sexier and more glamorous than rural West Virginia. Even local television was losing interest. Newspapers moved the story from the front page. It was over, at least in the public eye.

Gabi knocked on the open office door and leaned inside. "How's it coming?" she asked.

"Micah sent an information avalanche but it's worthwhile. It paints quite a picture."

"Mind if I join you?"

"Pull up a chair."

She joined him behind the desk and he clicked on the next video: a breaking news report of another shooting in Spring Creek, this time involving the police chief and a civilian. They had exchanged fire and both were injured. Again, details were unknown but federal authorities were said to be on the scene.

From there, the whirlwind began. Police corruption, drug trafficking, Japanese organized crime syndicates, and the eyes of the nation were focused on Spring Creek once more. No longer would the chief of the Spring Creek Police Department, a man named Darrell Sparks, be offering updates on the Ray Kessler murder investigation. Instead, after having been shot and badly wounded himself, he would be one of four law enforcement officials facing a litany of criminal charges.

The most shocking piece of evidence was next to be revealed to the world. A young woman in her twenties had inadvertently caught the murder of Ray Kessler on video. The video showed a struggle with a group of men later revealed to be the members of the Spring Creek Police Department. There was the unmistakable sound of a gunshot and the image of Kessler falling to the ground before the picture began to shake as the witness panicked and attempted to retreat but fell to the ground, which was later revealed to have broken the camera and alerted the conspirators in the distance.

Nick paused the video file after the airing of the shooting but before the inevitable discussion and analysis from the talking heads of the day.

"Wow," a wide-eyed Gabi said seeing it, along with Nick, for the first time. "That's the video that Dallas Taylor's daughter shot? No pun intended."

"Are you sure about that?"

"Okay, maybe a little," she conceded.

"That's the one," Nick said. "Lisa filmed it on an old Mini-VHS camcorder. We're talking the era right before smartphones and everyone watching and recording and posting everything all the time. It's amazing how much things have changed."

She leaned forward with her elbows on her knees and said, "What's next?"

Nick looked over to her and said, "I'd think you would be the last person in the world that's craving more excitement right now."

"I like a good adrenaline rush as much as anyone. Sue me," Gabi said and shrugged. "Open the next one."

"She just barks orders at me like it's nothing," he said as if she was absent from the room.

The articles and videos that followed revealed the complete depravity of the situation in Spring Creek in 2005. Two deputies had broken into the home of Ryan Clark and Adam Walton, the latter of which was dating Lisa Taylor, and stolen a copy of the video tape that they believed to be the original. When it was revealed that the evidence remained intact, Adam and Lisa were involved in an automobile accident that nearly ended her life.

Federal authorities were alerted to the situation by Clark, Walton, and Kevin Robbins, then the youngest officer in the Spring Creek department and the only one not involved in the Kessler murder. It was not until the discovery of the presence and influence of Yoshiro Sato that the full scope of the organization was brought to light. Under the direction of Chief Darrell Sparks, the police department was providing protection for Sato to use the rural location as a clandestine hub for his drug trafficking operation. An escape attempt imminent, Sparks was shot and wounded by Ryan Clark but not before firing upon Clark himself. Both men survived but the lives of all those involved were forever changed.

"How do you just get on with life after a tragedy like that, even fifteen years later?"

"I'm probably not the best one to answer that question, Gabi."

She touched his leg and said, "I know." After allowing the momentary gloom to clear from the air, she said, "Do we know what happened to all of these people?"

Nick shuffled through a stack of printed pages on his desk, separating them into two stacks. Working through the first, he said, "The major players are still living right there in Spring Creek, all grown up. Married, families, careers, it's the classic American dream." He moved on to the second stack and said, "Sparks is still in jail. Micah is digging up details on the others," then reclined in his chair and gazed out the window to his right.

"What is it?" Gabi asked.

"There's a lot more to know," Nick said. "I can read articles and court transcripts and watch videos until my eyes bleed but there will always be things that are only known by those who lived through it." He looked away from the window and back to Gabi. "Memories fade, people change, life clouds and clutters the mind, but some things stay with you forever. These people faced attempts on their life, national media attention, found themselves in the middle of an action movie plot, and decided to stay right where they are." He tapped his pen on the desk and said, "That's character. That's strength and resolve and confidence. It's pretty impressive."

"We still need to address the elephant in the room, Nick."

"Which is?"

"You tell me about Halcyon but not exactly what it is that you do. You open up the wall and show me a collection of weapons and a communication system but won't open up to me about details that have always either been hidden or avoided. You'll storm the fortress to get to me but keep a wall built around yourself so that no one can get all the way in."

"I'll tell you whatever you want to know. How's that?"

She stuck her tongue in her cheek and then said, "Okay. I'm holding you to that. No more secrets."

"No more secrets," Nick repeated.

"First question: How far does all of this go?"

"All of what exactly?"

"You and Dallas Taylor and Halcyon, all of it."

"Be forewarned. It's complicated, Gabrielle."

This time it was Gabi that reclined in her chair and locked her fingers behind her head. "I'm fairly intelligent and incredibly patient. Start talking."

Nick sat up in his chair and turned it so that he was facing Gabi. "I tell you what. Make your list. Think about what you want to know. I'll answer every bit of it on the way."

Skeptical and curious, she asked, "On the way where?"

"On the way to scenic Spring Creek, West Virginia. I need to have a talk with Ryan Clark."

19

Gabi shuffled through the small collection of clothing in the dresser in the guest bedroom, all of which were items left at Nick's, stolen from Nick, or purchased out of necessity and shipped overnight in the course of the previous week. "How long are we going to be gone?" she shouted down the hall to Nick in the master bedroom.

"Just a day trip," he said. "I hope," he added under his breath. A black v-neck short-sleeved workout shirt and matching pants comprised his attire. He arranged the printed copies of the materials on Clark and the remaining figures in Spring Creek that were provided by Micah and attached the stack and a black gel ink ballpoint pen to a clipboard.

Gabi appeared in the doorway, dressed in black yoga pants and a red performance t-shirt. "Do you ever wear anything else?"

"Practicality is crucial." He brushed the front of his shirt for effect and said, "It's far more comfortable than the tux."

She moved beside him and turned him toward the mirror. "We look like we just got back from the gym."

Looking at their reflection, Nick said, "We're beaten up, sore, and tired. It's essentially the same thing." He checked the time on his phone and said to Gabi, "Almost 10:00. Ready to go?"

"As ready as I'm going to be. Just tell me we're taking my car."

Nick raised his eyebrows, then turned away and walked through the door toward the steps.

"Nick!" Gabi said, following him. "You want me to go on a road trip in the Civic instead of a BMW?"

He stopped halfway down the stairs and turned to look at her. "That's a little elitist, don't you think?" he asked, waited for her silence to hang in the air, and then smiled.

Gabi looked askance at him and said, "What?"

Nick waved her forward and said, "Come outside." He led her onto the porch, through the front yard to the driveway, and stopped in front of the barn that stood on the left side, the weathered wood splintered in spots, the structure seeming to lean to the right. Ten feet high and wide on the front, twenty feet long, holes appeared in random locations but no light managed to peek through the boards. "What do you see?"

She hesitated, searching her brain for an answer other than the obvious, and said, "I see another old barn that should have been razed right after you moved in, Farmer Nick."

"You're absolutely certain?"

Her arms outstretched with resignation, Gabi said, "I'm filled with a combination of curiosity and dread that is almost unimaginable but let's hear it."

Nick scribbled a series of numbers at the bottom of the legal pad on the clipboard and tore off the bottom of the page. He held up the paper and asked, "Didn't you ever wonder why a broken down old barn would have a brand new breaker box on the side of it?"

Gabi looked at the box, then at Nick, and said, "Go on."

"Do the honors," he said and handed her the paper.

She walked to the side of the barn and opened the door to the breaker box, revealing a keypad identical to the one located within the bookshelves in the dining room, then typed in the ten-digit code that Nick had written on the paper: 2151624103.

Once again, there was a click followed by the sound of the activation of a motor and the doors began to open on the front when she pressed enter. Gabi stepped back just as the action initiated, then moved to the front of the structure. The interior was floored with concrete and fully illuminated by fluorescent tubes, insulated from the elements, climate-controlled, its contents concealed from external view. The walls of strategically placed and wholly unnecessary weathered wood and rusted tin roof on the structure served only to deflect undue attention and deter potential intruders as another layer of construction prevented the inside light from being emitted.

Parked inside the faux barn was a caviar black Lexus LC 500 coupe. Nick pressed a button on his key ring and started the engine.

Gabi stood with her mouth agape, her eyes wide, and turned toward a smiling Nick. "Are you kidding me? Has this been here the whole time?"

"The garage? Yes. The car? Sort of. It's a lease."

She walked inside the garage barn and peered through the passenger side window of the two-door luxury sports car. "Leather seats, premium sound, no rust. Why do you drive around in the Civic again?"

"Better gas mileage," he said from the driveway before approaching. "This is more of a special occasion ride anyway."

"Does a day trip to West Virginia qualify?"

"Considering recent events? Definitely."

"Am I driving?"

Nick slid on a pair of black sunglasses and said, "Not a chance."

Gabi smiled, sighed, opened the passenger door, and sat down inside.

Nick left Route 58 at Hansonville and turned onto Route 19.

"Black car, black leather seats, black dash. Did you buy this because you could blend in with your own car?" Gabi asked.

"Consider it extremely upscale camouflage."

"How far of a drive is this going to be?"

He checked the navigation display and said, "At present speed, a little over two hours. Why?"

She tilted her head back and to the left, looked at him, and asked, "No more secrets?"

"No more secrets."

"Good," Gabi said and rubbed her hands together. "That means a captive audience and plenty of time for questions and answers."

Nick inhaled and exhaled, slowly and deeply. "I already know which team I'm on," he said and increased his speed from 70 to 80 mph. "I'm ready whenever you are but just remember one thing."

"What's that?"

"The answers will be honest. Just don't expect to like, or even understand, them all."

"I expect that. Anything else?"

Nick deliberately focused straight ahead and said, "Promise me that nothing you hear is going to change the way you look at me."

She rested her hand on top of his on the gear shift and said, "Never."

"Don't make promises that you can't keep, Gabrielle."

This time she squeezed his hand. "Look at me." When he did, she said, "Never."

"Okay," he said, sitting still at a red light, and took a deep breath with his eyes closed. "Ask me anything you like."

"There's so much I don't know; all those things about Nick Burke that are avoided or mysterious or glossed over." She drummed her fingers on her leg and said, as if to herself, "Where to begin?"

"Start small."

Gabi glanced at the digital display and said, "Drive as fast as you want. I'll get all of my questions in."

"I have no doubts about that."

"I know you're originally from Iowa."

"Right."

"Tell me about where you grew up."

"In the south-central part of the state is the city of Pella, the largest in the Marion County but still not the county seat. It was the childhood home of Wyatt Earp."

Gabi nodded and started to say, "Which explains..."

"Which explains my middle name," Nick finished.

"The middle name of a gunfighter?"

"A lawman, a gambler, so many things. But Pella is much more than that."

Smiling, she teased, "Is Nick Burke about to wax poetic about his Midwestern hometown?"

"Nostalgia and sentimentality aren't weaknesses, Dr. McLane."

"I'm sorry. Go on."

"It was founded by Dutch immigrants in the mid-1800s. It's the home of Central College and the annual Tulip Time Festival. Years ago, after we left and came here, they built a replica of an authentic Dutch-style canal right in the middle of downtown: The water, the flowerbeds, all of it. It's called the Molengracht. I've only seen it once in person but it's spectacular, like stepping back in time and blending it with the present. My parents went on dates at the same local pizza joint on Franklin Street that they took me to when I was a kid. They got married at the Pella Opera House. That place is a part of me."

Gabi looked away and said, "We've never really talked about your parents."

"I know," Nick said. He waited a beat and whispered in repetition, "I know."

"Do you remember what you told me on side of the road yesterday, when we were looking at the headstones?"

"Which part?"

"You said that it should be unacceptable to be easily forgotten and washed away by the sands of time."

"Right."

She looked back at him and said, "I'd like to hear their story."

"You're right," Nick said. "Where should I start?"

Her tone soft, her smile warm, Gabi said, "Start at the beginning. How did they meet?"

Nick took a deep breath to calm his nerves. "October 19, 1985 in Iowa City."

"You have it down to the day?"

"It was college football season."

"Of course," Gabi conceded.

"Iowa was ranked number one in the country. Michigan is in town, ranked number two, for a mid-afternoon kickoff. The kicker hits a game-winning field goal as time expires to beat Michigan, 12-10, the crowd storms the field, and Iowa City becomes one giant block party for two days. My dad was a junior at the time. Mom was from Pella and was there visiting her friends, probably had to lie about where she was to do make it happen, and tailgated without ever going into the stadium. After the game, they both end up at The Mill, a mile away across the river. He strikes up a conversation, turns on the charm, and manages to get her number. They got married the next summer. A year after that, there I was."

"That's quite a story. Thank you for sharing it with me."

"It is, isn't it? I wish you could have met them. They would have loved you."

"You don't have to answer this..." Gabi started to say but stopped short of delivering the entire thought.

"It's okay. Go ahead." He let off the accelerator and watched as his speed dropped below the limit.

"What happened the night you lost them?" She squeezed his hand on the gear shift a second time.

"It was cold and rained all day. I mean, it poured for hours. Then right before dusk, it just stopped, like someone flipped a switch. The sky was bright orange and purple right before the sun started to set. It was one of those days when you could smell the rain leftover in the air. Classes were done for the day. I had fifteen hours that semester but Friday was an easy lead-in to the weekend."

He momentarily fell silent and began tapping his fingers on the steering wheel. "Nick, you don't have to keep going," Gabi said.

"No. It's okay. I need to," Nick replied. He looked to her in the passenger seat and said, "Really. It's okay."

"Okay."

"They drove to Radford to see me that night. I hadn't seen them in a month, just caught up in the madness of school and everything else that an eighteen-year-old junior in college has to do. We had dinner, sat in the living room at the house they were renting for me and talked and joked. They left after dark."

Gabi felt acid rush into her stomach. "I never knew you were with them that night," she said.

"I got the call an hour later, telling me to come to the hospital. They were on a two-lane road, out in a rural spot where it's flat and away from civilization, just trying to get home. The other car crossed the center line and hit them head-on. My dad saw him coming, slowed down, and moved as far to the right as he could but it didn't matter. Both cars went over an embankment but they were killed on impact."

Gabi sat in stunned silence, waiting for Nick to continue. When he did, he said, "The other driver wasn't wearing a seatbelt and was thrown through the windshield but survived. Someone drove by and saw the lights. When they got him to the hospital, his blood alcohol level was .17, more than twice the legal limit. If they stay five minutes longer, if they leave five minutes later..."

"Nick, don't do that."

He lifted his sunglasses and wiped a tear away before replacing them. "I'm not wrong," he managed.

"You're not right either."

"The timing of that night has haunted me ever since. I've tried to figure out what I could have done, or not done, to prevent it from happening. Should I have invited them that night or should I have gone to them? I've lamented the fact that we ever left Iowa and came here."

"How did you all end up here?"

"My dad's work brought him here. Mom could work anywhere. Higher education is always accessible. With the opportunity, the future, the new adventure, it seemed like a great idea to them. For all they knew, it was temporary; they could build and save and retire early and move back home. That's not the point. If they never leave, they aren't on the road that night. But..."

He broke off the sentence and Gabi waited for him to finish before asking, "But what? You can't stop the natural order of things, Nick."

"But if we never leave Pella to come here, I never find you. So the thoughts and the concerns and regrets are always moving and changing. There are nights when it's still just as real as the first one."

"And you've been doing this to yourself, in silence, ever since?"

"How could I not? I'm eighteen years old, closing in on college graduation and an immediate entry into graduate studies and a career and, in the blink of an eye, the world goes dark. My parents are gone, nothing makes sense, every plan, every vision of the future, is shattered. It's like standing on a house of cards during an earthquake, Gabrielle."

"I'm sure." Nick scratched the top of his head and winced at the silent consideration of the revelations to come, which caught Gabi's eye. "What is it?"

"My father was a planner, always ultra-prepared for almost any eventuality, positive or negative. So much so that a lower-middle class man who supported his family without being wealthy, made sure that every need and some desires were met, carried a million-dollar life insurance policy on both him and my mother."

Gabi quickly pushed herself up in the seat and said, "You mean…"

"That's exactly what I mean. Quietly, completely under the radar, I lose both of my parents in a flash and fall face-first into two million dollars."

"All through college, all through med school, every time I was having trouble and you were there to bail me out and you'd say, 'Don't worry about it,' with that glean in your eye. That's why. That's how. You never said a word."

"It changes the way people look at you, talk to you, work with you; when you know they know, every motive is questioned when it comes to those that give you reason to question their moral center."

"I hate to ask but what happened to the drunk driver?"

Nick increased his speed to 80 mph, hugging the line on the left side of the lane through the turn and back to the straight stretch. He pursed his lips and breathed through his nose. "A well-known local family, a misguided bleeding heart system, and a prosecutor's office that is more concerned with closure rates than anything else all led to an obvious conclusion: a sob story, a desperate cry for mercy that fell on judicial ears that should have been deaf, and the inevitable plea bargain. Even with multiple priors, he was sentenced to nine months, license gone for a few years, the standard issue rehab and counseling. It was a nightmare. He was out in six."

Gabi scoffed and furrowed her brow as disbelief led to outrage. "That's it?" she said, louder than intended.

"That's it. But justice has a way of finding people."

"How so?"

"He was dead a month after he got out; another car wreck, no one else involved, and not a single tear shed."

Not one.

She lowered her voice and rattled, "Good," then shook her head as if to clear it of its momentary darkness and asked, "What about other family? I've never heard you mention anyone else in all these years."

Nick slowed to a stop at another red light and said, "Dad was an only child, Mom had a brother that died right after he was born, all four grandparents are gone, extended family is either dead or entirely out of touch." He turned to her and added, "I'm it."

"And that's why you always say you're working somewhere out of town on holidays, isn't it?"

"About that..."

"Yes?"

"Remember the picture hanging in the living room?"

Gabi leaned forward, restrained by the seat belt, and cupped her face with her hands. Partially muffling the sound, she said, "You spend the holidays in Las Vegas?"

"As long as I'm earning money, it can be considered work."

"This is too much," she said, now sitting up straight.

"That's why I jumped at the chance to play in the poker game in Boston. It's nothing new to me. Let's face it. The caliber of player that spends Thanksgiving and Christmas at the casino is just begging me to take their cash."

"I can only imagine." After a pause, she said, "Wait a minute. The poker game. If that wasn't really a charity thing…"

"Pure profit," Nick said though a knowing grin. "Minus the entry fee that was borrowed from Dallas."

"Now we know who's buying dinner the next five thousand times." She narrowed her gaze and said, "Let's talk about something else. What's your net worth?"

Nick stuttered and managed to get out an, "I…"

"I'm kidding," a grinning Gabi interjected. "For now," she added.

"Don't worry. I was just scrambling for a fake number anyway." The remark earned him a smack on the leg. "What else?"

"I asked you something at the orphanage, right when Bret and Oso ran in, and you dodged it."

"Refresh my memory," Nick said.

"Why did Bret call you 'Hawk'?"

"Code name, nickname, whatever you want to call it; it's a Halcyon thing."

"I figured as much but why 'Hawk'?"

"Bret was brought in right after me, not long after he got out of the Air Force. Oso was still a couple of years away. One of the first things Bret learned about me was that I was from Iowa and I wore an awful lot of black with occasional gold."

Gabi nodded her understanding and said, "The Hawkeyes."

"I'm not a doctor on a sitcom in Korea so starting to call me Hawkeye would have been a little too on the nose. Hawk is what stuck because of that but he later amended his definition of it all, saying that it was appropriate because I had a tendency to try to watch over everyone."

"Like a hawk. He's not wrong."

"Before you even ask, Oso is the Spanish word for 'bear'. You saw him. It explains itself. Bret's is Eagle."

"That makes sense. He was in the Air Force."

"No, because he's bald," Nick said, deadpan.

Gabi threw her head back with laughter. "I needed that."

"I'm serious!" Nick reassured.

"Oh, I'm sure you are." She waited for the moment of levity to pass and asked, "Tell me about Halcyon."

"What more do you want to know?"

"All of it. What's it about? What do you do? Why do you do it?"

"Answer this question honestly. Really think about it before you do."

"Okay."

"Do you think that those who we so foolishly refer to as our leadership, on any level, truly care about the well-being of the general public beyond pandering to those who will either help them achieve reelection or pad their pockets in exchange for preferential treatment?" Gabi waited for him to continue. When he did, he said, "You work in medicine. You save lives. You are subjected to things that very few in the world will ever see and that happens to you as a specialist. The emergency room doctors and nurses, the pediatricians, the oncologists, their lives are filled with unspeakable horror, even if you consider only the things that are naturally occurring. Tragic events, genetic disorders, birth defects, they are all terrible things but they happen. It's a much different story when what you face is the result of a malicious act."

"Right," she said quietly.

"The innocent, the helpless, the powerless, the defenseless: Who stands up for them? Look around you. Look at our world. Look at the abyss that's progressively consuming every street corner of every city and town in every state. There is no such thing as immunity. Safety is now as much of a myth as privacy. When battles are won, when evil people are stopped, technicalities and gutless judges doling out bleeding heart so-called restorative policies release them back into the population to strike again. I'm not talking about someone selling weed or having a glove box full of unpaid parking tickets. I don't have to say the 'who' and the 'what'. You already know. They're everywhere. There is not a neighborhood free from them anymore and the ones that you believe to be the safe havens are the very ones that tend to harbor the worst. To protect and defend yourself and others is considered unthinkable in the modern era and yet those who are sworn to advocate and act on our collective behalf do nothing. To paraphrase Bret, can you think of an oxymoron more absurd than 'justice system'?"

"So where does Halcyon fit in?"

"Some misattribute the quote to George Orwell, others to Winston Churchill. There's no evidence to support either claim. No one really knows where it originated but the words resonate all the same. 'People sleep peaceably in their beds at night only because rough men stand ready to do violence on their behalf.' The problem is that what peace they once had is being ripped away from them, not by invading forces from overseas but by the domestic terrorist next door, sometimes in the next room. Domestic violence is an absolute epidemic, to a degree that there are untold millions of men, women, and children who are without a place to feel safe in the world, and they find themselves assaulted, their trust violated, by the very people who are supposed to stand by their side. Child molesters and rapists may not kill but they still manage to take the lives of their victims. Narcotics destroy the users and the family system that surrounds them but the dealers and the traffickers just stash the cash and move on with life."

"Useless air parasites," Gabi muttered.

"Some would shudder at the notion of their cardiologist saying such a thing but I'm in absolute agreement."

Gabi held up her hand as if to toast with an invisible glass and said, "Cheers."

"You don't rehabilitate a child molester. You ventilate them with nine-millimeter hollow-points."

"That's good. You should write that down."

"Gabi, there was an important lesson being taught when we were kids and we all missed it, right there at the end of every episode of *Scooby Doo*. We had the happy ending. The bad guy was caught. They all drove away in the Mystery Machine and moved on to the next case, crisis averted, roll credits. But before they leave, they pull off the mask of the perpetrator to reveal their identity and it turns out to be a seemingly innocent character from earlier in the story. That's the lesson. The scariest, the most dangerous, the most destructive monsters in our world are the ones who are right beside us, walking among us, hidden by their masks."

"Wow," Gabi said through a dramatic exhale. "I never thought about it like that."

"Why do we do what we do? To even the score, one small battle at a time rather than some futile attempt at a large-scale solution. Evil people don't need to be in prison. They need to be in the ground. It's another one of those mysterious quotes from history. 'The only thing necessary for the triumph of evil is for good men to do nothing.' I don't know if Edmund Burke actually said that at any point in time but I can assure you that Nick Burke believes it."

Gabi's phone began to ring and she declined the call without identifying the caller. "How long has all this been going on, Nick?"

"Everything you read about last night, all the videos and newspaper articles about what happened in Spring Creek all those years ago, that's why Halcyon exists. It was in the wake of all of that when Dallas decided that there were times when direct independent intervention was needed to deal with the worst that humanity has to offer. The timing was a perfect storm. It wasn't long after that when I lost my parents. Dallas is a shrewd and extremely well-connected businessman and apparently a kid that starts college at sixteen was something that was already on his radar. It started with a letter, then a phone call, then a meeting off-campus a few weeks later, and before I knew it I was the first piece of the puzzle, complete with a mission, a benefactor, a perfect corporate cover story and identity, and a blank slate ready to be filled with a combination of life lessons and skill sets that is absolutely chilling to anyone looking in from the outside."

Gabi scoffed, half-smiling, and said, "You were never a pharmaceutical rep a day in your life, were you?"

"Not one," Nick admitted. Then caught her eye and said, "I'm sorry."

"You did what you had to do," Gabi reassured him. "It's okay."

"If I could have told anyone, it would have been you."

"So what are you, Nick? Some kind of burned ex-spy?"

"Not hardly. We're not much for international arms dealers and government agencies. This isn't television. Come to think of it, the government would label us as criminals."

"What would you label yourselves?"

"Vigilantes with a noble cause and a large expense account. That's the best I can do."

"And there are no ties to the government whatsoever?"

"None. Halcyon exists free of the fetters of bureaucracy, politicians, rigged systems, paid-off public figures, and leadership that publicly condemns what they privately sanction and in which they often partake. That's why it works. We live in the shadows and enjoy walking into the places where angels fear to tread."

Gabi sensed momentum and progress in the narrative. "The trips overseas, the languages?"

"Some pleasure, mostly training. A covert excursion to train with a former Mossad operative in Israel or an ex-MI6 agent in London isn't something you broadcast, especially when you're supposed to be nothing more than a private citizen."

There was a moment of stillness as Gabi absorbed the wealth of new information. It was broken when she said, "The man at my house. Who was he?"

Nick checked the rear and side view mirrors, then eased into the right lane and slowed before entering the turning lane at the intersection. "I need to stop," he said.

Uncertain, Gabi said, "Okay."

He pulled the Lexus into a space at the vacant end of the Walmart parking lot, shifted into park, and unlocked his seat belt. "His name is Spencer St. Clair."

"Who is he, Nick?"

"In the early days of Halcyon, when it was just getting off the ground, Dallas was still fuming over what happened to Lisa, the failure of the system because of the corruption within it, burdened by the what-if questions and the answers to questions that get formed in your head by anxiety whether they're true, even reasonable, or not. Let's just say his approach was far less measured. It was a desire for aggression and revenge on those who were on the fringe of responsibility or simply reminded him of the kinds of people that were."

"Understandable," Gabi said.

"Of course. The problem with that comes when lines get blurred and opportunists find their way into your course of action. Enter Spencer St. Clair. He was well-traveled, smart, both intellectually and tactically, and experienced in the world of what espionage would call double agents. Corporate espionage, private investigations on behalf of good guys and bad guys, intimidation, unauthorized access to any number of facilities, the man did it all. He knew how to play both sides of the street for his own gain and it was his *modus operandi* from the beginning. He was never the leader or anything, just a contractor who was brought in for something international or when another hand was requested, and I'm sure he seemed like the perfect person to have around as long as he was on your side."

"Until someone figured out that he couldn't be trusted?" she asked.

"Until he decided to do as he pleased, place his own desires and loyalties and connections above all else. Some lowlife would get neutralized and he would risk everything, including the exposure of Halcyon or alerting authorities to what had happened well before we got out clean, just to steal money, items from the house, you name it. That's the danger of working with a mercenary. They have no cause. After a while, especially after more than a few close calls and risky decisions, I went to Dallas and told him that, in my still young and operationally naïve opinion, it was best to cut ties and let us handle things on our own. He did. Spencer knew who it came from and has never let it go."

"Of course."

"The fact that he is much better off doing things as he did for years later on never mattered. He held a grudge. He was slighted. He knew Dallas's bank account, his connections, his clout, and he saw bigger pieces, all the while forgetting that this was not a commercial exercise. I learned a lot from Spencer early on, some strategy and technique, but mostly how not to do things, who not to be, and how to retain at least a modicum of ability to sleep at night. Once he figured out that I refused to be who he was, there were lines that would never be crossed, a split was inevitable and I knew where Dallas would go."

"So why me?"

"He studied people. He listened to everything that anyone ever said in idle moments. Call it a photographic memory or perfect recall but if you said it, or if he saw it, he remembered it. Sociopaths are great at that. Anything you say or do or express or feel will be used as ammunition against you at some point. What did he remember most about me? That one person was both my greatest strength and my greatest weakness. If you want to get to Nick, get to Gabi."

Gabi allowed her head to fall back onto the headrest and said, "And that's why you never told me about any of this."

"You catch on fast, Gabrielle."

She let out a half-groan, half-grumble and said, "I don't even want to ask this."

"Oh, this should be good," Nick winced and said.

"Did Mia know?"

"Did Mia know what?"

"Any of this. All of it. Whatever."

"The more I think about things, the more I wonder how much Mia ever knew."

"About?"

"About me, about a lot of things."

"Have you heard from her, Nick?"

He carefully turned his left wrist that was still at the ten o'clock position on the steering wheel to see the face of his watch.

Gabi caught him and said, "Oh, don't even think about it. We have well over an hour to go. But if you don't want to answer that, I understand."

"No secrets."

"No secrets."

"Just an email a while back but it's been a long time. Months."

"I'm thrilled that were finally able to escape from the Mia vortex but do you even know where she is or what she's doing?"

"There are lots of answers to that."

"Pick one."

"I'd like to think that she's in a constant search for a house with no mirrors, hoping that she can live in a way that means never having to see her reflection and face her own reality, one that is a product of her own decisions, but I'm not sure I even give her that much credit anymore. How can someone simultaneously be a stranger and yet permanently ingrained into your mind?"

"What about the guy?"

"What about him? He's a dual-threat: ignorant and stupid."

"He's probably packing a Chinese corn cob anyway," Gabi said.

It was Nick's turn to slowly turn his head, wide-eyed. "That's quite a metaphor." The acknowledgement earned an accomplished shrug from Gabi. "He's just an anesthesiologist," Nick said.

"Really?"

"Really. Every time he did his job, she never felt a thing." It drew the biggest laugh of the day from Gabi, a sound that Nick had long listed among his favorites, the indication of Gabrielle's audible joy.

He waited for the moment of humor to subside and continued. "All I know is that having your status changed from forever to forgotten is one of the most destructive things that anyone can endure in this life."

Her hand, now in her lap, was placed back on top of his. "I know it is but, Nick, you have to understand something. People have a tendency to run toward practicality and convenience and the allure of what is easily accessible or a time-waster or some idealized version of something they believed that they once wanted or piqued their immature curiosities. But there is a major difference between the soulmate that you try to choose and the one that has been chosen for you. You only get one of those in your life and you will never find peace until you find your missing piece."

Nick felt his throat turn dry, unspoken words stuck at the base, and drank from the bottle of water in the cup holder. "Do you believe in that, in soulmates?"

"I do," Gabi said, flashing a reassuring, even knowing, smile. "The path to one another isn't easy and it's rarely short but the past becomes insignificant once you've found your forever. Deep down you know that you have to face and defeat every challenge, work through every lonely night, give your heart and your soul and your body to the one whose love transcends time and space rather than forcing affection and clinging to a sense of attraction to someone who will ultimately leave you feeling like you're a thousand miles apart while in the same room, all because they will never be the one, your one, and that fact is inescapable and no amount of fantasy or imagination or sense of adventure or temporary lust can change that."

In silence, he melodically spoke the words in his mind. "Only you can save me…"

His vision blurred with tears, a product of the unsaid words and unheard internal thoughts. He cleared his throat and asked aloud, "So you're saying that there's hope?"

"As long as there's breath, there's hope, Nick. All that's left is for you to believe." She stroked his hand rather than squeezing. "You're a poker player, Mr. McCormick. You know all about taking chances."

He pushed the button on the dash to start the engine. "I guess I'm just waiting for the right time to go all-in."

"You can't get the time back, Nick. Follow your heart."

He shifted the car into drive and left the parking lot, headed for the road. "I know you've heard this before but…"

"But what?"

"Someday."

20

Formerly known as Meyer's Grocery, the former owner sold out to a small regional chain in the year following the shootings in Spring Creek and moved to Florida to escape the resulting chaos. But when the larger company chose to close a number of locations to avoid bankruptcy, the space was purchased and saved by Dennis DeShong, the opportunistic former mayor of Spring Creek and owner of the only dry cleaning business in town, who crossed into nearby Monroeville for his latest venture, proving that his entrepreneurial instincts were of greater value than his political acumen. Regarded before the incidents as a centrist, non-confrontational, and generally weak mayor, his decision not to seek reelection came as a surprise to no one despite his lack of involvement in the corruption and killings, cleared of any wrongdoing or prior knowledge in the course of the investigation but made to look foolish for his ignorance in the process. His wife managed the dry cleaning. A general manager handled the daily operation of DeShong's Grocery store seven miles away. He existed only as a silent figurehead of both, a disgraced former local government official collecting a pension and enjoying the solitude of a private life lived outside of the public eye, free from unnecessary scrutiny and stress.

The supermarket was unusually packed for late morning, not yet noon. An incredulous Ryan Clark stood in the snacks aisle, staring at the product on the center shelf. "It just doesn't make any sense," he said.

Standing beside him, holding the plastic basket, his wife, Kara, said, "I really don't know why you're so worked up over this."

"Because it's Amish County popcorn."

"Right?" she said, looking at him and waiting for the drop.

"But it's microwaveable. You can't be both. Pick a team, fellas."

"I swear you get bothered by the weirdest things."

"And you married me anyway." He adjusted his thin black plastic glasses and smiled at his wife.

The hard blindside smack to the middle of his back sounded with an audible *whump* and nearly knocked his body forward into the shelves and the breath out of his lungs. "Mr. Clark!" the man said, louder than warranted by the situation and environment.

Clark steadied and turned to see the expected presence of Alvin Willis, the employee who sought him out for a handshake, greeting, and brief conversation during every visit. Once unkempt and disheveled but now proudly sporting a simple professional look, his beard now showing more white than gray, the aging Alvin bore little resemblance to the homeless black man who had been framed for the murder of Spring Creek police officer Ray Kessler fifteen years earlier. At twelve dollars per hour, he was the highest paid stocker of shelves at any grocery store in the region and the newfound employment and income had reaped dividends. Once gawky and thin from a combination of genetics and malnourishment, Alvin had added bulk throughout his frame, including a few extra pounds at his waistline. A studio apartment tucked away on the top floor of an aging office building in Spring Creek was subsidized by the city budget, one of multiple line items included in the settlement of the lawsuit, along with health insurance, physical and mental health care, and all utilities paid. The mass of the sudden financial windfall, limited by the shallow pool of resources within the town, was placed in a trust with multiple trustees and future beneficiaries at Alvin's insistence and funds were rarely withdrawn.

"Good to see you, Alvin," Clark said with a slap on the shoulder.

"Shew!" Alvin exclaimed with a high pitch, his hands on his hips. "It's good to see you, too, man."

"Everything going okay?"

"Cain't complain," the smiling Alvin remarked. "How you doin', Miss Kara?"

"I'm great, Alvin," Kara said.

"Well, I better go," Alvin said and disappeared down the aisle and around the corner.

Kara waited until Alvin was out of sight and said, "I'm always astonished that that's the same guy that was living on the street. He has all that money from the settlement, works here, and acts like nothing has ever changed."

"The man loves the simple things in life. There's something to say for avoiding complication."

Kara pursed her lips and said, "Was that a shot? That felt like a shot."

"That was not a shot, I assure you. You're not complicated. You're lovably complex." He raised his eyebrows and smiled as he looked at her.

"I'm not sure why but that's better," Kara conceded. "Are we about done here? Don't you have a deposition this afternoon?"

"I did. Harry Mace called and canceled this morning. The paralegal worked for three straight days prepping all the notes, tossing in a few suggested questions, arranging the exhibits, and Mace cancels. I can't stand the guy. The last time out he called opposing counsel an idiot and told the Assistant U.S. District Attorney that they were incompetent."

She leaned closer and asked quietly, smiling, luring him in, "So you're free all afternoon today?"

"I'm out of there by 2:00 at the latest," he spoke softly in response.

"I'm holding you to that. I'll see you at home," she said and turned to move toward the cashier at the front of the store.

"Insatiable," Ryan said to himself and took his first step to follow her.

Clark tapped the icon for the clock app on his phone and set an alarm for 2:00 p.m., an hour and ten minutes away, resolute on keeping his word, and dropped it on top of a stack of papers at the upper left corner of his cluttered desk.

It was the endless stream of mind-numbing paperwork that he hated most, even with a paralegal to bear some of the load. The reality of a career in law paled in comparison to the glitz and glamour of television, to say nothing of the extremely fast resolutions. Every case, criminal or civil, was wrapped up in a neat little package within an hour. Witnesses are blessed with perfect recall. Trials are a stage on which dueling attorneys perform for the jury, trying the cases on their own and swaying opinions with brilliantly crafted monologues that would leave even the finest bard hopelessly jealous. Opposing counsel is often rendered ineffective by virtue of excessive arrogance and a false sense of invincibility or suffers from a terminal case of incompetence, leaving them subjected to shameless mockery before the rolling of credits. The salaries are high, the stress levels low, each of the multiple homes beautiful, and the vacations to exotic locations frequent.

Not so in real life.

His compulsory involvement with criminal law during the trial of those involved in the Spring Creek Police Department debacle in his early twenties soured him on the field before so much as submitting an application for the College of Law at West Virginia University. Left to the world of civil law, the professional life of Ryan Clark existed in cycles of pleadings, discoveries, trials, and headaches. An increasingly litigious society necessitates corporate defense and it is where Clark specialized, challenging claims, negotiating settlements, and limiting losses in frivolous lawsuits for small and large businesses alike.

He was an equal founding partner of his firm, Clark and Bennett PLLC, which provided the southern region of the state with an array of legal services from general counsel to family law to estate planning, even occasional criminal defense of which he was not directly a part, allowing him to pick and choose his desired casework and, yes, premium vacation time while allowing two associate attorneys to sift through the stack of clients whose requirements were deemed more monotonous and less attractive. He reminded himself to remain thankful for his mostly enviable position on the most stressful days.

Clark turned in his office chair, removed his glasses, and rubbed the back of his neck before peering out the window that overlooked Main Street in Spring Creek. He felt the gradual effects of the approaching end of his thirties, mercifully still multiple years away but dwindling. More than six feet tall, his body was thin, lean without reaching the point of wiry. He kept his face clean-shaven and his light brown hair meticulously buzz-cut with trimmers and hoped that the inevitable thinning at the crown would be delayed for years to come. The suits were mostly similar, a classic black with a white dress shirt and a rotation of ties and shoes, a far cry from the relaxed casual wear that dominated a decade of his life that seemed as if it were a different life altogether. There was always the comfort of home for such things.

The intercom on the phone system buzzed and Clark picked up the receiver. "Yes?" he answered.

"There's a Nick Burke here to see you," the receptionist on the first floor said.

Clark quickly searched his mental lexicon for the name and drew a blank. "Does he have an appointment?"

"No, but he says it's important."

He checked the time on his phone. Five minutes after 1:00. "Send him up."

Thirty seconds later, following the sound of feet ascending the century-old hardwood stairs, the man in black appeared at the door and removed his sunglasses.

"Ryan Clark? My name is Nick Burke." Nick approached the desk and extended his hand, which Ryan shook.

Clark sat down behind the desk and said, "Have a seat." Nick did so in the chair on the opposite side and Ryan asked, "What can I help you with today?"

"The Sato family, among other things," Nick replied.

Ryan felt himself chill upon hearing the Japanese surname. Without responding, he stood, walked to the entryway to his office, and closed the door. He picked up the receiver and pushed the button for the intercom. "Hold my calls," he said to the receptionist.

"I'm sure it's still a sensitive topic but let's just say there have been some new developments," Nick said.

"How so?"

"Apparently his offspring favors the same kinds of illicit behaviors as his assuredly proud papa."

Clark tapped a pen on his desk and digested the alarming change of pace in his day. He unlocked his phone, opened his inbox, and texted three words to Kara: Get here ASAP.

Nick began with a detailed monologue then answered questions while Ryan scribbled an assortment of notes in a spiral-bound notebook. Kara entered the office halfway into the discussion.

Ryan rubbed his scalp and said, "Let me make sure I have this straight." He consulted his handwritten list. "Human trafficking, high-stakes poker, the Middle East, the illegitimate son of Yoshiro Sato, and porn?"

"I think that covers it."

Clark dropped the pen on the desk, leaned back in his chair and closed his eyes. "Are there any dirty cops, by chance? Maybe some drugs being illegally imported and distributed?"

"I've only spoken to one cop during all of this. He's not dirty. He's just an idiot. It's irrelevant."

"Does anyone know what happened to the old man?" Kara asked from her seat on the leather couch in the office.

Ryan deferred to Nick. "Not a trace of him in a long time from anything we've seen but Junior seems to have inherited the signature family traits. That's enough cause for concern."

"And who is exactly is it that you work for?" Ryan asked.

"I don't think we have time to get into that right now. We'll be here all night."

"Understood. So what do you need from us?"

Nick slouched in the chair and said, "Give me the rundown on what happened here all those years ago, what was going on that flew under the radar, the timeline of what happened, your knowledge and involvement; everything, but in an extremely abridged form."

"Everything was being distributed through the Japanese family that owned a restaurant here on Main Street. We knew all of these people and they knew us. We were regulars there. Helicopters come in, drop and pick up, and then leave, and no one had any idea what was really going on. It was an extremely minimalist operation. The police would turn a blind eye, take a cut, and make sure no one was ever the wiser. Things started to go downhill when a high school kid overdosed on coke and Ray Kessler couldn't take it anymore. He wanted out and ended up dead for his trouble."

Nick nodded along and, in a break, said, "Go on."

"Lisa, who is married to our friend, Adam, caught the shooting on video tape. Once they became aware of evidence that would directly tie them to what happened, it turned into a nightmare. They broke into the house and stole the tape. We were stalked, spied on, followed, and harassed. An attempt was made on Adam and Lisa's lives that was nearly a success. But until the very end, we all thought it began and ended with the shooting. No one knew anything else. But who do you go to with this when multiple levels are involved and you don't know who you can trust?"

"Probably the feds but you'd be surprised. How did you tip them off?"

"We used their aggression against them and pulled off a dead drop to someone they didn't know."

Nick sat up and, impressed, said, "Nice."

"They mobilized fast with what they knew but we couldn't assume anything. We'd later find out that they had been watching that group for a while but had trouble getting anything reliable on them. When they arrived at an unexpected time, we went down there to stall them."

Clark shifted in his chair and, without thinking, scratched his shirt at the chest. "I'm sure you know the rest."

"I do," Nick said. "No need to relive that part."

"Did I miss anything?" Ryan asked Kara.

"Nailed it," Kara replied.

"And you're telling me that you knew nothing of Sato or what they were doing until the very end?"

"Nothing," Kara answered before Ryan.

"Sato managed to shake free before the trial and no one knows what hole he crawled into. Once that dog and pony show was over, I graduated, went to law school, worked as an associate for a little while, and then we got married, came back here, and opened up the practice. It's a pretty boring story after the shot was fired."

"Excuse me?" a smiling Kara asked.

"Maybe 'boring' isn't the right word but you know what I mean."

"How about your friends, Adam and Lisa?"

"They got married right after that. They're still around, starting a family, working. I think we've all settled into life now. We're actually having dinner with them tonight."

"You're welcome to join us if you'll still be in town," Kara offered.

"That's very gracious of you. We'd be glad to."

"We?" Ryan asked.

"Gabrielle is with me."

"That must be who is waiting downstairs. Is she your…" Kara asked but stopped short of adding an official status.

Nick hesitated as he searched for the correct descriptive term, if there was one. "It's hard to describe exactly what we are but we'll be there. Thank you. What are we having?"

Ryan and Kara looked to one another in hopes that the other could provide an answer. Kara broke the awkward silence and said, "Probably takeout."

"Sometimes it's best. It exists for a reason."

"I'll give you directions before you leave," Kara said. "I love to host."

Gabi sat down beside Nick on one of the wooden benches provided to any and all patrons of the Main Street shops by the town of Spring Creek. Skies gray and overcast, the sun briefly peeking through before being obscured again, the air felt heavy with the potential for rain, even a thunderstorm. "This is a quaint little place, isn't it?" she asked. "If you didn't see the new cars you'd swear that time stopped at the city limits a long time ago."

"Look at the terrain," Nick said with his eyes on the steep hillsides in the distance opposite their vantage point. "At least I've got an upland valley where I am. They're all literally living on the side of the mountain, packed in close."

"Small town living in Appalachia." Gabi scanned the area again and focused east, away from the mountains and as far as the two-lane road stretched before disappearing into a gentle turn. "Look at the haze. It's going to rain."

Nick focused on Gabi as she spoke but missed the words and failed to respond.

She turned back and asked, "Did you hear me?"

He shook his head and said, "I'm sorry. What was it?"

Concerned, Gabi asked, "Where were you just now?"

He reached up and touched the mark on her cheek, almost completely healed but still visible to his discerning eye. Tightness formed in his throat. "That never should have happened."

"Nick, stop."

"It's not that easy." He took in a deep breath to settle himself and said, "Nothing like that will ever happen again."

"It all worked out," she said and touched his hand. "Did we learn what we needed to learn from today's trip?"

"Mostly, I think, but there could still be more to know. The dinner was a surprise but it'll be good to talk to the other two."

"Did you tell them about..."

"Nope," Nick interrupted. "Never give away your hand."

Three miles clear of the center of Spring Creek and located at the flattened apogee of one of the Appalachian mountains, Nick steered the Lexus coupe onto the smooth gravel driveway that wound in a semi-circle up to the home of Ryan and Kara Clark, moving closer to a sun that would soon set behind the trees that bordered the back side of the property. Their arrival would be ten minutes early.

The two-story, two-tone brick home with a front-facing two-car garage was expansive and dwarfed the small two bedroom single-floor house situated by the creek in the town proper where Clark and Adam Walton resided at the time of the first encounter with the Sato family. Both bays of the garage were filled but the external spaces were empty as they were the first guests to arrive.

Ryan opened the front door and stepped out onto the porch before they exited the vehicle.

"If you're going to live somewhere away from everything, this is how you do it," Nick said, admiring the structure.

"It's nice but I bet it doesn't have walls that open up when you type in a security code," Gabi replied.

"Point taken."

Ryan approached the car just as Nick and Gabi opened their doors. "We can just go around back. Dinner is on the deck tonight."

"You have to have a deck with a view like this. It's gorgeous up here," Gabi said as the group moved around the side of the house.

"It's a perfect night. Adam and Lisa should be here any minute. Kara is on her way back with the food."

Even in an environment that presented no known threat, Nick performed a perimeter scan behind his sunglasses as he moved, noting points of entry, looking for unexpected movement, glints of light from the line of trees, or sources of unnatural noise. Years of training and experience were not turned off by a mental switch.

"It's not Japanese takeout, is it?" Nick asked.

"You've got jokes," Ryan said. "Not bad. Italian, actually, from a local joint that has carryout pans that you wouldn't believe."

The deck formed a large half-circle, bordered by a matching railing; all built using pressure-treated wood and stained to match the darkest of the bricks from the house. A rectangular glass and aluminum outdoor dining table of modern design was situated in the third nearest the rear wall of the home, surrounded by ten matching chairs, leaving an arrangement that bridged the gap between a relaxing night under the stars and an exceptionally comfortable board meeting. Nick and Gabi sat beside one another on one side, their backs facing the glass doors, with Ryan at the end.

The sliding doors opened and Kara appeared. "Any wagers on how late they'll be tonight?" she asked as she set the bags on the table.

"Over-under is ten minutes," said Ryan.

"We teased them mercilessly last time so they'll be spiteful. I'll say under."

"We do this often," Ryan said to Nick and Gabi.

"Wine anyone?" Kara asked.

Gabi raised her hand as if signaling a server. "What are we having?"

"Pinot Noir now, Moscato later?"

"You're speaking my language," Gabi said, then added, "He'll have a water."

This is not a night to dull the senses.

"She knows me too well," Nick said.

"I'll have a Coke," Ryan said.

"I once heard a tasteless joke with that as the punchline."

"I've heard that one, too." Ryan grimaced as he recounted it in its entirety.

"I'll help you with the plates and glasses," Gabi said to Kara and stood to follow her.

Ryan watched his wife walk away and said, "I outkicked my coverage, don't you think?"

"To an extreme degree. Cheers," Nick said.

Almost nine inches shorter than Ryan, Kara managed to squeeze a wealth of intelligence, beauty, and sarcasm into a diminutive package. With olive skin, dark brunette hair, and bright green eyes, a reflection of her mixed-race Caucasian and Syrian heritage, Kara Morgan Clark had long stood in stark contrast to the predominantly pale populace of Spring Creek and the immediate surrounding area. Together for fifteen years, married for twelve, and friends for nearly a lifetime, her decision to build a life with Ryan was not one on which she had wavered a single time, even in the tempest of young adulthood and the initial struggles inherent to a shared life under construction.

"What's your story with Gabi?" Ryan asked Nick.

"One that's still being written," Nick said.

"Happy ending still pending?"

Nick tipped his water bottle to Ryan and said, "Exactly."

Ryan responded in kind and said, "Good luck."

"Much appreciated. I'll need it."

Ryan slid his chair back and stood. "Have a little faith. Love never fails."

"First Corinthians 13. Nice reference point."

"You know your Bible."

"Not well enough but that's always a work in progress."

Gabi and Kara returned to the deck, followed by Adam Walton and his wife, Lisa, the two remaining dinner guests.

"What's up, everybody?" Adam asked.

Adam and Lisa walked to the empty side of the table and Kara said, "Adam, Lisa, you've already met Gabi. This is..."

"Nick?" a shocked Lisa exclaimed. "Nick Burke? Oh my goodness!"

Nick stood and said, "It's been a long time, Lisa."

"You two know each other?" Ryan asked.

"Took the words right out of my mouth," Adam added.

Her expression still vacant, Lisa moved toward Nick and offered a friendly, familiar embrace. "It's great to see you but what are you doing here?"

Kara looked to Adam, then Ryan, then Lisa, and said, "Is someone going explain all this or not?"

Still looking at Nick, Lisa said, "Nick works for my father."

"You're a drug rep?" Adam asked.

Nick looked to Adam without moving his head and said, "Not exactly."

"Call it private security." To Nick, she said, "If you're here, something's bad wrong. What happened?"

Adam moved to her side and said, "Who are you again?"

Nick extended his hand and said, "Nick Burke. Nice to formally meet you." He looked to Lisa and said, "We've known each other a long time but haven't seen each other in over a decade."

"Should we go inside?" Lisa asked Nick.

"Who's going to hear us out here? I think it's safe," Ryan responded from the side.

"Who wants to tell them?" Kara asked.

Nick held up his hand and said, "Allow me. You two might want to have a seat."

"I'll stand," a stoic Adam said, standing with his arms folded.

With Lisa seated, Nick said, "Yoshiro Sato is still MIA but his son is not. He has his hands in any number of things and it has an international footprint."

"Sato," Adam murmured.

Nick continued. "His name is Daniel Staal. He took his mother's surname after what happened to you, started low-profile, and might have surpassed his old man in terms of the swath of destruction he's cut into humanity at-large."

"How so?" Adam asked.

"Daddy sold narcotics and electronics. Junior buys, sells, and trades human beings like currency," Nick answered to both Adam and Lisa.

"And plays high-stakes poker," Gabi said.

Lisa smiled and said, "You're still playing, huh?"

Nick tilted his head and offered a sly, "On occasion."

Lisa Walton, daughter of Dallas Taylor, was a natural blonde of the same shade as her husband, Adam. Tall and slender, her hair was no longer wavy as it was when they met but was now straightened and highlighted in a variety of ways that were largely dependent on her mood as well as the season, and paired with the alabaster skin that seemed reluctant to tan.

Six feet tall, distinguished by both physical and emotional strength, Adam Walton appeared to defy the natural process of aging. Beneath his bright blonde hair, his facial features were chiseled and a prominent brow protruded over his eyes. A life as a fitness fanatic and a desire to facilitate healing in others spearheaded the transition from a low-ceiling career as a personal trainer to one of greater potential and purpose in physical therapy. His life with Lisa was lived away from the extravagance that was offered by her father, with a restful and easily financed lifestyle politely mutually declined at the time of the wedding, opting instead for normality, rigid routine, and the personal pride of self-sufficiency.

"Let's go ahead and eat," Kara said. Ryan assisted in setting the table.

Nick recounted the recent saga of Lucien Murdoc, Daniel Staal, and Brann Cinema without including the name or exploits of Spencer St. Clair, its review unnecessary with Gabi sitting close by, after which he fielded questions.

"But you don't think any of this directly involves us?" Lisa asked at the conclusion.

"Absolutely not," Nick said. "There's no reason to."

Having gradually relaxed into the evening, Adam stated, "So this is more about fact-finding than anything."

"More or less. Obviously Daniel is well aware of his father's past because his legal name change happened right around the time of the trials but, unless Sato is pulling strings behind the scenes somewhere, there's no connection to him."

Her legs propped up and resting on the table, Kara sipped from her wine glass and said, "It all seems like a different life now." Looking away into vacant space, Ryan nodded along with her reflection.

Gabi refilled her glass and said, "Let's change the subject. Tell me about you-all."

The quartet from Spring Creek did exactly that, sharing life stories that led to mildly embellished tales and moments of levity that resulted in multiple faces turning various shades of red, a respite from the weight of the serious tone of hours past.

Nick checked the clock on his home screen and reluctantly informed the hosts and other guests that their evening was coming to a close. Handshakes, hugs, and farewells were exchanged as if the relationships were longstanding and another dinner, another evening, another meeting, was somehow inevitable.

"I'll walk you all out," Ryan said.

On the walk to the driveway, Gabi said, "This turned into such a great night. Thank you so much."

"It was a pleasure. You all be safe headed home," Ryan said. To Nick, he asked, "Can I talk to you for a second?"

"Of course," Nick said. He stepped away from the car and spoke softly, "What's on your mind?"

"Just sitting here tonight and talking about everything that happened back then, what's happening now – I don't know. None of it sits right."

"I'm sure. Flashbacks are powerful things. I saw you with a thousand-yard stare a couple of times."

Ryan looked down the mountain and said, "The thought of all of that in the past becoming part of our present is harrowing." He looked back to Nick and continued. "It was gone. It's been gone. That family, that operation, all of it was gone, and I know it doesn't look like there is a connection to any of us but what if there is?"

"There's no reason to believe there is."

"I have a wife. I want a family. The same is true for Adam and Lisa. These things can't be in our future, too."

"That's part of the reason we came here. We needed information but all of you also needed to be informed. It's all about the big picture."

Ryan handed Nick a business card with another phone number written on the back. "Call, text, whatever. Keep me apprised on everything going on."

"Count on it," Nick said.

Ryan returned to the front door and waved to Gabi as Nick started the engine.

"What was that about?" Gabi asked as Nick backed into an open space and moved forward down the driveway.

"What did you think? Did you like them?"

"Good night, good people, fun stories. They all have their heads on straight. I can't believe that's Dallas Taylor's daughter though. Why?"

Nick turned out of the driveway and onto the main road, accelerating quickly and setting the GPS for their destination. "We'll be seeing them again."

"You think?"

"I think."

"Why's that?"

"I don't know," Nick said. He switched on the radio and pressed the random key on the preset playlist on his phone.

The music began to play through the speakers and seven miles passed free of conversation.

"What now?" Gabi asked.

Nick allowed his head to fall backward onto the headrest and let out his breath. "Now, we go home."

21

His discussions with Daniel always resembled one-sided lectures from a domineering boss more than a dialogue, a conversation, an environment where open and honest discourse was welcome, even encouraged.

Instead, Lucien felt as though his words were being discharged from the earpiece into thin air with little hope of reaching their destination and that Daniel Staal spent his time on the other end of the line doing little more than waiting for his turn to speak. Hearing and listening were similar but not identical concepts, he thought, and Daniel rarely listened to him.

For the moment, Lucien was offering the same treatment to the young man who signed his paychecks and rolling his eyes throughout the process.

"... and I haven't heard from him since," Lucien heard Daniel say but missed the context along with the first half of the statement.

"I seem to be losing reception, *patron*," Lucien lied. Patience and interest as well, he didn't say. "Could you repeat that?" He closed his eyes and scratched the back of his head.

"You're losing the call? Where are you, Lucien?"

"I am seated on a bench outside of the tavern."

Staal allowed for the silence to indicate his skepticism, then sighed and said, "The last I heard from Spencer was that he was dealing with what he termed a 'security issue' that was discovered in Boston. That was days ago and he has been off the grid ever since. Calls go to voice-mail. His phone will not even ping."

"What is the security issue, Daniel?" Lucien asked. The use of his first name was a rare occasion.

"It doesn't concern you," Daniel snapped. "Do you understand the time table?"

"Yes, *patron*. But must this be done with such haste? With Spencer..."

"This is not a discussion, Lucien. I have told you my story but have I ever told you my given name?"

"No, sir," Lucien said. He shielded his eyes from the sun and watched for the arrival of his guests.

Daniel intentionally dropped the tenor of his voice and said, "I was not born Daniel Staal. My name is Daniel Kisho Sato, a surname that became toxic when I was a teen. I chose to dispose of his last name so that I could live as my own man, free of the bondage of the sins of his past, but my father saw a greater purpose in giving me the name Kisho, for it means 'one who knows his own mind'. I learned a great deal from him in my life. Do I sound uncertain to you, Lucien?"

"No, sir."

"A single misstep, one hesitation, a fleeting moment of uncertainty or debate, something done from anger, sadness, passion, or desperation, and we find ourselves in a downward spiral from which we may not escape. No, this is what will be done. Are we clear?"

"Yes, sir."

Daniel ended the call without speaking further and Lucien considered hurling his phone across Main Street, momentarily visualizing the series of bounces along the pavement in the manner of a stone skipping across the surface of a pond, but recalled the monetary value of the device and returned it to his pocket.

His presence ensured that Shelby would arrive first, well before Rae. He would meet with Allie at another time.

Shelby.

He pounded his fist on the bench, drawing a curious and critical look from elderly woman passing by.

It was difficult enough to watch her perform on camera with other so-called co-stars, be they male or female. To watch helplessly as she was shipped away to God knows where, her future supposedly bright but secretly uncertain, the future that he envisioned for her, with him, fading by the minute was devastating, physical ramifications ranging from the blinding stomach pain to the migraines, both of which were unprecedented until recent months.

He felt the arms drape over his shoulders and around his neck a split-second before he heard the voice.

"Hey!" Shelby said. She kissed his cheek and pressed her face to his, then sat down on the bench beside him.

Lucien managed a nervous smile and stroked her bare leg below her denim shorts, silently hoping that she failed to notice the trembling in his hand.

Her head on his shoulder, she nestled him close, caring nothing for onlookers. "What is it?" she asked without looking.

Lucien looked away from her, down the street toward an unknown and unimportant mark, and dodged the question. "Have you spoken with Rae?"

"She's supposed to be on the way." She rose up, ran her hand through his thin blonde hair and asked, "Do you want to go on in? There's A/C in the tavern. It's so muggy out here."

"In a moment," he said. Rae pulled her Prius into an empty space on the curb and opened the door. Lucien stood when he saw her and raised his hand to catch her attention. "All right," he said to Shelby and walked with her to the entrance.

He held the door open for Shelby and Rae to enter ahead of him, then circled in front of them and led them to an empty booth tucked into a corner on the rear wall.

Shelby and Rae sat opposite Lucien on the same side of the table and waited for him to speak.

"How's Allie?" he finally asked.

The two young women looked at each other before Rae answered, "She's filming a scene today. It's supposed to be her last one before they wrap things up. I thought you'd know that."

Her usual brightness absent, Shelby asked, "What's going on, Lucien?"

"Your travel schedule has been modified."

"Mine or ours?" Shelby said.

"Both of you and Allie as well." In his phone, he opened the calendar app. "I am still ironing out the details, as they say."

Uneasy, Rae waited for Lucien to look up from the screen and said, "Why the change? You said everything was set."

Lucien felt the pressure build in his chest and snapped, "It's not under my control," which caused Rae to lean back in her seat. He dropped the phone on the table, lifted his hands and said, "I apologize."

"This isn't like you," Shelby said. "You're worrying me."

Lucien was relieved when the bartender interrupted the conversation.

At the end of the table, Sienna leaned down and said to Lucien, "Hey there. You've not been in for a while. Can I get you all something?" Focused solely on the European blonde, the two women were rendered practically invisible.

"Just water for me," Lucien said and deferred to Shelby and Rae.

"Same," Shelby said. Rae nodded her agreement.

"Be right back," Sienna said.

"You know her?" a suspicious Shelby asked.

Monotone, detached from the moment, Lucien said, "She's usually working when I visit here. No need to be jealous." Realizing his error, he managed a nervous smile in a failed attempt to offer reassurance.

"It's so dark in here," Rae said to Shelby.

"I know. Just because it's a tavern doesn't mean you can't have a little light."

"It still beats that kitschy little place that was here before."

"Kitschy?" Lucien reentered the conversation and said.

"Yeah, it means tacky or cheesy or cheap."

"Then why not just say that?"

Rae scoffed but stifled her desired verbal response.

Tension building, Shelby said, "What's the matter with you?"

"I'm sorry," Lucien said to Shelby, allowing the apology to extend to Rae by default.

Looking only at Shelby, he failed to notice the return of Sienna. She slid three glasses of water onto the table. "Where's your friend?" she asked Lucien.

"I'm sorry?"

Smiling, Sienna said, "Your brash Aussie friend with the hat that was here with you before."

Lucien attempted to passively dismiss her. "He's on holiday, I believe."

"That's a shame. Tell him to stop by." To Shelby and Rae, she said, "I'll be back in just a minute and get your order," and left the table to tend to a customer seated at the corner of the bar.

"Take your time," Shelby said. When Sienna was out of audible range, she said to Lucien, "Are you in here a lot with your friend?" Rae looked away, vainly hoping to avoid the rising conflict.

Lucien felt his rate of respiration increase relative to the mounting stress. With a hint of annoyance, he answered, "It's no cause for concern. He's an associate from the company."

Rae rubbed the rim of the flesh tunnel in her right ear lobe and fixated on the salt and pepper shakers. "What aren't you telling us, Lucien?"

Lucien leaned forward, pressing his chest to the edge of the table, and spoke softly enough to be heard but not overheard. "The two of you, along with Allison and possibly two others, will be leaving earlier than scheduled. Arrangements are being modified presently."

"What?" Rae exclaimed. "How soon?"

"Three to five days."

"But Lucien..." Shelby objected.

Head tilted, he raised his hand, looked away from the table to check for curious eavesdroppers, and continued, "This was not my decision, nor is it yours."

"But my parents..." Shelby began to say.

Speaking over her, Rae said, "I have work. I was supposed to..."

Through gritted teeth, he interrupted, "Please." With their protests temporarily halted, he stressed in a whisper, "Do the two of you think that everything is up to me? There are those who I must answer to and who make no allowances for arguments or insubordination."

He watched helplessly as tears formed in the eyes of the one he desperately hoped to protect, tears of disappointment, fear, and over-whelming stress, the very things from which he desired to free her rather than cause her.

Shelby cupped her hands and covered her nose and mouth, the tips of her index fingers strategically placed at the inside corner of her eyes. Redness began to appear. Ignoring the friend and co-star seated next to her, she issued her plea directly to Lucien. Her voice shook and echoed inside of her hand as she said, "Don't make me do this."

His eyes locked with hers, Lucien felt as though time was grinding to a halt. He could hear the pounding of his pulse in his ears, his blood pressure rising to what he believed to be a dangerous level. He clenched his hands into the tightest fists he could muster, maintained them for a moment, and released, then repeated the process a second time. A psychiatrist had suggested the stress-relieving technique to him decades earlier.

"How do you feel about this?" Lucien asked Rae.

"It's not perfect but I know what I signed up for," she said. Looking at Shelby, she added, "But I understand if it's easier for me than for oth-ers."

"Excuse me," Shelby said as she slid out of the booth and rushed away to the restroom.

Scowling, Rae said, "Give her a break, Lucien. If anyone should be doing so right now, it's you."

"What do you mean by that?"

"Don't be coy. She just found out and you're not letting her process any of it. Don't be such a dick."

Lucien glared across the table and dismissed her chastisement. "Each of you was made aware of this several weeks ago. Don't act as if this is a revelation of some kind, Rae."

Having grown impatient with his excuses and incessant deflection, Rae said, "Come off it, Lucien. She already told me she's pregnant."

His frustration transformed into shock, followed immediately thereafter by an overwhelming rush of sadness. His eyes wide, his vision focused into a neutral space, the ambient noise of the restaurant sounded as though he had fallen into the deep end of swimming pool as the party on the deck raged on. He struggled to fill his lungs with air and felt the blood drain from his face.

Lucien looked in the direction of the restroom and back to Rae. "What did you say?"

Rae managed a nervous laugh before she realized the severity of her gaffe. She covered her mouth with her hand and said, "I thought you knew."

"Clearly not." He checked the hallway that led to the restroom a second time. "When did she tell you this?"

This time Rae looked away from the table and back to Lucien. "She took the test a couple of days ago. She swore she was going to tell you," she said in a hushed tone.

"Obviously not," Lucien whispered sharply. He rubbed his eyes and added, "Oh, *mon dieu.*"

"It's not quite what she signed up for either. You know?" She watched the restroom door open and said, "She's coming." The warning drew only a silent nod of acknowledgement from Lucien.

Shelby was still sniffling when she slid back into the booth. "I'm sorry," she said.

Rae draped her arm around Shelby's shoulders and pulled her in close for a one-armed hug. "Don't worry, girl."

Lucien remained involuntarily speechless, grasping at mental and emotional straws in the hope of finding a pathway through the fog and into the light.

Lucien Murdoc: Father?

He scoffed at first, but then allowed himself to romanticize the vision in his mind's eye.

A dramatic, unexpected but long-awaited exit from the life and lifestyle of which he had grown tired, a new love by his side, a future that many would view as comparatively dull but he would embrace as both restful and a new challenge by virtue of his lack of experience and the necessity of a change in both occupational culture and personal outlook.

His child would be sheltered from this world. No son would live only to exploit, to fuel the fires of lust and greed as he had done for more years than he could recall at the moment. No daughter would find herself bare and objectified and used, ultimately discarded, for the world to see.

He looked across the table to the young blonde who avoided eye contact with him and thought, "Like Shelby."

"Aren't you going to say anything?" Shelby asked through another sniffle. She wiped her nose and distracted herself with the social media on her phone.

Mouth closed, breathing through his nose, he tapped the heel of his hand on the edge of the table and mentally arranged the words in the proper order to the best of his ability. "Do both of you object to the upcoming arrangement overseas?"

"I'm here to be a performer, not a rental," Rae said.

"Shelby?"

He felt her leg begin to shake beneath the table before he saw the tears well up in her eyes.

"I..." Shelby started to say but stopped when Lucien raised his hand.

"I will do what I can to make alternate arrangements. Please be patient."

"Patient? Three days and you want me to be patient? What am I waiting for, Lucien?" Shelby exclaimed. The volume and intensity rose as she spoke.

"Trust me," Lucien said to Shelby without looking at Rae. "Please just trust me."

Her lower lip momentarily quivered, stifled when she pinned it under her teeth. Her voice cracked as she said, "I did."

Seconds of silence passed before Rae said, "I need to go."

"Okay," Shelby said and slid out of the booth to allow for Rae's departure.

"I'm leaving, too," Shelby said.

"Please stay here," Lucien said. He reached for Shelby's arm but she pulled it away and stepped backward.

"I'm leaving." Resisting the urge to cry, she sneered, said, "Let me know how soon I need to pack," and stormed to the exit ahead of Rae.

Five phone calls and three voicemail messages full of rising intensity and progressively spicier language were necessary before Lucien received a call in return, one that he answered after the first ring.

"I presume you have a good reason to be speaking to me in such an insolent tone," Daniel Staal said.

"Urgency can be mistaken for disrespect, Daniel."

"Lines can also be blurred, Mr. Murdoc. What is it?"

"There are changes that need to be made to the upcoming event that was arranged by Musad Khan." As he spoke, he heard Daniel maintaining a lighthearted conversation with an unknown figure in the room. "Are you listening to me, Daniel?"

Half-laughing, Daniel said, "Tell me again, Lucien. What's the problem?"

"The event for Musad Khan..."

"What about it?" Daniel interjected.

"I would like to know why you decided to close down the operation here and move forward in with Musad Khan so suddenly."

"I wasn't aware that you had any right or reason to know those kinds of operational details. That is well outside of your purview. You take orders, Lucien. You do not give them, certainly not from your highly specialized position. Do we understand one another? I haven't the time for this."

Lucien closed his eyes and breathed slowly, searching for a moment of calm before continuing the discussion. "Shelby and Rae will not be traveling, nor will Allison."

"Excuse me," Daniel said to the person who was sharing his immediate space and waited for the door to close. "What do you mean they won't be traveling?"

"There are dozens of women available to you who would be suitable for Mr. Khan and his allies. Find them and send them."

"Listen to me carefully, Lucien. Assurances have been made. The relevant flight plans have been filed. Once these things are in motion they are not to be stopped. Do you understand?"

"I understand but I do not accept," Lucien said.

"Someone has to be in a position of some kind of power in order to accept or decline, Lucien. This isn't an offer or a matter of opinion. You are being told what will be happening 72 hours from now, give or take a few. Is that understood?"

Standing in the bathroom, staring at the mirror, he took note of the determined look in his own eyes. "No, sir," Lucien replied flatly.

Daniel chuckled on the other end of the call and allowed his voice to whine with a blend of entertainment and disbelief on a long exhale. "Last chance, Lucien. You have been informed of the times, places, and plans. You have been told where to go and what to do next. You have been paid a large sum of money for these things and many others but you are an easily replaceable cog in the wheel of a machine that will keep running with or without you. Are you going to follow through with my directives or not?" The question hung in the air and Daniel said, "I suggest you only do now what you can live with later, Lucien. What is your decision? Yes or no?"

Lucien had not yet blinked. His phone buzzed in his hand, then a second time, with incoming text messages. He ran his free hand through his hair and dropped it to his side. Resolute, confident, defiant, he said, "No."

"Very well. You're fired, Lucien," Daniel said. "Best of luck in your future endeavors."

Lucien heard the tone that indicated the disconnection but held the phone to his ear for another five seconds, his gaze still fixed upon his own reflection.

For the first time that he could remember, he was proud, not ashamed, of the man looking back.

He swiped down to check the notification panel for the missed text messages.

Shelby.

He opened the inbox and read them aloud into the open room. "Why are you doing this to me? Please talk to me," he dictated to himself. Wishing she could hear, he responded, "I don't know."

He typed one sentence of a reply, cleared the window, and attempted the same task again before closing the window and opening his contact list. He tapped her name and initiated a call.

Shelby answered the call in silence, waiting for him to speak first.

"Come see me," Lucien said.

"I don't think that's a good idea right now," she whimpered.

"It will be alright. Just come here and speak with me."

"I'll be there tonight. I have some things to do. I love you."

The call was dropped before Lucien could return the sentiment in kind.

To be powerless was an alien concept. To live in fear was, in fact, no way to live. Options were assuredly few. An attempt to convince Shelby to seek a new life with him in a new land, away from the bedlam of the present and with eyes on the future, would take precedence but the effort to escape the reach of Daniel Staal would prove futile. It was only through his connection to Daniel that he was afforded the luxuries of corporate networking, ostensibly endless capital, and the resolution of problems without the lifting of a single finger by virtue of a single phone call or e-mail.

Now, he knew, he was on the opposite side of the combat zone, empathizing with those who had previously entered into war with Daniel Staal and found themselves overwhelmed, battered, wounded, and defeated in short order. He was in need of assistance, either by virtue of an equal but opposite force or a *deus ex machina* of literary proportion. The latter seemed to be of higher likelihood than the former.

"A security issue in Boston," he recalled aloud.

Lucien retrieved the phone from the pocket of his slacks and again opened the contact list, this time scrolling to the second half of the alphabet, sorted by first names, and stopped at the letter S.

He was not a religious man, nor a fan of American sports, but took time to appreciate the irony of what he knew was known colloquially as throwing a Hail Mary.

22

"My poor house," Gabi said with an intentionally-pouted bottom lip.

"It could definitely use a touch-up," Nick said. "Although some verbal gymnastics may be required in order to explain some of this damage to a curious contractor."

Laying eyes on her home for the first time since her abduction at the hands of Spencer St. Clair seemed surreal at best and harrowing at worst. Nick had returned in her stead in the days following the operation at the orphanage to gather a handful of requested essentials in hopes of delaying the inevitable flashbacks. She would go back when she felt that she could, she had told Nick, but with one stipulation: She would not go alone. Not the first time, anyway.

Standing in the driveway, Gabi said, "The last time I was here I was wondering if I would ever see this place again." She looked to Nick and said, "Or you."

"This can wait," Nick said.

"I'm not going to run away from my own house. Giving in to fear is no way to live. Come on."

They entered the kitchen through the garage and the unmistakable odor of mildew and mold seemed to form an olfactory wall into which they walked face-first, a product of the standing water that overflowed from the sink and into the floor as part of Spencer's effort to destroy the alarm system transmitter. The water evaporated after several days but the flooring was left warped and discolored, the first item to be noted on the list of necessary repairs.

Nick stopped after two steps, involuntarily recalling the sloshing of water under his feet on the day that he discovered that Gabrielle was missing, and scanned the room for further damage.

"How can evil people just take your home away from you?" Gabi asked rhetorically.

"The same way that they take lives from their victims without actually ending them. In some ways it's actually crueler to do so."

Gabi peered down the hallway into the living room and stepped slowly, as a stranger would, on her approach, unsure of what she may see in the light of day. The pile of pillows remained in place on the couch, the remotes on the table, the crumpled blanket half on the couch and half on the floor as it had been in the moments after she had been awakened by the wind-fueled crash of the door against the wall. Each sight sparked another reminder, another memory, another cue to touch a healing wound.

She stood next to the couch, her sight fixed on the spot where she had been at the moment of the breach, and said, "That's where I was. I heard the door slam in the kitchen and it woke me up." She then turned to the front door and said, "I got up and the second guy blocked me from getting to the front door."

"You don't have to paint the picture for me, Gabrielle. Living through it once is more than enough."

"Have you been upstairs?"

"Not since that first day."

"Let's go," she said and took the lead up the steps.

Nick followed but voiced his objection en route. "Gabrielle..."

Gabi stopped two steps from the top and said, "You can't protect me from this, Nick, and that's okay. Just be here with me and it'll be fine."

Nick gestured up the staircase and said, "After you."

Her path took a beeline to the master bedroom, including a momentary stop to inspect the numerous holes of small diameter and the associated dark red smear of dried blood that decorated the exterior wall, the latter of which she ran her finger across and checked the tip for residue.

Nick watched her move through the sequence and said, "You showed a lot of courage that night."

Without turning around, Gabi answered, "Fat lot of good it did."

"You're still here, aren't you?"

She nodded agreement and entered the bedroom. On his earlier visit, Nick had taken care to leave the scene intact, affording Gabi the opportunity to examine each piece as it lay. She knelt to collect the spent shells and lined them up on the dresser, deliberately arranged in the manner of a memorabilia display, then picked up the shotgun and returned it to its rightful place in the walk-in closet, concealed by the rack of clothing.

Turning her eyes back to the wall, Gabi forced a laugh and said, "At least I made him bleed."

"You did."

"Last time I saw him, he was flat on his back with a bullet hole between his eyes."

Nick stuffed his hands into his pockets and leaned against the door jamb. Looking up, he said, "He earned it."

As Gabi pulled an empty suitcase from the shelf at the top of the closet, she asked, "Which one of your team took that shot?"

His eyes still on the ceiling, Nick said, "I did. Point blank."

Void of emotion, Gabi said, "Good." She set the suitcase on the bed and opened the lid. "Do we know anything else about him or his brother?"

"Other than the fact that they've both recently relocated to a place with a much warmer climate? No. Why?"

"I was just curious." She stood in front of the rack of clothes in the walk-in and, in an attempt to change the subject, said, "I don't even know what to pack."

"Does it matter?"

"Which part?"

"The first."

"Probably not."

Gabi aimlessly browsed through the clothes in the closet before shifting her attention to another drawer in the dresser, both unsure and uncaring of what to pack, what to leave, or what to do. Despite the time of day, the sun beaming through the windows in mid-afternoon, she sensed the room falling into darkness, drawing her back to the night of her abduction. The shadowy figures lingered outside the door. Thunder shook the house. Lightning flashed the room and she flinched at the recollection.

Nick watched as her eyes grew distant. No longer searching for items to pack and transport, she was lost in a place beyond his perception. He stepped closer. Softly, he called, "Gabrielle?"

She turned slowly, her face blank, and mumbled, "Yeah?"

The wound on her face was now mostly healed, now a pink discoloration with hints of redness around the edge, but Nick brushed the place where it had been. "Flashback?"

She nodded and looked away for a moment, then back up to him again.

"There are going to be times that you go there," he said, careful to keep his tone calm. "Just don't let yourself stay there."

"Yeah."

"Easier said than done. I know."

She hooked his hand with her finger and lifted it. "At least I won't be alone."

"Never," Nick mouthed. He felt the phone buzzing in his pocket before the generic ringtone sounded and leaned his head back in disbelief. *Perfect timing.*

The name on the screen was unexpected but not unknown and he felt his stomach tighten. The call had most likely been forwarded from the burner phone, as he had designated weeks earlier, to his main line, only to ensure that the essential communications of the time would not be missed due to dead batteries or inadequate cellular signals.

That's not the name she needs to see on my phone right now.

"I'll be right back," Nick said and stepped out into the hallway.

"Okay," Gabi replied in a tenor that was more a question than an ac-knowledgement.

"Yes?" Nick answered.

"Is this Sean McCormick?"

"Yes."

"This is Lucien Murdoc. I presume you remember me."

"Yes."

"There's something I need to speak with you about and I'm afraid I must insist. It's rather urgent."

He walked slowly away from the door as he spoke, then pivoted and retraced his route. "If it involves a rematch at the tables, I'm afraid I've satisfied my appetite for competition for the time being." Glancing around the edge of the doorway to check for Gabi, he lowered his voice in hopes that she would not hear and said, "I'm sure there's no shortage of affluent men and women who would savor the opportunity to win Daniel Staal's money."

"Daniel Staal and his ilk are no longer of any relevance or concern to me."

Nick paused to process the revelation, thankful that his astonish-ment could not be seen by the caller, and said, "Very well. Before we go any further, please know that career opportunities are scarce at the moment, talented as you may be."

"I have no need for a job at this time, Mr. McCormick."

"Well, you sure didn't call to talk about the weather. I'm a very busy man. What's this about?"

Out of sight, yet only a handful of miles away, Lucien Murdoc was holding his breath and searching for words that held the possibility of forever altering his destiny. A familiar barrier stood in the way of his request, his admission of a need.

"Still there, Lucien?" Nick prodded.

"I have no idea who you are, Mr. McCormick, but I am absolutely certain that you are not who or what you say you are. What I do know is that I am in need of your assistance."

"Regarding?"

"Daniel Staal, the world he created, and the lives that he has polluted, formerly but no longer with my help."

"There are a number of law enforcement agencies, domestic and abroad, who would love for you to regale them with your tales. Why are you calling me rather than them?"

"Because the life and work of my former *patron* has been turned upside down since your encounter with him in Boston. His figurative and literal security blanket has disappeared and he is currently in the process of uprooting several of his present bases of operations. You are, as they say, the common denominator. Am I mistaken?"

"This is not a conversation to have over the phone." Gabi peeked around the corner in time to see Nick check the time on his watch. She offered an inquisitive head tilt as Nick said, "How free and able are you to travel?"

Gabi rolled her eyes and said, "Tell me later," and disappeared into the bedroom.

"Reasonably so, I believe," Lucien said to Nick.

"Call me back in an hour and I'll have a time and place for you."

"Very well," Lucien said and Nick heard the tone that indicated the termination of the call.

When the screen cleared, Nick pulled up the list of contacts and touched the icon to call Micah.

"What's up, bro?" Micah answered.

"I need a location."

"How soon?"

"Tomorrow afternoon."

"Requirements?"

"Avoid large cities and densely populated areas. Let's think old buildings with single primary points of entry and limited access to the others. An elevated position opposite the meeting location is non-negotiable. Let's find something that's not local but also not across the country and has an airport nearby that we can fly into. The other party will either be driving or chartering a flight into a larger airport and commuting in, so we'll be headed out tonight so we can scout and get set up."

The scribbling on a notepad was audible before Micah said, "Got it. How long do I have?"

"He's calling back in an hour."

"You're kidding me."

"That's why you're the best."

"Flattery doesn't make this any easier, Nick. Who are you meeting with?"

Nick waited for the sound of activity from Gabi, turned his back to the door, and said, "Lucien Murdoc."

"Whoa," Micah said, drawing out the word. "Hang on. What are you meeting him about?"

"I'll fill you in tonight. Right now, you know what I know."

"Does Gabi know?"

"What do you think?"

"I'll get you back in thirty minutes," Micah said and ended the call.

Nick took care to ensure that the pace of his return to the room was deliberate.

Folding and stacking items into the half-full suitcase, Gabi said, "Do I want to know?"

"Of course you do."

She stood up straight and said, "Okay. Out with it."

"I have to meet with someone that says he needs my help."

"Help with what?"

"I don't know yet."

"Where are you meeting him?"

"I don't know yet."

"When?"

"I don't..."

"Know yet," Gabi finished. "Do you know *who* you're meeting yet?" Nick grimaced and Gabi said, "Nick?"

"I feel like I know that accusatory tone far too well."

"You're deflecting."

"I'm meeting Lucien Murdoc."

"You're not serious."

"He says he's no longer working with Daniel Staal and he needs my help." He realized his error and added, "Well, actually, he says he needs Sean McCormick's help."

"You're not going through with this, are you?"

"Do I have a choice?"

"Nick, you cannot be serious!" Gabi shouted. "How deep into this do you want to get?"

"How much deeper can it go, Gabi?"

"Is that something you want to find out?"

"Are we going to keep conversing with dueling questions?"

The retort forced Gabi to crack a smile and allowed her to gather her thoughts and find a moment of calm amidst the rising tension. "What do you think you're going to accomplish?"

"I don't know yet."

"Oh, for God's sake," she laughed and said.

The cell phone began ringing again and Nick said, "Saved by the bell." He swiped the icon to answer and said, "That was fast."

"Found a spot. I'm texting you a link now," Micah said.

Nick tapped the link in the message and the satellite image zoomed in on the predetermined address.

"I can honestly say I've never heard of Millersburg, Ohio until this moment."

"That makes it ideal, my man."

"Where's the closest airport?"

"Holmes County. 4400 foot runway and three miles from the center of town.

"What's the timing look like?"

"It's an hour-long flight at cruise speed in the Cessna from your usual rural hub, virtually due north. You'll have a car waiting and a two hotel rooms booked. Drive time for your guest would be six hours; unless he charters a private flight into Columbus, in which case he'd still have a 90-minute drive."

Nick accessed the archived images taken from street level and said, "That'll work. We'll travel overnight. Nice job, Mr. Bruce."

"Should I send the convoy your way?"

"Absolutely. The complete set with all the accessories."

"Aye aye, Captain."

"Keep me posted," Nick said.

Nick tossed the phone onto the bed as Gabi zipped up her bulging suitcase. "You look surprised. What's going on?" she asked.

"Have you ever been to Ohio?"

"On purpose?"

"Fair enough. At least we're not driving," Nick said.

Lucien placed his return call ten minutes early.

Forgoing a greeting, Nick answered and said, "The Holmes County Courthouse in Millersburg, Ohio, northeast of Columbus, south of Cleveland."

"Ohio?" Lucien objected. "Mr. McCormick, I..."

"That was a statement, not an offer, debate, or negotiation, Lucien."

"I suppose I could fly into Columbus," Lucien said, mumbling more to himself than to Nick.

"You strike me as an extremely resourceful man, Mr. Murdoc. If it's important enough to you, you'll work it out."

"Very well. What time shall we meet?"

"The same time as every legendary showdown in the West: High noon. And Lucien..."

"Yes?"

"No surprises," Nick said and terminated the call without waiting for an acknowledgement or reply.

"Can't sleep?" Bret asked from the pilot chair.

Nick settled into the copilot seat, donned the headset, and said, "Not even close. Gabi was out the second we took off and Oso's got a game on his phone. What's our airspeed?"

"We're cruising comfortably at 225 with no traffic in sight. ETA is 1:22 a.m. Getting in and on the ground well ahead of the storm."

"Thank God for that," Nick said.

He felt safer in the confines of the first class section of a commercial airliner. Flying at a lower altitude meant clearer vision. A smaller plane meant a bumpier ride. Driving was preferred for the convenience, the relative anonymity, and the time for reflection. Efficiency was the lone benefit in his personal estimation, although the others onboard were sure to disagree.

The flight plan was filed by Bret before his conversation with Micah had ended. The first half of the route was a familiar one, so much so that the coordinates, airport codes, and related information were kept on a well-worn 3x5 index card that was rarely necessary. After the arrival at Mountain Empire Airport to allow Nick and Gabi to board, the Cessna 421C Golden Eagle was refueled and the hour-long straight shot to central Ohio commenced beneath the cloak of both darkness and relative secrecy. The arrangements made by Micah awaited them following the landing. Nick would work through the narrowly focused logistics with Oso in the early morning, following a couple of hours of sleep.

Bret looked over his shoulder to check for eavesdroppers and said, "Do you have any idea what we're walking into?"

"The man says he wants to talk, so we'll talk. Beyond that I'm as in the dark as we are at the moment. I've been back there reading up on the courthouse, getting a feel for the location."

"Are you sure there's not something more to it than that? Spencer lurking in the shadows or a bunch of Staal's henchmen ready to pounce?"

Nick looked at Bret and said, "No. But that's why you-all will be there."

"What about Gabi?"

"What about her?"

"Is she going to be with us out there or what?"

ENIGMA | 351

"I'm not saying she's going to be right on the frontlines with us but she's certainly proven herself capable and worthy to stand up for herself. You could ask Phil and Calvin but they're both roasting on a spit in the center of the Earth right now and she put one of them there herself."

"Zero doubt."

"It's also a Catch-22. If this is some kind of a ploy from Lucien and Staal just to get us to drop our guard so they can do God knows what, leaving her at home means leaving her isolated and that could be part of their design. Would I rather have her with us or sitting at home alone with Spencer on the loose? I'm not playing that game."

"I know she'll be just fine."

"So what's the problem?"

"Just make sure that your eyes are on Murdoc. We'll keep an eye on her. Don't let anyone or anything into your blind spot."

Bret held out his fist and Nick bumped it with his own. "I hear you."

"How in the world did Micah find this place?" Oso asked into his Bluetooth headset. "I live in Ohio and I've never heard of it."

"That's the biggest selling point," Bret answered in the call, lying supine with his head leaned against the wall just ten feet away from Oso. "At least they don't have a river that's polluted to the point that it's flammable."

Sporting a pair of silver aviator sunglasses and seated on a bench situated to the left of the courthouse, Gabi said, "So is this what it's like when you boys get together and work?"

"Basically," Bret answered.

"Not exactly," Oso said simultaneously.

"So which is it?" Gabi asked.

The line was silent for a moment until Oso said, "Consider this the easiest level of the video game. It's the little intro mission you do before the exciting one."

"Except we don't have cheat codes for extra ammo, invincibility, and walking through walls," Nick said.

Gabi looked 180 degrees around the area and asked, "Where are you?"

After a beat, Nick tapped her on the shoulder from behind. She flinched and gasped, then said, "I hate you," as he circled around her. Bret and Oso laughed on the line. "I hate you both, too," she said.

"This is a breeze as far as initiations go," Bret said.

Nick crossed to the side of East Jackson Street opposite the courthouse and took a seat on a wooden bench in front of a microbrewery, covered by a canopy. He checked his watch and said, "11:50. Do you have eyes on him anywhere?"

Bret and Oso were stationed directly above him. The row of gift shops, restaurants, and office spaces were staggered in height, either two or three stories high, but each shared a common feature: a flat rooftop. Under the shroud of darkness at 0400 hours, a wooden stairwell was taken from the rear of an adjacent two-story building, which led to a ladder that provided access to the third-story roof next door, an effort which was easier than either man expected. Few things were more valuable in battle than the high ground. Bret reminded Oso of that fact as part of their quiet ascent hours earlier.

Now on his knees, looking over the short brick wall that bordered the top of the building and down onto the street, Bret said, "Negative. But it's early."

"I'm sure he's here somewhere, watching and waiting," Nick said.

A mass of dark gray cloud cover was advancing from the west and, although the forecasted heavy rains had yet to fall, the sun was already obscured, casting a lowlight condition across the visible region. "It's getting dark," Gabi said as she opened the weather app on her phone. "Radar says we've got 15 minutes max until the storm cell gets here, and that's one menacing looking wall cloud. Tornado watch just got issued."

"She's a meteorologist, too?" Oso asked.

"Being the weather girl on channel eight doesn't have the same retirement package as cardiology," she replied.

Changing subjects, Oso said, "Did we fly here in a time machine? There's a parking lot beside the courthouse for horses and buggies." Through the chuckling on the line, Oso said, "I'm not kidding!"

"It's because of the Amish population," Gabi said straightforward. "There's tons of them in Holmes County. It's called the Amish County Byway for a reason."

"Micah must have forgotten to include that little nugget," Bret said.

"Even Micah can't out-research an inquisitive woman," Nick said.

The year of its construction, 1885, was embossed onto the rough stone walls at the center of the top floor of the Holmes County Courthouse. The building consisted of three floors, adorned with a statue of Lady Justice, blinded and holding her customary beam balance and sword, atop the colonnaded porch with Ionic columns at the main entrance on the northern side. The clock tower in the center of the structure was visible throughout town, colored in dark green and remaining functional more for the sake of tradition than practicality in the age of smart devices and immediate access to information and entertainment of any and all kinds.

Watching through binoculars from the rooftop above Nick, directly across from the courthouse, Oso said, "Eyes up, Nick. He's early and he's approaching. He's a block away, moving slow, and jerking his head around every time someone moves near him."

"ETA?" Nick asked.

"One minute. Ninety seconds if he gets held up by foot traffic."

Nick stood, found a gap in the slow moving traffic, and said, "I'm on the move," as he jogged across the two lanes. "Where is he?" he asked.

"He's stopped at a storefront and looking behind him," Oso said.

"Paranoid as a lab rat," Gabi added.

"It's just another Friday in a small Midwestern town," Bret sang instead of speaking.

Seventeen weathered and worn concrete steps, split in the center by a handrail and desperately in need of a fresh coat of brown paint, led to the main entrance on the second floor, narrowing as it approached the doorway. A small landing was formed after the first nine rows of the staircase and Nick sat down against the wall, facing down the street where he could keep Lucien in full view.

He pushed his sunglasses up on the bridge of his nose and said, "Anything seem out of place?"

"Just us," Oso said.

Lucien was out of sight as Nick felt his cell phone begin vibrating in his hand. "Oso, is Lucien on his phone?" he asked

"Negative. Why?"

"Because I've got a call coming in. Hang on." He checked the screen and saw the name and number of the unexpected caller and looked up to see Lucien moving through the Friday afternoon crowd and toward the courthouse. "Mute your headsets, everyone. I'm going to patch this in," he said.

"Got it," Gabi said. Oso and Bret, through experience, complied in silence.

Nick swiped the screen to answer the call, placing the conference call on hold before combining the two. "This is Nick," he said.

"Nick, it's Ryan Clark. You got a minute?"

"Two, at most. What's up?"

"A man was in town asking questions about the Sato family this morning. He brought up the police case here in Spring Creek. He says he was an independent investigator but it didn't have that feel."

Lucien was passing the Amish parking lot, now less than two hundred feet away. "Go on," Nick said.

"He was at Adam's clinic, which is a county away, first thing this morning. By the time he texted me about it, the guy was knocking on the door of my house. Kara was out but the video doorbell caught it. He left my office ten minutes ago."

Nick held up his hand and signaled for Lucien to continue forward.

Hearing no response, Clark asked, "You still there?"

"I'm here," Nick said.

"I thought the call might have dropped. Listen, I let this guy know that the Satos and the chaos they wrought were both long in the past and there was nothing more to say, but this guy was persistent. My secretary said all he did was charm her from the time he walked through the door, then he gets into my office and he's making every effort to passively identify himself as the most powerful man to ever emerge from the Outback."

When Lucien reached the bottom of the steps, Nick pointed to the empty space on the other side of the railing. "Say that last part again," Nick said to Clark without his eyes leaving Lucien.

"I left that part out. He's Australian, or at least he's affecting the look and the accent."

"Brown Panama, black band?" Nick lowered his voice and said, careful to prevent Lucien from overhearing.

"How'd you know that?" Clark asked.

"I have to go. Let me call you back."

"You got it," Clark said and disconnected.

Once the other three microphones were again live, Bret said, "Spencer."

"Who else?" Oso said.

"Mr. McCormick," Lucien acknowledged.

"What's all this about, Lucien?"

"To begin, the purpose of life beyond mere form and function."

"We could have had a discussion of existential philosophy through texts." Nick looked to the sky behind him and back to Lucien. "There's a storm approaching so if we could get on with it, I'd appreciate it."

"I have lived a life of adventure and pleasure and good fortune, Mr. McCormick. I have traveled the world, accumulated wealth, and bedded women who could appear on runways and magazine covers."

"Congratulations, I guess," Nick said. He made a show of checking his watch.

"I have also left a swath of destruction in my wake and forever altered countless lives for the worst, something I can no longer justify nor can I continue to act in concert with those who do."

Nick leaned forward and rested his forearms on his knees. "Do I look like a priest or a shrink? Take your confessions elsewhere, Lucien."

"What is it that you believe I do, Sean?"

"In layman's terms, you're a smut peddler, a middle management archetype in the underworld of the entertainment industry, and someone who considers his soul and the souls of others to be little more than currency for a barter system where every trade turns out to be one-sided. What did I miss?"

Lucien's expression turned stern. "I am not Daniel Staal."

"No, but you spent how many years as his enabler and loyal, fair-haired sidekick? Get to your point."

"Have you seen my work?" Lucien asked with a wry smile.

"I've heard of it. That's more than enough." Nick heard snickering in his earpiece. "The storm is getting closer."

"From the moment you traveled to Boston, Daniel Staal has seen quite a bit of his world set ablaze and the only notable change is your emergence and apparent influence. Whoever you truly are, I am in need of your help."

A rumble of thunder sounded in the distance and Nick tapped the face of his watch.

"Tomorrow afternoon, three of my former female colleagues will be boarding a small private jet, ultimately destined for what they believe to be an appearance at a special event overseas."

"Colleagues or co-stars, Lucien?"

"Are the terms not interchangeable?"

"You're a businessman and an on-screen performer so your experience in terms of screwing people is virtually unmatched. But office workers don't make appearances at events."

"Certainly not," Lucien admitted.

"What is it that you're so desperately wanting to ask but working so hard to avoid?" Lucien stood quickly, shoved his hands in his pockets, and turned away. "Turn around, Lucien," Nick said as he pushed himself to his feet and walked to the center of the steps. When Lucien complied, Nick leaned down onto the rail that separated their positions, he asked, "Where is that plane headed?"

"A series of connecting flights that will conclude in the Middle East."

Nick raised his voice and said, "Where in the Middle East?"

"Riyadh, Saudi Arabia, courtesy of Musad Khan."

"They're not coming back are they, Lucien?"

"It is possible that they may. However, the human beings who return will not resemble those who left."

"Dante should have created a tenth circle for people like you. Even the ninth circle doesn't suffice."

"I know," Lucien looked away and said.

"You still haven't explained what it is that you want."

"I need to know if you can stop this," Lucien cracked.

"Why? What are you looking for? Redemption?" Nick snapped in return. "How many people have you literally sold out and sent to their demise?"

Lucien engaged a staredown with Nick but failed to answer the question.

"Even megalomaniacs like Daniel Staal know to align themselves with intelligent allies and reward loyalty at all costs. What happened to you, Lucien?"

"The girl at the hotel," Bret said into the earpiece.

Nick tilted his head toward the rooftop across the street upon hearing the suggestion. When he looked back to Lucien, he asked, "Who's going to be on that plane?"

Lucien turned his eyes toward the ground and maintained his silence but a flash of lightning overhead caused him to recoil and look up again.

"She was at the hotel with you, wasn't she? The blonde girl that shuffled off to the car when we spoke in the parking lot, it's her, isn't it?"

Lucien felt his voice crack as he said, "Shelby." He exhaled a deep breath and said, "There are things you need to know about the man with whom I was formerly employed."

"Educate me but do it quickly."

"Very well. Staal is a pseudonym. His actual name is..."

"Daniel Kisho Sato," Nick interjected. "Illegitimate son of the disgraced electronics baron." He allowed himself a smirk of satisfaction.

"He inherited his business acumen from his father but shares the same innate fears and insecurities, as well. Only recently was the identity of his father disclosed to me. At the first sign of opposition, to say nothing of danger, he will flee, choosing to tear down and reconstruct rather than to stand and defend. He believes that course of action to be of less risk and of greater long-term benefit. He would remind those of us on whom he would occasionally rely for counsel that his father saw his own empire razed and found himself ostracized after only a single strategic misstep."

"You're toying with him, Nick," Gabi said from the bench.

Nick leaned closer and whispered, just loud enough for Lucien to hear, "Spring Creek."

Unable to contain his astonishment, Lucien felt his mouth fall open before he asked, "Who are you?"

Undeterred by the inquiry, Nick asked, "Is that what he's done in this situation? That's why this is such an urgent matter, with a 24-hour turnaround time?"

"It is." Lucien reached into the chest pocket of his dress shirt and retrieved a single page of white paper that had been folded into quarters. "This is all of the information that was available to me. Shelby passed it along this morning. Their initial departure will take place from a small public general aviation airport forty miles from Abingdon. Do you know it?"

"I do," Nick said. "Scheduled arrival and departure times, tail number, aircraft," he read aloud.

"MKJ?" Oso asked. Knowing he was watching, Nick nodded to confirm.

"Shelby and the others will be escorted to the site in a vehicle, more for institutional control and security than their own convenience. I'm afraid I cannot tell you how many guards there will be. There is, however, a complicating factor."

Seconds passed before Nick said, "I'm waiting."

"Daniel has chosen to accompany the party overseas. He will be there, as well. He travels heavily guarded and well-prepared for every eventuality."

Nick folded the paper and stuffed it into his pocket. "I would expect nothing less. Is there anything else?"

"Trust me. You know all that I know."

"Trust you?" Nick asked, half-smiling, eyebrows raised.

"Surely you trusted me to some degree or else you would not be here at present," Lucien said and showed a confident smirk of his own.

Nick removed his sunglasses, learned forward, and asked, "Did I now?"

"Given my association with Daniel Staal, how could you know for certain that you were not walking into an ambush, only to learn that my supposed termination was nothing more than a rouse? You took me at my word. There was undoubtedly a measure of trust, Mr. Mc-Cormick. Was there so much as a moment of trepidation?"

"Not really," Nick said dismissively. He touched his Bluetooth earpiece and said, "Show him," and tapped his index finger on his chest.

Lucien looked down to find a tiny red dot, intense and contrasting with his white dress shirt, courtesy of the laser scope mounted on Oso's Heckler & Koch SL8-1 rifle. A moment later, a second dot danced across his eyes as Bret slowly moved the barrel of his own weapon back and forth across Lucien's corneas. "If it's a trap, you die first," Nick said.

"Very well," Lucien said.

Nick shrugged his shoulders and heard Gabi stifling a laugh on the line.

"I can clip his ear from here," Oso muttered both to himself and the others on the call.

"Lock and load," Bret added.

"I think he's got the message," Nick said into the call, his eyes on the man who found himself in the pragmatic neutral space that lay between enemy by choice and ally by force.

The laser dots disappeared and Lucien pressed the palm of his right hand to his chest. "My heart is racing."

"Living in fear for your very existence must be extremely traumatic for you, Mr. Murdoc."

"It is," Lucien responded.

"Good," Nick said. "Perhaps now you can relate, in part, to those whose trust you betrayed and whose lives you have destroyed. Imagine how they felt in those moments when they surrendered the last of their hope." He considered giving the verbal command for Oso to fire a single suppressed shot, center mass.

"She is carrying my child, Sean."

"Whoa," Gabi said.

"Oh, man," Bret responded.

Thunder roared through the sky again, this time louder, deeper, and closer. Heavy rainfall was audibly approaching.

"Clock's ticking, Nick," Oso said. "We need some cover."

Nick stood, dusted off the seat of his pants, and slid on his sunglasses. "I believe we've reached the end of our time, Lucien."

He began to descend the stairs but stopped when Lucien shouted, "Sean! I need to know what you plan to do."

Nick stopped and looked skyward, turned to face him, and stepped over the rail to his side of the steps. "What I plan to do?"

"Yes."

"Knock his teeth down his throat, Nick," Gabi said.

"Nice," Oso replied to Gabi.

"Let me tell you what I don't plan to do," Nick approached him and said. A bolt of lightning flashed behind him and a deafening *boom* immediately followed, indicating a direct strike in close proximity to an object on the ground. A frightened Lucien shook and covered his head. He looked up to find Nick standing nearly nose-to-nose. "I do not and will not trust you but I will take you at your word regarding that last detail you revealed. If you are lying to me, you have one chance to come clean, right now, without consequence."

Shaken, uncertain, but desperate to convince, Lucien affected the finest baritone he could muster and said, "I would never lie about such a thing."

"Then I don't plan on allowing your unborn child to be placed at immediate risk, nor to be brought into this world without a father. I suggest you do the same."

Lucien felt his mouth quiver as he asked, "Even if that father is me?"

"Even if it's you, Lucien."

Nick again turned away and walked down the stairs, leaving Lucien standing in place as the first drops of rain began to fall, darkening the gray concrete walkway.

"What do you need me to do?" Lucien shouted, seeing only Nick's back.

"I have a suggestion that's anatomically impossible," Bret said.

"Does it end with 'off' or 'yourself'?" Gabi asked. She was up from the bench and moving toward the crosswalk at the intersection as she asked the question.

"Take your pick," Bret answered.

Nick stopped at the edge of the sidewalk, waiting for a break in traffic to cross. He turned for a final look at Lucien Murdoc and said, "Are you a religious man, Lucien?"

"I am not."

"Now would be a good time to start. Say a prayer, Lucien. He always hears the plea of a truly repentant man," Nick said and spun back around. He met Gabi at the corner, where they turned and disappeared down the block.

"We clear?" Bret asked.

"We're clear. The SUV is still in the alley. We're gone in ninety seconds."

Nick unlocked the doors and sat down in the driver seat, while Gabi claimed the passenger seat with no opposition. He started the engine and watched for Oso and Bret to appear on the ladder that led from the roof to the stairs on the adjacent building.

"Is he telling the truth?" Gabi asked.

"I think so but I've been wrong before. At some point, you have to decide to believe in someone or not. Right or wrong, I'll cast my vote on his side and hope it's the right call."

"So what are we going to do?"

"*We* aren't going to do anything."

"Nick…"

"Gabrielle, I'm not going to debate or argue this with you. I'm going to need you far more after this than I will during this."

"But what if you do need me during all this?"

"Then you'll be the first to know."

Bret and Oso stepped off of the stairs, hurried around the SUV, and opened the lift gate. They dropped their gear inside and jumped into the rear seats just as the rain began to pour, blown in sheets by gusts of wind that rocked the Suburban side-to-side and covered the windshield with high-pitched smacks.

"Just in the nick of time," Oso said.

Nick shook his head when he heard Oso and Bret chuckle in the back seat. "Every single time."

He drove out of the alley, turned right, and stopped at the intersection.

With the storm intensifying, rain standing in the roadway and claps of thunder rumbling every twenty seconds, the sidewalks were now clear, the patrons and workers having taken shelter.

Gabi touched Nick's arm and said, "Nick, look," and pointed to the courthouse.

Lucien remained seated on the brown concrete steps, his clothes drenched with rain, his face in flat affect, his eyes, mind, and soul visibly focused on a place accessible only to him.

"Is he okay?" she asked.

"Probably not," Nick said, "and that's exactly what he needs most right now."

Good luck, Lucien.

23

"Thank God. I should have just driven back," Nick said upon hearing the screech of the tires as Bret touched down on the runway.

"Oh, ye of little faith," Bret said. "We were out of the storm after twenty-five minutes. It's just a little turbulence."

"A little is more than enough. You're a madman." Nick took in the sights of the immediate area as Bret slowed the aircraft. "Everything is going to be a lot different when we see this place again tomorrow."

"If I understand this right, they've got superior numbers and fire-power along with prep time."

"Correct."

"And what do we have?"

"I'll have to get back to you on that one."

Bret finished relaying his information to air traffic control and said, "We're gonna be outgunned here, Nick. Bad."

"It wouldn't be the first time and I doubt it'll be the last."

"It's whatever. I need to get fueled up. What are they flying tomorrow anyway?"

Nick unfolded the sheet given to him by Lucien and said, "It's a Pilatus PC-24."

Bret whistled in lieu of a verbal response.

"Should I be impressed?"

Bret scoffed and said, "I am. A private business jet that can pull off takeoffs and landings with the same runway distance as this twin-engine prop? They've set it down and taken off from unpaved landing strips like it's nothing. Sign me up."

"What's that run you?"

"A cool ten or eleven million."

"You're right. I'm impressed."

"Tell Dallas."

Bret rolled the plane to a stop and Nick followed Gabi and Oso out the door.

"We need a bigger plane!" Oso exclaimed in a half-moan and half-yell that was only half-serious.

"Or smaller passengers," Bret said on his way out.

"I don't write the checks, sir," Nick said.

Gabi pointed to Oso and said, "I agree with him."

"You're used to flying first class," Nick said. The phone buzzed and the preview notification showed that a question mark had been sent by Ryan Clark. "I need to run into the terminal. I'll be right back."

As he hurried toward the entrance and Gabi shouted, "That better not be Mia!" Nick turned and sneered before opening the door and touching the icon to dial Ryan Clark.

"You seemed pressed for time earlier," Clark said when he answered.

"That's an understatement. Tell me everything that happened today involving your unexpected visitor."

"I've told you all of the high points. He kept things light, generic, but it was obvious that he was probing for more information. There was one thing that stood out."

"Which is?"

"He asked Kara if anyone had been around asking questions about the Sato family in recent memory and stressed that it was important for him to know if they had."

Nick closed his eyes and exhaled into the phone louder than intended.

"That doesn't sound good," Clark said.

"It's not. He's predicting moves."

"How's he doing?"

"Pretty well or else he wouldn't have shown up on your doorstep."

"Ryan, what's going on?" Nick heard Kara say in the background.

"I'm talking to Nick Burke about the man that was in town today," Clark said to Kara. "I'll be right back."

"Ryan..." she objected.

"I promise I'll fill you in on everything as soon as we hang up," Clark promised. A door closed then the ambient noise of the outdoors was heard. "I need to ask you something and I want you to be perfectly candid with me," Clark asked Nick.

"Ask away."

"Is my family in danger, Nick?"

Nick hesitated, considering the wealth of potential answers to Clark's question, all of which had the potential to be correct, and winced as he said, "Probably not."

"That's not the answer I was hoping for."

"I wish I had a better one for you."

"Who is this guy and how did he end up in Spring Creek?"

"His name is Spencer St. Clair. He's a sociopath, he's well connected, he has an insatiable desire for money and sex, and he's currently employed as the personal security for Daniel Staal."

"It sounds like you know him well."

"That, too, is an understatement. The less you told him, the better. The less he knows, the better. The sooner he's gone, the better."

"You said that you would keep me informed."

"I did. Your timing today was impeccable."

"How so?"

"Because I was about to have a meeting on neutral ground with Lucien Murdoc."

"Does he know who you are?"

"No. He still thinks my name is Sean McCormick but he has his suspicions when it comes to the rest of the details. Staal fired him when he started to become insubordinate and now he's ready to watch his old boss burn."

"Do you trust him?"

"Enough to see this through. But there's something I wanted to ask you. What happened that last day when everything went down all those years ago?"

"What do you mean?"

"At your office, you said you didn't put all the pieces together until the very end. But why did you go racing down there when you heard the helicopter arrive that night? Was it just the timing of it all?"

"It broke the pattern," Ryan said. "The more we thought about it and talked about it, the helicopter arrived at the same time, same day, over and over. When it was suddenly different, after all that had happened, that's an outlier that you don't ignore. The fact that we had gone to the lengths that we did meant that there was one chance for it to be done right or a lot of bad people could have turned into ghosts. When you know that, it's hard to justify doing nothing. Why?"

"It's fitting that you mention patterns because the same one is repeated. Cut-and-run, the Sato family way. Murdoc brought up the exact same thing today. But even the best patterns are predictable and that makes them vulnerable to countermeasures."

"Fair point. It sounds like a chess match."

"I'm more of a poker player but your metaphor fits, too. It's the same game on a different playing field when it's done the right way."

"What did Murdoc give you?"

"A plea for help, for one, followed by details on the when and where for the next Sato family disappearing act. The only difference is that Staal isn't running from the authorities and he legitimately believes himself to be invincible. He's literally flying three women overseas to serve them up to Saudi oil tycoons and their respective clans. It just so happens that Lucien has fallen head over heels for one of them and has finally seen the light."

"Praise the Lord," Clark said, referencing the country gospel standard. "And this is happening when?"

"Tomorrow afternoon."

"What are the odds that these people disappear as quickly as they came, Nick?"

"Staal will win the battle at hand and then retreat to safety and secu-rity so he can rebuild and allow the smoke to clear, and he will hire all that out."

"But…"

"But Spencer St. Clair leaves nothing unfinished."

"So what does that mean?"

"I don't know."

Unseen to Nick, Clark looked over his shoulder to ensure that Kara was not nearby and quietly asked, "Could you use some help tomor-row?"

Nick moved to the windows and looked out to the runway and the vast, open expanse that surrounded the airport. The ground to be cov-ered, the hiding places and numerous angles of approach, the potential pitfalls that lurked around every corner and in every dark room, lay un-seen in the fields, or stood concealed behind every tree, all seemed mag-nified a thousand times in the moment.

Gabi, Bret, and Oso loitered around the Cessna, waiting for him to rejoin them. She would not be there, he silently reminded himself. A three-man team to cover this space against well-trained, heavily armed, and potentially overwhelming opposition was less than ideal even with the element of surprise in their favor. He gritted his teeth at the idea of involving the untrained and inexperienced, namely a man who had already experienced a life-threatening gunshot wound and was married to a woman who preferred that he not suffer another.

"We could always use an extra set of eyes to watch our collective back. What did you have in mind?"

"Adam and I have been talking and we've come to a fairly simple agreement."

"What's that?" Nick saw Gabi, Bret, and Oso leering at him through the windows and he held up a single finger to acknowledge them and buy another moment of privacy.

"If any of this could present a threat to our families, to our way of life, or could reintroduce this element into our lives again, we want to be involved in the process of stopping it."

In the moment, Nick regretted his decision to drive to Spring Creek to speak with Ryan Clark and connecting the past with the present in the process. "That's not necessary, Ryan. Auxiliary support is welcome but your direct involvement is too high risk. Leave the past in the past."

"You don't see it, do you? The past was going to rear its ugly head again no matter what. This Spencer St. Clair was going to make his way to Spring Creek the first time someone asked the wrong questions about his boss whether you were involved in it or not. Make your plans, call the shots, but let me know what we can do and how."

Nick again looked to the runway and weighed the costs of involving two individuals who were new to Halcyon operations with the benefits of a much-needed temporary increase in manpower from three to five. The mental scale quickly tipped toward the benefits and he said, "I'll text you GPS coordinates for a staging location tonight. We'll have everything you need. Travel overnight and arrive before sunrise, if you can. As we hash out the operational details, I'll pass them along."

"Thank you, Nick," Ryan said.

"Thank me when it's over. You don't spike the ball until you score."

Fresh color copies of an aerial photo of the airport and the surrounding area sat on the table in front of Nick, Bret, and Oso.

"How are we going to pull this off, Hawk?" Bret rubbed his head and asked.

Nick flipped through the pages in the center of Gabi's dining room table and selected one that had been marked and notated earlier. He rubbed the back of his neck and said, "There's just so much open space to cover and so few of us to do it. Oso, you'll have to be on the ground for this, I think."

Gabi chimed in and said, "Their turnaround time will be fast. Land, pickup, leave."

"Just long enough to get packed up and refuel," Bret said.

"What are the specs on that jet?" Nick asked Bret.

"Cruise speed is around 500 mph, as opposed to ours at 280 mph in the 421. 2,000 mile range. Maybe the best avionics on the market. You're not going to like anything I have to tell you."

"I wasn't planning on an aerial dogfight between a jet and a twin-engine Cessna."

"That's not the problem. Once they take off, they're not limited to an airport. He can file a fake flight plan, disable the transponder, set that thing down on an unmarked landing strip somewhere in the Midwest while keeping the FAA mostly in the dark, take everyone to a commercial airport for their transatlantic journey as planned, and worry about explaining the fact that you dropped off the radar later."

"If they get that plane back in the air, we'll never find them," Nick said.

"If this was a TV show or a movie, we'd just go to a random warehouse, buy an RPG from a black market arms dealer and shoot the thing down when it's coming in to land," Oso said.

"And there would be 28-year-olds playing high school students," Bret said.

Nick shook his head and said, "Fuel tanks, collateral damage, undue attention drawn, federal charges; the list of troubles with that is virtually endless and then we really do end up in a movie with an inflated special effects budget. Imagine the kind of fun that would arise from an investigation into a private jet getting shot down by an RPG at an airport in a post-9/11 world."

He slid his phone to the center of the table, dialed the number for Micah, and activated the speakerphone. "Go," Micah answered.

"Quick question: Can you access the security camera system at the airport remotely?" Nick asked.

"Probably not but I'll look into it gently."

"Thank you, sir," he said before ending the call.

"The women are expendable to Daniel. He's proven that already," Gabi said.

"Go on," Nick replied.

"If all of your attention is on the plane and whoever is in it, they're dead. If you focus entirely on the women, Daniel and his guys will take off again and, like you said before, you'll never find them. So you have to decide which is more important, accomplish that, and hope for the best with the other."

"You're pretty good at this," Oso said.

"I've done it for years in medicine."

"What you're saying is that we're shooting for filet mignon and might end up with cube steak but at least we'll feel full," Bret said.

"What I'm saying is that the women being used as currency are far more replaceable than the seller's personal freedom. You know which one he will defend and which one he will dispose, and that's something you can use."

"Narcissism, avarice, hubris, and self-preservation: a personality cocktail that's volatile but predictable," Nick said. "Hand me a clean overhead shot." He drew two vertical lines on the page and said, "There's the range that's the top priority to cover," he said. Another line was drawn outside the previously drawn mark to the right and he added, "If no one else is there, we can block this point with a borrowed truck or SUV."

"Borrowed, huh?" a facetious Oso said.

"We'll manage," Bret said.

Nick circled a roadway in the center of the page and said, "There's a chokepoint," then circled a second space and added, "There's the refueling area."

Bret said, "We can track them online in real time. Once we get a visual, we can mobilize. Every second counts."

For ten minutes, Nick worked through the operational details with Bret and Oso and considered the involvement of Ryan Clark and Adam Walton.

With a fundamental plan in place, Nick said, "They arrive at 1100 hours, sixteen hours from now. We're in place and set up in twelve. We'll get everything we need from the farmhouse and convoy back here. Oh, and Oso?"

"Yeah?"

"Don't get pulled over."

24

"It's ten after five, Nick. Where are they?" Bret asked.

In contemplating where Clark and Walton might be, the potential causes of their delay, and the bevy of unknown factors that would soon be at hand and in play, Nick resisted the urge to call or text and maintained the agreed upon radio silence. "They'll be here," he managed to say.

They better be.

Oso opened an aviation app and said, "This says we've got a single-engine Cessna 172 inbound just after 0900 and outbound again 47 minutes later and nothing else until our special guests arrive an hour after that. The information on the plane isn't public so it's gotta be them."

"Access gets harder the later we get. Sunrise is our biggest enemy," Bret said.

"If I get quiet, I'm just adding up the list of federal charges and various felonies in my head," Oso half-joked.

"At least we'll have a lawyer with us the entire time," Nick said.

Bret blew out his breath and said, "If he ever gets here."

Overnight, the first immediately identifiable need was a temporary staging area with unrestricted access, close proximity, and for which early morning visitors would not be cause for alarm to passersby and nosy locals. A nearby truck stop was considered but instantly rejected, due to the bright lights, consistent traffic, and its position sandwiched between a convenience store and budget hotel, two hot beds for late-night wandering eyes. Their criteria were met by another location on

the opposite end of the map. Two steel buildings featuring nine holding containers with orange roll-up metal doors on each side composed
the entirety of the self-storage facility a mile away from the airport,
surrounded by grass and gravel, visually unassuming, and available 24
hours a day, perfect for the short-term needs of the early morning.

The SUV had been unpacked and parked on the side of the road between the airport and the storage lockers, in a wide spot in the road that
led to the overpass that spanned the interstate. Ease of access trumped
the desire to remain inconspicuous.

Nick held an overhead satellite image of the area in his hand, tracing
the perimeter of the runway and nearby buildings with his index finger,
then shook his head and said to Oso, "Any other time we'd have you a
perch somewhere."

Oso was taking an inventory of his equipment: the rifle, scopes, ammunition, cleaned and prepared as had been the case dozens of times
prior. He wiped the glass lens on a scope and said, "Don't sweat it. We'll
make it work."

"Headlights," Gabi said. "Are we expecting one car or two?"

"They didn't say," Nick answered.

"We've got two coming. Get ready."

"There's no reason for them to bring separate vehicles," Oso said.

The four hurried into the gravel row between the two buildings and
Nick touched his back to the corner nearest the roadway, facing away
from the approaching vehicles. Dressed in a black shirt and black athletic pants, as was his custom, he unzipped his black backpack on the
ground and pulled out a Glock 19 pistol, the magazine full, a round already chambered.

"Bret..." Nick said and motioned to the opposite end of the buildings, positioning him to flank the vehicles. Bret held a pistol of his own
and slinked around the corner.

*If that's not Clark and Walton, we're about to ruin someone's day and se-
verely complicate our own.*

The classic muscle car was the first to slow to a stop. Its outline was
clearly defined but the details were concealed by the lack of lighting on

the property. The rumble of the engine was unmistakable, even when idling. Behind it, an obsidian black Lexus GS 350 sedan parked in front of a row of storage containers. Ryan Clark exited the sedan first and eased the door closed. Adam Walton groaned as he got out of the muscle car but left the door open.

"Anybody here?" Adam asked in a voice above a whisper.

Nick stepped away from the corner and emerged from the shadows. "Good morning, gentlemen." When the passenger door of the Lexus opened and Kara stepped outside, Nick added, "And ladies." He spotted Lisa in the muscle car, curled up under a blanket and asleep.

"Not quite what we expected," Bret said.

"Can I talk to you a minute?" Clark asked Nick.

"Sure," Nick said and walked with him to the side of the lot that faced the interstate.

The two stood facing the four lanes of Interstate 81, traffic becoming heavier with commuters and truckers seeking an early start to their day, the beginning of the blue hour just beyond the horizon and seemingly just minutes away.

"I want to help…" Clark started to say.

"But?" Nick anticipated.

"It's a Catch-22. We bring Kara and Lisa and that's two more people to account for. We leave them at home and how do we know that this Spencer St. Clair isn't lurking somewhere close by? This seemed like the better of the two." Clark looked over his shoulder and said, "It seems like you agree with that sentiment."

"Why do you say that?"

Clark turned back around and said, "Because Gabrielle is right here with you."

"She's already had one run-in with Spencer. That's quite enough."

Clark stretched the tension from the drive out of his back and asked, "Any ideas?"

This time it was Nick who turned back to look at their makeshift staging area and said, "Actually, yes. Come on." To Bret and Oso, he said, "Get these two caught up on what we're doing." Then to Gabi, he said, "I need to talk to you," and led her back to the place where he had been standing with Ryan.

He stood silently for a moment, looking into the fields and rolling hills beyond the interstate, working out the sales pitch that he knew would not be well-received at first. When he turned his head to look at her, he found her looking out to the same place he had been, the moonlight falling on her face, her countenance at peace for the first time that he could recall in recent memory.

"I need a favor," he said matter-of-factly.

Without looking, she said, "I'm not leaving you, Nick."

"Gabi..."

"You're so predictable sometimes." She groaned in frustration and said, "I knew you'd do this."

"It's not what you think, Gabrielle. Hear me out."

"Why? I'm not some helpless damsel in distress," she said, making a show of fanning herself. "You said it yourself. The numbers are stacked against us anyway and you want to make it worse? Do you have a death wish or is there something you're not telling me?"

"Helpless? You?" Nick scoffed.

"It's a fair statement."

He gently turned her by the shoulders to face him. "If anyone has proven themselves, in every way that matters, it's you. You saved my life, Gabrielle. Believe me. I have no doubts when it comes to who you are and what you can do in this world. That's not the point."

"So what is?"

Nick lowered his voice to ensure that he could not be heard by anyone but Gabi and said, "We didn't expect Kara and Lisa to be here. Clark made a good point. It was either bring them along or leave them behind where Spencer could..." His sentence trailed off before he sparked her memory of her own encounter with Spencer St. Clair, an effort that he knew would be futile.

"What's the favor, Nick?"

"I love your heart, your soul, your passion, your never-ending concern for me, and your ability to alter every life that you touch. I even like your hoodie. I also have four other capable, skilled, and loyal people here to watch my back." He slid the Glock 19 pistol into the front pocket of her sweatshirt and said, "I need you to watch theirs."

She looked away and then back to him and asked, "How?"

"How effective are Ryan and Adam going to be knowing that Kara and Lisa could be in the crosshairs, dwelling on that, thinking about it when they should have their eyes on what's right in front of them? Now their presence becomes more of a liability than a strength to us."

"Right," Gabi said, nodding along.

"Get them out of here. They'll be safer with you than with us. These people have a long reach."

"Longer than Halcyon?"

"Maybe, maybe not, but enough that it should be acknowledged, understood, and part of anything that's planned. Go far, hide deep, pay cash, and take side roads. Any ideas?"

"I'll think of one," she said. She reached down and lifted his hand with hers and said, "Don't make me worry about you."

He leaned in and kissed her cheek and whispered, "You will anyway. We both know that."

His phone vibrated silently in his pocket and he checked the screen to find an incoming call from Micah. "This is Nick."

"Hey, I'm really busy. Call me back," Micah said and disconnected. He called back a moment later and said, "Just trying to lighten the mood, bro. Status check. What's up?"

Gabi was already moving back toward the storage units when Nick answered Micah. "Calm before the storm. I feel like there should be haunting music playing in the background. Any news?"

"Nothing new. Remote access to the security is a no-go but I just dropped you a rundown of what's there. You've still got one plane inbound before showtime but that's it. Have you thought about what to do about the workers or regular folks that might be on-site?"

"We'll get them under cover or out of the way. I don't know what else to tell you." He jogged back to join the others and saw Gabi standing to the side, her phone to her ear. "I'll check it out and get back to you once the sun's up."

"Good deal," Micah said before hanging up.

The bags of equipment were lined up against the side of one of the buildings, the tops opened, the contents still packed and sorted. Clark stood with Adam and Oso while Bret took inventory of the necessary items and to whom each would be distributed.

"You could take over a small country with this kind of firepower," Clark said.

"Better too much than too little," Adam said. He pulled an unmarked metal cylinder from the center bag and said, "What's this supposed to be?"

"Just hope we don't have to use it," Oso said.

"That goes for most of the rest of this, I assume," Clark said.

"Enough said," Adam answered.

Nick stepped beside Bret and said, "Pack a go bag for Gabi."

Bret stopped his inventory, stood, and asked, "For Gabi? What's up?"

"She's going to get Kara and Lisa out of here. I gave her my Glock but I'd rather her have some more options. Throw in a burner."

"You got it," Bret said and began picking individual items from each bag and packing them into another.

"Kara gets it, agrees, wants to do what's best," Clark said to Nick. "What about Lisa?" he asked Adam.

Adam nodded toward the car and said, "She's still out. I'd wake her up but which Lisa I'll get when she first wakes up is a coin flip. One night she fell asleep in the backseat, face down in a pile of coats and sweatshirts, and she was a bear when she finally got her oxygen levels back to normal. I thought she was going to knock my head off at one point."

"To be fair, you weren't helping," Clark said.

"Can't argue with that," Adam admitted.

Changing the subject, Nick said to Adam, "You definitely won the car battle." He activated the flashlight on his phone and moved it around the perimeter of the body.

"The 1968 Mustang GT California Special: Metallic blue, perfectly maintained, and an all-time classic. You're looking at one of 4,118 that were ever produced," Adam said. Nick watched his mood brighten as he spoke of his automobile.

"You wouldn't believe how he babies that thing," Ryan said.

"Can't say I blame him," Bret said from behind as he finished packing the spare bag for Gabi.

"Wait, what do you mean he won the car battle?" Ryan asked.

"Don't get me wrong. I'm a Lexus guy myself." He ran his hand across the hood of the Mustang and said, "Come on. I like the Middle Class Family Mobile just fine but a classic is a classic."

"I'll gladly take my amenities," Clark said. "It performs better than you think." He pulled a drowsy Kara close and said, "And so do I." She playfully nudged him away before pulling him back.

"I'll have to share the story of how I got it sometime," Adam said.

Nick smacked his shoulder, said, "It's good to see the brooding Adam Walton starting to fade out a little. Go awaken the beast and we'll get things sorted out," and walked around the building to find Gabi.

Adam helped a lethargic Lisa out of the Mustang and offered a brief explanation of what would soon happen along with the agreed upon reasoning. Her response was less than enthusiastic but preferable to the outright defiance he had expected.

Away from the group, Gabi pulled Nick aside. Grimacing, she said, "I've got a solution but I don't know if you'll like it."

"It doesn't involve your friend, the accountant, does it?"

She smiled and gave him a shove. "Shut up. No."

"Let's hear it then."

"My parents' lake house on Smith Mountain Lake is two hours from here. They're not there this weekend. It's safe. It's gated. It's secluded."

"I don't know," Nick said.

"If you're worried about these guys tracking us down, don't." A sly smile ticked upward at one corner of her mouth as she said, "It's not even in my dad's name so, unless they know the name of one of his paper corporations that was registered anonymously in another state, it's invisible. You said you swept the car for tracking devices or microphones. This'll work."

Nick scratched the top of his head and laughed.

"What?" Gabi asked.

"You're pretty good at this. It's about time your elitism and family affluence came in handy."

Gabi planted her tongue in her cheek and then said, "None of our walls open up when you type in a number."

"Point taken. Let's go fill them in and get you all on the road."

A concise rundown of the plan was followed by a series of hugs and handshakes and the exchange of best wishes. Gabi would drive them to the new location in her BMW X5, leaving Adam's Mustang and Ryan's Lexus sedan for the operation. Bret and Oso lingered at the storage units while the others took the short walk to the SUV as sunrise drew near.

"Don't do anything stupid," Kara said to Ryan.

"Mwah?" Ryan said, faking being taken aback.

"You've played hero once in your life," she said and touched the familiar and relevant place on his chest. "Promise me you'll just do what we've all talked about and nothing more. Come back to me."

He leaned down and kissed her. "I promise. Now get yourself somewhere safe and make sure there's a glass of something good waiting."

"I love you," she mouthed as she got into the front passenger seat of Gabi's SUV, and Ryan returned it in kind before the door closed.

On the other side of the vehicle, Lisa had shaken the cobwebs out of her head and was preparing for their departure. "Remind me again why this is your fight," she said to Adam.

"It's all of ours, Lisa. It started long before these guys were around. It's just coming around full circle."

"Be careful," she said and embraced him.

"I will, pretty lady," Adam said into her ear.

Nick placed the bag of supplies in the rear of the X5 and turned to Gabi, who was standing beside him. "You're all set," he said as he pulled the lid closed.

"Assuming everything goes well, this will finally be over," she said.

"Maybe. 'Over' is a subjective term. A war consists of many battles."

Facing him but looking over his shoulder and down the two-lane highway, Gabi said, "Are things ever going to be normal again?"

"Normal is subjective, too." He stepped to the side to enter her frame of view and said, "Once you went down the rabbit hole, everything changed. I'm sorry you got dragged into this."

Gabi lightly ran a finger down his forearm and said, "I'm not."

"Playing with fire and living in shadows isn't what your parents had in mind for you when you were growing up in the gated community and racking up academic awards at the private school."

"Privilege comes with a price, Nick. Maybe I'm exactly where I belong."

"You are," Nick said. "That much I know."

Seeing that Kara and Lisa were waiting inside, Gabi said, "We better go. I'll text when we get there."

"Turn your phone off and use the burner that's in the bag."

"Okay."

"There's a one-in-a-million chance that anyone will show up or anything will happen but if it does..."

"Nick..." Gabi said in an attempt to interrupt.

"If it does," Nick continued sharply, the pace of his speech increasing, "just get away. Don't try to stand your ground. Just get yourself and both of them out of there."

"Nick," she interjected again, this time more forcefully. With Nick momentarily silenced, smiling, she said, "You're trusting me with this. So trust me. Just focus on your business here. If something happens to you, I'll revive you just to kill you myself."

Nick wrapped his arms around her and lifted her off the ground, then sat her down again without speaking but still holding her tight.

"I'll see you soon. I love you," she said.

This time it was Nick that reached down and took her hand into his. "Gabi, just in case something goes sideways today…"

"Tell me later," she said and began to back away toward the driver side door.

"Gabrielle," Nick insisted in vain.

She smiled again, confident, reassuring, and said, "Tell me when I get back."

"Okay," Nick conceded.

He flinched when the door closed. He felt his chest tighten as the X5 pulled onto Lee Highway and disappeared into the quiet of the early morning, the skies streaked with orange and purple as sunrise approached. His throat tightened when he heard Ryan Clark say from behind him, "She's coming back, Nick."

"I know," Nick said. "We just have to make sure we do." He rubbed his face with his hands and said, "Let's get the license plates off the cars and start setting up."

"Do you think I'll enjoy prison?" Oso asked on the group phone call.

"Not if the guys in your cell block find out that your nickname means 'bear' in Spanish," Bret said.

Positioned at the top of a slope that overlooked the hangar and adjacent buildings on the left side of the runway, below the small-scale radar antenna, Oso blended into the landscape courtesy of his ghillie suit, a cheap throwaway rather than one of the four that he had crafted himself and put into use countless times during his time with Halcyon. His view of the terminal was partially obscured, the apron and tie-down areas less so, and the runway and taxiway were fully visible. He was, however, blind to the entrance of the hangar, an issue that prevented a perfect setup but was deemed to be of little importance in light of the brief period of time that Staal anticipated being present. He would have no need for the hangar, nor would those who were there to meet him.

A one-lane dirt road wound to the top of the hill but its access was restricted by the security fence that bordered the entirety of the airport proper, which forced Oso to sneak through private property and enter the space from the unprotected back side. Doing so moments before sunrise greatly reduced the chances of exposure but also increased the time spent in the suit with the sun bearing down and temperatures rising.

"Did you have any trouble getting up there?" Nick asked.

"It was a breeze," Oso said. "I just split a couple of houses, avoided the dogs, waved at the livestock, and ran up the side of the hill."

"You hate running," Bret said.

"It's better than climbing that fence. Once I got up there it was easy. The whole backside is totally unprotected."

"Speaking of backsides, you might want to protect yours if you end up in prison," Adam said.

A cacophony of laughter overtook the sound on the line and Oso said, "The new guys are already chiming in. Nice."

"I'm glad we're keeping it light before we commence the list of felonies and assorted federal crimes," Clark said.

"It's better than needless tension," Nick said. "You guys good?"

"All set up and ready to go," Clark answered.

"Bret?"

With the Mustang moved to the side of the road, directly across from the church, Bret was reclined in the driver seat. "Just waiting for the bell to ring," he said.

"Has anyone thought of how we're going to get these clowns out of the plane?" Oso asked.

"If you had encountered Daniel at the poker game in Boston, you'd know that it won't be an issue. He's a showman and those women are his property. He'll play it up. If he doesn't, we'll get him out of that thing somehow."

"We could go full-on junior high and lob firecrackers down there at them," Bret suggested.

"We'll think of something," Oso said.

Ryan and Adam were stationed at the aging but well-maintained Methodist church across the road from the airport terminal. Each man was armed, more for defense than for offense. From their position behind the building at the back of the lot, one at each corner to watch both directions of the highway, both the aircraft on final approach from the north and the vehicle of yet unknown make and model carrying Shelby, Rae, and Allie and their hostile escorts in tow, would be easily seen with a set of binoculars and a peek around the corner, at which point the advance warning would be relayed to Nick, Bret, and Oso.

The hours of waiting waned into mere minutes by virtue of preparation, strategic review, and small talk. The only other anticipated incoming flight, a single-engine Cessna 172 Skyhawk flown by a retiree in his mid-sixties with no passengers, arrived and departed within an 80-minute window, leaving the schedule clear for the only other flight scheduled for the day.

Nick had moved Clark's Lexus sedan to the main parking lot in front of the airport terminal and, like Bret, was reclined in the front seat with the engine running and air conditioning turned on. "Updates?" Nick asked into the line.

"Arriving on schedule according to the app. Keep your eyes on the skies, boys," Bret said.

"What the ETA?" Adam asked.

"Eight minutes but they're in a jet. Be prepared for less," Bret said.

"If anyone has anything they feel the need to say, now's the time," Nick said.

"It's getting weird to see a church nearby every time we get together to do something these days," Oso said. "Leave the religious buildings alone."

"Bad juju," Bret said in reference to Oso's superstition.

"Noted," Nick said. "Anyone else?"

"What's this going to look like, Nick?" Ryan asked.

"I was wondering that myself," Adam said.

"Once we begin, it's going to progress quickly. The faster it starts and finishes, the better it is for us. Longer duration equals more potential for disaster. The more noise, the more smoke, the more shots fired, the higher the likelihood that someone who lives nearby sees or hears something and makes a phone call, or that a driver on the interstate slows down to crane their neck to see the activity on the runway and decides to pull out a cell phone, or that a worker on-site gets caught in something tragic. All it takes is one bad turn and the clock begins to tick, and how fast it runs out depends on the response time of local authorities," Nick explained.

"So you're saying that that precision is our priority," Ryan said.

"Surgical precision," Nick said.

"Just like the orphanage," Oso said.

"Just like the orphanage," Nick echoed.

"Hang on. Orphanage?" Adam asked. "Are you telling me you-all launched an assault on an orphanage?"

"We did but it was for a good cause," Bret said.

"Do I want to know?" asked Ryan.

"That's a discussion for a later time. Let's get through this first," Nick said.

The binoculars raised, Adam said, "Eyes on the prize. We've got incoming."

"He's early," Nick said. "When he hits the ground, so do we. Any approaching vehicles?"

"None this way," Clark said.

Adam looked away from the binoculars and down the road. "Just a pickup headed this way." After a moment, he said, "They turned off. Clear."

Out of the Mustang, Bret was already moving, jogging up the secondary access road that led to the rear of the hangar and fuel station buildings, both of which were assumed to house at least one worker.

"Wait a second. White SUV headed this way. Bret, either get down or get clear," Clark said.

"Copy," Bret said, veered off the road, and knelt down.

"If they turn in, let me know," Nick said.

The white Chevrolet Tahoe slowed and turned left into the entrance to the parking lot behind the terminal. "They're coming now," Adam said. "Far right side of the lot, directly opposite you. Windows are tinted so I can't see in."

"Give me numbers and tell me as soon as they're inside the terminal. Bret, where are you?"

"Almost to the end of the service road, right behind the hangar. I can turn and go in either direction," he whispered just loud enough for the headset to pick it up.

"I've got a visual on you," Oso said.

The sound of the approaching jet engines increased suddenly as the Pilatus PC-24 descended and touched down onto the 5,200 foot runway. "The jet's on the ground," Clark said.

All four doors on the Tahoe opened at once and Adam said, "A driver and a passenger, both in black suits and shades. The three girls are in the between them. Five total. That's it."

"When they're all inside, we roll," Nick said.

Shelby, Rae, and Allie entered through the door that one of the guards held open for them, then the driver of the Tahoe before entering himself. "They're in," Adam said.

Nick opened the driver door of the Lexus, grabbed his backpack from the passenger seat, and quickly rolled out, taking a moment to move the seat upright again, a measure taken in case a sudden escape was needed.

Here we go.

On the runway, the jet was slowing to a crawl and moving toward the final turn onto the taxiway that led past the hangar and to the terminal. When the aircraft continued its slow progress past the fuel tanks and in front Bret's position, Oso said, "He's not refueling. They must have another stop after this somewhere within their range. I'm about to lose my line of sight on them for a minute. Nick, stay put. They're about to pass the tie-down spots and there's just a couple of single-engine puddle jumpers there. You're too much in the open with nowhere to hide."

"This last second nonsense has got to end," Nick mumbled. Then, speaking clearer, he said, "I'm going around. Ryan, Adam, keep an eye out."

"What are we looking for?" Adam asked.

"You'll know it if you see it."

This was not one of my better ideas.

Nick ran to the road and crossed the parking area to the right side of the terminal, pulled both straps of the backpack over his shoulders, and slung a cheap blanket over the three strands of barbed wire at the top of the fence that constructed the security gate.

"Wide is the gate that leads to destruction," he recalled from Sunday school and said aloud to himself as he locked his fingers inside the metal grate.

He quickly scaled the fence and dropped to the ground but was easily visible and sprinted to the side wall of the terminal building and heard his back slap against the bricks. "I'm blind here, guys," he said. "What's going on?"

"Coming to a stop right past the tie-downs," Oso said. "Terminal doors are opening and our guests are coming out."

A short, pudgy man in solid blue coveralls emerged from the hangar and began walking down the taxiway and in the direction of the jet, entering Oso's field of vision through the scope when he was halfway to the terminal. "Bret, keep an eye out. We've got a worker headed toward our guests. You'll have to account for him. We'll have to all go at once," Oso said.

"Copy that. We've got to go as soon as Staal is out, man."

"Another car just pulled up, Nick. Brown Range Rover. Just driver from what I can see," Adam said.

"Keep me posted. If bullets are about to start flying, get over here and delay him somehow."

"How?"

"Talk about the weather. Anything."

"He's just messing around on his phone for now. I can see the screen lit up. He's cut the engine," Adam said.

A guard was the first to exit the jet, dressed identically to the two guards that accompanied Shelby, Rae, and Allie, followed by Daniel Staal, dressed in the same manner as the guards save the sunglasses. His chemically produced blonde hair was styled straight back and fell over his ears, shining bright with the sun overhead. A third man stepped off next, a Caucasian man with neatly parted salt-and-pepper hair, clean-shaven, in a white dress shirt and tie but no jacket.

"Staal looks like he's in an Asian boy band from the nineties," Oso said.

"The pilot just got off but the engines are still running. Nick, this has to happen now," Bret said from behind the hangar. "Oso, are you ready?"

"Good when you are. Nick?"

"Ready as I'm going to be," Nick answered.

Daniel first approached Shelby, spoke briefly, then lifted her hand and kissed the back. He repeated the process with Rae but took the time to raise her arm and trace the outline of her sleeve tattoo with his finger, admiring the work and offering unheard compliments that left her smiling. He then moved on to Allie, who wore a sundress as opposed to Shelby and Rae who sported a t-shirt and low-rise denim.

"Staal's hair looks like yours, Walton," Bret said. "It's like he's an anime character."

"What's that supposed to mean? I can't see him," Adam said.

"He looks like he's spent way too much time in that peroxide sun."

The man in the blue coveralls approached the pilot and exchanged a friendly handshake as Daniel continued his conversation with the women who he would soon accompany to the Middle East.

"I'm moving," Bret said. He emerged from behind the hangar, climbed the short security fence and got back onto the ground quickly, then began a slow, casual stroll across the open space reserved for the small aircrafts that were based at the facility, two of which were secured opposite his position next to the terminal. His pistol was holstered on his right hip, out of sight from Staal and the guards.

The airport worker broke his conversation with the pilot when he spotted Bret. "What are you doing out here?" When Bret failed to stop or respond, the man began moving toward him and shouted, "Hey!"

"They don't like the random white guy in the backpack," Bret said.

The two guards assigned to Shelby, Rae, and Allie held their positions but did so with their backs turned to Nick, who stepped out from behind the wall, his Beretta 92FS raised, when he heard Oso say, "Staal's guards see Bret. Go now."

Nick leaned to look around the corner of the terminal just as the guard behind the women turned to scan the area behind him.

"Fire! Fire!" the guard shouted, a predetermined panic code indicating danger to Daniel and the others in the security team.

Nick dropped to a knee, looked around the corner, and fired a single shot into the leg of the guard, who dropped his pistol and clutched the entry wound.

At the same time, Bret said, "Cover me!" and broke into a sprint, headed toward the tied-down aircraft near the terminal.

Daniel's guard stepped away from his client and aimed toward Bret, following the moving target, but a well-placed shot from Oso ricocheted off the asphalt at his feet, forcing him to move closer and cover Staal. "I don't see him," the man said after searching for the source.

"I don't have a lot of options here, boys," Bret said, tucked into the corner of the wing and the body of the plane.

Nick rushed around the corner and drove his heel into the temple of the injured guard who had fallen to the ground, knocking him unconscious. The remaining sentry hooked an arm around Shelby and herded her, along with Rae and Allie, into the fifty-yard open space between the terminal and the jet but Oso fired two additional shots into the ground, causing the group to freeze.

"I'm still pinned down here," Bret said into the call.

The guard next to Daniel fired a single shot at Nick, who took cover around the corner for a second time, isolating himself from any further offensive action.

"We've got company," Clark said. "Anyone know somebody driving a gold Porsche Boxster?"

Breathing heavily, Nick asked, "What?"

"One just sped into the parking lot. Driver is out and ran inside. Thin blonde guy in a hurry."

Lucien.

"I'm losing my line of sight on people, Nick," Oso said.

All three women had retreated to the exterior wall of the terminal building and dropped to the ground. The door swung open and nearly struck Rae as Lucien exited on the other side. Holding a revolver, he pressed toward Daniel Staal, unaware of the remaining guard behind him.

"What's Lucien doing here?" Oso asked. "Nick, he's got a gun!"

Staal was huddled behind the attached airstair of the jet, a single guard shielding him from both sight and damage. The guard fired once at Lucien but missed high, the bullet striking and shattering a window in the terminal. Lucien ducked, shuffled to the left, and threw a shot toward the guard as he moved, which missed badly.

The guard nearest Shelby emerged from his position and fired twice, striking Lucien with both shots, first in the center of his back, then in the right shoulder blade. The energy of the bullets thrust him forward before he fell onto his chest, his face landing hard on the tarmac.

Nick spun around the corner and, finding the guard exposed and at an angle, fired three shots. The guard absorbed all three impacts and slumped to the ground.

"Lucien!" Shelby cried out. She ran to his side, rolled him onto his back, and brushed the hair and gravel and bits of tar from his eyes.

"Oso, take the pilot," Nick said.

Oso lined up the shot but a gust of wind initiated just as the trigger was squeezed and the round struck the pilot in the shoulder.

The man guarding Daniel reached behind his back and retrieved a green canister. "He's got something! Look out!" Nick shouted. When the guard turned to his right and tossed the can in the direction of the hangar, Nick said, "What's he doing?"

The object activated with a *pop* and dense violet smoke began to emanate, filling the air and concealing the location of the jet.

"That's what he's doing," Nick said.

"I'm blind, Nick," Oso said.

"Grab a pistol and get down here. We'll clean it up later." He quickly shed the ghillie suit, dropped the rifle, and extracted a pistol and extra magazine from his gear bag.

Rae and Allie were now beside Shelby and Lucien on the apron. Lucien was gasping for breath, his eyes wide, grimacing with each movement. "You're okay," Shelby said through tears. "Hang on."

Nick was moving behind them, headed for Bret's position to create the necessary interference to set him free. Oso had broken into a sprint past the hangar, passing the man in the coveralls who was now seeking shelter, running through the smoke and into the open space. He fired two warning shots, freezing the man near Daniel in place.

The pilot struggled to his feet. Blood had seeped through and saturated the upper left front quadrant of his white shirt. On the right side of the terminal, the wounded guard had regained consciousness and was attempting to reach the side of the plane where the man guarding Daniel was signaling to him, shouting unintelligible commands.

"Tell us what to do here, Nick," Ryan said.

"Stand by. We're going to need you."

Having moved to the same corner of the church building, Adam muted his headset and said to Ryan, "I'm headed inside. I'll get behind them. Where's the bag?"

Adam took the backpack, crossed the road, and sped toward the security fence, which he leapt and latched onto, reaching the top in two steps. A sharp point on the top row of barbed wire cut into his skin and ripped a gash into his forearm but he ignored the pain, as well the blood, and jumped down.

Clark ran in the opposite direction, through the grass and into the parking lot outside the terminal, where he removed a utility knife from his pocket and thrust the largest blade into each of the four tires of the Tahoe. The full-size SUV began to sink as the rubber flattened and Clark ran inside the building, the Taurus TH9 that had been temporarily removed from the Civic's glove compartment in his right hand as he moved, and reached the apron where he saw the women surrounding Lucien.

The pilot was helped up the steps and into the jet by Daniel's personal security agent, who then reached inside to retrieve a black canvas bag of his own. He pulled the tab on another smoke grenade and tossed it in front of him, then activated another and hurled it toward the terminal entrance. This time the canisters emitted thick grey smoke that enveloped the area.

"Get clear now!" Nick shouted into the earpiece to Bret and Oso, who met behind the plane that Bret had used for temporary cover and ran through the smoke toward Nick.

Before they could reach his position, set between their own and where Lucien lay wounded, the tab was pulled on a third canister, this one silver. It cut through the smoke and bounced on the ground toward Nick and the group around Lucien.

"Flashbang!" Nick exclaimed. "Cover your ears!" He jumped on top of Allie and Rae while Shelby attempted to cover Lucien, closed his eyes, and protected the ear without the Bluetooth earpiece. Still in the doorway, Clark heard the instruction and dove back inside the terminal.

The cylinder filled with a mix of magnesium and potassium nitrate exploded with a bright white flash and a bang of more than 180 decibels. Nick managed to look away in time to avoid the flash but the blast of sound left him momentarily disoriented, his ears ringing, and with symptoms that mimicked the sudden onset of vertigo.

The jet was lost behind the blanket of violet and dark grey smoke that was beginning to sweep over the taxiway and toward the runway. Unseen to Nick, Bret, and Oso, the men who remained outside hurried onboard and pulled the airstair upward and returned it into its secure position.

Clark inhaled and held a deep breath, covered his mouth with his shirt, and ran out to the apron. Before the door closed, he felt a rush of air blow past him in the opposite direction and saw the temporary jet-stream follow the path and swirl behind. He helped Nick to his feet and said, "You good?"

The ringing in Nick's ears prevented him from hearing Clark's question but he responded, "I'm fine. Stay with them. Have them call an ambulance for Lucien," and handed Ryan a clean burner phone from the front pocket of the bag. Clark nodded to affirm and, with his bag strapped over one shoulder, Nick ran through the purple cloud to his left to find Bret and Oso moving toward him.

Oso grabbed his shoulder and turned him toward the taxiway where the jet was moving toward the end of the runway, repositioning for takeoff.

"Come on!" Nick shouted. He led the two on a sprint up the taxiway, on a diagonal angle that would place them at the three-quarter point of the 5,000 foot runway. He sensed the worst of the temporary tinnitus subsiding and, into the earpiece, said, "Walton, where are you?"

"On my way. I can see you," Adam said, breathing heavily and running at top speed.

"Next to last turn onto the taxiway. Meet us there," Bret said.

The jet turned and aimed straight ahead, then began moving forward. Adam reached the position first. "I'm almost there," he said.

"We're en route. You have your bag with you?" Nick asked.

"I've got it. What do I need?"

"You should have a MAC-10 and a spare mag in there."

Adam dumped the contents of the bag onto the ground and said, "Got it."

The PC-24 was accelerating, needing only little more than half of the runway in order to take off. Nick met Adam steps ahead of Bret and Oso and pulled his bag free from his shoulder. "They're going to get airborne," he said as he unzipped the bag and pulled out his own MAC-10. "Fire everything you've got at them as soon as they get off the ground."

"I can try to hit them from here," Walton said and started to raise the weapon toward the plane.

Nick pushed the barrel down and said, "Not yet. That thing runs through a 30-round mag in three seconds and has terrible accuracy. We can't let any stray shots get past the plane and onto the interstate."

"Here they come!" Oso shouted through the noise.

The mix of smoke from the grenades was still hovering, now lofting over the runway and spilling out onto Interstate 81. "We're out of time!" Nick said.

Halfway up the runway, the jet lifted off from the ground and began to climb.

"Go!" Bret exclaimed.

Nick and Adam pointed the fully automatic MAC-10s just above ground-level and squeeze the trigger, firing more than sixty .45 ACP rounds in the direction of the fuselage as the aircraft surged upward. Bret and Oso emptied their fifteen-round magazines in their .40 caliber semi-automatics and quickly reloaded to fire again.

Nick swapped the empty MAC-10 magazine for a fresh one and fired the last of his supply overhead as the jet continued on and lifted toward the sky, joined by the rounds from Bret and Oso. "See anything?" Adam asked.

"I can't see what smoke is theirs and what smoke is from what was on the ground," Bret said.

"That pilot lost a lot of blood. He was staggering up the steps," Oso said.

The four watched as the jet cleared the immediate area then banked hard to the right. Rather than continuing to gain altitude as expected, its nose flattened and turned downward.

"Do you hear that?" Bret asked.

"Hear what?" Nick said.

"He's in trouble," Bret said and moved to his right in search of a clearer view.

They watched as the aircraft accelerated in speed but tipped further to the right and flipped over, an action that produced a high-pitched whine. The impact into the uninhabited mountainside resulted in an explosion that was seen a full second before it was heard.

"God in Heaven," Clark said into his earpiece.

"Yeah," Nick said.

"That's going to draw some attention," Bret said.

"Ryan, what's happening down there?" Nick asked.

"Lucien's fading," Clark said. "I'm doing my best but he took two in the back and he's in trouble." He stood and said, "We've got sirens screaming in the distance. Paramedics are on the way for Lucien but those sirens sound like fire and police. Time's up, guys."

"Oso, get back to the hill and collect everything. We'll pick you up on the backside," Nick said. To Adam, he said, "Get everything back in the bag," and then followed his own instruction.

"Got it," Oso answered and ran toward his elevated position where his rifle and supplies remained.

Already moving toward the apron with Bret and Adam following, Nick said, "Ryan, can you take care of the security inside like we talked about? You're the only one there."

"I got it," Clark answered. Ryan touched Allie on the shoulder with one hand, Rae's shoulder with the other, and said, "We were never here."

"Okay," Allie said, still shaken.

Rae nodded and Clark ran inside the building.

Nick, Bret, and Adam raced past the tied-down aircraft and to the portion of the chain-link security fence that led directly to the parking lot behind the terminal, thus bypassing the need to go through the building.

Bret scurried up the fence first, planted his foot at the top and jumped over the rows of barbed wire. Adam started to the fence next and, having seen the blood on his arm, Bret asked, "You good, man?"

Adam pulled himself upward and said, "I don't care," through the pain, copying Bret's action of pushing off of the top of the fence and over the barbed wire, then landing on the ground below.

Nick was last, having applied the same strategy, and dug the keys to Clark's Lexus from his pocket as Ryan exited the terminal. Bret palmed Adam the keys to the Mustang and said, "Your ride, you drive."

"We'll grab Oso on the way out. Stay on the air," Nick said. He turned to look down the road and saw flashing lights of both the blue and red varieties flashing in the distance, sirens wailing but drawing nearer.

Bret and Adam ran to the Mustang on the side of the road and started the engine. "Good luck, gentlemen," Bret said as he closed the door and Adam pushed the accelerator to the floor, spitting dirt and gravel behind the rear wheels as the engine roared to life.

Nick unlocked the Lexus and pressed the button for the trunk release, dropped the gear bag into the rear compartment, then sat inside and started the engine as Clark fell into in the passenger seat.

"First time I've ever been on this side," Clark said and pulled the seatbelt across his chest and waist.

"You only have to do it once," Nick said. "I like my LC 500 coupe better anyway." He backed out quickly, drove away from the main entrance and turned onto Lee Highway, speeding past the church building and following Adam and Bret in the Mustang. "Oso, where are you?"

"Coming down the hill now. Downhill is easier than uphill for guys like me," Oso said, his breathing labored.

"We're there in thirty seconds. Back door is open. Trunk is unlocked," Nick said. He looked into the rear view mirror and saw two fire engines and an ambulance ease into the parking lot. Ahead, two police cruisers approached at high speed but blew by them without slowing.

"Gravity is your friend, brother," Bret said from the Mustang.

Nick spotted Oso approaching and pulled to the side of the road. Oso dropped his gear into the trunk, slammed the lid shut, and fell into the backseat behind Clark.

"Hit it," Oso said.

Nick pulled back onto the roadway and checked the rearview mirror for any unwanted attention.

Clark caught the look and said, "We're going to be driving with our eyes on the mirrors as much as the windshield for a while."

"Splitting their attention between the scene at the airport and the crash scene will help fade the heat temporarily but it won't last long," Nick said. "Bret, you fly in here all the time. Who was the little guy in the coveralls?"

"No idea, man. Today's the first day I've ever seen him. He's got to be one of Staal's guys. He was way too friendly with them."

"Figures," Oso said.

Nick connected his phone to the Bluetooth system in the Lexus and unlinked his earpiece as Clark and Oso ended the call on their phones. Bret and Adam remained active on the line via their own earpieces in the Mustang.

"We'll rendezvous at the farmhouse," Nick said. "Before we get back on 81, we'll stop and get the plates put back on."

"We've got a restaurant that looks like a barn right here next to the on-ramp," Bret said. "Huge gravel parking lot."

"That'll work," Nick said.

Bret and Adam were out of the Mustang and waiting when Nick pulled into the gravel lot.

Two more fire engines roared by on a nearby side road, sirens blaring and fading in the distance, en route to the crash site where they would soon find a scene rife with mechanical and human carnage.

"We got out of there in the nick of time, huh?" Adam said.

Nick glared at Bret and said, "You told him to say that."

Laughing, Bret held up his hands in surrender and said, "Pure coincidence. You have my word."

The West Virginia plates were quickly reattached and the engines restarted. Nick, Oso, and Ryan Clark led Bret and Adam Walton in the Mustang onto Interstate 81.

"How far from here?" Clark asked.

"About an hour, give or take a few minutes," Nick said. The phone buzzed in his lap and the LCD screen displayed the incoming call from a private number. With Bret and Adam listening, he said, "I've got a call coming in from a blocked number. Ryan, when I answer it, call Adam back on speaker and have him start another conference call with Bret so everyone can hear."

On the third ring, Clark asked, "Got it. Any idea who it is?"

"Probably Gabi checking in on the burner. I told her not to use her phone. Here we go." He swiped the green icon to answer the call. "Hello?"

"It's been a while, Mr. McCormick. Or should I say Mr. Burke?" Nick heard the voice of Daniel Staal say.

Nick took a deep breath and exhaled slowly but silently and said, "Daniel. This is unexpected."

"That was quite a show you put on today, with a little help, of course."

"What do you want, Daniel?" Nick asked.

"Let's start with a rematch at the poker table and go from there, shall we?"

"Time and place, Mr. Staal. I'm available now, as a matter of fact."

Daniel forced a laugh and said, "I'm a little preoccupied with traversing the back roads of a place I have no desire to be at the moment, so I'll have to pass. What do you think you accomplished here today, Nick?" Taking a derisive tone, he said, "Do you think my business will suddenly collapse under this pressure that I've certainly never experienced before and never will again? Are those three girls that you left on the apron not replaceable? I'll have three more on their way across the Atlantic by the end of business tomorrow."

"You certainly are your father's son, Daniel."

"My father was wealthy but weak. My strength is a result of learning from his failures."

"Someone who claims to learn from his failures would have taken a more respectable path in life, don't you think? Whether it's by choice or by birth, you're an evil man."

The line fell momentarily silent before Daniel said, "You are not the man that you think you are."

"You better hope not," Nick immediately replied. He increased his speed as the conversation intensified, the speedometer climbing over 85 mph.

"Do you believe that you've won, Nick?"

"There is no such thing as victory in a war that never ends, whether it's with an enemy or yourself."

"He's always fancied himself a philosopher," Spencer St. Clair said in the background.

"Your old friend says hello, Nick," Daniel said.

The sounds of the vehicle moving onto the unpaved gravel shoulder of the road rumbled through the speakers. "What are we doing?" Daniel asked Spencer.

"I need to stretch. Humor me," Spencer said.

"I'll ask you again. What do you want, Daniel?"

Intense, angry, Daniel growled, "I want you to understand what kind of a firestorm you have created. Do you hear me?"

"I hear you," Nick said. He looked around the cabin of the Lexus and in the rearview mirror to the Mustang and said, "We all hear you."

"Good. This was one encounter, my man. But every ending is also a beginning whether you know it at the time or not," Daniel said. "You hear that?"

"I heard it. Just make sure you remember it," Nick said.

"Get out," Nick heard Spencer say to Daniel.

"Spencer..." Daniel objected.

Spencer opened the door and pulled Daniel outside. "Come on now," he groaned.

"Enough of this!" Daniel said.

"We don't drive a kilometer further until my money is in my account. Are we clear?" Spencer said.

Now disinterested in the verbal sparring with Nick, Daniel said to Spencer, "Your money was transferred upon your arrival. You can check for yourself."

"Very well," Spencer said. The line was silent as Spencer opened an app to check the balance of his account. "So it was. Thank you," he said to Daniel.

"Are you satisfied?" Daniel asked.

"Almost," Spencer said.

Confused, Daniel asked, "What is this?" When Spencer did not respond, confusion turned to panic and Daniel said, "What are you doing?"

A single gunshot rang out and blasted through the speakers in the Lexus. Nick turned down the volume on the sound system but slowly increased it again and heard two additional shots fired. The unmistakable sound of the body of Daniel Staal crashing to the ground in a heap of dead weight was followed by the rustling of the phone from off of the asphalt.

"Give my regards to the good doctor. I'll see you soon, mate," Spencer said and broke the connection.

Two minutes of silence passed before Oso asked, "What do we do, Nick?"

"Right now, there's another phone call to make," Nick said. "Did you all get that?" he asked.

"We got it," Bret said through the speaker of Clark's phone.

Nick opened his contact list and touched the icon to dial Gabrielle, who answered before the end of the first ring.

"Nick, thank God. Is everyone okay?"

"We're okay. It's over," he said.

"They're fine," she said to Kara and Lisa in the background. To Nick, she said, "What's next?"

"Just come home. I'll be waiting."

EPILOGUE

The popular dirt trail for hikers and mountain bikers situated in the New River Gorge in southern West Virginia measured 3.2 miles out and back. Shaded from start to finish and heavily trafficked by both locals and weekend tourists in the months that coincided with a cooperative climate, the visit to Long Point, 45 minutes from Spring Creek, had been recommended by Ryan and Kara Clark for the purposes of a single-day outdoor getaway.

"How much farther?" Nick asked.

Gabi checked her hiking app and said, "We're almost there. Don't quit on me now."

"Well, excuse me for still being a little bit sore. It was a long weekend. Flashbangs and smoke grenades and fence-climbing and gun-shooting..."

"Oh, my."

"I walked right into that one."

"Poor baby," she mocked. "Come on. The trail is getting narrow so we're getting close. I'm so glad there's not a crowd."

"That's why Kara said to get here early."

Nearing the end of the trail, a moderate downhill grade through a tunnel of in-bloom rhododendrons led to Long Point, the eponymous outcrop and overlook that features a panoramic view of the iconic New River Gorge Bridge that spans the gorge and serves as visual evidence of the collaboration between the engineering of man and the creation of God, leaving each visitor forever altered in mind and spirit.

Gabi's steps became shorter and more deliberate as she peeked over the steep sides before stepping onto the outcrop. Nick followed ten feet behind, his legs burning from the exertion and his mind dreading the incline on the return trip.

"It's beautiful here," Gabi said and snapped a photo of the bridge.

"It certainly is," Nick said with his eyes on Gabi rather than the landscape.

"Come here," she said as she turned around and pulled Nick close, then held up the phone to capture a photo with the front-facing camera. She checked the screen and said, "That's a good one."

"You don't take bad ones," Nick said. Gabi closed her eyes and forced a laugh but Nick refused to concede. "I'm not wrong," he said.

She snapped another photo of the gorge and pushed her phone into her pocket. "Have you heard anything about Lucien?"

"He's still in the hospital, still not much feeling in his legs but the doctors are hopeful. Shelby hasn't left his side."

"It's only been a few days. He's lucky to be alive at all but somehow it'll work out."

"I just keep expecting helicopters and a SWAT team to show up at the farmhouse and tell me that they'd like to ask me a few questions."

Gabi drummed her hand on her leg and asked, "Speaking of which, do I want to know how and why that hasn't happened?"

"You wouldn't believe me if I told you."

"After all this? Try me."

"The security systems at the airport, video and all, were operated and managed by a single publicly traded company. They were part of a corporate acquisition a few days ago. Controlling interest was purchased virtually overnight."

Fighting a knowing grin, Gabi said, "Don't tell me..."

"That company is now technically a subsidiary of Tayco Pharmeceuticals. Dallas even assigned someone in the company to facilitate the transition and look at everything that was now under their umbrella."

"Is it Bret or Oso?"

"Micah."

She rolled her eyes and said, "Of course."

"Ryan took care of what was on-site but all the high-end modern systems record onto a cloud server. Sadly, Micah discovered almost immediately that the footage from the airport had been corrupted and was unrecoverable."

Monotone, she said, "I'm shocked."

"Right?"

Looking out into the gorge, Gabi asked, "Where's Spencer, Nick?"

"I don't know. His plans are as unpredictable as his actions. He'll take his windfall and feed his vices for a while but he'll eventually surface somewhere, I'm sure. If not, consider it a pleasant surprise."

"That's a rather disconcerting thought," she said into the cool morning mountain air.

When she turned to face him, Nick said, "His fight is with me, and me alone, now. He learned a hard lesson about involving you in anything he says, does, or thinks."

"What am I supposed to do?"

"Fear does not prevent death, it prevents life. Personally, directly, you go back to doing what you do best."

"I'm not sure I know what that is anymore, Nick."

"It means a return to changing lives, saving lives, touching lives, and doing all of those things, and more, in the way that only you can."

"Just like that?"

"Just like that."

"What if that isn't me anymore? What if I don't have that fire and drive in me like I used to and I can't reach down and find it day in and day out?"

"Then you find another way, another avenue, another cause or purpose in life and you point everything in that direction and pray that God's hand is in it as it has been with everything else that you've done."

"You make it sound so simple."

"What can I say? I'm a simple man."

"You're anything but simple, no matter the context."

"I'll take your word for it."

Nick walked away from the edge of the overlook and to the cover of the trees at end of the trail.

"What is it?" Gabi asked.

He stepped back onto the outcrop and said, "There's something we need to talk about."

A look of concern fell over her face as she said, "Okay. What is it?"

"I don't know where to start."

"How about the beginning?"

Nick felt his eyes relax and lose focus as he thought back to the beginning, the moment in time of which she inadvertently spoke, the setting, the feeling, the zeitgeist, the connection. He saw the overcast skies of that day. He heard the sound of the water and felt the coolness of the breeze that it created. He heard the lyrics in his head.

Only you can save me...

"Nick?"

He eased back into the present and said, "It began one day when I was sitting at the fountain outside of Jefferson Hall," then looked to her and said, "It's been a whirlwind ever since," catching the light in her eyes that appeared at the mere mention of that day at Radford University.

"I remember that day," she said in a half-whisper.

"There are a million different things before, and even during, that day that would have prevented that moment from happening. If you had been on-time for class that day, if I had chosen a different section to be the teaching assistant..."

"If you had never left Iowa..." she added.

"Gabrielle, I don't know where I would be, or if I would be, today if you hadn't found me there."

"What's meant to be will always find a way, Nick."

"You can't outrun destiny," he said.

The high-pitched *ding* to indicate the arrival of a new message sounded through the speaker on his phone, followed by two more in succession.

"Do you need to get that?" she asked.

Nick pulled the phone from his pocket, checked the notification screen, and felt the pressure in his chest rising as he read the name before the message. The color drained from his face. His breathing grew shallow and rapid.

"Nick, who is it from?" She stepped closer and said, "Is it Spencer?"

Nick looked up and said, "It's Mia."

Gabi closed her eyes and said, "No. You can't go through this again."

The phone, still in his hand, began to vibrate as the sound of Mia's ringtone played and her contact photo appeared on the screen.

He held his thumb over the green icon to answer the call, then the red icon to decline it, and felt his pulse begin to race as he looked up at Gabi.

"Nick, please don't," she said. The ringtone began to play a second time and Gabi wiped the tears from her eyes. "We..." she started to say before looking down at the phone screen to see Nick swipe the red icon to decline the call.

Her eyes met his when she lifted her head. He allowed his gaze to linger for a moment, then looked to his right and tossed the phone over the side and listened to the device tumble into the gorge.

Gabi's eyes welled up once more and she said, "Looks like you're going to need a new one."

"I have everything I'll ever need right here," Nick said.

He placed his hands on her hips and drew her to him, then leaned down and, for the first time, pressed his lips to hers, feeling himself relax as she returned the action and held him around the waist.

She leaned back after a moment and said, "So is this the next chapter in our story?"

He considered her metaphor and said, "Maybe it's the first chapter of a new book."

Their eyes locked, Nick pulled her body close and whispered into her ear, "Only you can save me."

In response, Gabi whispered, "I'll be by your side."

ABOUT THE AUTHOR

Brad Cooper is a native and lifelong resident of West Virginia. In addition to his work as an author, he works in legal services, hosts multiple podcasts, and is the winner of 23 boxing championships as a trainer.

For more information on *Enigma* and upcoming projects, visit:
www.facebook.com/BradCooperBooks

Brad can be contacted directly via e-mail at:
BradCooperBooks@gmail.com

OTHER BOOKS FROM BRAD COOPER
Available at Amazon.com

FICTION
Guilty by Association

NON-FICTION
The Lifted Veil: Unlocking the Truth of the Christian Savior, the Jewish Messiah, and the End of the Age